FOREVER

Forlorn Series
Book V

Gina Detwiler

ALLY PRESS

First Edition
Print ISBN: 978-1-953290-44-1
eBook ISBN: 978-1-953290-86-1
Published by Ally Press

Printed and bound in the United States of America.

Gina Detwiler takes the concept of good vs. evil to ever higher levels, with action from the first line and imagery-packed scenes that permeate all the senses. Forever is more journey than novel, and readers will forget their current place and time as they become immersed in a world where angels, demons, and humans continue an age-old battle that begins with *Forlorn* (Book 1).

Susan Miura
Award-winning Author of *Healer* and *Shards of Light*

Wow! An incredible end to a fantastic series!!! Detwiler masterfully weaves one of many possibilities of Biblical prophecy, and makes you wonder how close to reality Forever might be. At times, it felt eerily close. Grace, Jared, angels, and demons traverse a treacherous "end of days" world and converge in Jerusalem for a final battle, making Forever an unputdownable read. If you enjoy end times stories where the hope of God always reigns supreme, don't miss the epic finale to the Forlorn series.

J F Rogers
author of *The Cursed Lands* and *Ariboslia* series

THE FORLORN SERIES

Forlorn

Forsaken

Forgiven

BEFORE: Jared's Story

Forbidden

Penny's Journal: Fortune Lost

Forever

ALSO BY GINA DETWILER

Ultimate Bible Character Guide

Ultimate Bible Character Devotional

WRITING WITH PRISCILLA SHIRER

The Prince Warriors

The Prince Warriors and the Unseen Invasion

The Prince Warriors and the Swords of Rhema

The Winter War, a Prince Warriors sequel

This book is dedicated to all those
readers who made it this far.

You are my heroes.

Psalm 2

Why do the nations rage and the peoples plot in vain?
The kings of the earth set themselves,
and the rulers take counsel together,
against the Lord and against his Anointed, saying,
"Let us burst their bonds apart and cast away their cords from us."

He who sits in the heavens laughs; the Lord holds them in derision.
Then he will speak to them in his wrath, and terrify them in his fury, saying,
"As for me, I have set my King on Zion, my holy hill."

Psalm 2:1–6

Part One
New Asgard

O daughter of Babylon
Doomed to be destroyed
Blessed shall he be who repays you
With what you have done to us.
Psalm 137: 8

Chapter One
Michael

I, Michael, prince of the heavenly host, guardian of Israel, have had just about enough of this.

How long? I ask again as the Golden Son takes to the sand for the main event of the day. Eighty thousand people spring to their feet, screaming his name and stomping so violently that the arena's steel rib cage, wrapped in a fake stone scrim, hums like the plucked strings of a lyre.

"Hail Baldyr! Golden Son! Destroyer!"

Camera drones swirl around him as he raises his sword to the cheering crowd, face tilted up to catch the light beaming through the prismatic glass awning. He wears little armor but an intricate gold pauldron over his right shoulder, leather straps bound across his broad chest, and a wide belt of gold links, each one a flame, around his waist. His expression is stoic, his blue eyes a perfect blank. Yet I see the contempt he hides behind the mask, the loathing for this place, for himself. For what he has become.

"Baldyr! Baldyr! Golden Son!"

His real name is Jared Lorn. Even he seems to have forgotten that.

The cheers turn to boos as his opponent ascends from a trap door in the arena floor—a colossal creature with a glossy, muscular body stained dark blue, a five-pointed metal star marking its chest. It brandishes a poleaxe, a long, sharpened spear with an axe blade on one side. Twisted horns protrude from its massive head, which has the aspect of a goat.

It calls itself Baphomet.

The goat-demon leaps high into the air on enormous, copper-tinged wings and flies about the arena, undeterred by the crowd's derision. Dark Ones ride upon its back and perch on its wings, screeching with hideous laughter.

Jared watches his opponent impassively, the dread in his eyes something only I can see. It has been nine months since his debut in this arena—a fanciful replica of the Roman Coliseum—as the trumpeted son of the Supreme Lord of the United Earth, Grigori Zazel. Nine months since he was killed by a supposed Israeli assassin then brought back to life by Zazel himself. All so Zazel could declare himself the new god of this world by raising his own son from the dead.

The boy was never dead in the first place. My job is to make sure he doesn't die again.

Baphomet suddenly swivels in mid-air, rips the star from its chest and hurls it at Jared. The star bursts into spangles of color as it spins across the arena with astonishing speed. Jared tries to duck, but the star seems able to track his movement and chases him, swerving just out of reach whenever Jared thrusts out his shield. Baphomet controls the star with its mind. The crowd gasps and laughs in equal measure as Jared runs, leaps, rolls, does everything in his power to avoid the deadly star. This is a new sort of weapon.

Baphomet attacks from the air, swinging and thrusting with the poleaxe as Jared struggles to evade both weapons. The Dark Ones try to distract him, whispering their curses, but they cannot touch him, for my Light protects him. Still, Jared is losing strength—he cannot keep this up forever.

Something else must be done.

Let it come.

I speak into his spirit, his soul. He hears me, though he doesn't understand. Baphomet pauses to acknowledge the crowd. The star flies toward its master briefly, then rounds for another attack.

Stand still.

Jared obeys, standing, lowering his shield. The star spins toward him.

Wait.

He waits, beads of sweat pouring down his face. The crowd gasps in shock. The Dark Ones claw and shriek. Baphomet laughs.

Now.

Just before the star is about to cut off his head, Jared thrusts out his shield. The star has no time to evade—it smashes into the shield.

The force of it knocks the boy off his feet. The shield is wrenched from his hand as the star bounces and flits over the sand, dragging the shield in a desperate attempt to free itself.

The crowd breaks into peals of laughter. Baphomet brays with annoyance. He dives toward Jared, poleaxe poised to impale him.

Jared springs up and bats away the poleaxe with his sword. Baphomet brays again and counters—Jared parries with two-handed swings. They fight furiously while the crowd shouts encouragements.

Baphomet is two feet taller and a hundred pounds heavier; his weapon far longer. He drives the Golden Son to his knees, then delivers a deep gash to his left arm. Jared falls sideways, blood pouring from the wound. Baphomet strikes again and again as Jared rolls on the ground to avoid the deadly spike. The crowd screams for blood.

I pour Light into Jared's right arm—he counters Baphomet's last strike with a mighty swing, cutting off the goat-demon's hand.

The goat screams as its hand, poleax and all, flies from its body and lands in the sand. Furious, it takes to the air, blood pumping from the stump. The crowd swoons as the creature rises high over their heads and then dives, its spiked horns aimed for Jared.

Jared lunges for the poleaxe, still attached to the severed hand. As the demon descends, Jared pulls the poleaxe upright. Baphomet sees too late, cannot reverse its momentum—the spiked tip pierces the top of its head.

The entire coliseum seems to go still for a long moment as Baphomet hangs suspended in the air, impaled on its own poleaxe. Then it collapses to the sand, convulsing, though not dead. The crowd screams ecstatically.

Jared pulls himself to his feet, picks up his sword, and sticks it into the sand by Baphomet's head. He clutches his bleeding arm and walks slowly out of the arena to thunderous cheering.

How long? I ask Elohim, the Lord of Hosts, as the crowd roars with ecstasy. *How long must we endure this?*

Elohim does not answer me.

Chapter Two
Helel

William West's eyes flutter as the gladiator battle unfolds around him in all its gory splendor. He's fully reclined in his overstuffed red leather chair, cigar clenched in his teeth, smoke rings curling around his bald head like halos. My, but he has gotten old—over a hundred by now. And so fat his bulk, wedged into the chair, spills over the armrests. How he disgusts me. I should have done this a long time ago.

I pause in the doorway, watching the battle—the Golden Son fighting the latest genetic monstrosity the Grigori have come up with: a flying goat? These arena fights get stranger and stranger. West draws on the cigar, making the tip glow red, then coughs asthmatically, chuckling when Baldyr gets speared in his arm.

I clear my throat. "Holo freeze."

The goat-demon stops in mid-swing with Baldyr on the sand, about to be skewered. That won't happen, of course. It never does. The boy never loses.

West blinks and takes the cigar from his mouth. He pushes a button on this chair to fold it upright.

"What is the meaning of this?" He sees me and scowls. "Oh, it's you, Amon. Why did you turn it off? It was just getting to the good part."

"I'll tell you how it ends. The champion, gravely wounded, makes one final heroic move and wins the day. They all end the same, Wincenty. What a bore. They could at least make it interesting. Chop off his leg or something."

"Still, I like to see it for myself."

I sit across from him on the hand-carved mahogany coffee table and select one of his cigars from the humidor.

West grumbles, adjusting his bulk in the recliner. "What is it you want that could not wait until our meeting tomorrow?" he asks gruffly. "Are you here about the GEM program again? I told you how I feel about it. I agreed with the limited use for the Peacemakers and the military, but it is not ready for employment in the general population."

"No, I've not come to talk about that." I carefully trim the cigar and light it with the marble cigar lighter next to the humidor. I puff until the tip glows. The burning sensation is quite pleasant. "I've come to accept your proposal to become your heir."

"I never made such a proposal."

"You don't remember? Hmm. That's not good, Wincenty. Not good at all." I blow a perfect smoke ring in his face. He coughs and waves the smoke away. "I remember when this happened to your father. Loss of memory. The beginning of the end."

West's small eyes grow even smaller. "My father? How could you know my father?"

"Oh, I knew him *very* well. And your grandfather and his father and so on. They have all served me faithfully, as you have."

"Served *you*?"

"Of course! Maybe you didn't know it. You thought you were serving yourself. That's always how it is."

"You are not making sense—"

"On the contrary. I make *perfect* sense." I take another gratifying puff of the cigar. "I brought the papers required. All ready to sign." I produce a folder of papers and set them on his lap.

He stares down at them. "What is all this?"

"Your financial records, accounts, holdings, power of attorney, last will, chairmanship of the Interlaken Group—everything signed over to me."

"The Interlaken Group? No, no. I have no intention of stepping down as chairman of the group."

"Wincenty, has your memory failed you again? Wasn't I the one who created the Cure as we know it now?"

"No, that was Darwin..."

"Speer. Well, he may have developed a miracle treatment to stop aging and cure all diseases known to man, but he was a small thinker. He cared only for his personal benefit, not the benefit of mankind. You had a higher goal. One that only I could help you achieve."

"Perhaps that is true," West concedes, "but you would never have been able to accomplish all you did without the Interlaken Group."

"Ah, dear friend, that is where you are wrong."

West looks straight at me and blinks. "What do you mean?"

"It was really the other way around, don't you see? I never needed you. But you did indeed need me. You think you were in charge, but you were just the useful idiot I chose as the face of my work. From the very beginning, it has been so, Wincenty. From the beginning."

I gaze into his eyes, unblinking. I show him the truth in my own eyes, feel them burn red like fire, reflecting in his beady irises.

He presses into the back of the chair as if he can avoid my searing gaze. Sweat breaks out on his brow, his jaw opens, the cigar tumbles from his mouth onto his enormous belly.

I delicately pick it up and snuff it out in the ashtray. "Now you see, don't you?" I say as kindly as I am able. "I don't know why you are so surprised. You always called me 'The Prophet,' didn't you? You boasted to your friends of my uncanny prescience. You claimed to have discovered me. No one need know otherwise. Sign the papers and turn your empire over to me. You are too old and too fat to be my slave anymore."

"But you said… I would live…"

"Forever? Did I really promise that? Hmmm, I might have exaggerated a bit. I'm not God, after all. Not yet anyway." I lean in, put my hand on his, my red eyes still locked on his. "I am the son you never had, remember? You trust me. You've given yourself to me, heart and soul. Now, you will give me the rest."

He nods, mute. I hold each document for him. With a shaking hand, he signs each one. When he's done, I take the pen and put it back in my suit pocket. Pockets are wonderful things. Humans are mostly scum, but they do have some neat ideas.

"Thank you, Wincenty. Might I call you Father now?"

"What?" His eyes pulse with confusion. "Oh, I don't—"

"I never had a real father—well, I did once, but that was so long ago, longer than even I can remember. Memory is such a funny thing, isn't it? Even for creatures such as I. How I wish I could choose to forget as some of you humans do. Forgetting… is a blessing. You should be glad of that, Wincenty."

I sigh and stand, snuffing out my cigar, and gaze at Baldyr, the Golden Son, lying frozen on the sand, clutching his bleeding arm, his face a rictus of pain. "He wins, of course. The games are rigged, just like everything else in this wicked life. You know about rigging the game better than anyone, don't you Wincenty? That is the secret to your success. You amassed a vast fortune with genetically modified seeds and used it to genetically modify humans. Your father would have been so proud of you. Your mother... well, it's a good thing she died before she knew how you turned out. You don't remember her, do you?"

West stares at me blankly. "My... mother?" His lip trembles slightly. His small eyes squint even smaller as if he is trying to picture her face.

I shake my head sadly. "No, I don't suppose you do. You were so young when your father sent you to America. But I remember her well. Such a meek woman. Devout. Doted on you. Perhaps she could have saved you." I pause for dramatic effect. "Nah." I bend over so my face is inches from his. "Goodbye, Wincenty. Have a nice trip."

"Trip? What trip?"

"Do not worry. It will be quick."

I place my hand upon his lumpy chest. I feel the blood flowing into and out of his heart as I draw his life force into me. My body warms as his heart falters; the beating speeds up and then becomes erratic.

West flails at me, trying to push me away. His skin becomes ashen; his eyes flutter. Red spots appear on his forehead. His mouth opens and closes, then goes slack. His mountainous body shudders and then relaxes as if melting into the chair. His eyes remain open, fixed on me, and I see all the questions running through his blood-starved brain. In the end, I see his understanding. He lets out one more, rattling breath.

I withdraw my hand from his chest, my own husk now radiating with the heat of his transferred energy. Such a delectable sensation. I straighten, gather the signed papers, and place them on his desk in a neat pile.

"My dear fellow, your heart isn't what it used to be. You really shouldn't watch these violent holos."

I say a command, and the gladiator battle picks up where it left off in the center of the room. As usual, the Golden Son overcomes his injury and defeats his adversary to wild applause. I can't take my eyes off the boy—such a beautiful creature. He will be mine in the end.

But first things first. The GEM. Now *is* the time.

"Loop," I say aloud. The match replays as I quietly leave the room.

Chapter Three
Jared

I step from the elevator into the garden, greeted by balls of light that hover in the air like small, burning suns, setting the overarching trees aglow. Mammoth white flowers shaped like the heads of wolves line the path before me. Snakes crawl by on tiny feet, and butterflies as big as birds flutter around my head. A rabbit sporting antlers peeks from behind a rock and hisses, baring fanged teeth. My father's creations become ever more bizarre.

"There you are." Vale, my brother, appears from behind a tree, dodging one of the floating lights. A tiny monkey no bigger than a rat, with pointed ears and a corkscrew tail, perches on his shoulder. "Thought you weren't going to show." The monkey chatters, a chillingly human sound, then jumps off Vale's shoulders onto the trunk and scrambles into the silvery foliage overhead.

"Sorry." I don't tell him it took the medi-bot extra time to secure the hydrogel seal to the wound on my arm. It still itches madly, and the healing infusions I need after every match make me lightheaded and jittery. I would have preferred a long hot soak in a tub and early bed to soothe my aching body, but my father insisted I appear at this party.

Vale wears a long red coat with an upturned collar, the same shade as his hair. He's letting it grow so he can braid it, like mine, a fashion among those aspiring to the arena these days. He's put some muscle on his sixteen-year-old frame, and there's a scruff of something on his lip. I resist the temptation to tease him about that.

"I saw the Beast Hunt." I give him a playful knock on the shoulder. "You looked good."

He grins and shrugs off the compliment. "Anyone can kill those poor, drugged-up creatures. But thanks—for talking Father into it."

"You deserve it. You've been training hard."

He straightens, his chin jutting slightly. "Father hasn't said anything. I hope he was pleased."

I pat his shoulder. "Of course he was. You'll be better than me in no time."

His eyes get big. "No way—"

Jarring laughter explodes from beyond the trees. The party is already in full swing. I draw a deep breath. "All right. Let's get this over with."

We walk together down the path to a wide marble-paved piazza studded with fruit trees, flower beds, and still pools. Hundreds of guests mingle and sip their drinks, their painted faces illuminated by the floating balls of light. Human-shaped robots roam the crowd, offering champagne in tall crystal glasses with spiraled stems and wide, pointed rims, made to resemble the New Asgard tower itself.

Women in glittering gowns with more glitter in their hair and on their skin gather in clumps like schools of iridescent fish. Around them strut those giant predators, the Grigori, fallen angels come to earth, all wearing bizarre costumes that make them look even stranger than they already are.

They were once Zazel's warriors, but now they live only for pleasure and extravagant self-indulgence.

Sariel approaches us, a bejeweled gold catsuit molded to his body, a pair of fake gossamer wings dripping with hundreds of diamonds. His gigantic, crescent-moon-shaped headdress adds two feet to his eight-foot frame.

"Well, if it isn't the Golden Son himself," he purrs, pausing to plant a kiss on my head. His gaggle of muscular slaves wearing only loincloths, all of them New People, eye me warily. They look so much like me, these white-haired men transformed by the Cure to be super-strong and practically immortal. Could it be that I am really one of them? "Fashionably late as always." Sariel laughs, an unnerving sound.

Armaros, small for a Grigori at only seven feet, sidles up to my other side. His hair is bright green and his body is covered with shimmering leaves so he looks like a bejeweled tree. He raises his arm toward me, showing off baubles of dangling fruit.

"Want a bite?" he asks with a gleaming smile.

"No, thank you." I take a step backward. Vale stifles a choking laugh.

"Let me." Sariel bends to grab one of the fruity baubles in his teeth. He makes noises of delight as he chews.

I turn away, only to be faced with a mammoth Grigori in dull black armor, his black hair hanging straight around his handsome, extremely pale face, his white, pupil-less eyes bearing down on me.

"Baldyr," he growls.

"Gadreel." I bow to him, avoiding his weird eyes.

He nods once, his bright red lips curling in what might be a smile. "You are not too badly hurt, I see." Gadreel sounds disappointed.

"I'm fine. Thank you for asking." I walk away from him quickly.

Vale catches sup with me. "Man, he's scary," he says. "And he really hates you."

"I've noticed that."

All the Grigori hate me, but then again, they hate each other equally.

"This piazza... is new," I remark.

"Father wanted the garden to look more Roman. It does, doesn't it?" Vale sounds pleased.

"Where is he?"

Vale shrugs. "Probably watching from his spire. It's his habit these days."

I glance up at Zazel's spire, one of ten that surrounds the garden, though his is by far the largest. He rarely shows himself in public anymore, appearing only as his gigantic avatar. I suppose it's all to perpetuate the idea of him being a real god.

We keep walking. Camera drones dart about like flies. Auroras spin and weave in the night sky above, swirling colors of red, green, orange, and purple. I wonder if they are real or a conjuring of Grigori engineers.

I get a whiff of jasmine—my father's queen strides into the piazza, accompanied by her freakishly handsome NP slaves. She's dressed in a lavish red gown that seems to be made entirely of rubies. Her red hair is piled high and held back from her face by a diamond-studded tiara. Cell-regeneration infusions make her look closer to thirty than fifty.

Shannon Snow. Grace's mother.

I pause, pressing a hand to my chest, as if to quell the sudden stab of pain. That's how it is when I think of her.

Grace. She was my wife. Now she's dead.

Beside Shannon is a younger woman in a plain green gown, her blond hair pulled into a severe bun. She looks out of place in this bizarre company.

"Who is that?" I ask Vale. "With your mother."

Vale shrugs. "Someone she knew from her Hollywood days."

"Hollywood?"

"When she was in movies, I suppose."

This is something I should know, and yet I don't. My memories have been fractured ever since I woke up in a cave in Switzerland a year ago with no idea who I was or how I got there.

"I'll bet she's one of your fans," Vale says, an edge of envy in his voice. "That's what they all are." He waves a hand toward the clutch of young women.

I'm instantly suspicious. Shannon has tried for months to set me up with women. Perhaps this girl is her latest ploy. Shannon knows who I really am, or who I was before, although I pretend I don't remember her. She wants a spy in my bed. This girl looks different from the usual suspects, who always resemble Grace in one way or another.

I grab two champagne glasses from a passing robot and hand one to Vale. We continue our stroll through the garden, passing by the Guardians who stand at intervals around the perimeter, watching us with their slitted yellow eyes, their cobra-like hoods fully expanded.

I continue scanning the guests—assorted oligarchs and billionaires, members of the Interlaken Group, along with their too-young escorts. Members of the Council of Ten, those that rule the ten unions of the United Earth. And the Grigori, about thirty of the one hundred fifty that now inhabit this world.

Wolves.

"There he is!" squeals an excited female voice. One of the starlets charges through the crowd, bumping into the girl in green and nearly knocking her glass from her hand. A general stampede of mostly shrieking women follows.

"It's him! Baldyr!"

"You were amazing today!"

"Baldyr! A Cubie please!"

Baldyr. After nine months, I am still not used to being called that.

They descend upon me, thrusting I-Cubes in my face for pictures. I glance at Vale, who looks on resentfully. I grab his arm and thrust it in the air.

"Let's hear it for Vale, champion of the Beast Hunt!" I shout.

"Yes! To Vale!" Shannon says, lifting her glass.

"Hail Vale!" The cries ring across the garden. Everyone laughs, toasts, drinks, and smashes their glasses onto the marble tiles. Vale grins, his face crimson.

The women natter on.

"What's it like to fight an NP Gladiator?"

"How did you get so strong?"

"Who does your hair?"

They beg for more Cubies.

"Just one picture so I can show my friends!"

I've learned to keep moving as if I have someplace important to go. I wish they would stop grabbing my arm because it hurts like crazy, though I have to pretend it doesn't. They think I am impervious to pain like the New People. Like the Grigori.

They don't know I am as human as they are.

Once I was a Nephilim, half-angel, half-human. No more. I'm not even sure how that happened. All I know is when I woke up in that waterfall, my angel powers were gone. Along with my memories. Most of them anyway. There are things I remember: Grace. The Abyss. Azazel, my angel father, once a prisoner of the Abyss, now the ruler of the world, Grigori Zazel.

Does he know? He must by now. He has to get reports on the daily ministrations of the medi-bots, the steroid injections, and the healing infusions. A true Nephilim wouldn't need any of that.

"I'm going to check out the food." Vale makes a beeline for the banquet table at the other end of the courtyard.

I start to follow him when someone grabs my arm. I gasp out loud and spin around, my hands balling into fists.

The woman in the green dress jumps backward with a half-suppressed yelp. "I'm sorry!" she says in a breathless voice. "I didn't mean to—I mean—"

"It's nothing." *Just a wound from a poleaxe.* I press my hand to my side.

"I'm really sorry." She's American, from her accent. The common language is Norwegian now, and Americans are worse at it than most. "I was just hoping to get a chance to meet you."

"Do I know you?"

"We met once, a long time ago. I was just a kid. It was in California."

"I've never been there." I keep moving. She follows doggedly.

"Actually, you were. Maybe you don't remember. If you would just stop for a second—please, Jared."

I stop dead. Among the few memories of my former life is my name. My *real* name. Jared.

I turn to look at her. Her lips purse, eyes narrowing. "So, it is you."

"Ah! Baldyr, I see you've met my stepdaughter!" Shannon appears suddenly, all sparkles and smiles, her arm snaking around the girl's shoulders. The girl stiffens visibly and forces a smile in return.

Stepdaughter?

"I just want to get a Cubie for the girls back in New York. He's not very cooperative." The girl throws me a look of warning and panic.

"He's like that, isn't he? I think he's just shy, really." Shannon forces a laugh. "Sally, there are some people I want you to meet." With a death grip on her shoulders, Shannon tries to steer the girl away from me.

"I'll be there in a sec," Sally says, gently disengaging from Shannon's embrace.

Shannon stands a moment, her face clouding and then clearing in an instant. "Of course, darling," she croons. "Don't be long." With a sharp look at me, she melts into the crowd.

Sally pulls her I-Cube out of her purse and scans her hand. "Camera" she says. Instantly the projection of a tiny screen bursts from the top of the small device.

"Say cheese." She aims the screen toward the two of us. I barely manage a smile before the projected screen flashes, replaced by a 3D image of the two of us. She touches the Cube again, and the image vanishes.

"Is there someplace we can talk?" she whispers as she slips the Cube into her purse.

I bite my lip. This could be dangerous. But it's a risk I must take.

"In my spire," I say. I hesitate before giving her the password she will need to get past the Guardiana. She nods, understanding. Then I walk away quickly, dismissing her.

I shouldn't trust her. She is Shannon's stepdaughter.

Yet, she knows my name.

"Hey!" Vale lurches at me, balancing a loaded plate in one hand while stuffing shrimp in his mouth with the other. "I brought you some." He grins, then stares at me, concerned. "Hey, Bro, you okay?"

Before I can answer, trumpets blare and timpani thunder so loud everyone shrieks and covers their ears. Vale jumps, spilling his plate of food. The garden fills with blinding light as if a meteor has suddenly descended from the heavens.

Above the cries of awe and fear, Gadreel shouts, "Kneel! The Lord has come!"

We fall to our knees as the light compresses into a single glowing circle surrounding the form of Grigori Zazel—his avatar anyway. He looks so real he could have just walked in, except that he is twenty feet tall. This is how he looked that day in the arena, when he raised me from the dead.

My memory of that day is still fuzzy. I've spent hours watching the holo feeds of my apparent assassination—the shooter rushing onto the arena floor and aiming a gun at my head; my body falling; sudden mayhem, people swarming over me, shouting; a close-up image of my face covered in blood. There's no way I could have survived such a wound.

And then my father, Grigori Zazel, descending from the heavens in his gigantic avatar and, in front of a hushed crowd of sixty thousand, bringing me back to life.

Was it real? Or a trick of some sort? The Grigori are capable of anything. Yet if it was real, I owe my life to Zazel. How, then, do I kill the one who saved me?

For that was supposed to be my mission. To kill Grigori Zazel—my father.

The Supreme Lord's white head is adorned by a crystal crown of ten spikes. His one golden eye—for some reason, he still sports an eyepatch—shines like a tiny sun. He wears a long white cape with a high collar decorated with jeweled snakes entangled in an intricate pattern. Beside him his favorite creation, a speckled lion with huge feathered wings, opens its massive mouth in a prolonged yawn.

"Welcome, my people!" Zazel lifts his arms. The cape falls away to reveal the rippling gold armor encasing his powerful body. "I come to congratulate my son, the Destroyer, the Golden Son, Baldyr on his great victory today. I am well pleased." He rests his single eye on me and smiles beatifically.

I bow to him. He may not be here in person, but no doubt he can still see me.

"How you have entertained us, my son. You've entertained the whole world! But I have not forgotten what happened nine months ago. How you were so ruthlessly attacked by that infidel assassin. I am not slow to act. The time for reckoning has come."

Suddenly Zazel's body seems to grow even larger, glowing brighter than the light that surrounds him. The trees, the vines, even the marble stones under our knees tremble and quake, causing fresh whispers of fear. I grab hold of Vale's collar to keep him from falling over.

Zazel's voice, always thunderous, now seems birthed from the earthquake itself.

"Listen to me! Hear my words! Strike the pillars until the foundations shake, shatter them on the heads of all the people. With the sword, I will kill the last of them; not one of them will flee; not one of them will escape. I am giving orders, and I will shake the house of Israel among all the nations as one sifts dirt with a screen, but no pebble will fall to the ground. All the sinners will die by the sword, those who say, 'He won't overtake us.' The mountains will drip blood, and all the hills will flow with it."

The last few words nearly break my eardrums. I shut my eyes as a scream rises inside of my mind, straining for release. The healed wound in my head pulses as if the bullet were still lodged there.

Just when it seems the entire tower will collapse, the shaking and tumult stops. I open my eyes. Zazel is gone, the light with him.

No one dares to move. The only sound is the faint buzzing of the drones.

Zazel's words hang in the air, reverberating like a mist. They were not his own words, they came from somewhere, probably from the Bible. Zazel loves to steal God's words for his own ends. But the Bible is illegal. Forbidden.

"What was that?" Vale is still kneeling amid his spilled food, his face pale as death.

I look down at him. "A prophecy." More than that. "A promise."

Murmurs rise as people totter to their feet. Several women have fainted. The Grigori burst into joyous laughter, drinking and smashing their glasses with renewed relish. Zazel, wherever he is, must be enjoying this spectacle.

I grab Vale's arm and pull him upright, brushing food off his coat. My body aches. My mind whirrs.

"It sounds like… war," Vale whispers, more excited than fearful.

"Yes," I say.

Zazel is going to wipe Israel from the face of the earth.

I was supposed to stop him.

I failed.

Chapter Four
Grace

For the twentieth time, I watch my husband battle demons.

Maybe it's been more than twenty. I've lost count. The video is fuzzy, transferred to VHS by our genius hacker Ripley and his hacker friends in the so-called Lollipop Guild. I strain to catch every move he makes, every thrust of his sword, every bead of sweat, every drop of blood. I wince and grab my throat when he's wounded; it's as if I can feel it. When the camera swoops in to focus on his face, I freeze the frame and stare into his eyes, that piercing, almost painful shade of blue, and imagine he can see me too.

The AngelSong buzzes in the back of my mind as it always does when I watch Jared fight. The song that is always in my head, the song that propelled him to save me from a school shooter all those years ago. A song that tames demons.

Can he hear it still? Or has he forgotten it, forgotten me, our life together, our marriage, our love?

He looks so different now—so much bigger, stronger, more… godlike. Yet I know inside he's the opposite. More human. More breakable. More killable. I see it in his eyes.

How is he doing this? More importantly, why?

For nine months, I've watched him perform in the arena for the world's pleasure. Is this what he was born to be? A spectacle? It seems he cannot escape it. The world once made him a rock star. Now he is a… a shooting star. This is partly my fault, I suppose. If he'd never met me, he could have continued living his life in obscurity. Maybe.

He wins, as usual. He never loses. Perhaps the games are rigged, as everyone seems to think. But their violence seems so very real. And Jared's suffering—that looks real too. Maybe it's just more Grigori fakery. Maybe I see what I want to see.

Above the arena, the sky fills with brilliant light. Auroras of every imaginable color flash across the screen, each one more brilliant than the last. Those are probably faked too.

Just like the day you were born, Jared. The day of the greatest aurora spectacle in history. Was that really an omen? A sign your birth would rock the world?

People say Jared is truly Azazel's creature now. They say Jared has finally embraced his role as Azazel's son, and I shouldn't be surprised, because I knew it was going to happen eventually. Only I don't believe it. Because he's human now. Isn't he? The more I watch him, the less certain I am even of that.

"Are you still mooning over Golden Boy?"

Penny's sharp voice in the doorway of the radio station makes me jump out of my seat. I slam my thumb on the monitor's power button and pull the headphones off my ears. "I was listening to the *Voice*," I sputter.

She walks over to me, arms folded. She's wearing a knit cap over her purple hair—where she manages to find purple hair dye I'll never know—and a cable sweater under her ubiquitous leather jacket. It's cold at night in the Black Hills this time of year.

"Aren't you supposed to be monitoring the radio?"

"I was." We take turns in four hour shifts on the short wave, scanning the channels for chatter, requests for help, or news from Oz, our nickname for the outer world. I usually do the night shift because it's quieter—more time to watch Jared's matches without interruption. "I was actually listening to the *Voice*." That's a podcast out of Israel that boldly proclaims biblical prophecy worldwide, a lifeline for those of us in exile, waiting for the end of the world.

"Is that so?" She grabs the headphones and puts them on. "I don't hear anything."

"It just ended," I say sheepishly, peering up at her as if she were my mom reprimanding me for playing video games when I should have been doing my chemistry homework. We used to be the same age, but now Penny is in her mid-thirties, and I'm just twenty-one. I lost a bunch of years when I went to the *There*—long story.

"You were watching *him* again, weren't you?"

I sigh. "He's my husband."

"Was."

"Till death do us part."

"He died. Like, more than once. Besides, you were never actually married. Not legally."

"We were so." Heat rises in my cheeks. "Just because we didn't have a piece of paper… we were married in the eyes of God."

Penny replies with a huffy breath. I know what that means. She blames Jared for what happened to Ralph and Emilia; she's convinced he ratted them out and got them arrested. I refuse to believe that. We still have no idea what happened to them, though Ripley and the Guild have done their best to find out. The fact that we might never know is an open wound in the pit of my soul.

"Did you just come to spy on me?" I ask.

"No, as a matter of fact. I thought you'd like to know that Noah is back."

"He is?" I jump up. "You could have led with that. Where is he?"

"In the chapel. He brought some new munchkins. I need to get your opinion about them."

Munchkins—her nickname for the refugees from Oz that find their way to the Rez.

"I can't leave. I'm on duty."

"Simon's coming to take over for you."

As if on cue, Simon appears in the doorway, huffing as if he'd run five miles. His scrawny arms are loaded with books which he balances all in one hand so he can push his glasses up his nose. Between the thick glasses and his thicker beard, his face is nearly invisible, other than a perpetually red nose.

"I'm here!"

I grumble, reluctantly ejecting the VHS tape and shoving it into my backpack. I keep the tapes of Jared's fights with me at all times; otherwise, they would probably disappear without explanation.

Simon takes my place in the chair, dumping his books on the desk and sniffling loudly. "Any chatter?"

"Not tonight," I say.

"Nothing from New Asgard?"

"No."

"So strange. The assassination attempt was months ago. What's taking Zazel so long to make a move?" Simon seems to be talking more to himself.

"Don't know."

Simon has always irritated me. Maybe it's his constant sniffling. Maybe it's because he thinks Jared is the Antichrist. That's just absurd. He says Zazel can't be the Antichrist because he's technically not human, and Jared was the one who sustained a head wound and came back to life. Never mind that Jared didn't do any of the other things the Antichrist is supposed to be doing. At least, not yet.

"Guess he wants to take them off-guard," Simon says, answering his own question. "They were ready for an attack nine months ago."

I sling my backpack over my shoulder. "Maybe Zazel's just afraid because he knows God is on Israel's side."

Simon barks out an annoying laugh. "I doubt that." He sniffs, puts on the headphones, and busies himself with the knobs and dials on the radio.

I sigh and join Penny at the door. We hop into the truck and drive the dusty road to the church, passing dilapidated trailers, pickup trucks, rusty vans, and the Quonset huts that house the newer residents of the Black Hills reservation. A few people wave from lawn chairs as they tend campfires. The smell of hot dogs roasting makes my stomach rumble. I haven't eaten since breakfast. A Twinkie. Or was it a Ding Dong? What I wouldn't give for a banana. Fruit is as rare as hot showers around here.

Penny seems to know what I'm thinking. "Come over to my place after. I've got a pack of dogs to roast."

"Sounds good." Meat is one of the few things we aren't constantly running out of.

"So what's your issue with the new munchkins?" I ask.

"I don't like the look of them."

"Why not?"

"Too... healthy. Rich looking. Mom, dad, two little kids. How many people in Oz are allowed even one kid, let alone two? Their story doesn't add up."

"So you think they're spies?"

"Noah doesn't think so. I'm not so sure. When was the last time a UE official defected? It doesn't happen."

"Maybe it does, sometimes."

"Yeah, maybe." Penny sounds doubtful. She quiet a moment, then says, "You know, even if Jared hasn't gone to the dark side, Zazel is still using him. And he's allowing it to happen."

"Maybe he doesn't have a choice," I say. "Or maybe something happened to him—to his brain. He was shot in the head. He died. Zazel brought him back to life. Maybe that... changed him."

"Ripley says it was a trick."

"The prophecy says the Antichrist will do signs and wonders."

"Simon doesn't believe Azazel is the Antichrist."

"Simon doesn't know everything. How many men have come and gone who were supposed to be the Antichrist? Nero? Antiochus Epiphanes? Hitler? Stalin? People said they were the Antichrist, but they were all wrong."

Penny makes a clicking noise with her tongue. "Ralph used to say they were all shadows of the Antichrist, like forerunners. I think that was the word he used. But the real Antichrist couldn't appear until there was a temple in Israel. And guess what? There's a temple in Israel now."

That's true. "Don't you find it odd that Zazel would allow that temple to be built, given how much he hates Israel?"

"When has Zazel ever done anything that makes sense?"

Penny swerves suddenly onto an even more rutted road. I grab the roll bar. A few minutes later, we pull in front of New Hope Church, an old clapboard building with a half-finished steeple. It was built by a group of Methodists who abandoned it during the pandemic. Inside, several people are stretched out on pews, asleep, using coats and other bits of clothing for pillows. So many people still don't have a place to live.

Blaine, our pastor, is seated with a small group at the front. They all turn to look when we enter. My gaze goes straight to the boy with the sandy hair, green eyes, and familiar dimpled smile. I break into a run.

"Noah!" I throw my arms around his broad shoulders. He hugs me, lifting me off my feet, chuckling against my neck. "Thank God you're back." I run my fingers over his stubbly beard; razors are scarce. It makes him look older, less boyish, but not harder. Never that. "I was getting worried. You're a week overdue. Trouble?"

"A bit." His words are still tinged with his native French. "But we made it back okay."

"Grace," says Blaine, standing up. "This is James and Emily Camden and their daughters Daisy and Rose. This is Grace. You might know her as M."

I gaze at the couple seated in the front pew holding two sleepy children. Emily is disheveled and red-eyed but well-dressed and not as hollow-cheeked as most of the people who come to us. The man, James, is tall and slender with the pale complexion of a government bureaucrat. Both of them are far too healthy looking to be Forbidden.

"Are you really M?" Emily says in a breathless tone. "We've been listening to you. So nice to finally meet you."

"I'm only a substitute. Filling in for the real M."

Emilia is M, not me. I won't give up hope that she will return. I focus on the children, who are nicely dressed like their mother, though a bit dirty.

"Not many people in the NAU are able to have children," I remark casually. They aren't Grigori children. The Grigori only sire boy babies.

"We were lucky," says Emily with a nervous look at her husband. "We were granted fertility treatments."

I can feel Penny tense beside me. Only top elites get fertility treatments.

"What were your jobs?" Penny asks.

"I was a primary teacher," says Emily.

"For WeLearn?" Penny says derisively. That's the Grigori school system reserved for children of the Grigori and favored elites. Emily nods, shamefaced.

"And you?" I ask, turning to James.

He hesitates before answering. "I used to be the deputy minister of the Bureau of Information Governance."

Penny sucks in a breath. I glance at Noah, who makes a motion that means, "just listen to their story first."

I turn back to James. "Why did you defect?" I ask. James clears his throat, always a sign someone is about to say something they don't want to say.

"I was in charge of... *revising* the results of research studies done for public release." James' voice is reedy with exhaustion. "I received a report on the side effects of the GEM."

"The what?" I ask.

"The GEM. The Grigori Eminence Marker. It's the latest innovation from the Interlaken Group, a biometric tattoo on the forehead designed to replace the subdermal chip. It's permanent, can't be removed, and connects a person's brain to the Neuro-Link network."

"Yikes," says Penny.

"So far, it has only been required for Peacemakers and other NPs," James continues, "but many people have gotten it voluntarily as a symbol of their devotion to the Supreme Lord. Besides, getting the GEM gives ordinary citizens special status and lots of extra crypto credits, a huge incentive. For a while now, there have been rumors that the GEM would be required of the general population, hence the report. So, I read it, and I was… shocked. One in three recipients suffered a severe reaction, usually a stroke or seizures, within a year of administration. Nearly half of those became permanently disabled or died. I was concerned. It was my job to either suppress or 'revise' reports like this, but in this case, I just couldn't do it. This thing sounded too dangerous." He pauses, licking his lips. "I sent it up-channel with a yellow sticker, which means I was advising a manual review. That's normal procedure. But apparently, in this case, it wasn't." He takes a deep breath, glancing at his wife. "The next morning, I received a Cube message saying I had to resign my position, effective immediately. I was being reassigned to delivery services."

"Delivering what?" I ask.

James shrugs. "It's always deliberately vague. We were told to move out of our apartment by the end of the week. There was a distinct chance we would be sent to WeCamp. It's a common progression. I should know. I was often the one who… facilitated such decisions." He lowers his gaze, ashamed. "Our only hope was to disappear."

"How many people have you sent to camps for information violations?" Penny asks sharply.

James sighs. "I thought I was doing the right thing—keeping people safe, protecting the public from the lies of the… Well, anyway…"

A moment passes. No one says anything.

"How did you know about the Yellow Brick Road?" I ask, breaking the uncomfortable silence.

"Our bureau was in charge of monitoring YBR misinformation that found its way onto the internet. You'd be surprised how often that happens despite the media blackout. We had to constantly shift the narrative to ensure people didn't get… infected. That's the word we used. The Forbidden were infecting people." He produces a handkerchief from his pocket and wipes his brow. He's sweating despite the coolness of the room. "In my research, I had learned about a woman who made quite a successful business helping people... disappear. I never acted upon the information. I'm not sure why. It seemed trivial at the time. Not many people escaped from Chicago. They were always caught—almost always. So, I contacted her. She refused to help me, thought I was a spy, like you. But she changed her mind when I offered to triple her fee."

"Do you know who that was?" I ask Noah.

"She goes by the name Glinda," he says. "Must be a free agent. She's the one who contacted us on the shortwave. Gave us all the details on where to find them."

"We did what she told us to do," James says. "We removed our chips—the woman gave us instructions on how to do that ourselves—left them on the kitchen table with our Cubes, and then left our apartment in the middle of the night. We went to my mother's house on the outskirts of the city and waited. Glinda was supposed to let us know when someone was coming, but we never heard from her again."

Emily continues the story. "We waited for a week. We were so scared, sure the authorities would find us before the YBR did. Then, one night, Noah showed up." She points to Noah with a grateful smile. "I couldn't believe it."

"He's the best," I say, touching Noah's arm. He blushes. I glance at Blaine, searching his face for his thoughts. He nods as if to tell me he believes them.

"You could have other trackers," I say. "So you'll have to go through our own examinations."

"Of course," says James. "Whatever you need."

I regard them a moment longer. Should we really trust these people? Every instinct I have says no, but then I think of those two little girls, and I know there's only one choice I can make.

I clear my throat. "Just so you know, this is a hard life. There are no amenities. There is very little privacy. We can't even guarantee you a place to live. And you'll have to work if you want to eat."

"We understand," Emily says.

Penny sighs loudly and turns to the pews. "Jackson?"

A teenager with a cloud of frizzy hair pops up, rubbing his eyes and yawning. Jackson has been Penny's shadow ever since she helped him and his family escape from Buffalo several years ago. "Yeah?"

"Jackson here will take you to the infirmary for your examination." Penny indicates Emily's bandaged hand. "And to make sure there's no infection."

"Thank you." Emily cradles her hand and winces.

"Yes, thank you—so much." James lets out a long-held breath.

"Come on, girls." Emily nudges the sleepy children awake. They rub their eyes and yawn as their mother and father lead them to where Jackson waits.

"So, what do you think?" Penny asks once the family is gone.

"I think they're telling the truth," I say. "Maybe not the whole truth."

Penny shakes her head. "The guy looks shifty to me."

"Everyone looks shifty to you."

"True." Penny sighs.

I turn to Noah. "You really think he's okay?"

Noah shrugs. "I believe he is sincere. And… repentant."

"Even if he isn't, saving those two children is the right thing to do," says Blaine.

"We'll have to keep a close eye on them," Penny says, then claps her hands and turns to me. "I'm going home to cook hot dogs. You want a ride?"

"I'll catch up," I say as she stalks out.

Blaine yawns. "I've got some praying to do. And sleeping. Noah, take the whole day off tomorrow, buddy. You deserve it." He pats Noah on the shoulder.

"Thank you." Noah smiles.

Blaine smiles at me before leaving through a side door.

I look at Noah. "So what else happened out there that you aren't telling me?"

"Nothing much."

I laugh. "Let me guess. You got chased by a drone and had to hide out in a cornfield for three days. Then you almost got arrested by Peacemakers in Chicago but managed somehow to escape—"

"I'm fine," Noah says, smiling wanly.

"It's getting worse out there, isn't it?"

He shrugs. "More road blocks, more drones. Seems like the NAU is trying to blockade all the main routes to the Free States. Maybe because of the news about this GEM thing now being mandatory."

"They don't want anyone escaping," I say. He nods. "Noah, you can't go out there anymore. What happens if you get caught? You'll get sent to a camp or worse—"

"I'm hungry," Noah says, interrupting. "Let's go eat some hot dogs."

Chapter Five
Jared

I gaze out the glass walls of my spire, counting stars. When did I start to envy them? Stars, birds, insects, the distant mountains—anything outside the window, anything free of walls. Even glass walls.

It's well past midnight. The aurora has faded or been turned off. I'm tired and hurting, but I can't go to sleep.

She should be here soon. I wait. I try to remember.

Grace. I search for her in my cloudy past. A few moments have come back to me: The day we met. I killed a boy that day. A boy with a gun. I did that to save her—because she sang. I don't need to remember the song because it is a part of my very being—the AngelSong.

Beyond that, our journey into the Abyss is the only clear memory I have. How long ago was that? The time between then and now is a mystery unsolved. Why did I leave her? Or did she leave me? What happened? When did she—?

No. I can't think about that.

"Dominus." Sabina, all six feet of Roman slave hologram, stands at the top of the circular staircase beside a bewildered Sally, clutching a green silk wrap around her shoulders. "Your guest has arrived."

"Thank you," I say.

Sabina promptly disappears.

Sally jumps and gasps, blinking in amazement at the empty space where a woman had just stood.

"She's not real," I say in English.

"What?"

"A hologram. You'll see a lot of them around here. Half the guests at the party tonight were probably holos. Grigori magic."

"Oh." She sighs, relieved, though still confused. She has switched to English as well. "Yeah, this is a very weird place. Why did she call you *Dominius?*"

"It's the way Roman slaves address their masters."

"Good grief."

"Would you like some water?" I go to a small table and pour water from a pitcher into a glass.

"Nothing stronger?"

"No, sorry." I hold out the glass.

She inches toward me, takes the glass, and sips loudly. "I knew the Grigori had advanced tech, but I had no idea. This is way beyond what we have in New York. Why exactly are we in your bedroom? I didn't come here for *that*."

"It's the only place with no surveillance. Zazel's concession to me. He hoped it would encourage me to have more... visitors."

"Did it?"

I shrug.

She moves around the room, holding the glass like a shield against her chest. "Nice view. Not much for furniture, are you?" She takes in the gigantic bed and the few curved benches hugging the glass walls. "What do you call this architecture? Modern icicle?" She notices the beat-up guitar sitting on its stand and moves to touch the strings. "I see you're still playing."

Still? "When I get the chance. It's another concession. Music is otherwise banned from the tower. Zazel believes it foments rebellion."

"Really? Well, I guess if the Sixties are any indication, he might be right." She gazes out onto the open expanse of night. "It's like being on top of the world."

"Yes."

"Not much privacy."

"Walls, darken," I say. Instantly the glass walls become solid white.

She looks at me, surprised. "Grigori magic?"

"I can make them into mirrors too."

"Bet you Grigori-types love that. Looking at yourselves in 360." She sits on one of the benches, examining its smooth surface. "What kind of wood is this?"

"Fake."

"Oh."

I study her, wondering how much I should reveal. "Why did you call me that name?"

"It's your real name, isn't it?"

I shrug. "I don't know my real name. I lost my memory."

"Really? Well, it was in California. I was just a kid. My dad was getting married to Shannon—"

"Your father was married to Shannon?"

"Yeah. My father was... Harry Ravel."

I stare at her, blinking.

"I see you're surprised," she says. "Yeah, the Special Counselor to the Supreme Lord was my dad."

"I'm... sorry." Harry Ravel was killed by the same assassin who shot me.

She shrugs. "Yeah, me too. We hadn't been on good terms for a long time. I never even got to talk to him before... Anyway, Shannon invited Grace, to the wedding—"

"Grace?" My heart nearly stops beating. *Grace.*

She gives me a strange look. "You remember Grace, right? Shannon's daughter? I mean, you two were in love. *Really* in love. You can't tell me you don't remember *that.*"

I swallow hard. "I do remember," I whisper.

"I thought so," she says with a grin.

"You said I was there? In California?"

"You were actually on tour with a band called Blood Moon. Ring a bell?"

I shake my head, though there is something familiar about the name.

"You wore an angel costume and went by the name Danny Loveless. You've had a lot of names, haven't you?"

"So what happened?" I ask.

"Well, it was all very dramatic. I discovered that Shannon was actually plotting to kill Grace, so I helped her escape."

"Wait. You're saying Shannon wanted to kill her own daughter?"

Sally nods. "She's always been kind of a psycho. She wasn't too happy with me, though, so right after the wedding, she packed me off to a boarding school. Then my father was elected governor of California and later president of the United States, back when that existed. He wanted me to come live at the White House, but by then, I didn't want to be anywhere near Shannon so I refused. I was in college anyway. But now I wish I had."

"Why?"

"Maybe I could have talked him out of doing what he did, resigning the presidency and coming here—to New Asgard. That was all Shannon's idea, I'm betting. Now he's dead. People around Shannon tend to end up dead once they've lost their usefulness." She takes a big gulp of water. "Are you sure you don't have anything stronger?"

I shake my head.

She sighs. "I live in New York now, working for the Bureau of Energy Conservation. I'm a lawyer, not a scientist. There are a lot more lawyers than scientists in the bureau. I thought Shannon had forgotten all about me, but then several months ago, she was in New York, filming her movie, and she called me out of the blue."

"Oh yes. The movie."

"Can you believe it? *Katrina Kross and the Curse of the Jehovians.* Who knew the world needed another Katrina Kross film. Jehovians—that's the UE's new term for the Forbidden. They love changing the names of things. Anyway, we went out to dinner, and Shannon was sweet as pie, acting like nothing ever happened. She invited me to come to New Asgard for the Grigori Games. As much as I hated her, I was kind of curious about you. I mean, you looked so much like *you,* but I couldn't believe you were the same person as that rock star I'd met so long ago. It seemed impossible, but I had to know. And, okay, maybe I was fangirling too. I mean, my friends were so jealous. Your fights are better entertainment than Zazel's speeches and the Grigori movies, which are pretty... Well, you've seen them, haven't you?"

I clear my throat. "I've seen them."

She nods in solidarity. "So I accepted. Shannon sent her personal Dragonfly to pick me up and everything. And I have to say, you definitely delivered." She pauses, looking at me with renewed suspicion. "Although now I'm beginning to wonder—was that really you out there? Or is that more Grigori magic? Holograms fighting holograms?"

"The arena is the one area where Zazel demands authenticity," I say. "For the most part."

She shakes her head. "Jared Lorn. I can't wrap my head around this. How come you aren't any older? Grigori magic?"

"Something like that."

"Are you really the Supreme Lord's long-lost son?"

"He thinks I am."

"How did you end up here?"

I sit beside her on the bench. Should I tell her about waking up in a cave among the Forbidden? Spending weeks with them, learning about their plight, and then agreeing to their plan to come to New Asgard and attempt to stop Grigori Zazel? No, I can't risk it.

"The only thing I remember is one day, I woke up in the wilderness, not knowing where I was or who I was. I wandered around for a while until I got picked up by a Peacemaker patrol. They tested my DNA and sent me here. I guess Zazel had been looking for me for a long time."

"Wow," Sally says. She stands and wanders over to the guitar, picks it up, and plucks some strings. "And you don't know what happened to Grace?"

I hesitate. "She's dead."

Her eyes widen. "Dead? Are you sure?"

"I've seen the records, the death certificate, everything. She died of the virus."

Sally plucks another string and sighs. "Is that why you're doing this?"

"Doing what?"

"Playing gladiator while Grigori Zazel destroys the world."

I move to her and take the guitar from her hands. "I don't know what you're talking about."

"Really? Is that how you're going to play this?"

I grip the guitar, my jaw tightening. "You don't know how dangerous it is to talk like that."

She laughs harshly. "Dangerous? You have no idea how dangerous the world has become, do you? You live in a glass tower with no care about what's going on in the rest of the world."

Shame floods me. She's right. I *do* have no idea. I set the guitar back on the stand, wishing I could get her to leave so I could sit down and play for a while, clear my brain.

She takes my arm and pulls me around to face her. "Okay, keep on pretending if that's what you want to do. Just remember that you are the only one who can. Some of us have to go back into that world and deal with it, you know? Most of us."

I look at her. "Tell me... What's it like?"

Her expression softens. She lets go of my arm. "I believed in them once. We all did. The Grigori. It sounded good. Peace and safety and all that... happy talk. I didn't know what they really meant when they said those words. I didn't know so many people would have to suffer. Once you've seen a thousand executions and ten thousand people sent to camps for the sake of peace and safety, you begin to wonder what sort of peace and safety you've bargained for."

"*How* many have been executed?"

"You mean you don't know? Or do you skip that part of the arena games, go to your dressing room, and get a massage? You probably don't even know the reason why most of them are executed—for questioning UE edicts, spreading 'misinformation,' worshipping a god other than Grigori Zazel. Or maybe they were just no longer valuable members of society. Too old, too sick, too... useless. Who knows? They don't even need a reason anymore." She breaks off, turning away from me. I sink onto the bed.

"I wish I knew what to do," I say lamely.

She rounds on me, her eyes flashing with anger. "You are the son of the Supreme Lord! If you can't do something, who can? You heard his little speech tonight. He's going to destroy Israel. And Israel is only the beginning."

"That was just... words. He rages all the time. But he does nothing."

"Are you so sure of that?"

I grit my teeth. "I never see him. No one sees him. I haven't spoken to him in months."

"Don't make excuses. If you can't do anything, then maybe you need to get out of the way and make room for someone who can."

Her words cut me like a knife. "I would die a hundred times over if it would do any good."

"Noble words," she says bitterly. "But words only." She heads for the stairs.

"I'm sorry," I say.

She offers me a grim smile. "Me too. I believed in you, Jared Lorn. I should know better than to put my hopes in superheroes. I'm leaving tomorrow. Going back to New York for Shannon's big movie premier. Don't worry. I'll be sure to tell her that she has nothing to fear from you."

Then she's gone.

Chapter Six
Grace

We roast the hot dogs on sticks over a campfire in front of Penny and Mason's trailer. No buns or condiments sadly. Penny goes for supplies in Custer or Rapid City once a month, but she's pretty frugal about what she deems important. Our gold supply has been dwindling rapidly.

"I've been saving this." Mason pulls a small collection of ketchup packets from the inside pocket of his jacket. "Liberated from a Wendy's on my last run. They may be kind of old—that Wendy's has been closed for a while—but ketchup lasts forever, doesn't it?"

Mason is a Scarecrow like Noah, one of those that go into Oz to rescue people who are trying to escape. But unlike Noah, he actually looks a little like a scarecrow. He's also in charge of vehicle maintenance on the Rez, so he doesn't travel as much as he used to. It's a full-time job keeping the vehicles running and scrounging for gas.

Penny and Mason got married when I was in the *There,* as we have come to call that other world, the spiritual world. That's where I first met Noah. I still don't feel altogether comfortable around Mason. It's hard for me to look at him without remembering the scrawny, drugged-out teen named Mace who tried to kill me—and Penny—in a satanic ritual. He still has the nose ring and the tattoos, but his eyes are no longer haunted, and a beard he rarely trims fills out his face. He always wears a knit cap over his wavy black hair. I have to admit that he and Penny are a perfect match.

Hooting with joy, I grab a packet and slather ketchup on my hot dog.

Noah makes a face. "What are you doing?" he asks.

"Oh, I guess French people don't put ketchup on hot dogs." I lick the last drops from the packet. "What *do* French people put ketchup on?"

"Only *pommes frites*."

"French fries," I translate for Penny and Mason. "French people have different words for everything."

"What do you put on hot dogs?" Penny asks Noah.

"French people don't eat hot dogs," I say. "They're food snobs."

Noah smiles a little sadly. "Not anymore."

We are all quiet for a moment. I remember Noah's sister, Mirabel, putting frozen squares of cricket-based "food" in a microwave and considering herself lucky. At least we eat real food here. Meat, milk, and eggs are still available most of the time, and the farmers who stuck to the land after the Grigori takeover still grow enough corn, wheat, and hay to keep some small ranches and pig farms going. We grow gardens along with the Lakota in the summer, but it's October now, and the gardens are done, and we're back to hot dogs and wild turkey for the time being.

"Have you heard anything from the neighbors?" Noah asks, peering over the fire to a hill in the distance where a fenced compound sits silent, a single light shining from the military-style lookout tower.

"Two of the women dropped by last week with a bushel of apples," says Mason. "Some kind of friendship offering."

"Not a bad one either," I add. We don't know much about the people who live in the compound other than they belong to some fundamentalist group that splintered off another fundamentalist group because I guess those guys weren't fundamentalist enough.

"We chatted a bit." Mason sticks another hot dog on a stick. I've never seen anyone eat as many hot dogs as Mason, and he's still skinny as a rail. "They call themselves Children of the Remnant, and they believe the Rapture is going to happen soon so they are getting ready to go."

"They're doing a lot of building for a group that thinks they're going to heaven any minute," Penny says sourly.

Mason chuckles. "I did a little scouting. Lots of young women with kids and teenage boys. The boys are doing all the manual labor; they work from sunup to late in the night. They're clearing a big patch of ground. Must be building something big."

"A temple?" Noah muses.

"Could be."

"Maybe a Tower of Babel," Penny says with a snort.

"Are they dangerous?" I ask.

Mason shrugs. "Security is pretty tight. Armed guards at the gate. I brought over some hot dogs, asked if they wanted any. They took the food, but they wouldn't let me in. They said all visitors have to be cleared by the Exalted One. I assume that's their leader."

I shiver. We knew when we left Oz that there would be a lot of other groups doing the same thing, all kinds of religious groups with their own set of beliefs and practices. But the Children of the Remnant sound especially creepy.

"I don't think they'll bother us," Mason adds, seeing my expression. "They seem to want to be left alone."

"Maybe we should be doing what they are doing." Noah puts another dog on a stick. He secretly loves hot dogs, I can tell.

"What do you mean?" I ask.

"Building walls. Arming ourselves. How long before the Ozzies come for us?"

"He has a point," says Penny. "The North American Union isn't going to ignore us forever."

"They let the Free States secede, didn't they?" I say.

"Yeah, that was then. How long is that agreement going to last?"

"Have you talked to the Tribal Council?" I ask Penny.

Penny rolls her eyes. "I've tried. They know the NAU isn't going to keep its word. They're used to the government breaking treaties. But Chief Dan says there's nothing we can do. How do you fence in a whole reservation? Besides, if they come, they will come from the air: Missiles. Drones. DEWs. Maybe even nukes. We're sitting ducks."

"We should move into the hills," says Noah. "Find some caves."

"I've suggested that. The Tribal Council doesn't think the NAU is going to attack us. They're starving us out, waiting for us to give up. That's what's happening in the Southern Free States. There's a rumor that Louisiana is going to return to the union. That will be a big loss of crop farms and oil refining. The rest of the South will probably follow."

"That could happen here," says Mason. "If we were to lose Nebraska—the governor there seems a little shaky—there goes most of our crops."

"We can't let that happen," I say. "We should be talking to the other stations, getting everyone on the same page. We've got to stick together."

"Problem is, the Forbidden aren't exactly the sticking-together type," Penny muses, peeling the skin off her burned hot dog. "All these factions, each with their own ideas. The tribes, the fundamentalists, the Amish, the

Separatists—who knows what other groups are out there? Some of them might not be too friendly. The state governments don't have a lot of control over the outliers. Never did."

This conversation makes me more and more nervous. Our situation is shaky at best. How long before we are attacked, either by the NAU or another separatist faction? How long before the Lakota throw us out? What will we do then?

Lord, protect us. A little longer.

***

Penny gives Noah and me a ride back to the church, where Noah will crash on a pew and I will sleep on an air mattress in the basement with a few other women. We've given up our own shelters to refugees.

We walk inside in awkward silence. There's so much unsaid between us. I know how he feels about me, and I can't deny I have feelings for him too. Confused, irrational, unwanted feelings, but feelings all the same. I am still Jared's wife, at least in the eyes of God. But Jared has become more and more an abstract idea rather than a breathing human, an image on the video screen, an icon for the masses, while Noah... Noah is here. Noah is real.

Like I said. Confused.

"I'll get you a blanket," I say. "There are extras in the basement." I run downstairs and return with two blankets and an extra pillow.

"Thanks." He takes them from me, yawning.

"Well, night, Noah. Sleep in tomorrow."

"Night."

I hug him. He holds me close and seems reluctant to let me go. I break away, my face going hot.

"Sleep tight!" I'm about to flee downstairs when Simon comes bursting in through the doors at the back of the chapel, gasping for breath.

"Grace! Hey, sorry to bother you so late, but... someone's on the radio. Sounds important."

"What do you mean?"

"Well, she needs help. Says she's in New York and she's in trouble."

I sigh. So many people are in trouble. "Shouldn't you be telling Ripley about this? He's the one in charge—"

"I was going to, but I still think you need to hear her message."

"Why?"

"Because she mentioned a friend who... she claims... was married to Baldyr."

My mouth drops open. I close my eyes.

Bree.

Chapter Seven
Jared

I don't sleep, my arm throbbing and my mind reeling. Sally's words reverberate in my brain.

You are the son of the Supreme Lord. If you can't do something, who can?

I get up, change the walls to glass, and look out. It's barely dawn. The sky is pink and cloudless, the city below peaceful and still. More like a painting than a breathing city. Is it real? It's so hard to tell anymore.

I wait until the sun is fully up, then take the circular stairs to the dressing room area to change my clothes. Sabina appears as soon as I'm dressed, loud and cheerful as usual.

"Good morning, Dominus. I hope you are well rested and had a nice evening with your new friend. What would you like for breakfast?"

"I'm not eating breakfast," I say. "I'm going out."

I head for the stairs. Sabina block my way, but I walk right through her, something I've never done before. Her image pops up again in front of me, over and over.

"Where are you going? You do not have training today. It's a rest day. You have no appointments scheduled. And you have not had a proper breakfast—"

I ascend to the elevator floor. A Guardian stands at the door, his cobra-like hood inflating when he sees me.

"Take me to the Supreme Lord," I say.

The yellow eyes glow as if from a power surge. "You have not been summoned," he says in his soft, slithery voice.

"I am the Son of the Supreme Lord. Do you dare to disobey me?" I hate the sound of my own voice saying those words.

The Guardian hesitates. For the first time ever, I sense uncertainty in him. I'd come to think of the Guardians as little more than robots, but they are human, if genetically and surgically modified. After a moment, he bows to me then raises his crystal spear to the elevator door. It glides open with barely a whisper. He steps aside so I can enter.

I don't ask where Zazel is at this time of day. The only time I've ever seen him in the flesh is in the garden. I've grown to like the garden, despite its sinister creatures; it's the only place where I feel as though I am outside of the tower, in the natural world. Vale and I used to sneak out into the city for underground music concerts in the old subway, but Zazel has since filled the subways with concrete. After spending an eternity in the Abyss, the Grigori have an aversion to underground places.

The elevator hurtles upward, sideways, then up again, telling me we are not going to the garden. My stomach clenches. I try to think of a prayer, a request for help from the true God. I think I knew Him once. Would He listen to me now? Sally's accusing gaze burns in my memory—*do something.*

Lord, if you haven't yet abandoned the world, tell me what to do.

I'm so preoccupied with my own thoughts I don't realize the elevator has stopped, the doors opened. All I see are clouds. For a frozen moment, I expect my Guardian to push me out into the empty air. Every day, I have lived in this place, expecting to die.

But the Guardian steps out first, and he doesn't fall. The clouds are a holo projection. I follow him into the sky as clouds swirl around me, changing shape rapidly as if in a time-lapse. They part to reveal a table laden with food and wine and a white chaise lounge floating in the fake sky. It contains my father, Grigori Zazel. He's practically naked, save for a towel around his waist, and surrounded by half-dressed women who are giving him a massage. One is combing his long, silvery hair.

I avert my gaze, embarrassed.

Beside the lounge, his lion growls at me, wings spreading, tail thumping the floor, a thick slab of meat in its paws. A few yards away, another animal, a large, shaggy bear-like thing with curved tusks and six stumpy legs, sits upright like a human, gorging on another slab of meat.

This is Zazel's spire. I've never been here before.

"Baldyr! My son. Come in, come in."

My father half rises from his prone position and beckons me. It's strange seeing him in person after the last months of his appearing strictly as his gigantic avatar. I wonder at the change in him. Not only does he look smaller, he seems… diminished somehow. Then I notice that the women are rubbing a bronzing cream on his skin, which has grown mottled and pale.

"Supreme Lord," I say with a bow.

"Call me Father. How many times do I have to tell you?" Without the effects that make his voice a sonorous boom for the masses, he sounds raspy and off-key, like a broken flute.

"Father." The word sticks in my throat. "Thank you for seeing me."

"I was going to call for you anyway, as it happens. Sit down. Please. Wine for my son!"

A stuffed chair covered in white fur emerges from the floor like magic. Robots swirl around me, pressing me firmly into the chair and placing a crystal goblet in my hand. Zazel downs his wine in a single swallow. I pretend to take a sip, keeping a close eye on the lion, who watches me unblinkingly. The bear thing tears at its meat, making loud chewing noises.

Zazel peers at me with his one open eye, a languid smile on his face. "I heard you had a guest last evening. How was she? You look as though you didn't get a wink of sleep." He laughs, a jarring, throaty sound.

"I didn't." I press the glass against my knee to keep my hand from shaking.

"I can't tell you how happy that makes me! My dear Freya was right. She thought that one would appeal to you. So, what can I do for you? Ask me for anything you wish. I am in a generous mood today."

There are times like these when Zazel sounds so normal, so human, so pleasant even, that it throws me off-balance. Is he really the monster I think he is? "Well, last night, after I heard your speech—"

"Ah, my speech! What did you think of it?"

I scramble for a response. "It was... powerful."

He grins. "I thought so too." He tosses away his goblet. It hits the glass wall with a startling clatter. I flinch at the noise. "I was going to tell you about it first, but then I thought it would be a fun surprise. You were surprised, weren't you?"

"Yes—"

"Good! I know you have been waiting far too long for your vengeance."

"*My* vengeance?"

"They killed you! My son! They must be destroyed. The missiles will fly in forty-eight hours."

My mouth goes dry. "Missiles?"

"Ten intercontinental nuclear missiles headed for Israel. The infidels will see a glorious display in the sky before they meet their end."

My head feels light and heavy at the same time. For a moment, I can say nothing. I can only fight to stop my hand from trembling and the wine from splattering all over the fake sky.

"It does not sound very—glorious." I search for words. *Lord, help me.* "Don't you want to ride into Jerusalem surrounded by your mighty Dragons with banners flying and hordes of warriors on parade?" The Dragons are Zazel's newest weapon, flying pulse lasers that will turn anything to ash. "A good show for the HoloNet? You can't do that after a nuclear strike. There won't be anything left to claim. And humans couldn't attend—all that radiation. You want a crowd of witnesses, don't you? A live crowd, not just... CGI. Do you really want to take possession of a nuclear wasteland? I thought you were Jerusalem's liberator, not its destroyer."

He sits up and stares at me, incredulous. For a panicked moment, I think I've miscalculated. He sees right through me. But then he settles back on his cushions, shaking his head.

"Liberator?" He smiles slyly. He likes that word. "Yes, that is true. I am a liberator. I am the savior of the world! But how can I subjugate Israel to my will without a great show of strength?"

"Perhaps you would consider... a meeting," I say. "A summit, of sorts. Go to Israel to discuss terms of surrender with the new prime minister—"

"No." His eye flickers. He looks away. "Wine!" He holds out a hand impatiently as a robot appears with another glass. "I meet with no human."

For a moment, I am flummoxed. Then I remember—he does not leave the tower. Ever since he took power, he has remained in his fortress, appearing only in his avatar form. I sense a tinge of fear in his voice. Do angels, for all their supernatural power, have limits on earth?

It comes to me then, as clear as day—what I must do.

"Let me go," I say. "I will take your place."

He looks at me, eyebrow cocked.

"It is *my* vengeance, after all." I hold my breath, gauging his reaction. Anger? Suspicion? His eye is unblinking, his mouth set tight. He's listening. "I am the one wronged. Imagine what it would look like to the masses—me offering an olive branch to your enemy. The world would be amazed at your compassion and grace."

He's up suddenly, pacing about. "You think Israel will bend the knee to me? It will never happen. She is as stubborn as she ever was. She must be annihilated. I have spoken. I am the Lord." He spreads his arms, encompassing the sky around him.

I stand as well. "Please... Father. Let me try. Reports from Israel say the people are turning against their government. Israel is isolated, low on oil. Their natural gas reserves cannot make up the difference. I can reason with the prime minister. Get him to see that you want to avoid war at all costs. You want to honor the treaty you made with Israel in the beginning, despite what that lone assassin did. All they need to do is join the UE. Then they will be under your protection."

"True." Zazel looks thoughtful. "True."

"We will be giving Davidov a graceful way out of his troubles."

"You must make him grovel." Zazel's voice is lower now, almost a growl. "Beg. He must know that I am his salvation."

I swallow. "Yes. Of course."

"And you must kill the *Voice*."

I step back, surprised. "The *Voice*? You mean, those podcasters?"

"They must be silenced. Forever." There is a lethal edge in his voice now. The podcasters known as the *Voice* operate somewhere in Israel, using verses from the illegal Bible to proclaim that Grigori Zazel is a false god. They had once roamed the streets of Jerusalem declaring their prophecies, but ever since Zazel declared himself a god, they have gone underground, somehow managing to get their message out on the internet despite heavy censorship. Their message has sparked protests in major cities all over the United Earth, yet the Grigori cannot pinpoint their location—they believe it is yet another dastardly plot of the Forbidden.

"Are they so important—?"

"I want them dead!" Zazel's voice echoes through the spire, making the glass walls shiver. His one eye turns fire red. He spins away from me and returns to his couch. "Tell Davidov it is a condition of his surrender that he turn them over to us—for execution." He downs another glass of wine and smashes it on the floor. "If he wants to save his people, he will do it."

I take a breath, hold it. "It will be done."

Zazel turns to look at me, his eye golden once more, the fire extinguished. "Good boy. I am so very proud of you, my son. You must speak to the council. Tell them of your plans."

"Me?" I swallow. "Wouldn't it be better coming from you?"

"If you wish to be my representative, you must do it yourself. Go now. Prepare yourself. I will call a meeting at once."

He dismisses me. I leave the spire, wondering if what I have done has made things better... or worse.

Chapter Eight
Grace

"I don't know if anyone can hear me. I need help. My husband—partner, I mean—and I, we're in New York. If the YBR is really out there... please help. I know who the Grigori really are. I had a friend who was sort of married to the Golden Son, Baldyr. At least, she used to be. Anyway, I need help. Can anyone hear me? Please—"

The recording stops abruptly.

"She got cut off," Simon says hurriedly as if to justify himself for not responding. "I thought she was crazy, just rambling, but then I remembered your... situation. Anyway, I didn't want to answer in case, you know, it was a trap. That's the protocol now. We can't always trust that people trying to contact us are—"

"Yeah, yeah, I know," I say irritably.

"Does she sound like your friend?"

The message was filled with static. The voice sounded deeper than I remember, but the inflections were familiar. It could be her. Bree, my best friend from my old life. Who else would know that Jared and I were married? And that Baldyr was really Jared?

Bree. Penny had told me she'd lost touch with her years ago. The last time I talked to her, she was just graduating from college. I was supposed to go to her graduation, but I missed it, because I went into the *There.* Fifteen years passed in that time. Bree married Ethan. And Grigori Zazel—Azazel—took over the world.

I missed everything.

I grab hold of the mic and press the button. "Hello? New York? New York, this is M. Are you there, New York?"

Static. I try several more times, to no avail.

"How do you know her? This... Bree," Noah asks.

I sit back in the chair, my mind returning to that day—that awful day. "From school. The Buffalo Arts Academy. I was sitting with Bree and Ethan when this kid burst in and started shooting. Ethan was horribly wounded, and Jared... saved his life. They came with us when we went to find Azazel in the Abyss."

"It sounds a little like her," says Ripley, scratching his beard. I'd woken him up to come and listen to the recording. He yawns loudly. "But it could be a plant. Someone trying to draw you out. Your mother, maybe?"

"I think my mother has forgotten I exist by now." I rub my hands over my face. "Can we get into New York?"

"No way," says Simon.

I look at Ripley for confirmation. He shrugs. "Manhattan is an island—limited access points, heavily patrolled. It's a fortress."

Desperate, I turn to Noah. He sighs. "It would be harder than Chicago. And Chicago was... hard."

"Yeah." I yawn. "Well, thanks, guys. You should all go back to bed. I'll stay here in case she calls back."

"Do you want me to stay with you?" Simon asks somewhat hopefully. "I don't mind—"

"No," I snap, then instantly regret my sharp tone. "No, thanks."

"Okay, fine." Simon gathers his stuff and heads out the door.

Ripley chuckles. "You're kinda tough on him, you know."

I sigh. "He just gets on my nerves."

"He's good though. Thorough. He caught that transmission. You really should thank him."

"Yeah, you're right. I will."

"Cool beans. Well, I'll see you guys tomorrow." Ripley exits, yawning.

Noah doesn't move.

"Go," I say. "I'll be fine."

"I'll stay." He moves a pile of books off a nearby chair and settles himself, looking very uncomfortable. "Just in case."

"Noah..."

"I'm not that tired." He makes his eyes big to show he's wide awake.

Such a liar.

I sigh and turn back to the radio, click the mic button, and repeat my message. Nothing but static answers me. I try different frequencies, but still nothing.

I think about Ralph and Emilia. Where are they? In a camp somewhere? Or prison? It galls me that there is nothing I can do for them. There's nothing I can do about Jared either. But this—Bree and Ethan—maybe there *is* something I can do.

At some point, I fall asleep, for the next thing I know, Noah is shaking me awake. I rub my eyes and gaze up at him blearily. "What time is it?"

"Morning," he says. His eyes are more hollow than the night before, yet he smiles his crooked, sweet smile. He puts a bowl of oatmeal in front of me. "Get it while it's hot."

I look at the food, my stomach turning. "Did I miss something?"

"No."

"Did you sleep at all?"

"Some. I found this." He holds up a wrinkled paper map. "It was in all those piles of junk on the shelf. Manhattan."

I move the oatmeal aside so he can lay the map on the desk. He points out the access routes into the city. There is the George Washington Bridge on the north end, the Holland Tunnel in the south, and the Lincoln Tunnel in Midtown, plus numerous ferries. Those would all be heavily guarded, if they were even running at all.

"We might be able to cross the Hudson farther north and work our way down to the city on the eastern shore, but we'd still have to cross a river at some point. There are over a dozen borough bridges, but most are probably closed."

I sigh. "What about a boat?"

"Yes, that might work, but drone coverage is pretty heavy around city centers."

I stare at the map, praying for some kind of revelation. "Wait a minute." I put my finger on the map. "The tunnels. The Lincoln and the Holland. There's probably no drones in the tunnels, right?"

Noah shrugs. "Maybe not. The Grigori have probably blocked the tunnels. You know how they feel about underground places."

"Yes, but... maybe they aren't completely blocked. We need to find out. I'll ask Josephine."

"At Camp Zero?"

"It's the closest station to New York."

Camp Zero used to be called Camp Hero, an abandoned naval station turned CIA outpost in Montauk on Long Island. Josephine, Darwin Speer's sister, has been there with two kids we discovered on our journey back from the *There*—it's a long story. I send a Morse code message to Camp Zero because Johnny, one of the kids, usually communicates that way. We get a reply from Johnny, who says one of their newer refugees—they have several, apparently—told them some people were getting out of the city through the Lincoln Tunnel, which was otherwise closed to vehicular traffic. It's not a lot to go on, but it gives us hope.

We spend the next hour trying to figure out a plan until Ripley comes in to take over at the radio.

"Any news?" Ripley asks, sitting in the operator's chair.

I tell him about Camp Zero.

"So you're really thinking you can get into the city?"

"We're working on it," Noah says.

"You don't even know if it was really her," Rip says. "Have you heard back from her?"

I shake my head. "Not yet. But she could call anytime. No hamming today, Rip. Keep the channels clear."

"Okay, okay. Anyone eating this oatmeal?"

"Help yourself."

Noah and I are about to leave when a voice crackles through the speaker. "Hello? YBR? Are you there?"

I seize the mic. "Yes! We're here! This is the YBR. Go ahead." I click off to listen, my heart pounding. For a long moment, there is nothing but static. And then the voice returns.

"Hi. I tried to call before. This is—"

"No names," I say. "Where are you now?"

"In... New York..."

"Okay, New York. What is your situation?" I try to keep my voice calm and businesslike. Is it her? Could it really be her?

"Well... um... we need to get out of the city before... My partner is sick. It's his heart. I think it's from the Cure infusions. I'm... scared. I don't want him to get any more infusions."

I take a breath. "When is his next infusion due?"

"Three weeks. And his Cube will automatically inform the clinic so he can't skip it. If he doesn't get it within forty-eight hours, he'll be fired from his job. We could lose everything."

"Okay, okay. Listen, just relax. Tell your partner to relax too. Maybe play a video game. Like... *Wrath of the Watchers*."

Ripley gives me the side eye.

There's a long pause on the radio. I think I've lost her.

"Did you say... *Wrath of the Watchers*?"

"Yes."

"Oh... God... who is this? Is this—?"

"Call me M," I say before she can say my name. Ripley chuckles. "You know that game?"

"Yes...yes...oh my god..."

"Okay, listen," I say. "We will see what we can do for you. In the meantime, stay close to the radio. Okay?"

"Okay." She's crying now.

I am too.

Chapter Nine
Grace

"New York? Are you there?" I release the mic switch.

"Yes, I'm here!" The voice is brighter this afternoon, definitely more like the Bree I knew. "I told my partner about what you said. He was surprised because the game was banned about five years ago."

That figures. Azazel didn't want a video game in which he was the bad guy. Ethan had created *Wrath of the Watchers* based on Jared's and my journey into the Abyss. He'd even won a prize at a gamer convention.

"Too bad. It was a great game," I say, even though I never played it. "Good thing you had a radio."

"My partner had it. It was his grandfather's. He said he should have thrown it away years ago, but you know him—I mean, *if* you knew him, you'd know he doesn't throw anything away."

Definitely Ethan. "How's he doing?"

"He's... weak. Can't seem to catch his breath. Chest pain."

"What do the doctors say?"

"They say it's probably due to the climate crisis. Extreme heat causes heart inflammation. But it could also be caused by herbal supplements, red meat, black tea, loneliness, taking too many naps, cold showers—"

"But not the Cure," I say.

"Everything but." She laughs bitterly.

"Okay, listen. We will get you out of there. Have you gotten the GEM yet?"

"No, not yet."

"Good. You will need to remove your chips."

"Remove? How?"

"It's a minor procedure. Use a very sharp knife. Either that or you can try to disable it with an electrostatic body charging device that you can make yourself. We call it a Zapper. We can get you the instructions if you want. And also, you will have to destroy your I-Cubes. A hammer works best for that. Or you can put in a water bath for twenty-four hours."

There's a long pause. Just when I think I've lost her, she says, "But if we do that, we can't get food… or anything."

"Right. Stock up beforehand. They can still track the Cube, even without the chips. As soon as they realize your chip is disabled, the Cube will alert the implanting office and they will be at your door within an hour. So just before you are ready to leave, you need to remove the chip, destroy the Cube, and leave them together in your residence."

There's another long pause, then her voice is weaker. "Okay. Okay."

"Okay. Listen carefully. Write this down. Genesis 7:4. Exodus 4:27. Acts 19:33. Exodus 2:12. That is our meeting place and time. Do you still have the book you need to figure this out?"

She pauses. "Yes. Yes, I do."

"We will wait for twenty-four hours."

Another pause. Now there is genuine panic in her voice. "I don't know if we can do this—"

"If you want us to help you, this is the only way." I keep my voice firm.

"Okay, okay. It's just so hard. I'm... scared." Her voice breaks off.

"I know you are." I pause to take a long breath. "Listen to me, New York. You've got to decide whose side you're on. Because you can't have it both ways. The world you live in is like a prison, where you can get free food, free housing, free health care... but you are not free. The world we live in is the opposite. Do you understand?"

"Yes, I understand." She sniffs.

"Tell your partner his life may be at stake."

"Yes... okay. I'll talk to him. I love him, but... well, you know what it's like... when you love someone, but they seem headed down the wrong path... don't you?"

I know what she's trying to say. "Yes, I do. But it doesn't mean we stop loving them—ever. We just keep going and pray for... a change of heart."

"Change of heart." She sighs audibly. "That's what they need."

***

"So you think it's really her?" Penny hands me a mug of coffee and sits opposite me in the little booth in her trailer. It's pretty rustic, but she's added some personal touches, like black-and-purple curtains, that fit her personality.

"Yes, I'm sure."

"New York." Penny shakes her head. "It's dangerous."

"I can't abandon them."

I've told Penny all about our conversations. She listened mostly without comment, a skeptical expression on her face.

"Well, I took a look at your plan. It's… iffy."

"Yeah, I know. But without a boat, it was the best we could come up with. I wish there was a way to contact Speer."

She snorts a laugh. "His boat is a little bit too conspicuous."

"But he has immunity. Peacemakers wouldn't touch that yacht." I sip the coffee and wince at the bitterness of it. "Do you have any sugar?"

"Ooh, yeah. I forgot you were a wuss." She gets up to rummage in a cupboard and produces a sugar packet. I dump it in my coffee. It's better now, though still nothing close to the lattes I used to guzzle. "So I guess Noah is going on this mission."

"Yeah." I pause. "I'm going with him."

She glowers at me. "Grace, that's crazy talk."

"Hey, I survived Samyaza and Moloch in the *There*. I'm not afraid of a bunch of Peacemakers." Just saying those names, Samyaza and Moloch, makes my insides smolder. I had blocked out the whole experience of the *There* after returning to the world, mostly because there were so many new shocks waiting for me: fifteen years had passed in the space of what I thought were a few hours. Just surviving those first few days kept my mind busy. But now, here in the Black Hills, with so much time on my hands and the evidence of my husband belonging heart and soul to the Grigori, those memories bombard me at all hours of the day and night. I had saved Jared from an eternal hell—for what? So he would fall into the arms of the enemy.

"You're going to get yourself killed." Penny drops her cup onto the table with a smack.

"We're all going to die anyway." The sense of doom, seared in me, bubbles to the surface every so often. "We're just waiting for the end, aren't we? So what difference does it make how it happens?" I push the cup of coffee away. No amount of sugar is going to help ease this bitterness.

"Where's your faith, Grace?" Penny chuckles a little and nudges my arm. "Sure, we know how this is going to end. But it's not death we're waiting for."

"Not us, maybe. But what about Bree? I don't know where her heart is now. If she's caught over there, it might be the end for her and Ethan. He was never much of a believer anyway. He went along with us just because he liked Bree, and it was kind of intriguing to him. But after all these years of Grigori rule? They've got control of people's minds, not just their bodies."

"Yeah, true," Penny says. "It's so weird. I mean, the first Cure made people practically superhuman, because it contained Jared's DNA. Total immunity from disease, super strength, near immortality. And yet those who got it, the New People, seemed to go crazy. They're all slaves or dead now, thanks to the Grigori. Or they're mind-controlled Peacemakers. But the New Cure seemed to do the opposite, make men weaker, more compliant, easier to control."

"All by design," I say. "That reminds me, anything new on James Camden?"

"He's sick." Penny pours more coffee into her cup. "Heart disease, like so many men on the Cure. We gave him a statin and some beta-blockers. It will help him for... a while."

"Oh." Those two little girls might end up as orphans after all. But James Camden still got his family out in time. "I've got to go," I say, getting up. "I've got a lot to do."

"Grace," Penny says.

I pause to look at her.

"Just... don't do anything brave, okay?"

I smile. "Don't worry. I'm the biggest coward I know."

Chapter Ten
Jared

I've never been to this room before. I'm not even sure it *is* a room, for it looks more like deep space, an infinite blackness lit only by pinpricks of stars and a gigantic replica of the solar system, each planet glowing as it orbits around a central sun. The movement of the planets makes the shadows shift on the immense round marble table intricately engraved with a map of the United Earth, divided into ten unions. The union lords seated at the table stare at me with expressions of suspicion and hostility. There are no women here, for the Supreme Lord does not allow females to hold positions of power. Those women who objected to this policy were never heard from again.

I know what these men are thinking—I am an entertainer, a gladiator, the Supreme Lord's Golden Son. I have no business conducting a council meeting. I would agree. I take a breath as I sit on the Cobra Throne, a mammoth chair of solid gold shaped like the hood of a cobra. It's placed at the north point of the table just under the sun so that the light from that burning orb shines fully upon it. Two Guardians stand on either side of the chair, the biggest of Zazel's bodyguards. Twenty more Guardians form a circle around the table, spears in hand.

"Where is the Supreme Lord?" asks Devon Newman, the ruler of the North American Union. He's a tall, handsome man with a thick slab of dark hair and a dimpled smile, a face made for the HoloNet.

"I will speak for him today." The chair itself is cold and hard as ice, and I feel all wrong sitting there, yet I have to play this role if I am to convince these people I can lead in my father's place.

"You? The gladiator?" Farad Hassan chortles a laugh. The Middle Eastern ruler always looks angry, even when he's smiling.

"Yes. Me. My father has charged me with executing our plan for Jerusalem."

Hassan's smile disappears. He says in a more conciliatory tone, "Ah, yes. Tell us how the Supreme Lord will proceed with the attack on Israel."

"I didn't say anything about an attack. There will be no attack."

Murmurs and gasps move around the table, the union lords exchanging disdainful looks.

"What do you mean, no attack?" says Lee Zuolin, the Chinasian ruler. He is a squat man with reflective round glasses that conceal his eyes.

I grip the arms of the cobra throne. "I plan to lead a delegation to Jerusalem to negotiate Israel's surrender."

Silence. The lords stare at me in disbelief.

Hassan springs up. "This is not to be. We were promised! We agreed to let them build their temple as long as Israel was wiped off the face of the earth!"

I have to hide my shock. Was this what Zazel was planning? The Middle East Union had been severely depleted by the Alliance war against Israel. Zazel had taken advantage of their weakness by forcing them off the Temple Mount and removing the Dome of the Rock to make way for the new temple. Israel had thought that some kind of miracle. Now, it seemed, there was no miracle after all.

"The Supreme Lord wants Israel to join the United Earth peacefully," I say. "He desires peace."

The room erupts, everyone shouting at once. Hassan throws both fists in the air. I try shouting over them, to no avail. In desperation, I reach for a spear from a nearby guardian and hurl it into the air. It hits one of the planets—Mars, I think—which drops out of orbit and smashes onto the marble table, the resin outer shell breaking open and spilling the contents of the liquid bulb within. Sparks fly and bounce across the tabletop. The rulers gasp and dive for cover. I wait until calm returns and all eyes are on me once again.

"Listen to me," I say slowly. "Once Israel submits, the other holdouts will quickly follow. The African, Baltic, and American rebels will come to heel. The whole world will be united for the first time in history. All without bloodshed. The Supreme Lord is a god of peace."

The words taste bitter in my mouth. Yet I must speak them. To prevent war. Prevent countless murders. This is all I can do.

"Israel will never surrender," says Hassan savagely. "They must be destroyed! There can be no other plan!"

"I must agree," says Newman in his raspy voice. "Israel has proven itself an enemy of the United Earth. Time and again it has launched unprovoked attacks on its neighbors. This is our chance to eliminate the threat once and for all."

"Here, here," says someone.

"We were promised!" Hassan seems about to launch himself on top of the table.

"We do not accept this plan," shouts another ruler.

"Do you *dare*?"

It is not my voice but Zazel's they hear. His head appears in the center of the table, amid the ruins of Mars, rotating slowly, eyes burning fire. Did they think he wouldn't be listening?

"You dare to question me? And my son, my chosen one? Who do you think you are? Who put you in your place? Who will take you down in one fell swoop should the mood strike? This is my son. Obey him as you would me!"

The avatar vanishes. The room is silent once more. Hassan sits slowly, straightening his turban. The other rulers stare at the table.

I clear my throat. "I would like a few members of this council to accompany me so that the Israeli leader knows I have the support of the council. I have selected Lord Newman of the North American Union, Lord Haraldsen of the Scandinavian Union, and Lord Godunov of the Russian Union for this mission." Zazel had chosen these three. They seemed odd choices to me, but I did not raise an objection.

Haraldsen, tall and thin with pale eyes and hair, has no reaction to the news. He rarely speaks at all in these meetings. Godunov, a bear of a man with a thick beard, looks positively furious. Only Newman seems pleased with his selection.

"We will leave tomorrow." I stand up. "To the Supreme Lord, may he live forever." I thump my chest with my fist. Reluctantly, the ten union lords shuffle to their feet and do the same.

I breathe in fully for the first time. I was able to convince Zazel and the Council of Ten to go along with my plan. Now, I just have to convince Prime Minister Yosef Davidov.

Chapter Eleven
Helel

I watch from afar as she strolls down the red carpet, waving to her throng of fans, her smile made more radiant by the flashing lights of camera drones. The premier of her film, *Katrina Kross and the Curse of the Jehovians,* is about to begin. It was my brainchild, though she doesn't know it. She will soon.

She takes her seat in the packed holotarium with a thousand others. It's a gigantic, dome-shaped space where the holo film unfolds all around the audience in brilliant 4D, complete with real lasers, wind, rain, lightning, thunder, and even small explosions. The audience is thrilled, and often terrified, as Katrina Kross and her army of GEM-tattooed freedom fighters subdue the monstrous Jehovians (my new term for the Forbidden, much more sinister sounding), and branding them with the GEM, turning them into docile, worshipping sycophants. It ends with a spectacular aurora that fills the entire space with color and light. There is no plot to speak of, no character development, no clever twists or profound revelations. Still, the spectators are on their feet by the end with a resounding ten-minute ovation.

At the afterparty at the Marquee, disco music throbs through gigantic speakers and colored lights rove around the sparkling crowd as Shannon holds court in her favorite booth, accepting accolades from her fans and fellow cast members. I wait my turn.

"Ms. Snow," I say formally, bowing as if she were royalty. "Allow me to introduce myself. I am Amon H. Doyle."

How beautiful she is, with that fire red hair and those luminous green eyes. The others in the booth with her, her NP bodyguard, her little band of sycophants, eye me warily. Shannon's gaze is more glazed—she's had a bit too much to drink.

"Oh, hello," she purrs in her throaty voice and waits for me to compliment her. She has no idea who I am.

"Allow me to congratulate you on your triumph. I've longed to meet you in person. I was a very close associate of William West. He always spoke of you with great affection."

At the mention of West's name, she straightens slightly and blinks, more attentive.

"Oh, poor William," she says. "I was so sorry to hear of his passing. So sudden."

"Yes, it was quite unexpected. We all thought he would live forever." I glance at the others in her company, who continue to stare at me as if I were a creature from another world, which, as it happens, I am.

The bodyguard inches closer to his charge. I take a step backward. "I don't wish to disturb you on your celebratory night, but I would like to extend an invitation—to dinner—at my apartment tomorrow evening. Just you. Alone." I pull a card from my jacket pocket and hand it to her.

She glances at the card without taking it. "I appreciate the offer, Mr. Doyle, but I already have plans—"

"I will send my car for you," I say, leaving the card on the table. "And call me Amon."

Her green eyes harden slightly. "As I said, Amon, I already have plans—"

"Cancel them. Trust me, you will not regret it. Nine o'oclock."

I hold her gaze, unblinking. Her mouth tries forming the words of refusal again, but she doesn't speak them. "All right," she murmurs. "I live—"

"I know where you live. See you tomorrow, Miss Snow. May I call you Shannon?"

"Shannon is... fine..."

"Have a lovely evening, Shannon." I bow again and turn my back on her, though I can feel her watching me as I walk away.

***

She comes. Of course, she does.

I hear the bell ring at my penthouse on the ninety-sixth floor of 432 Park Avenue, the Toothpick Building, considered by some to be the ugliest building in New York. I bought it because I knew she would love it. She could not resist anything so extravagantly tacky as the Toothpick. I purchased a great deal of real estate in the city after the pandemic and the Rages decimated the population and reduced the survivors to abject poverty. Cleaning up the tent cities on the streets and in the subway tunnels has proven a nearly impossible task, but little by little, the riffraff have been either executed or sent to camps.

My butler announces her—a human butler, as I don't go in for robots. Slaves should know they are slaves and feel the bitterness of slavery. A robot could never do that. Manning is an old codger, a college professor once, one of those useful idiots who promoted all the progressive ideals the Grigori brought to bear. Now, he is a slave. Our world has no use for college professors.

Knowledge is superfluous. Information changes so constantly that nothing is worth knowing anymore. Even history is constantly being rewritten.

"The lovely Shannon Snow," I say as she enters the room. No sign of the bodyguard. That's good. She's wearing a shapeless red dress, her hair bundled into an austere bun, a small black purse clutched in her fingers. Why the puritanical look, I wonder? What has that mad demon Azazel done to her?

"Hello, Mr. Doyle." She blushes slightly, so very charming, averting her gaze.

"Amon, please." I take her hand and brush a kiss over her knuckles. Her arm stiffens, though she doesn't pull away. "Thank you for coming." As if she had a choice. It's the rare human who can resist me. "Congratulations again on your sterling performance. The film is already a smash hit, breaking box office records."

She looks at me and smiles. She likes what she sees. I'm young, tall, and devilishly handsome, pardon the pun. I've chosen a face she would be drawn to—piercing blue eyes and jet-black hair. So like her former husband's and most of her lovers—except for one.

"Thank you." Her voice is faint. The scent of jasmine wafts over me. I breathe it in, enjoying my sensory ability. This human frame brings so many unexpected pleasures.

"Do come in." I lead her into the huge living room. She gapes at the size of the apartment, then is drawn to the bank of windows on the far wall.

"Lovely view," she says. "So many new buildings. I hardly recognize the skyline."

"You don't care for Grigori architecture?"

"It's very... uniform."

"Uniformity is an underappreciated quality." I stand beside her, very close. I feel her stiffen. "Before, it was all haphazard, uneven. Now, it is quite... symmetrical. Perfect, wouldn't you say?"

"Yes... perfect. Almost *too* perfect."

"Soon, the human population will match the perfection of the cityscape. The children of our WeBirth programs are now reaching their prime. All the Grigori do anymore is sire children, after all. But our cloning program, WeClone, is also starting to show positive results. Within ten years, this city will be teeming with people but without the... imperfections of before."

"Uniform people?" She smiles wryly. "You said 'our' programs. Are you a part of this?"

"Well, I don't like to boast, but I invented most of the innovations the Interlaken Group has initiated."

She stares at me. "You? I thought William—"

"He enjoyed taking the credit, of course. He was the face of the Interlaken Group and its main source of funding. I preferred to stay in the shadows. For a time." I smile at her. "I have other interests as well. Film, for instance. It was I who produced your movie. I even wrote most of the script."

Her eyes flash. "*You* did?"

"I knew you were just the woman we needed to help us initiate the next phase."

She hesitates, stepping back from me. "The next phase?"

"Oh, where are my manners? Let us make ourselves comfortable, shall we? I haven't even offered you a drink." I lead her into the sitting area, a collection of gray leather couches and chairs sprawled between the huge windows and the modern fireplace. A thick orange rug warms the herringbone wood floor. Shannon's gaze lingers on the grand piano, a modern confection of exotic wood wrapped in red leather with a skeletal black lid that resembles a dragonfly's wing.

"This piano is so—unusual," she murmurs, running a finger over the pure ivory keys.

"A work of art, isn't it? Do you play?"

"No. My daughter does. Did."

"I didn't know you had a daughter," I lie.

She gives me an appraising look. "I'm surprised. You seem to know a great deal about me, Mr.—Amon."

"Apparently, there are gaps even in my knowledge. Please. Sit."

She sits primly on the edge of the cushion, crossing her ankles, hands folded on her lap. That makes me smile.

"Champagne Cocktail?"

She raises an eyebrow. "How did you know—?"

"I saw you drinking it last night." *And many other nights as well.* I snap an order to Manning, who disappears through a doorway. Sitting beside her, I stretch out my legs and let out a long sigh.

"Are you enjoying your new life in New Asgard?" I ask as casually as I can. "How is the Supreme Lord? He hasn't made a personal appearance in quite some time."

"He is well." She smooths her dress nervously. "Very busy, of course."

"Yes, I would think ruling the world is a full-time job. But you must see him more than most, am I right?"

She glances at me, wondering if she should tell me the truth or lie. I can read her so plainly. The butler reappears with her drink, saving her the trouble of answering. She takes the tall, delicate glass with murmured thanks and sips. "Oh, my. This is very good."

"*Louis Millenium Cristal Brut*," I say. "Created originally for Tsar Alexander in 1876. This vintage was made to commemorate the victory of the Grigori in the Alliance War. Only two hundred bottles in circulation. I have ninety-nine of them."

"Oh my…"

"You were saying? About Zazel? He treats you well?"

Her shoulders stiffen, the glass at her lips. "Of course."

"I'm glad to hear it. From what I have heard, his only interest these days is that loutish gladiator he calls his son."

Her eyes dart away, fingers gripping the glass until her knuckles go white. She doesn't reply.

"I'm rather surprised you haven't taken care of the situation yet—" I move closer to her on the sofa and speak into her ear. "—as you took care of your former husband."

Her eyes snap to mine.

I chuckle. "Cyanide, wasn't it? A good old-fashioned method. How lovingly you cradled dear Harry in your arms after he was shot by that assassin—*your* assassin. You wept over him so convincingly that no one noticed the needle you plunged into his neck. And the body was cremated without an autopsy—your orders, of course."

Her champagne glass tips dangerously. I take it gently and set it on the coffee table. Then I take her hands in mine and lean even closer to her.

"I'm not here to judge you. In fact, I applaud you. Harry was not the one. *You* are."

"One… what?" Her eyes pulse.

"What is it you want, Shannon? More than anything? Freedom? Influence?"

"I already have that."

"Yes, you appear on the HoloNet wearing a certain dress, and the next day, every woman and many men all over the world are wearing it. Is that the sort of influence you crave?" I stroke her hair. "You want him to love you, don't you?"

She sucks in a breath, holds it. I move ever closer.

"All your life, you have longed for love. You had it once. A man named Charles Silas. He loved you. He would have died for you. He *did* die for you, in fact. But only because you killed him. You didn't do a very thorough job of that, unfortunately. That's the funny thing about you, Shannon. You crave love, but when you get it, you throw it away. You kill it. Why is that, do you think?"

"How can you know… about Charles?"

"As I said, I don't blame you. I applaud you. You've always done the necessary thing, the thing others would not have the courage to do." I pull the pins from her hair so that it falls free around her shoulders. She gasps softly, her eyes fluttering. I press a hand to the side of her neck. "You have made a career of pretending to be someone you're not. Now is the time for you to show your true self."

"My… true… self…" She repeats the words like an automaton.

We are very close now, my cheek brushing hers. *My Mysteria. Can you hear me?* I speak not aloud but in a sending, a wordless thought into her heart, her spirit. Her true spirit. Mysteria, the Queen of Babylon. She moans softly, her head falling back onto the cushions. I rise, pull her up, and sweep her into my arms. *I have waited so long to hold you again.* I carry her to the bedroom.

Chapter Twelve
Grace

We're on our way to New York.

The bed of our rusted-out, primer-colored pickup truck is loaded with gas cans, enough to make it there and back—we hope. We're a rolling tinderbox. Noah keeps the truck below fifty to save fuel and stay under drone radar, avoiding highways where drones are more prevalent. Still, an old gas-powered truck on the road these days stands out like a Maserati at an Amish funeral. We drive at night and hope the dull gray truck will be virtually invisible despite the headlights.

I navigate from a paper map. I've never been great at maps, and following Noah's route highlighted in yellow is like escaping from a maze.

"Hungry?" I ask Noah. We're an hour into the trip.

He smirks. "Already?"

"Driving makes me hungry. And also fear. Pretty much everything makes me hungry."

"Sure."

I pull two granola bars from my backpack and hand him one. "One hundred percent cricket free." I snort a laugh.

"Thank you."

I take a bite of the granola bar—Quaker Oats, only six months past the expiration date.

"That code you gave your friend about the plan," says Noah, "the Bible verses? What were they?"

"Oh, that. Genesis 7:4—seven days. That was the timeline. Exodus 4:27—Aaron. Acts 19:33—Alexander. Exodus 2:12—kill. The Weehawken Dueling Grounds, where Aaron Burr killed Alexander Hamilton. Ethan is a history buff. He'll know that monument is right on the other side of the Lincoln Tunnel."

"Clever. Who is Aaron Burr? And Alexander—?"

I keep forgetting Noah is French. "They were two guys in the Revolutionary War. Hamilton said some nasty things about Burr, and Burr got mad and challenged him to a duel. Hamilton shot at the ground, but Burr shot to kill." I crumble the granola wrapper. "Like a Twitter feud today. Except with guns."

"Or like saying something against the Supreme Lord and getting your head chopped off," Noah says darkly.

"That too." I glance out the window at the blackness. "How much longer?"

"About twenty-four hours."

"Ugh."

We stop in a wooded park just before the Iowa border. It's still dark, but the sun will be up soon, so there's no point crossing the border now. Noah parks on a dirt path under some trees. We get out and stretch, take care of business—that's the girls' tree, this is the boys' tree, I instruct—eat more snacks, and try to sleep in the truck's cab under some threadbare blankets we've brought along. I have a hard time sleeping, listening to Noah's gentle snores, worrying about every possible thing that can go wrong. Pray more, worry less—that's what Emilia would say. Penny too. Why do I always do the opposite?

Also, it's pretty darned uncomfortable sleeping in a truck.

I'm just dozing off when I hear a rumble, like an engine. I sit up straight, eyes wide open, and grab Noah's arm to shake him awake. The noise grows louder. Something is coming toward us. Then a bright light shines through the windshield.

Chapter Thirteen
Helel

Ah, but she is a marvel, my Mysteria.

To have her all to myself is a glory beyond imagining. I have waited thousands of years for this moment—to watch her as she sleeps, red hair sprawled on the pillow, red lips inviting me to bite. In the cold light of morning, the fine lines around her eyes and mouth are more visible. I cast a hand over them, erasing them from my sight.

She must feel it—her eyes fly open.

"Good morning." I pull away, smiling. "Sleep well?"

She gasps and jerks upright. "What… happened?"

"Calm yourself, my love. You are safe here with me."

She lets out a breath, her eyes softening as she gazes at me. "I thought it was a dream."

"A good dream, I hope?"

"Yes… very good." She smiles warmly.

"I'm glad to see you relaxing finally. You were a little tense last night." I call out. "Slave! Coffee! Scones! Immediately!"

Manning appears as if he's been standing outside the door for hours, bearing a tray of coffees and pastries. He crosses the room, the cups jittering, sets the tray on the bedside table, then straightens with an audible sigh, relieved he made it safely.

"Not there," I bark. "Bring it here, where my love can reach." I grin at the sudden consternation on his face as he is forced to pick up the delicate tray again. Panic sets in as he is unable to find a safe space to sit it down. The man can barely breathe. I laugh and take the tray from his hands.

"Go clean the kitchen floor with your tongue," I say.

He bows, mumbles his thanks, and hurries out.

"How you torture the man," Shannon purrs.

"Creatures like him are made for torturing. Coffee?" She sits up, leaning against the headboard, as I hand her a cup already loaded with cream and sugar.

"I never take cream—"

"Of course you do. And have a scone. They're the best in the world. Full of butter and sugar."

She stares at the scone, biting her lip. "Oh, I shouldn't. But... I am rather hungry." She takes the scone from my hand and bites into it. Her eyes flutter. "Oh my... that is so good."

"Didn't I tell you? Eat up, for we have much to do today."

"Really?" She looks at me, mouth still full of scone.

"You must begin your publicity tour. For the movie. Interviews, podcasts, HoloNet appearances—I have them all lined up."

"I didn't realize—"

"You are vitally important to the work of the Interlaken Group, you know. Surely you realize that your movie was not *just* a movie."

Her eyes widen. "What do you mean?"

I take the rest of the scone from her hands and set it back on the tray. I pick up a napkin and wipe her mouth. "The Jehovians are not fictional inventions. They are the true enemy we fight. Your movie was made to spread the word about the danger they pose. We are in the midst of a brand-new pandemic. A virus of the mind. The Jehovians spread this virus with their blasphemy about the Grigori and their proclamation of some other god who has dominion over their lives. We must not allow the population to become infected by these toxic ideas. People must be saved from themselves. You will help them understand this truth and convince them to get the GEM for their own protection."

"So the GEM really works like it does in the movie?"

"Of course! It is virus protection for the brain; like a firewall, it shuts out any harmful or counterproductive information. It is the culmination of years of research and billions in funding from the Interlaken Group, combined with the genius of Grigori technology. Not to mention my own modest contributions. People must understand that getting the GEM is more than just a public duty; it is an act of worship."

Her eyebrows rise. "Worship?"

"Worship of the Supreme Lord, who loves them with all his being and sacrificed everything for their sake. He came down from high to save them. For this, they owe him their allegiance."

"Oh, I see..."

"That's why you must be the one to tell the people about this incredible innovation. You are the paramour of the Supreme Lord, his queen, if you like. The people adore you. You're popular and glamorous, a movie star. Folks nowadays don't know the difference between reality and make-believe.

It's all the same. As I told you last night, it is time for you to show your true self. For the movie star to become the reality star."

Her eyes seem to glow; her smile lights up her face. How radiant she is when she catches fire.

"Of course, I will do whatever you say... but Zazel will not be happy if I don't return—"

"Don't worry about Zazel. I will deal with him."

"You will? But how do you... do you even know him?"

"Of course, I know him. I've known him forever."

"Really? He's never mentioned you."

"Does that surprise you? When has Zazel talked about anyone except himself? And that gladiator son of his, of course. Zazel's interests are singular, to say the least."

"Yes, I suppose that's true." Her tone is forlorn, a woman abandoned by the man she loves. I reach out to her, take hold of her chin, and turn her face toward me.

"I will handle Zazel. Don't worry." I kiss her mouth as gently as I can, holding back.

She pulls away suddenly. "What about my son? What about Vale?"

I drop my hand from her chin, frowning. "What about him?"

"He is the rightful heir. I want him to assume his place."

I wave a hand dismissively and get up from bed. Coffee spills onto the sheets. "Don't worry about Vale. I will make sure he gets what he deserves." I take her in my arms once more. "My love, you and I are going to save the world."

Chapter Fourteen
Jared

"That went well."

Sabina greets me when I return to my spire. I scowl at her as I exit the elevator and head to the circular stairs. How does she know what happened anyway? Is this whole place one giant hive mind?

When I get to the dining room floor, I have my answer. A huge figure wearing a voluminous black cloak sits at the table, gorging on a pile of lobsters. He glances up when I arrive and throws back his hood so I can see his garishly painted white eyes.

"Gadreel," I say, frozen at the top of the stairs. "What are you doing here?"

"Thought I'd stop in for a bite," he says sardonically, picking up a lobster and cracking it open. His long hair is the color of polished pewter today—his shoulders are the width of a sofa, accented by the spikes in his armor. He slurps meat from a claw and throws the carcass over his shoulder. A robot scurries in to clean up the mess. "I watched your performance. Nice spear skills. The robots are apoplectic about losing a planet. It's thrown off the rotation of the entire solar system. I hear Mercury has already collided with the sun."

"I'm sure they will sort it out. What do you want?" My throat is so dry I can hardly speak at all, yet I cannot let this man—angel—know how scared I am.

"I am coming with you. To Jerusalem."

I let a moment pass before answering. "That would not be a good idea. Your presence would be seen as a threat."

"That's precisely why I am going. You need *someone* to look threatening. Your union lords certainly won't scare anyone. And you will more than likely lose your nerve. I am bringing ten Dragons."

"Ten Dragons? Then they will know we mean to annihilate them."

"That is because we do. Should your negotiations fail, the prime minister must understand the consequences."

"Was this my father's idea?"

"Zazel always has a contingency plan."

I slump down at the table, feeling defeated once more. Dragons will destroy any hope I have of a peaceful negotiation. I need time to think.

Sabina appears instantly, asking what I would like for lunch. "Anything," I say. "Except lobster."

She nods with a wary look at Gadreel and disappears again.

"I am concerned about... my father," I say as casually as possible. What does Gadreel know of his condition? A robot appears with a plate of calamari and a bottle of champagne. Gadreel grabs the bottle, tears out the cork with his teeth, and guzzles the contents. "He does not look... himself."

"Zazel has been too long in the sun," Gadreel says, tossing the empty bottle over his shoulder. It shatters against the glass wall. "Our kind were not meant to stay so long in this… atmosphere. But Zazel loves the light too much. It's taking its toll."

That must be why I rarely see the other Grigori, except at night. The sun. The light. Zazel's earthly body cannot tolerate it.

"But it doesn't matter," Gadreel adds hastily as if he knows he has told me too much. "His mind is not affected. He will always be in control." He wipes his mouth.

I gaze at the calamari without appetite, wishing it was something else—chicken wings. That makes me think of Grace. I push the thought away.

"If you come," I say, finally, "you must keep your Dragons out of sight. Unless I give you a signal. This can't look like an invasion."

"Of course, Golden Son. Whatever you say." Gadreel's tone drips with sarcasm. He casts the remnant of his lobster shells onto the floor. The robot spins around, frantically sweeping up the mess. Whoever knew angels were such slobs?

Gadreel stands, tossing the chair aside like a bundle of matchsticks, and I am struck by the size of him once again, his head nearly grazing the glass ceiling.

I sigh. "Remember, stay out of sight unless I call for you."

"As you wish." He bows mockingly. "I await the command of the Golden Son."

Chapter Fifteen
Grace

"Under the seats!"

Noah and I dive for cover under the dashboard. My heart is beating so loud that I think whoever is in that other vehicle must be able to hear it, too. After a moment, the beam of a flashlight roves through the driver-side window.

"Hello? Anyone in there?" The voice is female, with a twangy accent.

A woman's face peers through the glass. Middle-aged, wearing a red-and-green checked hunting cap. "Hey there. You folks lost?"

Noah looks at me, then sits up and rolls down the window a crack. "No... just taking a break."

"Okay, then. Just wanted to make sure you weren't... well, Shepherds have been lurking around these parts in old pickup trucks. Can't be too careful, can you?'

I emerge from under the dash as a man joins the woman. He's older than her but equally friendly-looking, though he has a shotgun crooked over one arm.

"I'm Carol, by the way. This is Ben."

Ben lifts his free hand to wave. "Howdy."

"I'm Joshua. This is Sarah," Noah says. We never use our real names while on a mission.

"Where you two headed?" asks Ben.

"Sioux City," says Noah. "Picking up supplies."

"Well, you're not far, then," Carol says. "Why don't you come to the house? Just through the woods. Get some hot grub if you like."

"Thanks," says Noah. "But we're fine here."

"Are you sure?" Carol frowns a little. "Like I said, Shepherds and Peacemakers are all over this area. You'd be safer at the house. After all, there's no place like home!"

That's a YBR code phrase. I look at Noah. His eyes flicker at the phrase, but he doesn't respond with the answering phrase. Instead, he just shakes his head and smiles politely.

"Thanks for the offer anyway," he says.

Carol hesitates, then shrugs. "Please yourself, then. Nice meeting you two! Stay safe!" She and Ben tip their caps to us, then return to their truck.

"I know you're being extra careful, but they knew the code—"

"Shhhh." Noah shushes me. He turns the key to start the engine. He's staring through the windshield at the other truck, barely breathing.

"Noah—"

"Quiet."

We hear the other truck start up. Then it slowly backs away from us.

I let out a breath. "See? I told you they were fine—"

The engine roars; the truck barrels straight for us.

Noah throws the shift into reverse, spins the wheel, and hauls our truck backward and sideways. My body flies forward into the dash and then snaps back against the seat as we careen into a ditch, the engine still revving. I cry out at the jolt of pain in my neck.

"Get down!" Noah pushes me under the dashboard as an explosion of noise shatters the windshield. I hear myself scream as tiny bits of glass shower down on us like an ice storm. Noah pulls something from under his seat—a gun. He springs up and shoots: one, two, three, four, five, six. The shots nearly break my eardrums. He's down again, next to me, panting hard. Outside, a woman screams.

Noah wrenches his door open and jumps out. I sit up, brushing away the glass, to see Carol running down the dirt track in the glare of the other truck's headlights. Noah sprints after her. I get out of the truck and creep over to the other vehicle, where Ben is still in the driver's seat, leaning back, his face a mass of blood. He doesn't move.

I swallow hard and race after Noah, who has tackled the woman, putting all his weight on her to keep her down. She stops fighting, though she's still panting and cursing loudly.

"Are you okay?" I ask Noah, checking for wounds.

He nods, though he's breathing hard and his face is flushed. I wonder if he knows that he killed Ben.

"How did you know?" I ask. "About them..."

Noah turns the woman over onto her back. Her hat has fallen off, revealing a tattoo of six small, iridescent dots arranged in a triangle on her forehead.

"Is that the GEM?" I peer closer.

"Shepherds wear hats to hide them from their quarry," Noah says. Shepherds are Peacemakers specially trained to hunt down Forbidden.

"But they seemed so nice. So normal. They don't look like NPs."

"I guess their starting to use regular humans now." Noah searches the woman's pockets, finds her Cube, and smashes it to pieces. The woman winces as if in pain. Does she feel her Cube being smashed through her GEM? "Help me get her up."

Together, we pull the obstinate woman on her feet, Noah holding her arms behind her back.

"Which way to the house?" Noah asks her.

She points with her head, cursing him as she does. We walk for ten minutes through the woods into a clearing where a simple white farmhouse stands alone in a field. As soon as we pass through the front door, I smell death. A man and a woman lie in pools of dried blood on the kitchen floor. The real Ben and Carol. I kneel beside the dead woman and brush her hair out of her face. Her eyes are open, staring. I close her eyelids, swallowing the rising bile in my throat. I say a prayer over them both.

"You killed them?" I look at the Shepherd woman. "Why?"

"They're Jehovians," she replies. "That is what they deserved."

"Find some rope or tape," says Noah. He holds fake Carol while I search the house and find a roll of duct tape in a drawer. Noah pushes the woman into a kitchen chair, and we bind her as tight as possible. She struggles against the bonds, but she can't break them. Definitely not an NP.

Once she is secure, I turn to Noah. "The guy… is dead." I speak gently, not sure of how he will react. Has he ever killed anyone before? He rarely tells me what happens on his missions. Maybe this is why.

Noah takes a long breath and points to the bodies. "We should bury them."

Noah finds a shovel in the garage, and, as the sun rises, we dig two graves in the garden, where the soil is looser. We carry the bodies out place them in the newly dug graves, covering them with dirt. Tears fill my eyes, even though I didn't know these people. They could be Ralph and Emilia, who might be lying dead somewhere, perhaps in an unmarked grave. I pray they are still alive, that there is still hope.

We stand over the graves for a moment. I feel like we should pray or say some sort of memorial. Instead, I start to sing *Amazing Grace*. Noah stares, silent, his face a mask. I think he's still in shock.

We search for food in the kitchen. There are cans of beans in a cupboard and hot dogs in the fridge so I cook some franks and beans while Noah gathers up what supplies he can from the house—ammunition, two rifles, gasoline, matches, cans of food. Ben and Carol must have been preppers. The Shepherd watches us intently, her upper lip curled in a sneer.

"Where are you really going?" she asks.

"Like I would tell you," I say, stirring the franks and beans.

"Trying to 'rescue' someone? You're fools. Both of you."

"I'd rather be a fool than... whatever you are. You killed two innocent people in cold blood."

"Wasn't me. Anyway, those two came at us loaded for bear. We were just defending ourselves."

"You were in their house. They had every right."

"Rights? Ha. No such thing anymore. You Jehovians need to learn that lesson. And you will, once you quit worshipping that fake god of yours."

"So you really believe Grigori Zazel is a god?"

"*The* god," she says proudly. "The only true god."

Her words fill me with dread.

Noah returns. I spoon franks and beans into two bowls. We sit at the small kitchen table and say a quick prayer over the food. I think about giving some to fake Carol but decide against it. She's probably already eaten plenty of the real Ben and Carol's food supplies.

"What do we do with her?" I whisper while we eat. "We can't let her go. She'll report us. And we can't take her with us, not with that tattoo on her forehead."

"Maybe having her with us would be a good thing," Noah says.

I look at him.

He shrugs. "She's one of them. If we pass through any scanners or drones get too close, they'll see the GEM and let us go."

I shake my head. "They'll be able to track us."

"Yes, but they will be tracking a Shepherd. Not fugitives. I think they will not bother with us, at least for a while. Until we get close, anyway. Then we will separate from her."

"We'd have to take their truck," I say.

"Even better. They won't be suspicious. We could even drive on the highway."

"Really? That would be awesome." I hesitate. "But what about the...the guy? In the truck. Won't they know he's dead?"

Noah thinks about this. "I'm not really sure. His GEM will be offline, but they won't know why. Shepherds stay off-grid when they're in the field. Part of their cover. They act like... us." He smiles. "Don't worry. Everything is going to be fine."

If I had a nickel for every time he said that...

Chapter Sixteen
Helel

The interview is with a perky blond named Katy McCarthy on GNN, Grigori News Network. Shannon is nervous; she much prefers facing the public as a fictional character than her real self. In the dressing room, I take her hands and speak to her gently, whispering all the words I want her to say, writing them on her memory.

Once on stage, she lights up like the sun itself, her smile radiant and warm. She and Katy have a lovely rapport. She even spills some secrets about the Supreme Lord that everyone is dying to know.

"Does he ever take off his armor?"

"Well… sometimes."

Wink-wink.

Then she speaks my words. "The reality of our time is that there is an enemy out there, a very real enemy, those who are trying to destroy all that the Supreme Lord has created for our benefit. The Jehovians are real. They have sparked violent protests all over the world. There are factions hiding out and planning attacks upon our civilization. But what's worse is they try to infect people's minds with lies about the Supreme Lord. Everyone is in danger. Everyone needs protection."

She goes on to describe how the GEM was created with super-advanced nanodot technology now available to all people, no matter where they are or their economic status. She explains how it is applied—quick and easy, perfectly painless.

They play a holo I created of people with the GEM laughing, playing, and enjoying life to the fullest. The GEMs on their foreheads sparkle like diamonds.

"Isn't it so pretty?" Shannon says once the holo ends. "What's even better is that wearing the GEM shows one's love and devotion to the Supreme Lord. He proved he was truly our deliverer by saving us from the Rages and the ravages of war. And he raised his own son from the dead! He is truly God. It's only with his protection that we can survive the Jehovian onslaught."

"They are so sparkly! Are you going to get one, Shannon?" Katy asks effusively.

Shannon glances at me. "Of course I am! I can't wait. I just didn't want to butt in line. Everyone should know that as soon as you get your assigned number, head to the imprinting office. Don't miss your chance! You must stay protected from this deadly Jehovian virus that is infecting people all over the world."

Katy rushes into the dressing room as we are preparing to leave. "Oh, Shannon, I just wanted to tell you that was like the best interview ever. You are so fun. And so intriguing."

"Oh, thank you." Shannon smiles.

Katy gushes on. "I can't wait to get the GEM. I actually got my number this very morning!"

"Perfect! Better hurry. The lines will probably be long."

"Oh yes." Katy glances at me, her smile fading slightly. "I don't think we've been introduced. Are you her manager?"

"In a sense." I put my arm around Shannon to lead her away. She evades me grasp, still focused on the interviewer.

"I hope you'll come back on soon," Katy says. "Tell us more about the GEM and about the Supreme Lord—"

"I'd love to—"

"We will think about it." I yank on Shannon's arm, drawing her to the door. She winces at my grip. "We will be in touch."

"What was that all about?" Shannon says once we are outside. She rubs her arm.

"We have a schedule to keep," I say.

"You hurt me."

"Did I?" I take her arm and kiss it tenderly. "I'm so sorry."

She pulls away, looking around. "Stop that. It's… I don't want… people are watching. The cameras are everywhere."

"Are you ashamed of me?" I give her a wounded look.

"No, of course not. But Zazel…"

I laugh at her look of consternation. "Do you really think Zazel would be jealous? How much you overestimate him. Zazel loves all women. And none. You don't really believe you are all that special, do you?"

Shannon's face crumples at my words.

"Poor lamb." I take her in my arms before she can protest and kiss her long and hard. She tries to pull away as the camera drones click all around us, but I hold her fast. Inside, I am laughing. Zazel's bound to see this. I wish I could see the look on his one-eyed face when he does.

I release her and steer her into the street, where a small crowd has gathered, some with Cubes out taking pictures, others with pens wanting autographs. Seeing her fans, Shannon recovers herself, smiles broadly, poses for Cubies, and signs her name on movie posters and even a few arms. I have to drag her away from her fans to make our next appointment. She does not mention Azazel again.

Part Two

Jerusalem

The Lord builds up Jerusalem,
He gathers the outcasts of Israel.
He heals the brokenhearted
And binds up their wounds.
Psalm 147: 2-3

Chapter Seventeen
Jared

Jerusalem feels like… home.

I've never been here before, yet it seems as though I have always been here. I wonder why that is. Perhaps it has something to do with my peculiar ancestry. Or perhaps it is just being outside of the tower, away from New Asgard, that has me so exhilarated.

Our limousine drives through the newer part of the city to the prime minister's compound, a dreary, post-modern castle built of sand-colored Jerusalem stone, surrounded by a high wall. A huge crowd greets us as we pull up to the front gate, and I brace myself for stern opposition. To my great surprise, the "protestors" carry signs of welcome and praise for the Grigori leader and his "Golden Son."

"Your popularity extends even to the enemy," says Godunov wryly. "Or is it their fear speaking?"

"This is good," says Newman. "Public opinion has turned against Davidov. This will make our job easier."

"You think Davidov will be swayed by public opinion?" says Haraldsen wryly.

"He will be swayed by the Supreme Lord's Dragons," Godunov retorts. I scan the sky for Dragons but see only the surveillance drones following our caravan.

We pass through the gate into the courtyard of the compound, where a soldier opens our doors. A short, balding man greets me as I step out of the vehicle.

"Lord Baldyr, welcome to Jerusalem." He speaks English; the Israelis have not complied with the Grigori directive of forcing everyone to speak Norwegian. "My name is Yaakov. I will show you to your rooms and then offer you a light lunch. The prime minister will be pleased to see you at dinner."

"I wish to see him now," I say.

Yaakov gives me an startled look. "My great apologies, my lord, but the prime minister is unavailable at the moment—"

"Take me to him." I glance at the union lords. "My colleagues will attend your lunch."

Yaakov stands moment, looking from me to the others, unsure what to do. When no one comes to his aid, he says, his voice quivering slightly, "Well then, as you wish, of course, Lord Baldyr." Yaakov motions to the guards to take Godunov, Newman, and Haraldsen away and then beckons me to follow him.

We enter the building and step into an elevator—small and slow compared to the tower—which takes us to a floor of wood-paneled walls and dark red carpet. Several people stop and stare at me as we walk through the dimly lit hallway. Others duck into offices and close their doors. I don't blame them. In this cramped space I look even more like a giant.

Yaakov stops at a double door at the end of the hall. He knocks. A brusque voice on the other side answers. The bald man motions me to wait a moment, then goes in. I hear muffled voices, one distinctly annoyed, and then Yaakov returns, his forehead bathed in sweat.

"You may enter," he says, opening the door wider for me. I have to duck through.

The room is large but dark, with wood paneling, a low ceiling, and black leather furniture. A man wearing camo pants and a cable-knit sweater with leather elbow patches sits in a chair, one ankle crossed over his knee. His face is unshaven and his curly black hair hasn't been combed in a while. Two men wearing suits stand on either side of him. All three men turn to look at me.

Yaakov comes to my side and addresses the man in the chair. "Prime Minister, may I present His Highness, Son of the Supreme Lord, Baldyr."

Yosef Davidov's expression is one of annoyance rather than awe. He sighs, uncrosses his legs and rises to his feet. "Lord Baldyr, welcome to Jerusalem," he says in the least welcoming tone ever. "I am sorry, I am not quite prepared to greet you at the moment."

"I can see that." In fact, the man looks like he just rolled out of bed, yet there is an air of command about him, even in his apparent exhaustion. "Nevertheless, the matter is urgent. I've come a long way."

After a moment, Davidov nods. "Give us the room." Yaakov and the aides file out, eyeing me as they go. Two armed soldiers remain at the door.

"Where is your detail?" Davidov asks me once we're alone.

"I didn't bring one."

"Ah. Your... species... doesn't require bodyguards, I suppose."

It's an insult, but I don't respond. I find his rudeness almost refreshing. It's clear he doesn't think highly of the Grigori. He's taken a hard stance against the UE since his election, unlike his predecessor, and he has suffered for it. Now it appears his own people are turning against him.

"I bring tidings of peace from my father, Grigori Zazel, Supreme Lord of the United Earth. Though he believes we are justified in using deadly force against your country, we wish to make peace first."

A wry smile plays about on Davidov's weathered face. "How kind." He offers me a seat and sits himself.

I sit, still feeling as though everything in this room is much too small and dark. I've become so used to the tower, to the Grigori proportions of everything.

"So. You come to offer peace? On what terms, I wonder?" His directness is disconcerting.

I clear my throat. "Israel must join the UE. Your back is to the wall. You have no allies, few resources, and a military that is, while quite capable, minuscule compared to ours. Your people seem to agree with me. They have been suffering because of your isolation. The way I see it, you can resist us and be destroyed, or you can come to terms with us and live."

"And why does Grigori Zazel care so much about my people to spare our lives?"

"He doesn't," I say. "But I do."

He stares at me. "So this was all your idea? This little tête-à-tête?"

"Your population has been cut in half since the pandemic and the Alliance War. Not to mention the current embargoes you are facing. Can you afford to lose more?"

He's quiet now, though there is a certain smolder in his eyes that tells me he's doing all he can to hold in his temper. Then suddenly, he breaks eye contact with me and rubs his hand over his face as if enormously tired. "If you expect an answer this moment, I cannot give you one. We will talk more at dinner. It will be small, just a few of my cabinet ministers. And my wife, Shira. She is, I'm almost ashamed to say, a fan of yours." His bare hint of a smile breaks some of the tension between us.

"I'll be delighted to meet her." But I am thinking of Gadreel's Dragons. Where are they? How much time will he give me?

"I've arranged a tour of the temple tomorrow. If you are interested." He sounds more conciliatory, suddenly. I smile and nod.

"Of course, that would be fine. But—I must ask another favor."

"What is that?"

I take a breath. "The *Voice*. I want to meet them. Can you arrange that?"

He takes a long time before answering. "You are speaking of those podcasters, I assume?" I nod. "I have no way to contact them directly, I'm afraid. Even Mossad has been unable to track them down. We suspect they are not even in Israel."

"I'm sure you have some way to reach them," I say, staring him down.

He sighs. "I will contact my intelligence director and see if he has any ideas." He pushes a button on a box by his chair, and Yaakov reappears almost instantly. "Yaakov, please take Lord Baldyr to his quarters." He says "lord" as if it were distasteful to him.

I follow the small man out of the office back to the elevator, two soldiers at my heels. Yaakov faces the doors as we ride, humming a little to pass the awkward seconds. When the doors finally open, he rushes out and scampers down another hallway. He stops, opens a door, and ushers me inside.

No glass walls; these are made of plaster. The windows are narrow, and the ceiling is low. The bed seems extremely small with a plain, gold coverlet. There are no robots, no AI servants, no holograms. So this is how the non-Grigori world lives.

"I will fetch you for dinner. Please ring if you need anything at all," says Yaakov.

"Ring?" I look at him.

He hesitates, amused by my confusion. "Yes, the phone there." He points to a contraption on the bedside table. "Pick it up and ask for whatever you need. I shall be back in two hours to see you to the dining room."

"Thank you."

I sit on the bed and glance around the room. There's a large shiny black box sitting on a dresser. I wonder if it is a video-displaying machine. I've heard of them. I get up to touch the screen to turn it on, but nothing happens. I should have asked Yaakov how to work the thing. I root around in the drawers until I find a small handheld device with several buttons. I push button after button until the black screen bursts to life.

It's a news program about a protest occurring in a large city. The announcer speaks in Hebrew, but I hear the English words *New York City*. Protestors swarm Times Square, holding signs that say *Freedom* and *Down with the UE*. The picture changes to yet another city. Several more cities are displayed. Apparently, the Israeli news is trying to show its people how the world is turning against the Grigori and the United Earth.

I pull out a small Cube from my luggage and call Gadreel. A moment later, he appears in a beam of light, only a small image that flickers slightly, not nearly as good as the holos in the tower. Still, I feel his heated gaze upon me.

"Did he agree?" he asks me without a greeting.

"Not yet. We will talk more tomorrow."

"Tomorrow?" He scowls.

"There is a dinner tonight. Tomorrow, we will go to the temple for a tour."

"This is taking too long."

"You must be patient. Davidov is reluctant, but he is under terrible pressure. He will concede. I promise you."

"He must agree by tomorrow. No later."

"It won't be a problem. Do not make a move unless you hear from me."

"If you say so, Son of Zazel."

I close the connection—Gadreel disappears. No doubt he will tell Zazel what I've said, twisting the story to make me look weak and ineffective. I should call Zazel myself, but I can't bear the thought of talking to him now. Instead, I call Vale.

"How's it going?" he asks. He's got headphones around his neck—listening to music against the rules again.

"Nothing so far, but I talked to Davidov. He's going to be tough. How are you? How's the training?"

Vale shrugs. "Good, I guess. I'm hoping to fight in the Grigoralia games in December. Maybe even get a real gladiator match."

"Keep working, you'll get there," I say, though it hurts my heart to think of him in the arena against a real NP gladiator. "Have you talked about it with your mother?"

"No, she's in New York doing interviews and stuff. For her movie." He rolls his eyes. "She'll probably say no anyway. She doesn't think I'm ready."

"Well, mother knows best," I say. "Seriously, there's no hurry—"

"You don't think I'm ready?"

"I didn't say that—"

"Well, I'm ready, I know I am." He sounds petulant. "You'll see."

I smile. "Okay, Vale, I believe you. I'll see you in a couple days and maybe we can spar a little."

His face brightens. "Really? That would be awesome."

I sign off and lie on the bed, wondering how I can stop Vale from ever getting into the arena again.

***

The dining room is long and narrow, with just enough space on either side to pull out a chair and sit. One side is all windows, though the curtains are closed. A huge abstract painting takes up the opposite wall. I am seated on the left side of Davidov, his wife next to me. He wasn't kidding about her being a fan. The bleached blond woman with red lipstick peppers me with questions throughout the meal, which consists of lentil soup, a mixed grill of lamb, chicken, sea bass, and roasted eggplant. I'm saved from answering mostly by Newman, who maintains a steady commentary on all that he sees wrong with Davidov's leadership.

"The people do not seem to agree with your decision to resist the UE," Newman says. "In order to be an effective leader, you must be of the people, by the people, and for the people."

"*For* the people?" Davidov retorts, moving food around his plate with a fork. "Is that what you are?"

"Everything I do is for the people. To keep them safe," Newman replies with a lift of his chin.

Davidov lets out a small chuckle. "And you think your people are happy now that they are so safe?"

"They ought to be."

"When was the last time you spoke to them?"

"Who?"

"To your people. Or any person in your… union?"

Newman picks up his wineglass to take a sip. Classic stalling move. "I hear from people all the time."

"Do you?"

"Of course. They are always welcome to write to me, or call, or email."

"And you respond?"

"My office responds personally to every query."

Davidov does not pursue this any further. He seems to know there is no point.

"You looked as though you were badly hurt in that last bout with the Baphomet," whispers Shira, lightly touching my arm.

"Not too bad," I say, inching my arm away.

"It was thrilling," she says with a slight giggle. "When will you fight next?"

"I suppose... the *Grigoralia* in December."

"Oh, is that a new holiday?"

"It's the celebration of Grigori Zazel's birth."

"So, instead of Christmas, you mean?"

"Yes." I swallow a piece of lamb lodged in my throat.

"Oh! I'd love to see that in person. Could you get us tickets?"

"Shira, leave the poor man alone," Davidov says before I can respond. "You know they won't allow Jews anywhere near New Asgard."

"Oh." Shira's smile fades, her shoulders slump. "I hadn't thought of that."

"Well, if our talks go well, perhaps the Supreme Lord would make an exception," says Eli Galant, the foreign minister. He's a good-looking man with peppered, gray hair and a genial personality. He was the first to grasp my hand in greeting when I came into the room. I sense Galant is leaning toward joining the UE. He wants security for his people, and he knows Israel's defense systems could not withstand a war with the Grigori.

Galant's eyes bear down on me with great interest. "Tell us. How does a champion of the arena become a politician?"

"I act only in my father's name," I say, knowing this question would come up.

"So this has nothing to do with the attempt on your life?" asks Yitsak Cohen, the Minister of National Security. His round face, frameless glasses, and dimpled smile belie his reputation as a freedom extremist who vehemently opposes alignment with the UE. "In which a Zionist was falsely accused?"

"It was not an attempt," I say. "I was dead. The Supreme Lord brought me back to life. And the assassin *was* a Zionist. That has been confirmed."

Cohen snorts under his breath. "According to you Grigori—"

"Yitzak," Davidov says warningly.

"I understand you will be touring the temple tomorrow," Galant breaks in. "You will be quite amazed—"

"No one told me this," says Cohen. "Why was I not informed? Security will be problematic."

"I've already called in the Border Guards," Davidov says.

"Why did you not tell me?" Cohen sputters with indignation. "I cannot be responsible—"

"Just relax, Yitsak. Everything will be fine."

The meal proceeds with stilted conversation punctuated by many awkward silences. Davidov seems utterly uninterested in entertaining his guests, while his ministers grow increasingly uncomfortable. Shira asks questions about my arena fights, and Newman comments repeatedly on how great things are in the NAU, leaving out any mention of the astronomical crime, skyrocketing suicide rates, and the drug epidemic. Godunov seems only interested in the food, while Haraldsen picks distastefully at his meal and says nothing.

Davidov gets up to leave while dessert is being served. "My apologies," he says, not in the last apologetic, "but I have some matters to attend to. My detail will see to your transportation to the Temple Mount in the morning. Shira."

Shira rises reluctantly and bends to whisper in my ear, "See you tomorrow—" Davidov takes hold of her arm and pulls her away. An awkward silence follows their exit.

"What do you think of the malabi?" asks Galant, sticking a spoon into his dessert. "It's a national dish in Israel. The flowered scent comes from the rose water..."

He drones on about the pudding. I don't listen, thinking of other things. Dragons and temples and war. And if I can do anything to stop it.

Chapter Eighteen
Grace

When I wake up, the sun has nearly set. Panicked, I run into the kitchen.

"Why didn't you wake me?"

Noah glances at me from the kitchen table, where he is cleaning a gun. Judy—that's the Shepherd's name—squirms in her chair, still tied up. "You looked so peaceful. No worries. I'll sleep in the truck."

"That means I'll have to drive. And I don't drive pickup trucks. I don't even like to drive regular cars. You know that."

"Well, you will have to get used to it."

"What about her? Who's going to watch her?"

"She's going to be taking a nice, long nap."

"How's that?"

He pulls a bottle of prescription pills from his pocket and jangles them in front of me. "Apparently, Carol had trouble sleeping too." He frowns a little, looking at the bottle, probably thinking of poor Carol. Her sleeping troubles are over. I see from the reading material in the house—lots of

Bibles and religious books—that she and her husband were believers. They are with Jesus now. That's a comfort, at least.

"I'll go get the truck." Noah stands and stuffs the pills in his pants pocket. "And take care of that other problem. Then we can load everything up and go." He hands me the gun. "You know how to use this, right?"

"Yeah. I go to the range just like you." It wasn't that long ago that neither one of us would even touch a gun. But times have changed.

Noah checks Judy's bonds, then heads out through the screen door. It squeaks and slams shut. That screen door was probably just one of the many familiar sounds of ordinary life in this house, before the Grigori came. Before Ben and Carol got killed by Shepherds. It makes me sad to think no one will hear it again.

I sit opposite Judy, holding the gun on my knee.

"I need to go to the bathroom," she mumbles.

"Great. You'll have to wait until Joshua comes back."

"I've got to go now."

"Sorry, can't help you."

She grumbles and swears under her breath.

"You used to be one of us, weren't you?" I say after a moment.

She looks at me, then looks down. "Yeah, I fell for the lie for a while."

"What lie?"

"That Jesus was the Son of God, saving the world." She laughs coarsely. "I was dumb. But I'm not anymore."

"You think the Grigori can save the world?"

"They saved us from the New People Rages. They gave us peace and prosperity. Your God never did that."

"Is that what you call this? Peace and prosperity? I'll tell you why you turned. You were starving. You were desperate. You didn't like being an outcast, hunted and deprived. So you went to them. They needed women to play these roles. And you knew the Forbidden. You knew how they traveled. You knew where to find them. You made a deal with the devil."

"You're the devils. I see that now."

"Right after they put those dots on your forehead, right?"

"It had nothing to do with the GEM. I knew already."

"You know, Indian women wear a dot on their forehead to signify marriage. I guess that means you're married to the Supreme Lord. His bride."

She smiles at that, genuinely pleased. "Yes. I'm his bride."

"But the dot—the Indians call it a Bindi—is also known as the Third Eye. The person who wears it loses all sense of ego and individuality and becomes one with the universe." Ralph told me that once.

"I am one with the universe and with the Supreme Lord," Judy says, lifting her chin. "I feel sorry for you to be so... lost."

"It means you aren't a person at all anymore," I say. "You are a... a cog in a machine. A single cell in an organism. The Supreme Lord doesn't even know your name."

"The Supreme Lord knows all." She glares at me with such venom I feel it in my bones. She jerks her hands as if to break her bonds. But her bonds are deeper than even she imagines.

Chapter Nineteen
Jared

I wake up, gasping.

Just a dream. But this felt like more than a dream. It felt like… a warning.

I lie in the darkness, still gulping in air, the images and feelings of the dream reverberating in my brain. I was walking on a hill through a dense grove of trees, their thick trunks twisted and gnarled, their spidery branches tipped with tiny silvery leaves and small, round clusters of fruit. Olive trees. It must have been the Mount of Olives. Not how it looks today—a barren hill filled with tombs—but as it was in ancient times, before the Romans cut down the trees to pave the way for their invasion.

It was very dark, but a light shone through the branches from the top of the hill. I felt drawn to the light and started to run toward it. The light grew brighter and brighter. Then there was a terrible noise, a rumble from deep inside the earth. The trees shivered so hard that all their olives fell from the branches. Slimy olives smacked me in the face; I raised my arms over my head. The ground under my feet gave way, and I started to sink along with the trees themselves. I fought and struggled to stay above, but the earth seemed to be pulling me under until the ground closed over my mouth and my head, and I could no longer breathe.

That's when I woke up.

I stare at the ceiling, which seems so oppressively low. Why do I suddenly feel... trapped?

Unable to sleep, I turn on the video-displaying machine. I scroll through the various channels using the handheld device, but all the shows are in Hebrew. I turn off the machine. The clock by the bed has a radio. I turn it on and fiddle with the tuning knob.

Suddenly, a voice blazes loud and clear from the little box. The voice speaks in Hebrew, but for some reason, I can understand every word.

> *"Next I wanted greater clarity about the fourth beast,*
> *the one that was different from all the others*
> *and utterly terrifying with its iron teeth and bronze claws.*
> *As it ate and crushed, its feet smashed whatever was left over.*
>
> *As I watched, this same horn waged war against*
> *the holy ones and defeated them,*
> *until the Ancient One came.*

The second voice speaks.

> *"So you must know and gain wisdom about this...*
> *After the sixty-two weeks, an anointed one will be eliminated.*
> *No one will support him.*
> *The army of a future leader will destroy the city and the sanctuary.*
> *His end will come in a flood,*
> *but devastations will be decreed until the end of the war."*

I realize with sudden clarity that this must be the *Voice*. The podcast that terrifies my father. As I listen, I begin to understand his fear. There is a chilling power in the words spoken, which are clearly prophecies from the forbidden Bible. This is the podcast that has caused riots all over the world.

> *"When their kingship nears its end,*
> *and their sins are almost complete,*
> *a king will step forward.*
> *He will be stern and a master of deception.*
> *At the height of his power,*
> *he will wreak unbelievable destructions.*
> *He will succeed in all he does.*
> *He will destroy both the mighty and the people of the holy ones.*
> *Along with his cunning, he will succeed by using deceit.*
> *In his own mind, he will be great.*
> *In a time of peace, he will bring destruction on many,*
> *opposing even the supreme leader.*
> *But he will be broken— and not by a human hand."*
>
> *He will be broken and not by a human hand.*

That is what Zazel fears most, why he wants the *Voice* destroyed. And I am to aid in that destruction.

I get up and dress. The sleepy guard rouses when I open the door, drawing to attention.

"I need to speak to the prime minister," I say.

The guard's mouth opens and closes. He looks away and then back at me as if he thought maybe I was talking to someone else. When all else fails, he pulls a radio from his belt and says something in Hebrew. Once he gets a curt response, he nods and tells me to follow him.

He takes me via elevator to a lower floor, and then we walk down a long, winding hallway and up a flight of stairs. At the end of another hall are double doors that appear to lead to a different building. The carpet is worn, and the doors are of carved wood. Davidov is standing at the end of the hallway, dressed as he was at the dinner, waiting for me.

"Can't sleep?" he asks wryly.

Now that I'm here, I don't even know what to say or where to begin. Should I tell him about my dream? He'll think I'm crazy. Or will he? The Jews have a long history of dream revelations.

"You need to evacuate the city. As soon as possible."

Long pause. Davidov stares at me.

"Why?"

I take a breath, let it out slowly. "I think… something bad is going to happen."

He continues to stare at me as if I'd grown a second head or perhaps lost the one I had.

"Come in," he said after a moment. "I'll put some coffee on."

I follow him through a cramped sitting room and into a small kitchen. He directs me to sit at the table and busies himself at the stove.

"Is this… your residence?"

"The Shin Bet does not allow anyone outside my family to know where I live." He fills a kettle with water and sets it on a burner. "This is a… convenient meeting place." He spoons coffee grounds into a French press. "So tell me about this revelation of yours."

"It was a dream."

He pauses and turns to me, frowning. "A dream? You are here because you had a dream?"

I nod, swallowing. "This dream—felt very real. I think it was a warning."

"Of what?"

"Some sort of disaster. Earthquake, perhaps or... something else." I should tell him about the Dragons now, but I don't.

"There has not been a major earthquake in Jerusalem in over a hundred years."

"Maybe you are due for one."

"And why would God—assuming this dream came from God—tell *you* about it? Why not a rabbi? Why not me?"

"I don't know."

Davidov purses his lips. The kettle whistles. He turns off the stove and pours the steaming water into the press. He sets the lid and carries it to the table, where he sits heavily and looks at me.

"Why are you here, Baldyr, son of Zazel?"

"I told you. I had a dream—"

"No. I mean, why are you *here*? In Jerusalem? You know I will never accept this offer of yours, don't you?"

I sigh. "When I met you yesterday, I guessed you wouldn't."

"No doubt your father knows it, too. Why this charade? So you can tell the world you tried to reason with me, but I would not listen? So you can destroy Israel with a clear conscience? Perhaps that is *really* what your dream was about." He presses the knob at the top of the press. It sinks slowly down. "I am damned either way, aren't I? If I accept your offer, Israel will disappear slowly instead of quickly, as it will do if I refuse. In either case, Israel will cease to exist. You offer me the coward's way."

I shake my head. "Is it the coward's way to want to save your people from certain destruction? Israel is small, and the UE is great. You're right. You *don't* stand a chance."

Davidov pours the coffee into the two cups without responding. I pick up my cup and take a sip. It's as bitter as his words. He leans back in his chair, running a finger around the rim of his cup, not drinking. "If it will make you feel better, I will consult with the Geological Survey Center, but I know that Jerusalem does not lie on any fault line that would raise concern for a major earthquake."

"Except for the fault line that runs through the Mount of Olives."

He gives me another long look. "Geologists are divided on the significance of that fault."

"But you know your scriptures, don't you? Wasn't it Zechariah who said, 'The Mount of Olives will be split in half from east to west—' "

"How do *you* know our scriptures?" he asks sharply. "Did you Grigori not ban the Torah, the Prophets, the entire Bible?"

I can't tell him about the cave I once lived in with the Forbidden and the nightly sermons about prophecy and God's plan for the world. Instead, I shrug. "That doesn't mean such works are not still… accessible."

He stares at me for a long moment, his pupils pulsing. Then he picks up his coffee cup, drains it, and drops it on the table with a clatter. How is he able to down that bitter brew in one gulp? He stands, and I stand as well, sensing our meeting is over. He scrubs his hand through his hair, a gesture of exhaustion, and turns for the door.

"I will take your warning under advisement. Good night, Son of Zazel."

Then he is gone.

The sleepy soldier escorts me back to my room. I lie down on the bed, but I don't sleep. Afraid of dreams. Afraid of what fresh horror they might reveal.

Chapter Twenty
Michael

It is morning. The sky is a dome of unbroken blue, fading to gold where it touches the outline of my beloved city, Jerusalem.

Since the beginning, I have been this nation's protector. I have seen it rise and fall, burn to ash, and emerge anew, strong and resilient, nearly as eternal as the God who placed His hand upon it. Today will be a day for ashes, a hard day. But a necessary one. I have gathered my host from the far reaches of the heavens. We cannot stop what will happen—Elohim has spoken—but we have a part to play.

A line of black cars winds its way through the crowded streets around the new Mount Zion, past the ancient ruin called the City of David, and slows to a stop at the loop before the Western Wall Plaza. Lines of Israeli police and Border Guards made up of army reservists push back hordes of onlookers as Jared and his entourage emerge from the cars.

He looks like a giant among these people, tall and regal in his white, high-collared coat with the golden snakes embroidered at the hem. The crowd hushes, as if witnessing a god in their midst. He pauses to gaze up at the sky, squinting in the sunlight. His eyes are still unused to the undiluted light, but the smile on his face is genuine, natural. He knows the blue above him is real, not a conjuring of the Grigori.

He is more at ease today. Perhaps because Yosef Davidov has sent out an alert advising residents to evacuate the city. The reason given is "possible catastrophic seismic event within the next twenty-four hours." Many people are taking the warning seriously and are headed into the hillside. Yet a large remnant flock to the Temple Mount to get a closer look at the famous Golden Son.

None are aware of the ten Dragons, parked just over the treaty line in Jordan, beyond the Dead Sea, awaiting orders.

Davidov is already in the plaza, his wife by his side, surrounded by a platoon of Border Guards and his own security force, the Shin Bet. He greets Jared and the union lords with a handshake and a forced smile as camera drones whir around them. They pass through the sea of people to the wooden walkway that leads to the Temple Mount. Shira stays close to Jared's side. Newman lags behind, waving and smiling for the cameras as the crowd shouts enthusiastically, "Hail to the Supreme Lord! Hail to Baldyr the Golden Son!" Dark Ones hang over the crowd like a blanket, obscuring faces, trying to block our Light. I send angels to keep them at bay.

The sun beats down on the white stone of the new temple, now called the Millennium Temple, making it appear illuminated from within. Some call it the Grigori Temple, for it would not exist without the intervention of Grigori Zazel, who ended the Alliance War and forced the Muslim nations to give the Temple Mount back to the Jews. The leaders of Islam had formally acknowledged Zazel as the Madhi, the One Who Guides, the crusader who would conquer all the world. They even consented to moving their shrines from the Temple Mount to Jabal Thawr Mountain, a holy mountain near Mecca, whose caves had once served to hide Mohammed from enemy tribes. Zazel had promised them a triumphant return and the annihilation of Israel—only one of those promises he intends to keep.

I bristle, watching these fragile humans swarm over the Temple Mount, seemingly unaware of the ground on which they stand. This is sacred ground, Mount Moriah, later called Mount Zion, where Abraham brought Isaac to sacrifice, where David bought a threshing floor and built an altar to stop a plague he had caused by demanding a census. I was here when Solomon dedicated the first temple, smaller than this one but infinitely more beautiful, and when it was destroyed by the Babylonians less than four hundred years later. I was here when the second temple began, some seventy years later, though it was a paltry shadow of Solomon's glorious work. I saw Herod embellish that temple five hundred years later, only for it to be destroyed by the Romans within a century.

Now they have done it again. Do they imagine this temple will stand when others have fallen?

Jared's smile fades as he gazes upon the gleaming white building with its magnificent stonework, high walls, and elaborate gates. His brow furrows; something disturbs him. He does not remember Samyaza's temple in the shadow world, the place where he died and his body was taken over by a demon. Yet that event still marks him in a way he cannot fathom. He puts a hand unconsciously to his chest in answer to a sudden ache.

Suddenly, a voice booms over loudspeakers at the south side of the Temple. Not any voice. The *Voice*. It was not Davidov who persuaded them to come here today, though he made an effort. It was Elohim Himself.

Black hoodies and white plastic masks obscure the faces of the two men. They shout their prophecies as a crowd gathers around them, mystified and curious. Jared takes several steps toward them, straining to hear the words, which are not a warning but, strangely, a plea for mercy.

> *"But now, my Lord, our God—*
> *you who brought your people out of Egypt with a strong*

hand,
making a name for yourself even to this day:
We have sinned and done the wrong thing."

I listen for the response of Elohim, readying for His command.

The crowd becomes hostile, shouting and throwing stones at the two men, who seem unperturbed. I send my angels to protect them from the swarm of descending Dark Ones. The two men shout even louder, raising their arms and speaking in unison.

My Lord, please! In line with your many righteous acts,
please turn your raging anger from Jerusalem,
which is your city, your own holy mountain.

My Lord, listen! My Lord, forgive!
My Lord, pay attention and act! Don't delay!
My God, do all this for your own sake,
because your city and your people are called by your name.

The crowd reacts with unrestrained violence. They try to attack the men but find they can't—my angels repel them, push them back like an energy force. Some fall as if struck by lightning. Others cry out in agony as if they'd been burned. All begin to rush around in a kind of madness. Police and Border Guards attempt to break up the mob. Camera drones dart about, recording everything.

Davidov grows agitated by the distractions. He tugs firmly on Jared's arm, forcing him away from the scene. Jared turns back reluctantly, and the procession continues around the outer courtyard of the temple toward the Golden Gate. This is where Yeshua entered Jerusalem on a donkey to show the world who He was.

There is more history here than the tour guide tells. It was once known as the Gate of Mercy, for every year on the Day of Atonement, the priests would send a goat out into the wilderness heaped with the nation's sins "to Azazel." Azazel always took this to be a sacrificial offering to him, whereas, in truth, the Israelites were sending their sins where they belonged—the demonic realm. For them, the desert has always been a place of evil, a place to be overcome. Like all the fallen, Azazel still thinks he was unjustly condemned.

The tour guide explains that Muslim invaders blocked off the Golden Gate during the Crusades. It is the only gate of the Old City to remain sealed. Jared stares at the gate long after the tour guide has moved on. Davidov nudges him gently to get his attention.

The guide leads the group around the temple's south side to the main entrance, the Beautiful Gate, which is so huge it takes four men to open it. They enter the high-walled outer court surrounded by a colonnade partitioned into several smaller spaces. The tour guide describes in effusive tones the wonders of this new temple, how it was a near-perfect replica of Herod's temple, down to the number and size of the stone blocks. At the opposite end, steps rise to another gate that leads to the inner court, where the huge brazen altar stands. Beyond that is the Holy of Holies, the enclosed inner sanctum.

The raucous noise of the crowd outside the temple escalates, forcing the tour guide to shout. The delegates and union lords look around uncomfortably, wondering, perhaps, why Davidov doesn't order his men to remove the *Voice* from the Temple Mount.

Jared pauses before entering the inner courtyard. He turns around to see the two masked men standing at the entrance of the Beautiful Gate. They shout in unison; they are speaking to him.

A single, very small horn came out of one of the four horns.
It grew bigger and bigger, stretching toward the south,
the east, and the beautiful country.
It grew as high as the heavenly forces,
until it finally threw some of them and some of the stars down
to the earth.
Then it trampled on them.
It grew as high as the very leader of those forces,
taking the daily sacrifice away from him
and overturning his holy place.
In an act of rebellion, another force will take control of the
daily sacrifice.
It will throw truth to the ground and will succeed in every-
thing it does.

Jared is frozen in place, the words like the sting of a scorpion, paralyzing. The tour guide has moved on to the Nicanor Gate. Davidov tries, without success, to get Jared's attention. The *Voice* continues, relentless.

And he shall make a strong covenant with many for one
week,
and for half of the week he shall put an end to sacrifice and
offering.
And on the wing of abominations shall come one who makes
desolate,
Until the decreed end is poured out on the desolator.

Davidov grabs Jared's arm and spins him around. Jared blinks as if awakening from a dream. Davidov directs him up the steps to the gate. Jared hesitates, then steps into the inner court.

Suddenly, a dreadful whine sounds overhead. Everyone looks up. Ten mighty Grigori Dragons approach from the east in formation, hulking black machines shaped like preternatural beasts, each with four hinged arms that unfurl as they close in over the Temple Mount, tips glowing white.

The crowd outside hushes; the people in the temple courtyard gaze up in wonder.

"What are they?" Davidov says.

"Dragons." Jared stares at the flying machines darkening the blue sky above. His body shakes, his eyes pulse. "Get everyone out of here!" he shouts to Davidov as he runs toward the Beautiful Gate. He is face-to-face with the *Voice*.

"You need to leave," Jared says. "Everyone! Get off the Temple Mount! Now!" No one listens—they are gazing at the monstrous machines overhead, wondering what they mean.

The *Voice* speaks, softly now, so only Jared can hear.

> *There will be great suffering*
> *such as the world has never before seen*
> *and will never again see.*
> *If that time weren't shortened,*
> *nobody would be rescued.*
> *But for the sake of the ones whom God chose,*
> *that time will be cut short.*

The Dragons fan out, three hovering over the Temple Mount, the others moving into the Old City. Jared watches, helpless, the words forming on his lips. *No, No No...*

Davidov emerges from the temple with his Border Guards. "What is happening?"

The *Voice* shouts the last of their prophecies, raising their arms high.

O God, the nations have invaded Your inheritance;
They have defiled Your holy temple;
They have laid Jerusalem in ruins.

The two masked men fall to their knees in prayer.

A tremendous boom comes from the Dragon directly overhead. A thin beam of white light shoots from one of its tentacles, aimed at the *Voice*.

The two men are suddenly bathed in a halo of fire. They glow like angelic beings for a split second before their skin bubbles and blackens, and their clothes explode into flame. Their bodies collapse on the ground, writhing in agony as blood and tissue burst through their charred skin. Their masks disintegrate, exposing their bulging eyes. The *Voice* is finally silent.

The onlookers nearest the two men shrink away from the gruesome sight, too terror-stricken to scream. Then all the Dragons begin to fire, their pulse lasers raining down hellfire upon the Temple Mount. People scream in agony as the heat from the lasers boils the water inside the bodies. Others fall into the gigantic holes burned into the pavement. Dark Ones dart everywhere, glorying in this growing horror. I hold my forces back, waiting for orders.

"Get everyone out of the temple!" Jared shouts to Davidov, who is frozen in place, unable to comprehend what he's seeing. Jared turns to the Border Guards. "Get them out!"

Two Border Guards rush back into the inner court to retrieve the rest of the delegation. But none of them will obey.

"We'll stay here!" says Newman. "It's safer in the temple!"

"No!" Jared shouts. "Come out!"

"Come out!" Davidov shouts. "Shira!" He lunges through the Beautiful Gate, but Jared holds him back.

"Don't go!"

"Yosef!" Shira appears at the Nicanor gate. She takes several steps toward her husband but stops, undecided. Too late. A pulse laser explodes upon her, turning her to mist.

"Shira!" Davidov falls to his knees.

The rest of the delegation disappears in a blistering barrage of laser fire. The entire inner court is consumed by smoke.

Jared drags a weeping Davidov away from the gate.

Dragon fire is everywhere. Those still alive stampede for the overloaded walkway, which sways and bends like a reed. A support beam snaps. Then another. The air is dense with wails and cries as the walkway collapses into a cloud of dust, taking hundreds of people with it.

Jared drops down to Davidov's side and throws an arm over his shoulders. He can do nothing now but comfort the prime minister and wait for the end.

And then a new voice booms from the heavens.

> *"Thus says the Lord! I will make the land a desolation and a waste,*
> *and the pride of her strength shall cease;*
> *and the mountains of Israel shall be desolated,*
> *so that none shall pass through.*
> *And they shall know that I AM THE LORD,*
> *when I have made the land a desolation and a waste*
> *because of all their abominations which they have committed."*

It is the voice of Grigori Zazel.

A bright light appears in the sky, splitting the blue, like a solar eclipse. Those who are staring upward shriek and cover their eyes as if their retinas have been burned. The radiant light soon takes the form of a man—a god. The image of Grigori Zazel, his avatar standing a hundred feet tall, descending from on high and coming to rest on the roof of the Holy of Holies. His arms are outstretched, a sword in one hand, a scepter in the other.

> *"How your betrayals defile you!*
> *I cleansed you, but you didn't come clean from your impurities.*
> *You won't be clean again until I have exhausted my anger*
> *against you.*
> *I, the LORD, have spoken!*
> *It's coming, and I'll do it. I won't relent or have any pity or*
> *compassion.*
> *Your punishments will fit your ways and your deeds!"*

The great hologram of Grigori Zazel sinks slowly into the roof of the Holy of Holies.

Now is my time to act. I gather my forces at the Golden Gate, the Gate of Mercy. We sing, our Song breaking through time, space, and eternity into the very stones blocking the gate, exciting electrons, sending protons reeling. The Song that shatters the Veil, breaks through worlds. Ten thousand angels sing, commanding the stones to crack open, crumble into powder, dissolve into mist. The humans cannot hear us, but they witness the effect with fear and trembling. For the first time in six hundred years, the Golden Gate is open.

Jared is the first to move, pulling Davidov to his feet. "This way! Follow me!" He races toward the Golden Gate, shouting as he goes. Survivors obey, stumbling forward, still in shock yet desperate for escape. Davidov shouts commands to those soldiers still alive.

"Follow him! Through the gate!"

The Border Guards, grateful for orders, corral everyone still on their feet toward the gate. My angels form a shield around them as they charge

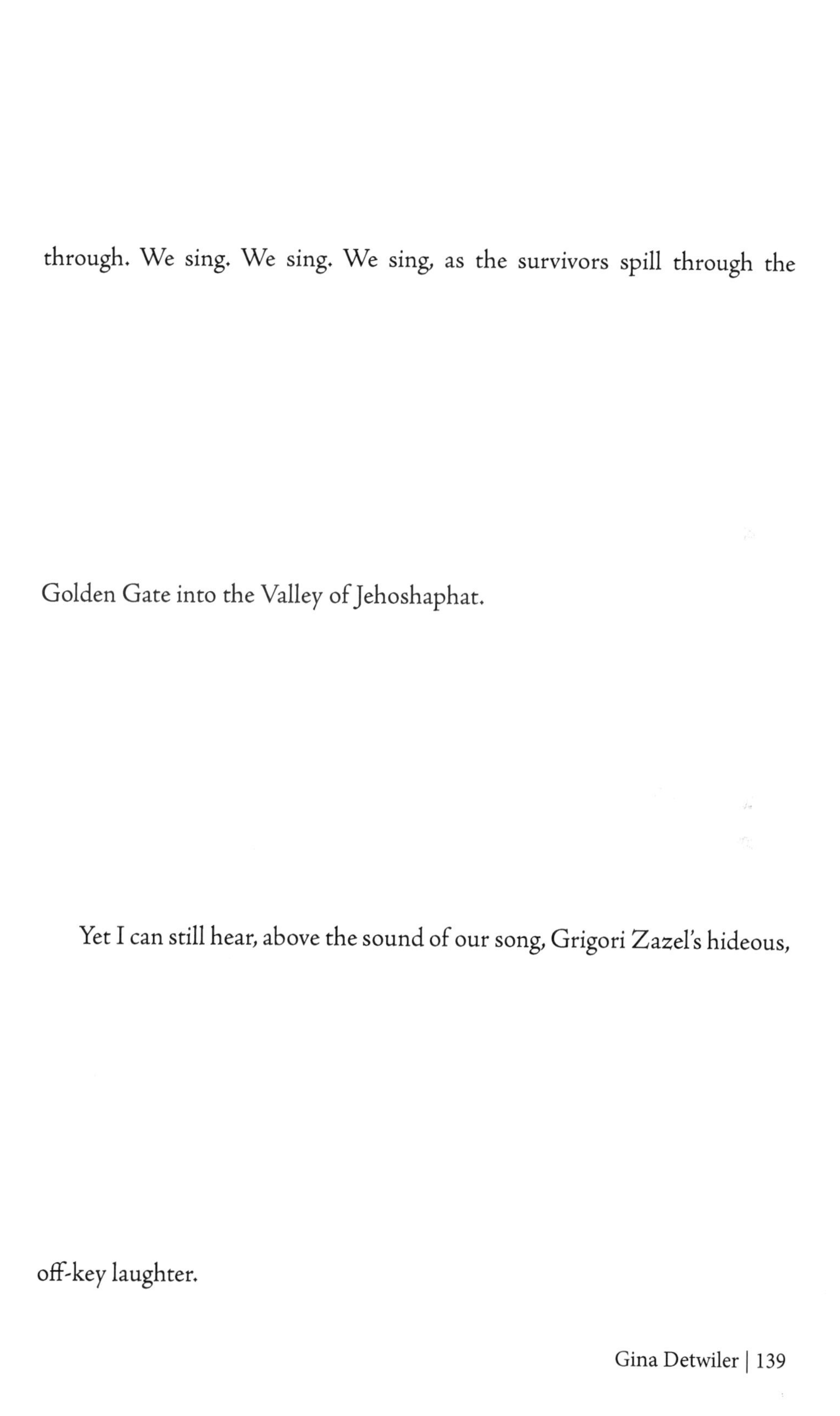

through. We sing. We sing. We sing, as the survivors spill through the Golden Gate into the Valley of Jehoshaphat.

Yet I can still hear, above the sound of our song, Grigori Zazel's hideous, off-key laughter.

Chapter Twenty-One
Grace

Noah makes Judy sit in the front seat, her hands and feet still bound with duct tape, and waits until she swallows the sleeping pills. He even checks her mouth to make sure she did it. Noah surprises me with how badass he can be; he's such a gentle soul most of the time. But this is his world now, the world of the Scarecrow, and he takes no chances. Especially with me doing the driving.

Noah shows me how to operate the truck, which still has remnants of fake Ben's blood on the dash, despite Noah's efforts to clean it. Fake Ben's name was Seth, according to Judy. He'd been enlisted from the camps because he was old, and the Peacemakers needed more agents who looked like Forbidden to be Shepherds. How bad must it have been in the camp for him to make that choice? I can only imagine.

Once I feel comfortable driving the truck without crashing into anything, I pull out of the woods and onto the main road, headed east. Noah lies down in the back seat, his arms wrapped around the shotgun as if it were a teddy bear. More guns lie on the floorboards. He's not taking any chances.

The sleeping pills work wonders on Judy, who snores like a lumberjack. I have to admit it's nice driving on smooth highways rather than winding back roads and dirt tracks. Perhaps our encounter with fake Ben and Judy was a divine intervention. I only wish it hadn't cost the lives of two innocent people.

It's mid-afternoon when Noah wakes up and tells me to pull off so we can refill the gas tank and take a bathroom break. That's music to my ears. I pull onto a side road and turn off the engine. This rouses Judy, who says sleepily, "What's happening?"

"Bathroom break."

"I don't see any bathrooms."

"There's a girl's tree and a boy's tree."

Noah refills the tank from his gas cans while I lead Judy into the trees. Her feet are just wide enough apart that she can take tiny, shuffling steps, but because her hands are bound, I have to help her with the rest of it, which is not my favorite thing. She's still pretty groggy, though, and doesn't give me any problems. She even giggles as if what we're doing is somehow hilarious.

We take turns driving through the night. Judy becomes surly when the drugs wear off, telling us how "they" are going figure out what's going on and we're all going to get "neutered." Apparently, that means something new these days, like a lot of words.

We get to New Jersey without any major issues, definitely a new experience. Noah decides it's time to part ways with Judy, in case we run into any drones that might be tracking her GEM. He follows a sign that says Great Swamp Wildlife Refuge, which lives up to its name. Noah drives into a thicket of trees and turns off the engine.

"So you're just going to leave me here?" Judy slurs as we prepare to hike out. "Tied up like this?"

"We'll leave you some food," Noah says. "We'll be back in a couple of days."

"If they find me here," Judy says, "I can tell them all about you and where you're headed."

"You don't know where we're headed."

"Sure I do. New York. Where else?"

Noah pauses, glancing at me. Then he says flatly, "You're wrong."

"You can't leave me here." Her expression changes suddenly. Her chin trembles and her eyes blink as if she's trying not to cry. "If they find me, they'll kill me."

Both of us stare at her.

"Kill you? Why?" I ask.

"Because… I failed." Her voice cracks. "I got captured. I lost my Cube. The penalty is death."

I grab Noah's sleeve to pull him aside. I whisper so Judy can't hear. "We need to take her with us."

"Are you crazy?"

"We can't let her die."

Noah's face reddens. It occurs to me I've never seen him angry before. "And if they track her? They will find us too. We're headed into the most populated area of the country—"

"I know all that. But what if they kill her? Are we going to let that happen? I mean, if we lose our humanity, what else have we got?"

He's silent for a moment, staring at something in the trees that I cannot see. He runs a hand through his hair and sighs deeply. Then he opens the tailgate of the truck and starts rummaging through the boxes of stuff we'd taken from the farmhouse. He comes up with a roll of aluminum foil and some duct tape.

"What are you—?" I ask.

He doesn't answer. He wraps several sheets of aluminum foil around Judy's head, ignoring her protests, and secures it with the tape.

"Is that really going to work?" I ask.

He glares at me. "Probably not, but it's all we've got. Let's go."

Chapter Twenty-Two
Jared

It's all a blur, like whoever is operating my body is someone else, not me. I sense a presence, familiar yet alien—the same presence always with me in the arena, guiding me, telling me what to do when I have nothing left.

We had burst through the Golden Gate after watching it miraculously open before our eyes. No one who witnessed that could have had any doubt about who did it. But instead of heading up the Mount of Olives, which seemed to be what happened in my dream, I feel directed to stay in the valley. Perhaps there is more protection here from the Dragon fire, but in any case, the Dragons do not come after us. Gadreel's deadly machines continue to fire upon the city. The screams of the dying reverberate in my ears.

"Where are we going?" Davidov asks breathlessly, echoing my thoughts.

"We'll follow the valley," I say, though in truth I have no idea.

"How far?" Davidov asks.

"How far does it go?"

"To the Dead Sea."

"That far."

Davidov doesn't protest. He looks despondent, emptied of hope. He's probably thinking about his wife, whom he watched turn to ash before his eyes. I know what he's feeling. But I have no time to comfort him.

He turns to his soldiers. "Keep everyone together. Tell them not to drink from the stream. It's polluted. They'll get sick."

I glance down at the narrow stream that runs along the very bottom of the valley, banked on either side by lush grass, the only healthy vegetation for miles around. We are all thirsty; the temptation to drink this water will be very great. But Davidov is right; the valley is filthy, choked with trash.

We move as fast as we can through the outskirts of the city into the desert, surrounded by nothing but rocks and hills dusted with scraggly shrubs. I hear people moaning and complaining of heat, thirst, and exhaustion. Some are wounded, suffering from burns. We can't stop now. Who knows when the Dragons may come after us. I'm kind of surprised they haven't already.

Perhaps Gadreel doesn't know we've escaped. Or he has something else in mind for us.

An hour into our journey, I call a halt for rest. People collapse where they're standing, gasping for breath. Many moan in pain. They aren't going to be able to run much longer.

"Are there any shelters in these hills?" I ask Davidov.

Davidov blinks as he gazes around him, like he's only now understanding where we are. "There's caves. A few Christian monasteries. Most of them have been abandoned since the rise of the Grigori."

"Which one is closest?"

He thinks for a moment. "Perhaps… Mar Saba. Near the Dead Sea. At least another three hours."

"Is there water there?"

"There are cisterns. And a spring."

I take a long breath. "Tell them," I say. "Tell them we are headed to Mar Saba. It's a long walk, but there will be water there. They must keep going."

"You have to let them rest—"

"The longer we remain out here, the more danger we're in."

"But the Dragons didn't pursue us—"

"It's not the Dragons that worry me."

"What then?"

I don't reply. I don't want to say it aloud.

A few minutes later, Davidov's soldiers have the people on their feet and moving again, albeit slower than before. The heat of the day is fully upon us, the sun high overhead. It claws at us, drags us down. Just for a moment, I wish for my angel powers to return. I could carry them all.

You can carry them. I pray this to whoever is guiding me. *Please, carry them.*

Tell them to sing.

Sing what?

A song of ascent.

I turn to Davidov. "Get them to sing," I say. "The song of ascent."

"You think they can sing? They can barely breathe."

"Please."

He sighs, then starts to sing. He sings in Hebrew, yet for some reason I can understand the words.

I lift up my eyes to the mountains—
where does my help come from?
My help comes from the Lord,
the Maker of heaven and earth.
He will not let your foot slip—
he who watches over you will not slumber...

His voice is remarkably strong and clear. After a few minutes, others join in, haltingly, then growing in strength. I join the song as well, allowing the music to work it's way into my body, soothing my aching muscles. I move a little faster. Soon, we are all moving without effort, our lungs no longer screaming for air, our limbs no longer weighed down by exhaustion.

It feels as though we are flying.

The valley becomes a canyon, so narrow we have to move in twos and threes. Davidov points ahead—I see the monastery of Mar Saba, a walled fortress spilling down the mountain, overseen by a crumbling tower.

At the sight of the monastery, many following us break into cheers. The cliffs are high around us now, the stream deeper. We are so close…

An earsplitting buzzing fills the air, like a million swarms of bees. I look up to see several white bulbous drones weaving thick streams of smoke in the sky, nearly blocking out the sun. Everyone stops to gape in wonder at this strange, hypnotic performance.

"What are they?" Davidov asks.

My insides seem to melt. This is what I feared. "Rainmakers," I say.

He looks at me. "Rainmakers?"

"They are generating clouds, which they will inject with silver iodide to make rain." I swallow the growing lump in my throat. "We need to hurry."

We pick up the pace to the monastery, though because of the narrowing of the valley, we are even more disjointed than before. I look up frequently, watching the clouds turn from white and puffy to black and thunderous. Within minutes, fat raindrops begin to fall.

At first, the people sigh with pleasure, the rain cooling their faces and tongues.

"Tell them not to drink it," I shout to Davidov. "It's toxic. It will make them sick."

Before he can give the order, people shriek and choke from the bitter taste of the rain, which quickly progresses from a drizzle to a downpour. Each drop feels like a tiny flame boring into my skin. I'm thankful I am wearing a jacket, but many of these people have only T-shirts on. The growing torrent nearly drowns out their cries of pain.

I push them harder, begging them to keep moving. Water streams down the cliffs and puddles around our ankles, rising quickly to our calves. It's like twilight now. Between the rain and the darkness, I can barely see Davidov's face. People shriek with fear, straining to keep from being washed away in the fast-moving current. Many pray out loud for deliverance.

Look up.

I raise my gaze despite the burning rain. What I see is impossible—a figure perched on the edge of the cliff, shining like a star, holding a flaming sword high in the air. Then there are more of them, all along the cliff edge on both sides, their bodies swathed in white, their faces bathed in fire.

Do I imagine this? Is this the hallucination of a man about to die? The water rises to my knees, the current threatening to push me over. People cling to each other, heads bowed to the storm. *Look up!* I want to shout. But there is no point. They will not see.

With a mighty roar, a sudden rush of water spills down from the top of the ridge, headed straight for us.

"It's coming," I shout.

"Brace yourselves!" Davidov orders. Cries and shrieks fill the air. I crouch low and close my eyes, waiting for the deluge.

It doesn't come.

I open my eyes and blink several times, for I can see nothing—the whole world seems filled with light, as if the sun were inches from the earth, obliterating everything.

And then I see them—the angels—they have formed a cordon around us, holding back the water.

I want to shout to Davidov—*look! Look at this!* But I can't move, can't speak, my whole body frozen, as if this moment exists outside of time. I can only watch. And shake with awe.

A voice comes out of the light.

And the serpent cast out of his mouth
after the woman water as a river,
that he might cause her to be carried away by the stream.
And the earth helped the woman,
and the earth opened her mouth and swallowed up the river
which the dragon cast out of his mouth.

The rain stops. The light fades. I stand straight, still trembling, yet no longer with fear.

"What… just happened?" Davidov is looking at me, mouth agape. I don't answer. I don't trust myself to speak.

Others rise from their bent positions and gaze up at the sky, serene and blue once again. The clouds are gone. Even the water at our feet has receded, absorbed into the earth. For a long time, no one speaks.

Then someone starts to sing. Others join in, growing in strength, their voices infused with wonder and joy.

The Lord will keep you from all harm—
he will watch over your life;
the Lord will watch over your coming and going
both now and forevermore.

Chapter Twenty-Three
Grace

Two hours into our walk to Weehawken, I regret my decision to bring Judy. All she does is complain.

"You barely feed me, you fill me up with sleeping pills, you wrap my head in foil, and then you expect me to walk fifty miles," she grumbles as we trudge through dense woods.

"It's not fifty miles," I say. "It's twenty-five. And you're eating as much as we are."

Suddenly, Judy stops walking. Her eyes pulse, and her whole body shakes with convulsions. She falls to the ground, her body flopping like a fish out of water.

"What's the matter with her?" I shriek.

"She's having a seizure." Noah drops to his knees and turns Judy onto her side. He takes off his jacket and puts it under her head. "Help me hold her down. Keep her from hurting herself."

I kneel beside her and grab her legs to keep them still. After a few minutes, the tremors subside. Judy looks like she's unconscious.

"Is she going to be all right?" I ask, my voice shaking.

"I think so."

"Where did you learn this stuff?"

"I was a firefighter. We were trained as paramedics."

Judy starts to moan. Noah turns her onto her back and shines his flashlight in her eyes. She make a face and feebly bats him away. "Get off me." Her voice is slurry. She blinks and gazes around. "What happened?"

"You had a seizure," Noah says. "Has this happened before?"

"Once or twice."

"Since you got the GEM?"

She nods slowly, her brow furrowed. "My head hurts bad."

"The tattoo must cause some neurological problems," Noah says.

"They said… it was just a side effect," Judy says. "It would stop after a while."

I scoff. "Of course they would say that."

"Can you walk?" Noah asks.

"I… think so." We help Judy to her feet. She seems a little unsteady, but she shrugs off our help. "I'm fine. Let's just get this over with."

Judy walks like a toddler taking her first steps. Noah walks beside her, rifle slung over his shoulder, reaching out to steady her when she wobbles. Our progress slows, and we reach the park well after dark. Still, because we could drive during the day, we're early for our meeting with Bree and Ethan.

We nestle under the trees just below the platform of the Weehawken monument, exhausted and hungry. We eat granola bars in silence. Noah leans against a tree with the gun on his lap, away from Judy and me. He's still mad. I move over to him.

"Thank you," I say.

He looks at me; his eyes, barely visible, soften a little. "For what?"

"For... everything."

"Maybe you should kiss him," says Judy with a snarky laugh.

"Keep out of this," I snap at her. "No one asked your opinion."

"What's with you two anyway? I sense tension."

"Be quiet."

She chuckles and curls up on her side, laying her head awkwardly on her bound hands. I try to sleep, avoiding Noah even though it would be a lot warmer, snuggling up to him. Not that he looks like he wants to be snuggled up to at the moment.

"I'm... sorry," I say.

He looks at me and sighs. "I'm not mad. I'm just... worried." He turns his attention to the starless sky. Looking for drones, no doubt.

"They don't fly at night, do they?" I whisper.

"This close to the city, they have drones equipped with night vision. And if they suspect we are in the area, if they *have* been tracking her..." He doesn't finish.

"Won't the trees give us cover?"

"Maybe."

I'm pretty sure I'm never going to sleep, no matter how tired I am. Instead, I pray.

Lord, please, protect us. Make us invisible.

Judy starts snoring. At least one of us is getting some sleep.

I try to imagine where Bree and Ethan are now. Are they making their way through the tunnel? What if Josephine was wrong, and they can't get through? What if Ethan is too sick or weak to make the trek? What if they misunderstand my clues? What if we can't get back to the truck or get caught... So many what-ifs.

Stop thinking already.

"I lived in New York once. Did you know that?" I say aloud.

Noah grunts in reply.

"Yeah, it was a long time ago. Feels like a century. I thought the city was like a magical place, a fairy kingdom. Where all my dreams might come true."

"Why did you leave?"

"My dream turned into a nightmare."

Noah sighs. "Seems like all dreams are nightmares these days."

I shiver at the tone of his voice—so bleak. "God will protect us," I say, "no matter what happens."

"Yeah."

In these alone times, I think of Jared the most. My husband. The Nephilim boy who rescued me, whom I tried to rescue. Was he now completely in the grip of the Grigori? Was he the Antichrist? All those horrors I could deny during the day came back to haunt me in the sleepless nights.

I remember the prayer I prayed with such fervor when I was falling through cave waterfalls, clinging to Jared's back—Levin's prayer from *Anna Karenina,* which for some reason got stuck in my mind forever:

Lord, protect us and save us!

***

The whir of a drone overhead stirs me from my doze. My head aches, my back aches, my legs ache—I take an inventory and find there is not a single part of me that doesn't hurt. But that sound, it makes me forget my pain.

Noah gets to his knees, gun ready, and peers through the trees. I join him. We watch as a surveillance drone drops to the monument platform and spins slowly, red lights blinking, scanning the area. Noah and I duck. Noah grabs Judy's head and forces it down as well. *Lord, make us invisible.* I can't see Judy's GEM because of the foil. Can the drone still detect it?

The drone rises and flies away. I let out a breath.

"Do you think it saw the GEM?" I ask.

"I don't know," says Noah. "But we can't take a chance. We have to move."

"But this is the meeting place."

"We should go into the tunnel." He consults the paper map. "Drones can't track us underground."

"How do we get to the tunnel without being seen?"

"Follow me." Noah shoves the map into his pocket and starts down the slope toward the railroad tracks below. Judy and I scramble after him. We walk along the tracks for a short time, staying under cover of the trees, until we come to a huge factory-like building of brown brick.

"This is the ventilation tower for the tunnel," Noah says. "There should be a way to get into the tunnel from here."

Before I can ask any questions, he moves to the rear of the building and navigates through the dense tangle of overgrown shrubs. He finds a broken window and helps Judy and me through before climbing in himself. The interior is dark and stuffy, filled with a warren of pipes and giant fan turbines. Noah pulls a small flashlight from his pocket and turns it on. We wander for several minutes until we find an elevator shaft with no elevator.

"Great," I say. "How do we—?"

Without answering, Noah puts the flashlight in his teeth and launches himself onto the steel skeleton of the shaft. He waves to us and climbs down. I have to undo Judy's bonds so she can climb.

"Now's your chance," I say. "If you run, I can't stop you."

Without a word, she grabs hold of a steel beam and starts climbing. I follow. The beams are so rusty I'm sure they will disintegrate as soon as I touch them, but I manage to get to the bottom without falling.

All I see is a viper's nest of pipes and machines. Noah walks around, searching for something. Judy and I follow so closely we're practically on top of him.

"There's got to be a door," Noah mumbles. "Ripley said there would be one."

"Ripley? So you planned this?" I ask.

"I plan for contingencies." He stops dead. Judy and I run into him. "There."

I peer over his shoulder to see the beam of the flashlight shining on a narrow steel door with a push bar. Noah pushes, but it doesn't budge. All three of us throw our weight against the metal door, and after several shoves, in which I almost dislocate my shoulder—at least it feels that way—it gives an inch. We keep pushing and shoving and growling at the door until it opens enough so we can squeeze through.

"That was not fun," says Judy.

"This is it," Noah says. The Lincoln Tunnel.

It's eerily dark but a bit cooler, though the air smells musty. I rub my aching shoulder. Noah shines the flashlight upon a dingy tiled wall, a narrow curb, and a roadway of broken blacktop. Otherwise, the tunnel appears to be intact.

Noah takes out a compass and shines the flashlight on it. "We'll head to the New Jersey entrance," he says, pointing with the light. "Wait for them there."

We walk along the narrow curb in single file until we reach the walled-up entrance and look for an opening. There is a hole in the blacktop underneath the concrete barrier just big enough for a person to shimmy through.

Surprisingly, the Peacemakers didn't notice that. Maybe they're not as vigilant as we thought they were.

"What do we do now?" I ask.

"We wait," Noah says.

So, we wait.

And wait.

And wait.

Chapter Twenty-Four
Helel

Jared Lorn.

We had him trapped! And yet he escaped. With survivors.

How was this possible?

I can think of only one name.

Michael.

It is time to pay a visit to my old friend.

As my Mysteria sleeps, I exit my human frame and journey to the desert place. There he is, with his army, perched upon the ridges overlooking the Kidron Valley, where a desolate band of humans stumble about helplessly. His guardians try to block me, but Michael signals them to let me through.

"You were expecting me?" I ask, settling in beside him.

"I knew you would come, eventually."

Michael doesn't even look at me. He is gazing at the Human One, the Forsaken One, Baldyr.

"You think you have him, but you don't," I say. "He's mine. He's always been mine. Just as all his kind belonged to me."

"He is not yours or mine. He belongs to Elohim." Michael's voice is sonorous, so beautiful it makes me want to weep for the voice I once had. "It is up the Him to decide his destiny."

"Oh, yes, I forgot," I say, my own ruined voice dripping with sarcasm. "You still answer to Him. No matter what idiotic plots He comes up with. For all your vaunted power, you are still just a tool, an instrument. A *slave*."

His Light flairs slightly, though he doesn't speak. I try a different approach. The one that worked so well on those two imbeciles in the Garden.

"It doesn't have to be that way, you know. You could be free to choose your own path. Do what you want. You don't have to be tied to Him or those pathetic meat puppets down there. You could soar. Don't you even think about that? Doesn't it ever cross your mind?"

He is silent a moment, and I think I have him. Then he speaks.

"Never."

His Light is nearly overwhelming. I feel myself disappear inside of it.

"Michael," I whisper, even the voice I have fading. "Do you not remember how we sang together as creation loomed before us? So much beauty, then. So much promise. So much glory. We were like brothers. We were alike, you and I. If you had stayed with me, we could have ruled the world together. But you chose..." I pause to indicate the humans below, "...*this*."

"I chose life. You chose rebellion. You chose death."

"I chose freedom!" My rage bubbles up, yet my Darkness, as great as it is, cannot overcome his Light. I lash out, prepared to do battle, as we have done before, so many times.

"Get behind me, Satan." His words cut me to the core, bind my power so I am unable to move. How I *hate* that name.

"Fine, then!" I move away, try to regain my strength. "Do you think you can win with those useless knuckle-draggers holding you down? Your so-called saints. I leave you to them. Waste yourself serving those helpless carbon-eaters, those stupid, brainless lumps you call the human race. Sad, really. I feel sorry for you. When will you realize that He has played you for the fool?"

Michael suddenly explodes to his full form, his Light now so bright and terrible it knocks me from the tower. I wait for the strike, anticipating, salivating at the mere thought of it. *Yes, do it! Do it!*

He does not.

"Do. Not. Dare."

That is all I can get from him. Michael knows me too well.

I laugh. "It was worth a try." I am fading now, my Dark shriveling, burning up in his Light. "Good luck with your little band of human excrement. What do you have there? A hundred? With many millions already dead. And your pretty acolyte down there is going to shepherd them? Is he a Moses? I got Moses, you know. I'll get him, too."

"You did not get Moses." Michael's Light recedes. I knew the mention of Moses' failure would hurt him.

"Ha! Moses was not allowed into the Promised Land for his disobedience. I did that. Don't get me wrong, I love these little games we play. What else do I have to do anyway? Just remember, no matter what you think you can do to me, I *always* find a way."

Before he can strike me again, I escape, back to my human form and sleeping princess.

It is morning. I sit beside her on the bed. She wakes.

"Amon," she says drowsily, stretching. "What are you doing?"

"Watching you sleep. My favorite activity." I smile and plant a kiss on her forehead. "Coffee?"

***

The delightful extermination of the *Voice* plays over and over in every corner of the world. Zazel is throwing endless parties, celebrating his conquest of Jerusalem and the elimination of those pesky podcasters. He has ordered the bodies left to smolder on the Temple Mount so that all the world can see that he did what no one else had the guts—or the ability—to do. And he has brought the cameras inside the Holy of Holies to demonstrate his ascendance as the one and only god.

I must make sure he doesn't get a big head about this. It was all my idea, after all.

Now that Jerusalem has been decimated, Azazel sends out his Dragons to complete the task of putting an end to the resistance. In every major city and the Forbidden States, Dragons rain down hellfire. From my window in the penthouse of the Toothpick building, I can see the pulse lasers burning from Wall Street to Times Square, eradicating those who dare to protest our new world order. What a lovely scene.

Azazel is not the only one unleashing his wrath on the nations. The Eternal One has chosen this moment to mete out His own punishments. Earthquakes rattle the cities from sea to shining sea, and volcanos long dormant burst to violent life. There are floods in the mountains and snow-storms in desert places. Wildfires ravage huge swaths of land. The seas rise to drown islands and coastlines. Nature turns against man. Alligators crawl out of swamps to attack hapless pedestrians. Foxes and coyotes sneak into houses and make off with small children. Venomous snakes slither into bathrooms through plumbing pipes. Sharks loom up on beaches to snap off limbs of unsuspecting bathers. House pets turn vicious, kill their owners, and roam the streets in large packs.

People begin to ask the question, "Is the universe turning against us?"

Not the universe, you wretched mouth breathers. It is your God who turns against you. Your precious Holy One judges you and finds you wanting. This is not my doing. Oh, no. I do not judge. I do not condemn. That is the purview of the great Elohim. Had I been in charge, or should I say, *when* I am in charge, things will be different. Everyone will be able to live as they please—those that are allowed to live, of course. There will be no rules except the ones I make up.

"What is going on?" Shannon joins me at the window to watch the fires rage across the city. "Are we under attack?"

"Don't worry. We're safe. Just getting rid of the vermin." I plant a kiss on the side of her head. "You must get ready for the Met Gala. I bought you a dress. It's in your room."

"The Met Gala is still going on? Even with all this happening?"

"Of course. Why would it not?"

She shrugs, smiling shyly. "What is the theme this year?"

"I believe they are calling it 'Gaga for Grigori.' It's Grigori fashion all the time, these days. Your dress is made with twenty-four-carat gold thread and reveals more than it conceals, as all good Grigori outfits do."

"It must have cost a fortune."

"It did. But you are worth it." I kiss her. She responds warmly. "I have another surprise for you," I murmur in her ear. "One I think you will definitely want to see."

"Oh?"

"It will be here tomorrow, I believe."

Chapter Twenty-Five
Grace

We sit hunched against the concrete barrier of the tunnel, counting the minutes, then the hours. Every once in a while, Noah turns on the flashlight and shines it into the darkness in hopes of seeing movement, two people coming to meet us. We see nothing but scurrying rats.

"Something's happened," I say. "Maybe they can't get through. Maybe they got caught."

"We can wait a little longer," Noah says.

"Maybe we missed them. They might be at Weehawken right now, waiting for us. We should go back—"

"Grace," Noah says with a tired sigh, "we can't do that."

"Then… I will go to the other end of the tunnel and see what's going on."

"No—"

I cut him off. "You stay here in case they show up. Look, I'm just going to go walk to the other end of the tunnel and see if they're coming. Maybe they got lost or something. I'll come back. I promise."

"I'll go," says Noah. "You stay with her—"

"No, I'm going. They're my friends. I got us into this."

Noah opens his mouth to argue, then shuts it with a sigh. He hands me the flashlight and the rifle.

"Keep it," I say, taking only the flashlight. "You might need it more than me."

Noah sighs again. "The tunnel is a mile and a half long. It will take no more than an hour to walk to the end and back. If you don't return in one hour, I'm coming after you."

"Fine."

I turn on the flashlight and walk away, as resolutely as I can, into the darkness of the Lincoln Tunnel.

My footsteps echo eerily against the tile walls. The tiny beam of the flashlight seems to go only a foot or so before dissolving in darkness. What is that Bible verse about the Word being a lamp unto my feet? I get it now. It's not a headlight, showing you what's ahead. It's a tiny light, showing you the next step.

Lord, show me the next step.

I walk faster as if I can outpace the fear, the dark. The tunnel is straight and surprisingly empty. No way they could have gotten lost. So what happened? Did Ethan have an attack? Were they unable to get away from the safe house?

My heart races, thinking about all that might have gone wrong. What if they were arrested and had to tell the Peacemakers about us? In which case, I should turn right around and go back to Noah. But I can't. If there's even a chance I can find them, I have to try.

Finally, I reach a dead end—a concrete block wall covers the tunnel entrance. I search around but find no gaps or holes to crawl through. No wonder Bree and Ethan didn't come through the tunnel. If there had been a way through on this side, it's gone now.

If only Jared were here. He could break through these concrete blocks in a heartbeat.

I bang on the wall in utter frustration, tears running unchecked down my cheeks. *Why, Lord? Why? To bring us here only to lead us to this dead end? Why did this happen?*

I search again—still nothing. I need to get back to Noah. He'll be coming after me if I don't go soon—

Pray, Grace.

I stop dead and spin around, certain the voice was real. I swing the flashlight in all directions but see no one. *Pray.* I drop to my knees and close my eyes, holding the flashlight between my closed hands.

Okay, Lord, what do you want me to do?

I wait for an answer. Then something comes into my mind—a story. And words: *Cast your net on the right side of the boat.*

Cast my net? What net? What boat?

The story is about Peter fishing all night but catching no fish. Then, when Jesus shows up and gives him that command, he catches so many fish his boat starts to sink.

Cast your net.

I examine the wall again, inch by inch, pounding on each individual concrete block. Nothing moves. The longer I'm at this, the worse my frustration. By the time I get to the bottom row, I'm furious, frantic. I start kicking the blocks, battering my toes.

Then something gives.

I pause, blinking away tears. I drop to my knees and push against the block with both hands. It moves slightly. Desperate now, I sit on the ground and stomp on the block with both feet, shrieking at the top of my lungs. My feet throb with pain, but the block gives a little more each time I hit it. Finally, I knock the block out of the wall. A light from the other side bursts through the hole.

I make a noise of triumph and squeeze myself through the hole. It's just big enough for a skinny person, but all of us Forbidden are pretty skinny now.

I get up and brush myself off. The road slopes upward, flanked by high walls. No Bree or Ethan. No one at all. Dull booms reverberate in the distance, and the sky above is streaked with black smoke. It looks as though the city is under attack. Is that why they didn't come?

Hope dies in my heart. They aren't coming. They might be dead for all I know. I squeeze back through the hole, replace the block, and start to head back, brushing away tears.

Where is your faith?

There's that voice again. Didn't Jesus say that, in the boat, in the storm? When the disciples thought they were going to die?

I turn back to the barrier. I kneel before it and clasp my hands together.

Lord, please protect them. My friends. Please. Bring them here. Please.

I have no more eloquent words than these. Five more minutes, I think. I'll give them five more minutes. Maybe ten. I keep praying.

Rap, rap, rap.

Something is knocking on the barrier from the other side. I jump up, my heart racing. Muffled voices—I can't understand the words. Could it be them? Or someone else? Peacemakers?

Only one way to find out. I shove the concrete block out of the hole and stick my head out.

"Bree?"

A woman with short brown hair stares down at me, her mouth open. Her companion freezes, cane in midair where he had been hitting the wall.

"Grace?" says the woman.

"Bree!" I wiggle out of the hole and throw my arms around her. We jump up and down together, laughing. It really is her. She looks so different. She's older now though still pretty, despite the worry lines on her face and the short bob haircut. She always had the most beautiful brown hair and the biggest brown eyes. She's wearing a puffy overcoat over jeans and a white sweater that fails to hide how thin she's become. Was it worry for Ethan? Or are people in Oz as food-deprived as we are?

"Sorry I missed your graduation," I say when I can speak words again.

"Yeah, only fifteen years late," says a reedy male voice.

I pull away and turn to Ethan. His once thick curly hair is now sparse, and his eyes are droopy, though he no longer wears his signature coke-bottle glasses. He was always on the scrawny side, but now he looks emaciated. His jeans are baggy, and his heavy sweater hangs on him as if he were a hanger. I hug him gingerly, afraid he might break.

"Ethan. Thank God you both made it. I was getting so worried."

"We almost didn't," says Bree. "The whole city is under attack. Everything is burning. So many people dying—" She breaks off, covering her mouth with her hand.

"Dragons," says Ethan. "New Grigori weapon. Ultra pulse lasers." He coughs and clutches his chest.

"We need to get going," I say. "Go through this hole. We'll catch up once we're safe."

Bree gets down on her knees and shimmies through. I hold Ethan's cane while he works his way inside. Then I push the cane in after him.

"Stoppe! Ikke beveg deg!"

I spin around. Three huge Peacemakers on hoverbikes descend, their scary-looking guns leveled on me. I stand in front of the hole, blocking the Peacemakers' view.

"Go," I hiss. "All the way to the end of the tunnel. My friend Noah is waiting. Hurry!"

"Grace!"

"Go!"

One of the Peacemakers leaps from his bike and comes toward me. I press myself against the wall, my heart racing. He's wearing a full helmet and face shield that obscures his features. His black uniform looks like armor. He raises his forearm, where his scanner is attached, wrenches my arm, and scans my hand. The light flashes red. He shouts something in Norwegian.

"Sorry, no speakee," I say.

The Peacemaker switches to English. "What is your name?"

"Wilma Flintstone," I say.

The Peacemaker raises his forearm to my face. The hologram of a camera pops up and takes my picture. I try to scrunch up my features to avoid facial recognition, but I know it probably won't work. The Peacemaker is motionless for a long moment. Then he lowers his arm and gazes at the readout. I'm not in the UE tracking system, but they probably have pictures of me in their database.

After a moment, the Peacemaker looks at me again. "You are Grace Fortune, leader of the rebel Jehovah faction, Yellow Brick Road."

"Well, I'd hardly call myself a leader. More of a facilitator—" I hope stalling will give Bree and Ethan more time to get away. "That's some nifty gadget you have there, by the way. Don't even need a pocket for that."

"You are under arrest."

"What's the charge? Loitering? Breathing?"

"Treason."

He spins me around and wrenches my arms behind my back. I feel the pressure of zip cuffs and all the flippant remarks I had ready to launch fizzle and die. This is real. This is happening. A bag goes over my head, plunging my world into darkness.

Lord, protect me and save me.

Chapter Twenty-Six
Jared

Two elderly monks in black cassocks and tall hats block our entrance to the monastery. Apparently, women are not allowed inside—something about Eve and temptation. Apples are also forbidden for the same reason.

Davidov argues with them until the monks finally relent, and Davidov's soldiers usher the refugees into the main courtyard of the monastery. Davidov wastes no time organizing the survivors into groups to fetch water and tend to the wounded. He seems wholly different from the man I met in Jerusalem—energized, almost happy. This is his true vocation, taking action, dealing with real problems rather than playing politics.

Once they've gotten water, the people search for shade and rest. Davidov tells me to lay low while he deals with the monks—my presence seems to disturb them even more than the women.

I decide to scout out the compound and am soon lost in the complex warren of buildings. I wander through tiny chapels, prayer rooms, courtyards, and balconies. I search the storerooms and find only a few sacks of couscous and dried lentils. The gardens contain a few anemic fig trees and a handful of vegetable plants. How will we feed these people?

Huge murals cover the walls of the main church, each one a riot of color, depicting Bible stories and the daily life of the monks. The desiccated body of Saint Saba, the monastery's founder who died fifteen hundred years ago, lies on display in a glass case.

In another room, hundreds of skulls are displayed in neat rows—martyrs of the many attacks the monastery has endured from Persians, Arabs, Jews, and Palestinians through the ages, according to the placard written in several languages.

I climb the staircase that leads to the high tower at the top of the mountain, the Justinian tower, hoping there might be stores of food there. But it's a library containing scores of ancient manuscripts, books, icons, and artifacts, all caked in dust. More stairs ascend to a rooftop observation deck that offers a magnificent view of the Kidron Valley and the Dead Sea over the ridge to the east. This was a place of fire and brimstone once, thousands of years ago, when Sodom and Gomorrah fell to the wrath of God. It must have been like Jerusalem when the Dragons rained down burning lasers upon us. Azazel trying to imitate God.

I gaze at the steep, forbidden canyon we traversed to get here. An impossible feat. How did we do it? Not in our own strength, I'm certain of that. It is late afternoon; the sun slants on the desert-colored stones of the monastery, turning them bright gold. It's like a scene from heaven. For the moment, there is peace.

"I hope you aren't planning to jump."

I spin around, startled by the voice. A man stands behind me, his face shrouded by the hood of a black cassock. A hermit? None of the monks wore cassocks like this.

"No." I hesitate. "I was just looking."

"There is much to see, isn't there? And yet so little. This is how we live, seeing what others cannot see."

I peer at him, wondering at his words. "I'm not sure I understand."

"You will, in time. I sense you wish to make a confession. I am here, if that is your wish."

"My confession?" I think about this. "Yes. I must confess. I am not the son of the Supreme Lord. I am an impostor."

"I see."

"I thought I was helping by coming to Israel, by forcing Davidov into making a deal with the Grigori. But I see now that was not only foolish it was… evil. I did exactly what Zazel wanted me to do. And now I've brought all this trouble on these people."

"But you rescued them."

How does he know what I did? Did Davidov talk to him? "I might have helped them escape death, but for what? To die here in the desert?"

"Have you still so little faith? You think the One who fed six hundred thousand in the desert for forty years cannot feed these people?"

I take a step toward the monk, trying to see his face. "What should I do?" I sense this man knows the answer.

"Tell Davidov to take them to Petra."

"Petra? It's a hundred miles from here."

"A hundred and fifty. Do you not know the prophecy? The land of Edom is spared the wrath of judgment. That land is on the other side of the Dead Sea. What used to be known as Jordan."

"I will take them."

"Not you. You will return to Jerusalem. To prepare for the final battle."

I stare at the hooded man. The voice no longer sounds the same as it did before. It is the voice of command, of glory. The voice of…

"Michael," I murmur, closing my eyes.

When I open them again, the monk is gone. Did I imagine him? Was there even someone speaking to me at all?

Shouts of delight filter from below. I peer over the edge of the rooftop—what I see fills me with awe. The straggly fig trees, devoid of fruit when we first arrived, are now green and leafy and so loaded with figs that the branches bend nearly to the ground. People swarm the trees, grabbing figs and stuffing them in their mouths. I smile for the first time in a very long time.

You think the One who fed six hundred thousand in the desert for forty years cannot feed these people?

I leave the tower and find Davidov, who is standing on a balcony overlooking the garden, watching the feeding frenzy.

"I thought we had our share of miracles this day," he says, sounding wonderstruck.

"I think," I reply, "that we haven't seen anything yet."

He's silent a moment. "Did you know about those... Dragons?"

I take a breath. "Yes. I'm sorry. I never thought... Gadreel betrayed me. Zazel betrayed me."

"Why would your father attack us like that, knowing you could die as well?"

I sigh. "He wanted me to die."

Davidov turns to me, eyes wide. "Why?"

I meet his gaze. "I'm not who you think I am. My name is... Jared Lorn."

"You are not the son of Grigori Zazel?"

"I was... well, it's hard to explain. I went to New Asgard to try and stop Zazel. I failed at that. But I think he knew what I was up to. He never wanted to negotiate with you. He just used me to... destroy Jerusalem. Kill two birds with one stone." I pause, taking a long breath. "That was his plan. But God had… other plans."

Davidov shakes his head. "Yesterday, I would have called that nonsense. Today…" Tears spring to his eyes. He puts a hand over his face as his shoulders shake.

"I'm sorry about your wife." It's a paltry thing to say, but I have nothing else.

He gathers himself, then raises his head to look out over the view again. "I don't pretend to understand this. But now is not the time to ponder. What are we to do with all these people? What is the plan now?"

"You must take them someplace safe. Petra."

His eyes widen. "Petra?"

I nod. "There are plenty of caves, there is water, and the Siq is easy to defend."

"Defend? Will Azazel attack again?"

"Yes, most certainly. He's not done with Israel."

"Petra." He mulls this over. "It's a long walk."

"I know."

"And what will you do?"

"I will go back to Jerusalem. Gadreel is still there with the Dragons. I have to deal with him."

"Alone? You're mad."

I smile. "I won't be alone."

***

As night falls, the refugees find nooks and crannies for shelter, for there isn't enough room in the buildings for the three hundred who escaped with us, including twenty Border Guards. The monks invite Davidov to a supper of boiled lentils, bread, and goat cheese. He brings me along, and after explaining the situation, the monks accept my presence despite their misgivings.

Davidov tells them of the events of Jerusalem. They listen in silence, neither surprised nor awestruck.

"This is to be expected," says a small, withered monk with a long, gray beard. "It has been foretold."

"Foretold?" Davidov cocks an eyebrow.

"You have not read the prophecies of the Apostle John? Or of our Lord Jesus Christ?"

The prime minister shakes his head. "We are not taught the Christian scriptures," he says.

"Our Lord promised that the prophecies of Daniel would come to pass." The old monk clears his throat and recites from memory.

> *"So when you see the abomination of desolation*
> *spoken of by the prophet Daniel,*
> *standing in the holy place*
> *then let those who are in Judea*
> *flee to the mountains.*
> *Let the one who is on the housetop not go down*
> *to take what is in his house,*
> *and let the one who is in the field*
> *not turn back to take his cloak.*
> *And alas for women who are pregnant*
> *and for those who are nursing infants in those days!*
> *Pray that your flight may not be in winter or on a Sabbath.*
> *For then there will be great tribulation,*
> *such as has not been from the beginning of the world*

until now, no, and never will be."

There is a look of amazement on Davidov's face. And worry too. "So, we are not finished, then."

The old monk chuckles. "There is much trouble ahead. But do not fear, Prime Minister. The Lord protects those He has chosen."

"Do you mean the Jews?" Davidov scoffs. "How has God protected the Jews? Through the holocaust? The Rages? The Alliance War? This latest attack? Jerusalem is in cinders, Priest. That is how God protects His people." His tone has turned bitter.

"All is not what it seems," says the monk, a gleam in his eye. "Have you not been spared? There is work for you still."

I understand Davidov's ambivalence. Why would God allow the city to be destroyed yet make a way of escape for barely a handful? I should know better than to ask these things of God.

We sleep in a small dormitory that looks like it hasn't been used in years. It takes an hour to sweep it out and wipe away the cobwebs. I consider the words of Jesus as I try to sleep. At least it isn't winter. Not yet.

I awaken before dawn to loud bleating outside the window. An amazing sight greets me—hundreds of goats surround the monastery, munching on sparse grass and nosing their way through the entrance. People gather to stare in wonder, many shouting praises to God.

The Lord provides.

Davidov is soon corralling the goats and organizing the people who can cook and tend herds. Several women invade the monastery kitchen, cleaning it out and preparing to cook meals. The fig trees overflow. Even the gardens have sprung miraculously to life. The monastery has no electricity, so groups of men and children go in search of wood for the cooking fires. Other groups are assigned to fetch water from the spring near the base of the monastery.

I pack a small bag of water and figs and prepare to return to Jerusalem.

"You're leaving now?" Davidov says from the doorway of the dormitory.

"Yes."

"Walking?"

"Yes." I glance at him. "Something wrong?"

"I've been thinking."

"Yes?"

"About the walk to Petra. It's too far. It will take too long, too much time in the open. Besides, most of these people would not make it."

"You have a proposition?"

He grins—he looks surprisingly charming when he does that. "There is a military installation outside of Jerusalem. There will be trucks there."

"The Dragons have probably destroyed it."

"Perhaps. But maybe not all of it. They were likely more interested in missile sites and the advanced tech. It's possible some vehicles survived." He pauses. "I'm coming with you, to Jerusalem." He holds up a hand before I can object. "My soldiers will keep order here until I return. But I must go back. I must see about those trucks. And if there are survivors, those who escaped the Dragons in the city—it's my responsibility."

I can see by the look on his face that he will not be dissuaded. I sigh. "Fine. Can you leave now?"

"First thing in the morning," he says. "I have a couple of things to take care of today. And you could use another day of rest."

Chapter Twenty-Seven
Grace

I'm in a cage. Like a dog in the pound. It's so small I can't even sit upright. Prisoners occupy the other cages that are stacked around me, but they are all silent, motionless. I'm not even sure they're alive. A sickly green bulb hanging in the narrow aisle between the rows of cages shines on their prone, curled-up forms.

A loud humming noise comes from somewhere, like an appliance that's about to die. I rattle the bars and cry out, though I can't hear my own voice over that piercing hum. I give up, finally, and curl into a ball, covering my ears. This is the sort of thing that makes people go insane.

Lord, protect me and save me.

Hours go by. Every once in a while, I rattle the cage again, just for fun. In between bouts of rattling and crying, I imagine all the terrible things that are about to happen to me. Mainly death. Will it be a firing squad or guillotine, the favored execution device of the Grigori, who claim it's more humane than other forms of murder? Or maybe they will send me to WeCamp where I will labor twenty-three hours a day and get pummeled with Grigori talking points until I lose my mind or die. Maybe they will torture me first. For information. Like they do in the movies. Pull out my fingernails, one by one. I shudder at the very thought of it. Can I joke through that? I doubt it.

Lord, protect me. Save me. Get me out of here.

No. Save *them*. Get *them* away safely. Noah, Bree, Ethan. Get them home. If that happens, then all this will be worth it.

Was it Judy's GEM that gave me away? Probably. At any rate, this was all my fault. If we hadn't taken Judy with us... But it is too late to do anything about that now.

As the hours drag by, I begin to wonder if they won't just leave me here, in this cage, like they seem to have done with all the others, until I am shriveled and forgotten.

That might be the worst ending of all.

***

A light appears from somewhere, followed by the tread of heavy boots. I sit up and grab hold of the bars, straining to see. Two Peacemakers appear in the sickly light. I recoil at their masked helmets as they stand in front of my cage.

"Time for a bathroom break?" My stomach is cramping, but I refuse to use the bucket in the corner. One of them reaches his arm toward my cage door, and it magically opens. Before I can move, he reaches in, grabs me by the arms, and hauls me out roughly.

"Hey, take it easy," I mutter. He barely gives me time to untwist my legs before dragging me down the aisle of cages to a door at the end. I squint in the bright sunlight.

"Oh, you're letting me go? That's big of you." I try to keep my voice from shaking.

I feel the press of something cold and hard in my back—a gun, maybe—as I'm pushed toward a sleek, silvery vehicle hovering a few feet off the ground. Dragonfly. So I'm being shipped somewhere else—a camp, most likely. I don't know whether to be relieved or disappointed.

The door opens vertically, and the Peacemaker forces me inside. It's dark. There are no seats, just an empty metal shell. It reminds me of Samyaza's prison. A dense and palatable emptiness.

I sense the Dragonfly moving, lifting, spinning through the air. My stomach lurches. I hear only a steady whir, like a real dragonfly. I try to imagine myself somewhere else, walking in the woods, Jared at my side, coming to a lake where dragonflies land on the surface of the water, spinning their wings. *Jared…*

A gentle, almost imperceptible bump, and then the whirring stops. The door yawns open with a faint whoosh. I expect to see the walls and barbed wire of a prison camp. Instead, I see only the sky, streaked with a crazy pattern of elongated black clouds, like the chalk marks of an angry child.

And then I see something I never expected to see in all my imaginings.

My mother's face.

"Grace?"

I gape, certain I am hallucinating or maybe dead and in hell. Did they kill me without my even knowing it?

Her green eyes flash; her red lips part in a happy smile. "It is you. I can't believe it."

What is she doing here? Why does her face look so… fake? Maybe she is just one of those AI avatars, not really there at all.

She reaches to grab my hand. She's real, all right. I flinch away from her, scuttling backward until I hit my head on something hard. I wince at the pain.

She laughs lightly at my resistance. "You're perfectly safe, Grace. I won't hurt you. I'm just so glad you're back. You're alive! It's a miracle. Please, come out."

Her arms reach for me. After a moment, I creep forward and allow her to help me to the steps. Wind lashes my face, and the light is so bright my eyes water. I glance around to see the tops of buildings on either side. We must be on the roof of a very tall building. Shannon pulls me into an embrace. I endure her suffocation, overwhelmed by her floral scent, the smell of treachery.

"I'm sorry for all that fuss," she says when she finally releases me. "As soon as they told me they arrested you, I demanded they bring you straight to me."

I still can't think of anything to say. *Thank you?* Somehow, that doesn't seem appropriate, given the circumstances.

Shannon's face tilts, and her eyes narrow slightly. "Grace, are you all right? I know this is a lot to take in. You've had quite a time of it. Come on. Let's go inside." She wraps her arm tightly around my shoulders and steers me away from the Dragonfly to a metal door at the far end of the roof. We go through and into an elevator with sleek, blond wood paneling. I'm glad to be out of the wind, yet I'm still so disoriented I don't know what to make of any of this.

"Where are we?" I ask finally.

"You'll see."

The elevator doors open upon a palatial scene grander even than the Central Park apartment I lived in with Shannon all those years ago. It must take up the entire top floor of the building. The floors are shiny and blue; they would make a good skating rink.

"Here we are!" Shannon says brightly. "Make yourself at home."

I look around. A piano shaped like a prehistoric gnat occupies the center of the room, surrounded by various modern sofas and chairs arranged more like a doctor's waiting room than a person's home.

"You live here?" I ask, still in shock from seeing my mother—*my mother*—again. I'm probably still in the cage, asleep, dreaming, having a nightmare. I pinch myself to see if I will wake up.

"Not exactly," Shannon says. "This place belongs to my friend, Amon. Wait until you meet him. He's really the one who got you out. Amon!"

A man appears in a doorway. He's tall with dark hair, wearing shaded glasses that mask his eyes. He moves strangely, more shadow than man. I didn't even hear his footsteps. He smiles at me, and I take an involuntary step backward, sensing something unnatural in that smile, in his whole presence.

This man is not human.

I'm not sure where that thought came from, but I know it must be true.

"Well, there she is," says the man. He sounds human enough. I can't pinpoint where his accent is from. "The prodigal returns."

How strange he would reference a Bible story. People in Oz aren't supposed to know those stories anymore.

"Amon!" Shannon beams, taking his arm and bringing him closer to me. "Grace, this is Amon H. Doyle. You've probably heard of him. Or maybe you haven't. He's quite famous now— author, philosopher, scientist, and the new chairman of the Interlaken Group. He produced my movie, too." Her voice trembles a little as she says these words like she's madly in love with him—or she's terrified of him. "Amon, meet my long-lost daughter, Grace Fortune."

"How do you do, Grace Fortune?" Amon steps toward me and bows formally. "What a miracle to find you are still alive. Shannon was certain you were dead." He says this as if he wished it were so. Or is that just my imagination?

I look at my mother. "You thought I was dead?"

"Well, yes. There were reports... all misinformation, I suppose." She laughs awkwardly.

"Put out by the Jehovians," says Amon, a coldness in his voice that sends a shiver down my back. The AngelSong hums at the back of my brain. I have a strong urge to sing it out loud. "Lucky for you, as chairman of the Interlaken Group, I am informed of all arrests of high value targets." He smiles in the most charming manner. "They didn't want to release you, of course. You are quite a prize! But I would do anything for my dear... Shannon." He puts his hand on the side of her face. I want to gag. "So you were on that reservation in South Dakota all this time? Well, it's a good thing you got out of there when you did."

My skin prickles with heat. "What do you mean?"

"Oh, I guess you don't know. There was a Dragon attack just this morning. The entire reservation was destroyed."

My head swims. I have to struggle to remain upright. "Destroyed?"

"These latest protests and riots could not be tolerated. We had to eliminate the poisonous source of these toxic ideas. It meant breaking the treaty with the Free States, of course, but the YBR was becoming much too divisive. If only you and your friend had kept to yourselves. Ah well." He sighs heavily. "Just think... had you not ventured to this city, your purpose being to rescue your two friends, you would be one of the charred victims on that reservation."

Charred victims. Penny. Mason. Blaine. Ripley. The children...Daisy and Rose. All of them.

Sickness lurches from my stomach into my throat. My knees buckle. But I cannot fall. Not yet. Not yet.

Doyle's smile fades. "I see I've upset you. I'm sorry about that. But you must understand. It's for the public good."

"I'm just so grateful you weren't there." Shannon rubs my arm. "So grateful to have you back again."

I want to cry, spit, rage, collapse in a heap of tears. I turn to Doyle, jutting my chin. "I think I would prefer if you sent me back to prison. If my friends are dead, I want to die with them." I pull my arm away from Shannon and walk to the door.

"Grace!" Shannon gasps.

"That's too bad," Doyle says coolly. "Here we thought you would jump at the chance to be reunited with your husband."

I spin around. "What did you say?"

"Your husband," he says, emphasizing each syllable as if it were a separate word. "Baldyr. Or, as you call him, Jared Lorn."

My throat constricts. I cannot manage even a single breath. "Jared?"

"Yes, that's right!" Shannon chimes in. "Come to New Asgard. We can leave tonight. Jared will be waiting for you."

"Does he know… I'm here?"

Shannon laughs. "Of course! We told him we found you and promised to return you to him."

I should wait, pray, seek the Lord's direction. But I know I won't. My friends are gone; they are with the Lord now. Noah… Noah should be taking Bree and Ethan back to the Rez. They'll find it in ashes. Maybe they will discover survivors. Maybe they will stay alive somehow. But Jared… If there's even a slight chance I will see him again, I must take it.

I take a deep breath, then nod.

***

We ride to New Asgard in Shannon's tricked-out Dragonfly, a shiny, boomerang-shaped airship. The inside is all softness and comfort, with built-in couches with thick cushions, long-haired fur rugs, and soft lighting. It takes off vertically and then speeds into horizontal motion, yet it's so quiet it hardly feels like moving at all. Like being in the space shuttle—in space.

Shannon talks the entire time—she seems to need to fill the cabin with sound as if that will overcome the vacuum between us. I half listen, remaining as sullen and detached from her as possible. I still feel as if I'm in some twisted dream. My thoughts stray to Penny and Mason... all the rest. Their last moments. What did they see? What did they feel before...

The Song continues to buzz in my head, louder than ever.

Doyle, still wearing his sunglasses, sits close to Shannon, his hand always on her knee or stroking her hair, except when he gets up to get her another glass of wine. She's had three so far. He treats her like some prized Pomeranian, a special, beloved pet. Shannon told me he was West's right-hand man, his "Prophet" and the architect of the Cure and the GEM. It seems Doyle was the man *behind* the man behind the curtain.

What would Darwin think of this? Is he listening to the news as he sails around on his yacht? Does he know what his miracle treatment has wrought?

I pull at the collar of the shirt Shannon gave me to wear—the tiny beads around the top edge chafe my skin. At least it's clean, as are the jeans she gave me. Very expensive. I admit I don't mind wearing them.

"We should be landing soon. I'm sure you're anxious to see Jared again." Shannon gives my hand a squeeze. I pull away. "This is going to be such a surprise for him. When was the last time you saw him?"

I think about that last time—in the *There*, when he lay dead in my arms. At least, I thought he was dead.

"A year, maybe?"

"How did you two get separated?"

I shrug. I'm not going to tell her about *that.*

Shannon takes my silence for pain and clutches my hand again. "None of that matters now, does it? Everything is good now. And you will meet your brother Vale. He's a sweet boy. Almost sixteen now. We will have such a family reunion."

Vale. I remember him from the holos. His red hair, his black clothes, his slumping posture. My brother. Go figure.

The Dragonfly lands so smoothly I hardly know when it's stopped. I step onto the pavement of a huge courtyard. The shining tower of New Asgard looms over me. It's hard to believe something so ethereal and beautiful could be real. It reminds me of a gigantic tree with a spiraling trunk that unfurls its branches at the very top. That's where the garden is, I presume. The famous Garden of Grigori, Azazel's recreation of Eden.

Jared is not here to meet me. Instead, creepy-looking snake-men march out of the arched foundation of the tower in single file. Guardians. So they're real, too. I couldn't imagine people like this could actually exist. If they *are* people. They are at least seven feet tall, all with inflated hoods around their heads that make them look like cobras. Their bare upper bodies are covered in tattoos of snakes, and their lower bodies are encased in skin-tight leggings that look an awful lot like scales.

They form a ring around us, each one holding a tall, sharpened, translucent spear. I cringe inwardly at the sight of those spears, so like the zircon crystals I remember from the Abyss. Several camera drones swirl around our heads, their red lights blinking.

"What's going on?" I ask.

"Oh, I'm sure it's just... the welcoming committee," Shannon murmurs, though her voice trembles slightly. She moves closer to me and grips my shoulder. I don't see Doyle anywhere. Where did he go?

One Guardian steps up to me. "Grace Fortune, leader of the Jehovian faction known as the Yellow Brick Road," he says in a slithery voice. "You are under arrest for crimes against the United Earth."

I spin around to face Shannon, whose mouth has dropped open.

"No," she says shrilly, stepping in front of me. "This is my daughter. I brought her here."

"Orders of the Supreme Lord. She is to be arrested, tried, and executed for treason."

I should have known.

Two Guardians grab my arms, their grip so tight I want to cry out. I bite my tongue. Shannon protests loudly as a bag comes down over my head—this again. In the blackness, I am dragged away as Shannon screams my name. I want to scream too, but my voice feels frozen in my throat.

Shannon's voice fades as new sounds emerge, harsh voices echoing in some vast space. We must be inside the tower. I hear the ding of a bell and then I am falling, dropping so fast my stomach lurches into my throat, though my feet are still on the floor. What is happening?

The wild motion stops, and I am dragged again, the air now close and musty. The two Guardians thrust me forward and I am thrown onto a hard floor like a sack of flour. The loud slam of a heavy door reverberates in my ears. Then silence.

After a long moment, I sit up and remove the bag. It does little good. Everything around me is black.

Chapter Twenty-Eight
Jared

Davidov is holding two horses by the reins. He grins. "Found them at a nearby farm. Thought it would make the trip go by faster."

I gaze doubtfully at the animals. They are not much bigger than ponies. One is chestnut with a sad, misbegotten air; the other looks more sturdy, with a shaggy gray coat.

I point to the gray. "Will that one carry me?"

Davidov shrugs. "Arab stock. Tougher than they look. Do you ride?"

"I guess we'll see, won't we?"

He chuckles. "I also have these." He holds up two black cassocks. "The monks lent them to me. You can't go back into Jerusalem dressed like that."

"I suppose not." I take off the white coat, now so filthy it looks brown, and put on the black robe. It's very wide but reaches only to my knees.

Davidov shrugs. "It was the biggest one they had." He turns to his captain, a wiry man with a trim mustache named Uri. "Make sure no one leaves the monastery grounds. I will return in a couple of days."

Uri nods, giving me a sour look. The soldiers don't trust me, nor do they like their boss going off to Jerusalem in my company—alone. But Davidov has insisted they stay behind.

We mount the horses, me much more unsteadily than Davidov, who has a natural grace in the saddle. He shows me how to guide the horse with the reins and use my legs to move it forward. My mount requires a lot of prodding.

"So perhaps there is something you are not good at, after all," Davidov jokes.

I follow the prime minister through the canyon until it widens into a narrow valley. The sky above is blue and clear, with no sign of Dragons or Rainmakers. Perhaps Zazel is too busy in Jerusalem to think about coming after me.

We ride side by side, a stilted silence between us. Finally, Davidov speaks.

"Your fights, in the arena. Were they... real?"

I glance at him, though he's still looking ahead, watching the uneven terrain underfoot. "They seemed real enough to me."

"I just wondered. It is so hard to tell what is real anymore."

"So you have watched my fights?"

"My son did." He pauses. "He's dead."

"I'm sorry."

"He died in his sleep. Six months ago. Seventeen years old. Heart attack. All too common since the Cure."

"Did you take the Cure?" I ask.

"I did. Once. It made me so sick I never got the later infusions. But I recovered. Many don't. Especially the younger men, the teenage boys. So many dead of heart ailments and cancers, those who are the healthiest among us."

"Is that why you oppose the UE? Because of what happened to your son?"

"That's where it started."

We are silent for a while. Then Davidov speaks again.

"Have you considered how we are going to get into the city without being seen? Assuming your Dragons are still there."

"I was hoping a solution would present itself," I say truthfully.

Davidov chuckles. "I have an idea."

"What is it?"

"Many years ago, a roadway was discovered underneath the remains of the City of David—that is the oldest part of the city. They call it the Pilgrim's Way, the road leading from the Pool of Siloam to the Temple Mount. My predecessor had the road excavated and opened it as a tourist attraction."

"And it is… underground?"

"Yes." He looks at me and smiles. "Jerusalem is an ancient city, which means it has many layers, one city built on top of the other. You can go from the Dung Gate to the Damascus Gate completely underground. The Grigori don't like underground places from what I hear."

"True enough."

"If there are survivors in the city, they will probably be in the tunnels. That's where they hid during the Roman conquest. Jerusalem has been fought over, conquered, burned, and destroyed many times, yet it endures. The whole world will fall. But Jerusalem will stand. *Must* stand."

When the sun is high overhead, we stop to rest, letting the horses drink water from the stream. It won't hurt them, Davidov says. They've ingested far worse. We sit on rocks, cooling our legs in the stream, and eat figs.

"You have seen battle yourself," I say.

"Not nearly so glamorous as yours," he replies, tossing away the fig stem. "I was a tank commander in Tel Aviv during the Alliance War. We mostly retreated once the dome was exhausted. But we held our line in Jerusalem. We thought those were our last days—until the Grigori came. And Israel fell for the lies and signed a peace treaty with the United Earth to end the Alliance War. My predecessor believed the Grigori were sincere when they promised peace. Most people did. Besides, what choice did we have? The Grigori had saved us. And for a while, it seemed to be the right thing. The Temple Mount was restored to us against the wishes of the old United Nations and the enemy nations surrounding us. We were allowed to build our temple. But now I see why. We were building the temple for *him*. Grigori Zazel." He glances at me. "We were both deceived."

I nod, saying nothing.

He stands up, stretching out his back and arms. "We should be going. There is much to do before the night falls."

I mount my horse, and we ride again together with a certain ease between us. No more strain in the silence.

Chapter Twenty-Nine
Helel

I sit on a white sofa and pour tea into a china cup as Shannon flails about in a glorious rage.

"How could he do such a thing? Arrest her? My daughter? What is he thinking?"

"Perhaps he is thinking that she is an enemy of the UE," I say blandly. "The loss of the *Voice* and the YBR are a death blow to the rebellion. Not to mention the Dragon attacks on the protestors."

She turns to look at me. "Did you know he would do this?"

I bat my eyes innocently. "Never crossed my mind. Like you, I only thought to reunite the girl with her long-lost husband."

"And Jared isn't even here," Shannon says, flouncing on the sofa beside me. "She'll blame me for this. She thinks I lied to her. Again. I'm always the bad guy in her mind."

"Have some tea," I say, handing her the cup. "Calm down."

She takes the cup, rattling on its saucer, and looks down at the brown liquid. "Will he really kill her?"

"Oh, yes. No doubt. Probably at the Grigoralia. All the most prominent executions take place then."

She drops the cup onto the coffee table. "I must speak to him."

I shake my head. "It won't do any good. He's quite made up his mind—"

"I must speak to him!" She jumps up and calls for an AI servant to relay the message to Zazel. I go to her and try to embrace her, but she jerks away from me.

"You don't blame me, I hope," I say soothingly, my hands on her shoulders, "for what that beastly Zazel is doing. Do you?"

She turns to look at me. "No... no... of course not."

"Good. Come here now. Let me hold you." I feel her relax at my touch, warming to me as she always does. "There, there. Everything will be all right—"

"The Supreme Lord will see you now," the AI servant announces.

Shannon stiffens and pulls away. "Now? Good."

"I will come with you," I say as I follow her to the door. "Perhaps I can be of help."

***

The Supreme Lord lounges in his favorite hammock, his winged lion at his side. His long body arches lazily, the white robe draped artistically over his massive shoulders.

"My love, my dear beautiful Freya. How I have missed you."

He holds out his arms for her. I sense her wanting to run to him—I hold her back, keeping my gaze on Azazel. He has not yet acknowledged my presence, though he is acutely aware of me. We have not occupied the same physical space in quite some time. I sense his smoldering wrath. No doubt he knows what I have been up to with his queen.

"My lord," Shannon says, her voice quivering, "you have arrested my daughter."

He draws his arms back and puts his hands behind his head. "I did. She is a traitor, darling. She may be your daughter, but she is my enemy."

"My lord, please, I beg you, spare her life."

He smiles. "You beg me? I would like to see that."

"See what?"

"See you beg."

Shannon hesitates. Then she breaks away from me and approaches him slowly, drops to her knees and puts her head on the floor. "Please, my lord, please, spare my daughter."

I have to look away, I am so disgusted by this sight.

"Hmmm," Zazel says. "Not bad."

Shannon remains prostrate. I turn back and watch Azazel's one eye perusing her.

"I might consider your request. Although, I am a bit surprised."

Shannon glances up at him, still bent over. "Why, my lord?"

"Well, I would assume you wanted your son Vale to be named my heir. Isn't that your most fervent wish?"

Shannon sits back on her heels, her head tilted in curiosity. "Yes, but—"

"With Baldyr gone, Vale would become my one and only son. But only if you are completely loyal to me. I can't stand disloyalty. That's the one thing I will not abide." He swings his legs over the side of the hammock and leans into her, looking deeply into her eyes. "Do you want that for Vale?"

"Oh, yes. Yes! Of course, I do. But Grace..."

"Loyalty, my dear. That is all I require." Azazel reaches out to stroke the side of her face. "She is not your daughter any longer. She is the enemy.

Do you wish to plead on behalf of an enemy? I would consider that very disloyal."

"Oh... I..."

"Say it with me. She. Is. The. Enemy."

"She. Is. The. Enemy." The two of them mouth the words together, over and over. Gradually, I see Shannon dissolve before my eyes. And Mysteria returns. My Mysteria. Azazel smiles deeply. "There. See how easy that was?" He pulls her up to him and kisses her mouth. She melts into him. Zazel's one eye focuses on me as they kiss.

When they finally part, the Supreme Lord addresses me for the first time. "Well, my friend... *Amon*... thank you so much for bringing my love back to me. It's been... quite a long time, hasn't it?" He continues to stroke Shannon's face and throat while he speaks, glorying in the rage he produces in me, yet his smile never wavers.

I give him a stiff nod. "So it has."

"You are looking well. Much younger than the last time I saw you. How do you do it?"

"You are too kind, Supreme Lord. Come, my dear, let us leave the great lord in peace..."

"No." Azazel's voice hardens slightly. He turns his one-eyed gaze to Shannon. "Stay with me, *my* love. It's been so long. You may go, Amon. Thank you for your... *service*."

That word burns through my human frame, threatening to break open flesh and bone. Servant? Me? How dare he? But I cannot give him the satisfaction of my anger. I breathe in, containing the fury, forcing my lips to a smile, my head to bow. Then I turn on my heels and saunter out of the garden, blocking from my mind the image of my Mysteria in Azazel's arms.

He will pay. How he will pay.

Chapter Thirty
Grace

I sing the AngelSong aloud, certain no one in this evil place will hear me, but perhaps Jared will. *Jared, where are you?* Every moment, I expect to see him come through my prison door. Yet all I see is unrelenting darkness.

I feel around the space. The walls and floor are smooth and cold but not like metal, more like hard plastic. There's a door with a tiny window in one wall that's hardly big enough to put my fist through. There's a cot with a thin mattress made of rubber. No blankets or pillow. I lie down and close my eyes. Perhaps I can sleep. Sleep would be a blessing.

Light. So bright it hurts. I sit up straight, covering my eyes to protect them from the sudden onslaught. No sleep, I guess. What now?

Once my eyes adjust, I look around the room. It's like a cell in a mental hospital—white walls, floor, and ceiling all molded together with no sharp edges. There's a small table with a tray. Looks like a grilled cheese sandwich. Even a little vase of fake flowers. Nice touch.

I peer out the door into a long, dimly lit hallway. "Anybody out there? Can anybody hear me?" Nothing. "I want to see my husband, Jared… Baldyr!

I'm his wife! I demand to see him now!" No answer except my own echoing voice. I go back to the table and pick up a half sandwich. It looks good—perfect, in fact. And it's warm like it just came off the griddle.

"Do you like the sandwich? We understand that you former Americans love grilled cheese. I asked for it special."

I drop the sandwich and spin around. A tall woman stands before me in a tight-fitting black jumpsuit with a black cap tilted on her head. She looks like something out of a magazine from the sixties.

"How did you get in here?"

"Do you like the sandwich?" she asks again. She's speaking English, which surprises me.

"Yeah, sure. How did you get in—"

"But you haven't taken a bite."

I realize she isn't actually looking at me, just in my general direction. I walk close to her and put a finger on her shoulder. My finger goes right through. I jump back, alarmed. What is this thing?

"Who are you?" I demand. "You aren't real."

"Of course I am, silly. I'm your assistant while you are staying with us. My name is Sandy." She smiles brightly.

So this is some sort of... hologram. Right here in my cell.

"You serve people in prison?" I ask, walking around her to see if I can disrupt the image somehow. I can't. She's a full 3D image, so realistic it's scary.

"Protective custody," she says, though she doesn't turn with me, "for your own safety."

"Right. Well, I want to see my husband."

"Husbands are not a known entity to me," Sandy replies, a puzzled look on her fake face.

"Jared... I mean, Baldyr. I want to see him."

"Baldyr, son of the Supreme Lord, is not available at this time."

"Where is he? Can't you call him or something?"

She is still for a few moments. Maybe her handlers are processing. "Baldyr, son of the Supreme Lord, is not available at this time."

"Well, then I want to see my moth—I want to see Shannon. Freya."

"Freya, consort of the Supreme Lord, is not available at this time. Perhaps I can help you?"

"I need to talk to her. Get her a message. Something. I need to know what's going on. Can you give her a message?"

Silence. The hologram keeps smiling.

"I said, can you give her a message?"

"I'm afraid that I cannot at this time. Ask me again tomorrow. Please enjoy your grilled cheese. I had it made special for you. Because Americans love grilled cheese. I also learned to speak English so you could understand me. I hope you like me. I like you." She beams again. "Let me know if there is anything else I can do for you." And with that, she vanishes.

That was weird.

I pick up the grilled cheese again. The inside is all soft and gooey. It *does* look good. And I *am* really hungry. When was the last time I had a grilled cheese? How many eons ago? I take a bite. The cheese has a strange texture and tastes like... melted plastic. Definitely not real cheese. But I finish the whole thing, because I'm hungry, and who knows when I'll get another chance to eat? Scenes of movie prisons in totalitarian regimes come to mind—people left to rot in cells for decades, forgotten, starving, going slowly insane. Will that happen to me? I'm determined to make sure they don't forget about me.

I go to the window and shout through the little hole. "Helloooo, Sandy! I'm done!"

No answer.

"Yoo-hoo! Sandy? What's for dessert? Anyone? Hello!"

After several minutes of shouting and getting no answer, I sit on the bed. A voice comes over a loudspeaker, a soft female voice just like the hologram, saying something in Norwegian. A few seconds later, the lights go out.

I lie on the cot and stare into nothing.

And I hear a voice, gravelly and strained, echoing in the dark. "I can hear you, Grace."

Chapter Thirty-One
Jared

We wait until dusk to scope out the military post called Ariel—why does that name sound so familiar? The place seems deserted. Evidence of Dragon damage is everywhere; buildings are hollowed-out husks. We don't hold out much hope as we ride to the motor pool.

Most of the vehicles have been damaged beyond repair, but not all. Davidov finds five still intact—two armored personnel carriers and three Sand Cats, smaller utility vehicles designed for desert driving. They even have full gas tanks.

"I told you," he says proudly. "These don't carry weapons, so the Dragons didn't target them. Now we just need drivers."

"And more fuel," I say.

The fuel pumps were destroyed, but one fuel truck, parked inside a garage for repairs, remained untouched. And full of fuel.

"Another miracle?" Davidov asks wryly.

"Manna from heaven," I reply.

He laughs. "We'll scrounge up some gas cans and take as much as we can back to Mar Saba with us."

"Are there any other fuel sources between Mar Saba and Petra?"

"There's an outpost south of the Dead Sea. My hope is the Dragons didn't go there."

"I thought Israel was out of fuel."

"Not quite. When I became prime minister, I reversed the ESG rules from the previous administration and opened up oil reserves in the Golan Heights. The Grigori don't know about that."

We leave Ariel close to dusk and continue our trek until we get to Silwan, the sprawling neighborhood on the slope of Mount Moriah. We dismount at the bottom of the hill. I pat my horse's neck and thank him for the ride. Davidov slaps them on the rump, and they both take off.

"Will they be all right?" I ask.

"They will go back to their home," Davidov says.

In the distance, I can make out the outline of the Temple Mount and the twinkling lights of hovering Dragons overhead. Only three in the air right now. The rest must be on the ground somewhere. They have to take turns, for a Dragon can only hover for a few hours at a time before needing to fly or land.

We walk up a steep road, passing burned-out shops and houses, several snarling dogs, but no people. The air itself feels eerily still. There is not even a whiff of breeze. We pass through some barricades, then descend several stone steps to a courtyard and eventually come to a large pool. This must be the Pool of Siloam. There's people here. Several dozen men, women, and even children gather on the steps and wade in the water. Davidov reaches out his hand to stop me.

"Better they don't see your face just yet. Can you make yourself look a little... shorter?" He chuckles, then takes a deep breath and steps out of the shadows into the pool area.

I pull my hood over my head, keeping it as low over my face as possible, and follow.

People turn to look at us. Some gasp and grab their children in protection. Others recognize Davidov and cry out in relief. He says something in Hebrew that puts them at ease. A few men come forward to speak to him. I stay well back from them. Davidov glances at me as he speaks, probably offering some explanation for who I am. The men eye me with suspicion.

Finally, Davidov turns and beckons me to join him. He motions for me to take off my hood. When I do, everyone gasps in horror. Davidov says a few more words, perhaps telling them what happened on the Temple Mount. They relax slightly, though they keep their distance.

"We will speak English now for the sake of my new friend." Davidov looks at me. "I told them what you did. Do not worry. They say they were at the Western Wall when the attack started and escaped through the tunnel that connects to the Pilgrim's Road. They were lucky. No one caught in the open survived. They said it was... very bad." His voice cracks as he speaks.

I nod. "I will go."

Davidov shakes his head. "It is too dangerous."

"If Zazel's avatar is still in the temple, then Gadreel is there."

"He will kill you."

"He will try."

Davidov sighs. "All right. I am going to find more survivors. I will take some of these men with me. Come back here before morning—if you can."

***

I walk slowly up the limestone steps of the Pilgrim's Road, smoothed from years of trodding feet. The tunnel is wide with an arched ceiling of steel beams, making my footsteps echo. Displays of first-century market stalls line the path, decorated with baskets of plastic food, stuffed goats, and pigeons.

I sing the song of ascent as I walk, the song we sang in the wilderness. The same song the pilgrims sang every year on Passover, as they walked this very road to the temple.

> *I lift up my eyes to the mountains—*
> *where does my help come from?*
> *My help comes from the Lord,*
> *the Maker of heaven and earth.*
> *He will not let your foot slip...*

Lord, please don't let my foot slip.

Once away from the entrance, the path grows dark, and I have to feel my way, inching for the next step. I should have brought a flashlight. As I near the end, I hear music. Not sacred hymns or praises choruses—this music is forceful and discordant, driven by pounding drums and the grinding scream of electric guitars. What is going on there?

I emerge near the the Western Wall, which has collapsed in several sections. The parts of bodies—feet, arms, and even heads—protrude from the rock piles, caked in dust so they appear like pieces of broken statues in the moonlight. I climb the crumbled stones to the Temple Mount, avoiding body parts as best I can.

I pause at the top and take in the scene—it's like something from a nightmare. People—I *think* they are people—dance and scream along with the awful music, scantily dressed or completely naked, bodies and faces painted in ghoulish colors. They raise their hands toward a glowing figure hovering above them in a white costume with preposterous golden wings. Gadreel. He's singing as he dips and sways over the manic revelers, his voice going from a high-pitched screech to a cavernous growl. He leers at them with his white eyes and bright red lips, driving them further into a frenzy of wild dancing while others writhe on the ground, performing obscene acts upon each other.

If there is a hell, this might be it.

I pull the hood over my head and make my way through the gyrating bodies, fighting off the many hands that claw at me, tearing at my robe. It's like wading through a river of leeches.

I come to the place where the *Voice* fell. They are still there, those two slain men, their blackened bodies now covered in rotten fruit and garbage. The revelers give them a wide berth, but the camera drones continue to circle them. Zazel wants the world to see what happens to those who dare speak against him.

Three more of the leeches attach themselves to me. Teeth sink into my calf; a tongue swipes at my neck. Sickened, I shake them off and hurry for the temple.

The Beautiful Gate has been torn away. Burned bodies litter the outer court. I chanting and head through the Nicanor gate to the inner court, where Shira and the rest of the delegation died. There is no sign of their bodies. The brazen altar churns smoke into the night sky.

But there are people here. Some sort of ceremony is taking place. Several priests in red robes wearing masks stand in a circle around a bound, hooded figure wearing nothing but a loincloth. His skinny body is covered in bloody stripes. He sways on his feet.

More bound and hooded prisoners are kneeling outside the circle. They are bent over, their heads to the ground, as two priests whip each of them with a long cord, shouting incantations.

A priest with a black sash—perhaps the high priest—steps into the circle and puts one hand on the standing victim's head. He produces a knife in his other hand and slashes the victim's throat. I put my hand over my mouth to stifle my gasp. Another priest produces a cup to catch the spurting blood as the hooded victim collapses. Two more lift the body and carry it up the steps to the brazen altar.

They are sacrificing people.

I don't think. I rush to the priest with the knife, grab it from his hands, and throw him to the ground. He snarls something unintelligible through his mask. The priest with the whip comes at me, ready to lash at me. I grab the end of the whip in midair and yank on it hard, pulling the priest off his feet. He sprawls on the ground and shrieks as I grab the whip from his hands. I spin around and crack the whip several times, screaming at the other priests.

"Get out! Get out!"

I continue cracking the whip and yelling until all the priests scurry out of the court. I suck in a breath and drop the whip and the knife, my hands shaking. I fall to my knees, my legs suddenly too wobbly to hold me.

I hear moaning and turn to see the victims struggling with their bonds. I pick up the knife and approach the one closest, a teenaged boy. He balks when I come near, holding the knife. I open my hands.

"I'm not going to hurt you," I say. "Let me cut your bonds."

After a moment, he offers his hands to me. I cut him free. He continues to stare at me with wide, fearful eyes.

"What's your name?" I ask.

"N...Nasir," he says.

"Okay, Nasir, help me with the others."

He turns to the woman beside him, a small, frail older woman whose back is horribly torn from the whip. "Imma. Imma." His mother.

I cut the woman's bonds and hand the knife to Nasir so he can do the rest. Four boys around Nasir's age, three woman, and one older man. I take off my robe and rip it into pieces so they can cover themselves.

"You must all get away from here. Quickly," I say.

The older man stares at me. "I... I know you."

Yes, he knows me. Son of the Supreme Lord. I'm the one responsible for all of this, in his eyes. What little good I am doing here to help will never undo the damage I have done.

"Go now. use the Pilgrim's Road to get to the pool." I glance nervously at the Dragons overhead. Then I turn away from them, pick up the whip again, and go into the temple.

This was a place one reserved only for priests. A holy place. Now it is a house of horror.

The carcasses of dead animals—pigs mostly—litter the floor while revelers wallow in their entrails, gorging on their internal organs, smearing blood over themselves. I bend over, gagging on the overpowering stench. Blood seems to cover every surface of the temple—the floor, the columns, the lampposts. One woman shrieks as she pulls what looks like a heart from a dead pig and thrusts it into her mouth.

The priest with the cup of blood stands before the gigantic avatar of Grigori Zazel, which glows like a beacon in the place where the Holy of Holies ought to be. The priest chants something incomprehensible as he pours the blood upon the altar where the avatar stands.

Zazel opens his arms wide and shouts, "I am the Lord, your God! You shall have no other gods before me!"

The priest and the revelers bow low and shout, "Zazel is our Lord!"

I crack the whip. "Get out! All of you!"

They look at me blearily, eyes pulsing with drugs and lust. They don't move. I stalk around, ranting at them, cracking the whip until they stumble and crawl out of the temple. Some I have to throw out bodily, for they seem unwilling or unable to move on their own. None offers much resistance. One woman—or perhaps a man—hisses at me and pretends to claw at me, but then scurries away before I can respond.

I make my way to the altar, to Zazel's avatar, stepping carefully to avoid slipping on the blood-soaked floor. *Lord, don't let my feet slip.* The priest with the cup is still there, a look of defiance on his face.

"Get out," I say.

He bares his teeth. "You may not enter the Holy Place—"

I wield the whip, wrapping it around his neck. He drops to his knees, the cup clattering to the floor. He holds up his hands in surrender.

"Please! Don't kill me! Please!" He grovels.

I unwrap the whip. He scurries out, slipping and sliding on the bloody floor.

I look up at the face of my father.

"Azazel!" My voice echoes.

For a moment, nothing happens. Azazel is perfectly still, as if the mechanism operating him had stopped working. I hesitate, uncertain. Perhaps I'm wrong. Perhaps he can't see me or hear me at all. Perhaps he is what he appears to be, an enormous statue without thought or sight.

But then the head moves, lowering, and the one golden eye focuses on me. "Who dares speak to me?" The voice is thunder and lightning all at once, a storm of sound.

I swallow hard, forcing my voice to stay steady. "I am Baldyr. Your son."

"I have no son. Baldyr deceived me. He betrayed me. He is dead."

"I'm not dead," I say. "And it was you who betrayed me. You sent me here to make peace. And you... you killed thousands. You wanted me dead, too. Now you are sacrificing people to yourself?"

"I am simply fulfilling the prophecy. *His* prophecy. Did you really believe you could stop me? Who do you think you are?"

The voice propels me backward. I struggle to stand up against it, to not collapse in terror.

"I am your son!" I shout. "You betrayed me."

He bursts into peals of laughter, the sound like the screams of demons in that echoing space. "I betrayed *you*? Have you not been lying to me all along? You were my son. Once. But no longer. Did you think I didn't know? That I don't see everything that happens in my tower? Were you such a fool to believe that because all the world loves you, I do too?"

It takes a moment for his meaning to become clear to me. "This was always your plan?"

"To sacrifice you? Of course. What else are sons for?" He laughs again, the sound like daggers in my brain. "Poor Baldyr. You could have been great. Immortal, like me. A god. Even human, as you are. Instead, you chose... *them*. You think you are not dead? But you are. To me. To the world. No one saw what you did. The holos have been wiped clean."

Could this be true? Yes, of course it could.

I gather my voice again. "What will happen when Baldyr does not compete in the games? What will you tell the world then? That you killed your own son?"

"But Baldyr *will* compete in the games," he replies, calmer now, almost amused. "You think you are not... replaceable? Stay there, in the forsaken land, with the forsaken people. Stay and die a traitor's death in the wilderness. Just like all those who tried to oppose us. This is where their bones lie."

I want to scream at him, cry out, pummel his form with my fists. Yet there is nothing I can do. He is not even really here. He's a hologram. I've done what I can in denying him his sacrifices. The stench of the carcasses makes my head swim. I have to get out of here—

Suddenly, the temple is rocked by a massive explosion. Chunks of plaster and stone fall from the ceiling. Piercing screams come from outside. The giant avatar of Zazel flickers.

"What is this—" Zazel's voice cuts out as if muted, though his mouth continues to move. His image flickers several times, then disappears altogether.

Another explosion knocks me to the floor. Plaster and beams fall all around me. I get up and run, dodging falling debris. I run to the inner court, expecting to see the Dragon overhead firing again, searching for me. But the Dragon is gone.

I make my way through the outer court to the Temple Mount. People scream and run wildly, trampling each other. Huge piles of burning metal are strewn all over. The Dragon crashed? Gadreel is nowhere to be seen. Thick yellow dust permeates the air. It stinks like… sulfur.

Amid the screams, I hear singing.

People are gathered around the bodies of the *Voice*. The people I freed. They kneel, holding hands, singing softly, as if they were entirely alone in the world, an oasis of serenity amid the chaos.

If the Lord hadn't been for us—
let Israel now repeat!—
if the Lord hadn't been for us,
when those people attacked us
then they would have swallowed us up whole
with their rage burning against us!

I run over and stare at the two dead men. They are bathed in a circle of brilliant light that doesn't seem to have any source.

Their chests rise and fall. They are breathing.

Hands twitch, legs slide together, knees bend. Burned, bubbled skin smooths out and becomes healthy flesh. Their faces are radiant—so bright I cannot make out their features. They rise from the ground as if pulled by some invisible string. Up and up they go over our heads. Revelers stop and stare in horror and amazement. The two hover a moment, vertical now, and raise their arms in the air as if declaring victory. Gasps of awe and wonderment explode all around us. The song grows louder, filling the dusty air with the sweetest of music.

> *Bless the Lord because he didn't*
> *hand us over like food for our enemies' teeth!*
> *We escaped like a bird from the hunters' trap;*
> *the trap was broken so we escaped!*
> *Our help is in the name of the Lord,*
> *the maker of heaven and earth.*

The *Voice* disappears in a halo of light so bright it burns my eyes.

The revelers turn to each other, questions on their lips. A woman puts her arms over her breasts as if suddenly horrified that she is naked. Others stumble away, struck by some nameless fear. Still others laugh and rush in to stand on the spot where the two bodies lay as if offering themselves to whatever force is at play.

Another thunderous boom nearly bursts my eardrums. The ground trembles violently.

"The sky is falling!" someone shouts, and the revelers scatter in all directions, frantically searching for cover, using each other as shields. Balls of fire crash all around us, cratering the stones, turning everything to ash. I gag as sulfurous smoke fills my nostrils. Someone steps on me. I look up to see a man fall to his knees nearby, vomiting uncontrollably. I cannot see much beyond him; the air is so thick with yellow dust.

Yet the little group I rescued continues to sing as if nothing is happening. Not one piece of shrapnel falls upon them.

I struggle to my feet, dazed. A young woman grabs hold of me, her face painted with streaks of red and yellow.

"Help me!" She mouths the words, unable to speak. Blood spurts from her neck, where a steel rod protrudes. Her eyes flutter, and she falls against me, dying in my arms. I lay her on the ground.

What is this? Meteorites? But these are not ordinary meteorites. The yellow dust. The smell. Sulfur.

This is brimstone.

The other Dragons have taken to the air, shooting pulse lasers into the sky—but at what? One by one, they are destroyed, exploding into shards of metal that fall upon the unprotected revelers, slicing and burning through flesh and bone. The ground convulses, huge cracks opening in the pavement, sucking in screaming people. I think for a moment that the entire Temple Mount will collapse into a great hole, taking us with it.

Yet the song of those rescued rises above it all.

The people who trust in the Lord
are like Mount Zion: never shaken, lasting forever.
Mountains surround Jerusalem.
That's how the Lord surrounds his people
from now until forever from now!

I kneel beside the boy named Nasir, taking his hand. I join in their song until the fire stops falling, and all the world is silent. It seems like hours.

On the horizon, a faint promise of dawn rises.

We stop singing. A great wind suddenly washes over us, clearing away the choking dust. In the gathering dawn, I gaze at the devastation around us, the piles of ash where people once danced with glee. I turn to the temple.

There is no temple. Just a mountain of rubble.

"The Lord destroyed it." Nasir looks up at me and smiles.

I nod, rise to my feet, and stare at the ruined temple. The older man comes up to me and touches my shoulder.

"I know you," he says, just as he said before.

I feel the heat rise up my neck, the shame. Before I can answer, he says something else.

"I… remember you. Jared Lorn."

Chapter Thirty-Two
Grace

"You know my name?"

"Everyone knows your name," says the voice with a rasping chuckle. Is this another AI trick? The voice sounds real enough, but then so does Sandy's, more or less. "You will soon see that they love to play holos of Grigori exploits and enemies to the prisoners. Capturing you seems to have made them extremely happy."

A strange thing for a bot to say. "I can't imagine why."

"You are the daughter of Freya and the wife of Baldyr. And you are a Jehovian, the leader of the YBR. That makes you a fine prize."

I decide the only course of action is to play dumb. "I don't know what you're talking about."

"Really?" Another chuckle. "You're too modest, Grace. Emilia would be proud of you."

Emilia. I swallow a lump in my throat. They know about her too?

"I don't know anyone by that name," I say. "I think you have the wrong person."

"Do I? Oh, that's a shame. I thought you were Grace Fortune. She was a dear friend. I remember the first time I saw her, standing with my son Jared on the steps in front of that school. The girl with the frizzy red hair, scared to death. Jared had quite a time getting her into the PsychoVan, as I recall."

Jared. School. PsychoVan. *PsychoVan.* No one could know about that except...

"Ralph?" My mind whirls, going in several directions at once. Leaping to unfathomable conclusions. I clutch at the wall as if I can reach through it somehow and touch him, see him. "Ralph? Ralph? Is that you?"

"Yes, it's me, Grace." He sounds suddenly sad.

"Ralph. I... what... how...?"

"It's as much a mystery to me as it is to you, my dear. Perhaps it was the Lord's doing; what do you think? That I should end up here. They plucked me out of the camp yesterday and whisked me here with no explanation. Grigoralia is coming up soon. The great Zazel's birthday celebration, where they execute all the prisoners who managed to survive a whole year in the mines. Or perhaps Zazel knows of our connection and decided to play a cruel trick on both of us. I am almost grateful to him. I have waited all these years to find you again. I had given up hope that you were still alive."

"Ralph," I whisper, tears now streaming down my face. I keep saying his name. "I can't believe it. I thought you were... When I got back, you were gone. You and Emilia. They had taken you away. We've been looking for you..."

"And I missed your return by mere moments. Life is cruel. Well... that night, yes, they raided the Hobbit Hole and arrested us. Emilia and I were sent to a camp in the Yukon, where we worked at a rare earth mineral mine—neodymium and yttrium. It turns out those elements are highly toxic. Emilia got sick within a few months. They told her if she took the Cure, they would send her to a hospital for treatment, but she refused." His voice breaks, and he doesn't speak for a while.

I fall to my knees, my breath caught by a sob. "Emilia," I whisper, thinking of all our long talks over her famous hot chocolate—Emilia's Liquid Love, Bree called it. Her meatloaf and beef stroganoff, Jared's favorite. The way she made even the dark, underground dwelling we called the Hobbit Hole feel like a home.

Penny told me how Emilia had masterminded the whole YBR thing and created the character of M, the voice on the shortwave that told people the truth about what was happening. Emilia was always more than she seemed.

"I'm sick as well," Ralph says. "Throat cancer, I suspect. Difficult to swallow. I haven't been able to eat much. You would be amazed at how skinny I am now! I don't think I will make it to my own execution. What a pity."

"You are not going to die," I say, defiant. "As soon as Jared finds out we're here—"

"Jared… I don't know him anymore." Ralph's voice is full of grief. "I fear he's lost."

"No, he isn't." I set my jaw. Hearing the despair in Ralph's voice sends me nearly over the edge. "Even if I go to the guillotine, and he's up there watching me die, I won't believe it. If he had really become the enemy, I would feel it. I know I would."

"I pray you're right," Ralph says with a long sigh. "There is always hope, I suppose. Something I have long abandoned. But hearing your voice… it has revived my hope a little."

"Even if he doesn't, Shannon will. She was angry when they arrested me. She didn't expect that. She'll help us."

"Shannon has a divided heart," Ralph says. "Always has. Whenever she takes a step toward the light, something draws her back to the darkness. Someone, perhaps. The demon that still has hold of her."

"The Whore of Babylon," I whisper.

"She tries to fight it, but she always loses. Because she can't commit. She can't give up all the demon has given her—wealth, fame, power, the favor of powerful men. Those things are still too important to her. And then there's her son, Vale."

"Vale." I say the name like it's a swear word. "My brother. Half-brother. Don't remind me how twisted all this is." I let out a breath. "I thought the worst thing that could ever happen to me was that school shooting. Now, here we are, all these years later, in a prison awaiting execution for imaginary crimes. I guess I was wrong."

"Remember, Grace. We serve a great God who has a plan for those who give up their lives for His sake. Death is not the end."

Death is not the end. I know he means that to be comforting, but just now, it isn't.

Please, Lord, just let me see Jared. One more time. I could die gladly if I knew he was really still mine. And yours.

Chapter Thirty-Three
Jared

I stare at the man in disbelief.

"How do you know that name?"

He chuckles. "Forgive me. I didn't mean to alarm you. You might find this hard to believe, but... I met your wife, Grace, in the... *other* place. I am Ari by the way."

Ari proceeds to tell the most outrageous story I could ever have imagined. Grace and I had gone into the spirit world—the Other Place, he calls it—to rescue our friends, Darwin Speer and Josephine. Those names mean nothing to me. Ari was trapped there along with six other Singers—those who have the gift of the AngelSong. The Watcher, Samyaza, held them in some sort of prison, but Grace rescued them, and they helped her rescue me. Samyaza had killed me and then used my body for the demon-god, Moloch.

"It was all very confusing, and I can't quite tell you all that happened, for the details are fuzzy. I do remember that Grace managed to release you from Moloch, but you were still quite dead when we got out of there."

"How did you get out?"

"I have no idea. The whole place was collapsing, then there was a bright light and the next thing I knew, I was in a kibbutz in Israel—the very place I had grown up. But you—what happened to you?"

I tell him how I awoke in a cave with the Forbidden. He chuckles at that.

"It seems we were all sent to where we were most needed."

We were *sent?* I had not thought of that before.

"Perhaps it is a blessing you don't remember how that happened," Ari says. "But how did you end up in New Asgard? The son of the Supreme Lord, that devil?"

I tell him the story. "I was supposed to stop him. I ended up helping him," I say bitterly.

"You cannot thwart His plan," Ari says, chuckling. "I had never been a faithful Jew—I was a nuclear physicist, after all—but after that time in the Other place, I became a devoted Christian. Trust and obey—I have learned to do this the hard way. We Messianic Jews are not well-loved here in Israel. We are constantly harassed. Our churches are vandalized on a regular basis. It's only gotten worse since the Grigori… listen to me going on. I'm sorry. What about Grace? Where is she?"

I hesitate. "She's dead."

"Dead? No, I don't believe that."

I look at him. "You don't?"

"She was very much alive when we left the Other place. And if you're here, then she must be too."

"But Zazel said… I saw the death certificate, I saw the video of her funeral…"

"And such things cannot be forged? You, of all people, should know that the Grigori are masters of deception. Why would you believe anything Zazel says?"

I pause, considering this. Why *did* I believe it? Perhaps because to believe she is alive and knows what I've become would be even worse?

I shake my head. "If she is alive, then where—"

I'm interrupted by a screeching noise that nearly shatters my eardrums. I spin around to see a blackened form rising from the temple ruin in a shower of sparks and ashes, taking the shape of a monster.

Gadreel.

His wings have been burned to stumps, one arm is missing, and half his face is melted, all but his eyes, which focus on me with the predatory intensity of a crazed owl. His mouth opens, revealing sharpened teeth. He's human, angel, and wild beast all molded together in one horrifying stew of evil.

And he's very angry.

At me apparently.

"Get these people out of here," I tell Ari as I dash away from the group. Gadreel flies toward me, screeching like a beast from nightmares. I search desperately for a weapon, pick up a stone and throw it at his head. He staggers but recovers quickly. I lift a piece of concrete and hold it up like a shield, but he bats it away as if it weighs nothing and reaches with his one good hand to grab my neck. He lifts me off my feet, squeezing so hard I feel my eyes nearly pop out of my head. I swing around and stick a finger in his bulging eye. He shrieks and releases me; I fall hard, feeling something crack. A rib? A backbone? I see his fist coming for me and roll away, barely in time. I scramble and shift as he pounds the ground all around me, just barely missing me. The pain in my chest makes it almost impossible to breathe.

I pick up another stone and throw it, hit him on the shoulder. He barely notices. Even wounded and burned as he is, he's still an angel and far stronger than I will ever be. Desperate, I grab his foot and hang on, pulling him off his feet. He collapses with a crash on a pile of rubble but kicks me off, swings around, and suddenly he has me by the neck again. He slams me down into the rubble so hard my entire body seems to shatter. My breath is gone now. Pain shoots from the small of my back into the tips of my fingers like lightning, followed by a spreading numbness. Gadreel shrieks again and leaps for me, his fist poised to finish me. I try to lift a hand as if that will hold him off. I can't move.

The fist never falls. Suddenly, Gadreel is off me, suspended in mid-air, his blackened arm and legs flailing against some force I cannot see. And then I do see—Michael, his pale armor shining, his flaming sword thrusting into Gadreel's blistered body. The dark angel shrieks in anguish as his body vaporizes from the point of the blade, turning to red mist carried off by the wind.

Michael descends to where I lay and looks at me. I expect him to rebuke me for my stupidity; instead, he puts a hand on my chest. I feel my skin tingling, heating, the bones of my back crackling and burning as they knit together. Numbness turns to stinging needles of pain. I gasp and breathe through the pain until it finally begins to subside. Michael lifts me and sets me on my feet.

"Thank you," I say. It seems inadequate.

"You really thought you could take him on, Human One?" He shakes his head. "Perhaps your success in the arena has gone to your head."

"I'm sorry—"

"Never mind that. Take care of them." He points to the survivors, who stare at me with shocked expressions as if trying to piece together what just happened, make some sense of it.

"Can they see you?" I ask.

"Some of them, perhaps," Michael says. "Most saw you defeat a monster from the Abyss. They will remember that. They are your army now."

"Army?" I shake my head, glancing at the forlorn group. "They are not an army."

"Oh, but they are, Human One. You will see. More will come. Gather them in the City of David."

"The City of David? You mean, the excavation site?"

"The true Mount Zion. Where David first conquered the Jebusites. Where he made his capitol and built his palace. You will make your stand there."

With that, Michael vanishes in a flash of light. I blink, once again unsure what just happened. Did I dream it all?

I walk to the wounded people huddled together, staring at me. In their eyes are a thousand questions, but no one says a word.

"Let's go to the pool," I say. "We will talk more there."

Chapter Thirty-Four
Helel

Zazel is beginning to get on my nerves.

There was that business with Mysteria—she has gone back to him. Fool woman. Now he gloats over his conquest, thinking he has the better of me.

Worse, we have lost Gadreel and his Dragons, and the temple was destroyed, all because of a little brimstone. I've seen this movie before.

Our adversary has not limited his attacks to the temple, however. Brimstone showers have struck all over the world, poisoning rivers and lakes and nearly all freshwater sources except for a few underground springs. I've had to commandeer all the bottled water plants in the Ten Unions to make sure New Asgard does not suffer.

What does Azazel do? He lounges in his garden with his lion and his other abominable creations as if he had not a care in the world.

Luckily, the Eternal One's reprisals have driven more people to get their GEMs. That and the fact that the virus has made a resurgence, this new variant producing painful boils that eventually turn septic. It will not be long before all those still living will be bowing in worship to the Supreme Lord, their minds completely taken over by—me.

There is another problem I must take care of now. The problem of Baldyr. We have scrubbed the video feeds of the Temple Mount, erasing the Golden Son from every frame. He was never there. He did not rescue people from the burning city, nor did he lead them into the desert.

But that is not enough. Grigoralia is coming, and Baldyr must perform in the games. The world must believe that he is still one of us.

I seek out Vale. He is not in his spire, nor is he anywhere in the tower. That means he has snuck out again, taken his hoverbike into the city as he used to when he attended music concerts in the subway tunnels.

I go into the city, prowling the streets and calling his name. I find him, finally, lying on a pile of trash next to a derelict building, wearing his Grigori mask disguise, his clothing soiled as if he hasn't changed or washed in several days. I approach and rip the mask from his face, startling him awake. I grab him by the collar and haul him to his feet. His mouth opens; his eyes go wild.

"Hey, man. Be cool. Want some sugar cubes? I got whatever you need..." His gaze is unfocused, bleary. He's high as a kite.

"Shut up and listen to me." I shake him to get his attention. "I am a friend of your mother's. She's been looking for you everywhere."

"My mother? She couldn't care less about me." He opens his backpack and pulls out a handful of pills. He's about to shove them in his mouth when I slap his hand away.

He yelps, shaking his hand. "Hey, man! Not cool."

"I have something to tell you. You need to be sober to hear it."

"Fine. Whatever."

"It's about Baldyr."

He looks at me, his eyes more focused now. "I don't want to talk about him."

"Too bad. It's time you knew the truth. Baldyr is your real father."

I wait for the predictable response—shock, outrage, disbelief.

Vale blinks, then bursts out laughing.

I scowl at him. "It's true," I say. "Your mother and he have both been lying to you. What is worse, Baldyr used you. He pretended to be your brother to get you to trust him, then he betrayed you. He betrayed us all."

Vale stops laughing. He stands, swaying slightly, his expression unreadable.

"No. It can't be. He's too young..."

"He's much older than you think."

Vale's mouth opens and closes several times. His face crumples—he starts to cry. So pathetic.

"Enough," I say, shaking him again. "I'm going to tell you what will happen now. Stop blubbering and listen. Can you do that?"

After a moment, his sobs subside. He wipes his eyes, sniffs, and looks at me.

"Good. Your father is a traitor. But the world cannot know what he has done. It would be a disaster. Therefore, you must take his place. You must *become* him."

Vale blinks, shakes his head. "I can't—"

"Yes, you can. Isn't that your deepest wish, after all? To *be* him? The great and glorious champion with the world at his feet? The Golden Son? The Destroyer?"

He swallows. "I guess so."

"There! See? I am your fairy godmother, making all your wishes come true."

"But how—?"

"Close your eyes. Be very still. Think about being him, Baldyr. The man you revered. Imagine him vanquishing every bestial challenger in the arena. Every creature on earth cheering for him. Think about what it would be like to *be* that man. You can be whatever you want to be, Vale. That is the one inviolate rule of this world. Imagine you are him, and you will become him."

A smile creeps across Vale's face as he imagines himself in the body of Baldyr, drinking in the roar of the crowds and the adulation of Zazel, who had always ignored him. I place both hands on his head and breathe on him, pouring my spirit into him. He transforms before me, gaining height, muscle, beauty, his hair fading from red to white. I delight in his metamorphosis, though it taxes me greatly. My own human shell withers as the power leaves me.

"Keep your eyes closed," I say with the last of my voice. "Believe, Vale, believe." I must disappear for a time until I can regain my strength. With my mind's eye, I can still watch him.

After several minutes, he opens his eyes. He looks around and realizes I am gone. His gaze travels to his hands. He turns them over as if not recognizing them. His sleeves are suddenly too short, his trousers straining at the seams. He walks, then runs down the street, skirting the homeless encampments until he finds a shop window that is not broken or boarded up. He looks into the glass, staring at his reflection for a long time.

***

The planets have disappeared, all but the sun, which shines upon me as I sit on the Cobra throne and look down upon the seven union lords seated around the gigantic table. They gaze at me warily, wondering who I am and what I am doing in Zazel's place. But I see fear in their eyes as well. I've remade myself since my encounter with Vale. I'm taller, stronger, fiercer. My face is hard a stone; my eyes gleam. I am feeling more myself.

"Greetings, Gentlemen. Allow me to introduce myself. My name is Amon H. Doyle." I smile menacingly. "I am the chairman of the Interlaken Group and personal advisor to the Supreme Lord. As he is unavailable at the moment, I will be conducting this session in his absence. So, what questions do you have?"

"What does the Supreme Lord plan to do to avenge our comrades?" Morales, leader of the South American Union, asks. His voice trembles. The death of the three union lords has rattled them all.

"Vengeance will come in time, Lord Morales. The Supreme Lord has declared an official day of mourning, with all the necessary pomp and circumstance. And the Great One himself will take over the rule of the Russian, Scandinavian and North American Unions."

"But what is the Supreme Lord going to *do?*" says Gascon, the European Union ruler, stroking his pointy goatee nervously.

"All will be revealed," I say. "You must be patient. The Supreme Lord is in control."

"We saw the holos," says Kabua, the South American Union ruler. He's small and muscular, wearing a colorful shirt and matching cap. "We saw what that gladiator, Baldyr, really did. It is clear the Golden Son has turned against his father."

"Nothing could be further from the truth," I say. "In fact, the Golden Son is at this moment training in New Asgard for the Grigoralia celebrations."

Kabua makes a face. "I don't understand. How can he be here if he is still in Israel with the rebels?"

"He was never there."

"We all saw him!" shouts Morales.

"No, you didn't," I say levelly, staring the man down.

Morales blinks several times, then looks away. No one else tries to contradict me, but I see the uncertainty in their expressions.

"I see you are all under the strong delusion that Baldyr has betrayed us. I can assure you he has not. Whatever you saw in the news media or on the HoloNet was probably some conjuring by those disgusting Jehovian pigs. It was a complete and utter lie, and I will prove it to you. Come to the training center tomorrow and see the man for yourself."

Chapter Thirty-Five
Jared

Davidov rises to greet me when I emerge from the tunnel. He gazes at my disheveled condition and that of the half-naked people with me and shakes his head.

"What have you been up to?"

"I found them at the temple," I say. "About to be sacrificed."

Davidov's eyes go wide. He runs a hand through his tangled hair. "What happened up there? We saw fire falling from the sky. Was it the Dragons?"

"The Dragons are gone."

"Gone? What do you mean? How?"

I guide my charges to the pool so they can wash their wounds. The others there rush in to help them.

I turn back to Davidov. "The temple is gone too."

He stares at me. "No... What happened? What was that fire in the sky? A meteor?"

"Not exactly."

"I see." Davidov's mouth forms a tight line. He nods as if he understands. "And what happened to you? Did the temple fall on you?"

I smile slightly. "If I told you I got into a wrestling match with a demon, would you believe me?"

Davidov shakes his head. "I knew you were mad."

Ari's voice can be heard telling the others what he witnessed at the Temple Mount. Some glance at me wonderingly. Others shout praises to God.

"Why would God destroy his own temple?" Davidov asks.

"It was not His temple," I say. "These people need medical attention."

Davidov nods. "The hospitals are deserted. But you may be able to find bandages, antibiotics."

"Good. You found survivors, I see?"

"Yes, a few. We have enough drivers for the trucks."

"You should go as soon as possible."

He looks at me. "You are not coming?"

I shake my head. "I am staying here."

He frowns. "Why? What can you do here?"

"I don't know. But I have to stay."

"Alone?"

"I won't be alone."

"No indeed!" Ari comes to my side, a shawl wrapped around his shoulders. "I will stay also. There will be others as well. This is where the final battle will take place."

"The final battle?" Davidov looks doubtfully at Ari. "What are you talking about?"

"Armageddon."

"Oh, that." Davidov chuckles. "Don't you Christians believe that will be at Megiddo? That's a hundred fifty kilometers from here."

"A mistranslation," Ari says. "Armageddon has often been translated as Mount of Megiddo. But there is no mountain at Megiddo, is there?

Armageddon means the Mount of *Assembly*. Mount Zion. Here in Jerusalem."

Davidov stares at him then shakes his head. "You Christians are all mad."

"I stay also!" Nasir shouts. Several others voice their intentions to stay as well. All the ones I rescued from the temple, plus a few others.

Davidov surveys them, bemused. "You think you can stop the Grigori? You and this small remnant?"

I glance at him. "Isn't there a story in your histories of a group of farmers who drove the most powerful army in the world out of Israel?"

"You speak of the Maccabees."

I nod.

Davidov's eyes widen. He shakes his head, chuckling. "Definitely mad."

***

"This pool is likely where the Church was born," says Ari once Davidov and his group have left. He lies on his back in the water while I dip my feet in its coolness. Michael healed my broken body, but the aches and the bone-deep exhaustion remain.

"Oh?" I say idly.

"This pool was huge, the size of two Olympic-sized swimming pools. It is the only place where three thousand people could get baptized on the Day of Pentecost. The day the Holy Spirit came upon the believers."

I try to imagine that day—three thousand new believers rushing into the waters of this pool to receive the gift of the Holy Spirit.

"The Pharisees and the Sadducees must have lost their minds that day," Ari says with a laugh. "They thought they had taken care of the Yeshua problem at his crucifixion. Little did they know that they had unleashed a movement that would still be on fire two thousand years later."

"Ironic."

"Here's another bit of irony for you. People used to claim that Herod the Great built the Pilgrim's Road, but no, it was built by Pontius Pilate." Ari chuckles. "That Roman blackguard, the one who killed the Messiah. Pilate. Perhaps it was out of guilt for all the Jewish lives he took. Pilate has always been a curiosity to me. A cruel ruler who hated the Jews, yet he wanted to spare Yeshua. Tried over and over to let him go. This is what I have learned about Yeshua since I came to know him personally. You can be for him or against him, but you cannot be indifferent. You must make a choice. Pilate tried to find a middle ground and failed. I believe he never got over that. Some say he committed suicide. Others claim he and his wife became Christians. I like to believe that."

Ari begins to sing the song of ascent in a strong and sonorous voice.

I lift up my eyes to the mountains—
where does my help come from?
My help comes from the Lord.

I stand, allowing the song to seep into my aching limbs.

My help comes from the Lord.

The Lord. The One who sent Michael to lead me and guide me. Why me? All that Ari has told me of my forgotten past whirls in my brain like electrons hurtling around a nucleus. I was dead. A spear through my heart. I didn't die. Yet a part of me did. The angel part of me. The part I've always loathed, tried to deny. My cursed soul. I was a man split in two. Am I only half a man now, or have I been made whole? Was my death a true healing or merely a cutting away of the broken parts? Even now, I cannot trust myself. I must trust only in Him. The Lord who directs the angel armies. The Lord who has brought me to this place. The Lord who called me by name.

Chapter Thirty-Six
Helel

I have a small viewing stand constructed in the training center so that the union lords—and Shannon—can watch the new, improved Baldyr be put through his paces by his two burly NP trainers. Vale plays his role with relish, though he is far more brutal than the former Baldyr ever was. The session ends with the two NPs howling in pain on the floor, one with a broken jaw, the other with a bone sticking out of his leg.

Shannon clutches her fists together tightly and winces each time Vale smashes his opponent or stomps on his head. I have told her that Vale went through a cutting edge procedure to achieve his new look, but she is as yet unconvinced.

"That's not my son," she says as the medi-bots swoop in to tend to the wounded. "He was never so.... sadistic."

"Yes, well, the procedure did make him a bit more... energetic," I say mildly. "We are still working out the kinks. But we will get it under control, I promise."

"What have you done to him?"

"We made him the champion you wanted him to be," I reply.

She shakes her head. "I need to speak to him. To be sure he's really my son."

"Of course."

The union lords are suitably convinced that this was the real Baldyr and whatever they saw on the HoloNet was some sort of Deepfake.

Once they are gone, I call Vale over to us. He comes reluctantly, still quivering with the violence of his bout, looking more than ready for some new opponent to devour.

"Vale?" Shannon says tentatively.

He gives her the coldest of looks. "Mother." His voice has changed, become low and flat, toneless.

"Is it really you?" She reaches a hand out to touch him.

He flinches and bats her hand away.

Her expression clouds. "What is the matter? Why do you—?"

"Why did you lie to me?"

"What? I don't know what you're—"

"You told me Zazel was my father. You lied." Vale points to me. "He told me the truth."

Shannon whirls on me, her eyes wide with shock. "What did you tell him?"

"What you should have told him a long time ago," I say. "It's better this way, trust me."

Shannon returns her gaze to her son. "Vale, please, listen. I love you. I wanted to protect you. That's the only reason... everything that happened before... it doesn't matter. You are Zazel's heir. That's the important thing."

"When did it happen? You knew Baldyr all those years ago? How?"

"None of that matters, I'm telling you!"

"It matters to me!" Vale's fists clench, and his whole body trembles. For a moment, I think he's going to hit her. I step between them.

"Easy, boy," I say under my breath. "Keep it under control. What I just saw was overkill. If you can't act more like the real Baldyr, people will become suspicious. Deep breath now, my boy."

I breathe in, and he breathes with me. His fists unclench. But he still rests his smoldering gaze on his mother.

"Stay away from me." He stalks away.

I feel sorry for her for one small moment. She stands there, watching her son flee from her, the one person she loves in the world, the one person she would have given her life for. But it had to be done.

I take her hand. "Come, my love. Let us go to your rooms, have a drink, and relax a bit. I know how to make you feel better." I pull her to me.

She draws her hand away. "No."

I look at her. "No?"

"Zazel… Zazel has asked for me to come to him."

I clench my jaw, forcing my body to remain calm. "Then I will come with you. There is something I need to speak to him about."

***

Zazel is in his hammock, watching the holo of Vale's bout as Shannon and I enter the garden.

"He looks like him, but he doesn't fight like him," Zazel says, downing a glass of wine. The area around his hammock is littered with broken glasses. He's probably been drinking all day.

"He needs some refining, I admit, but we have plenty of time before the games." I pick up a grape from Zazel's dining table and pop it in my mouth. So Roman, lounging about on hammocks, eating grapes. Except for the winged lion, perhaps. Real Romans would have been so jealous.

"He's… so different," Shannon murmurs.

"Ah, love. Come to me," Zazel purrs.

Shannon obeys, brushing aside pieces of glass so she can kneel next to his hammock. Azazel pets her as if she were a dog. I turn away, disgusted.

"Where is he now?" he asks. "My true son? The Betrayer? Is he dead yet?"

"Not yet," I say. "But he will be. Soon enough."

"Tell me, Amon, how did we manage to lose Jerusalem? You said your plan was foolproof."

I bristle at his sarcasm. "What, that old Sodom and Gomorrah trick? It was to be expected. Shows we got to Him, though, doesn't it? He is not so almighty as He thinks He is. He might have destroyed our Dragons, but not before the Dragons destroyed two-thirds of the population. The rest have fled. All that's left is the Betrayer and a few stragglers. Jerusalem is no more."

"But he lives." Azazel's voice has become a growl. "He *lives*."

"He's nothing," Shannon says soothingly. "He'll be dead soon—"

"He lives!" Azazel springs up from his hammock, tossing Shannon aside. She shrieks as she falls into a pile of broken glass. Azazel seems not to notice. He continues raging as I pick Shannon up and brush off her bloodied hands.

"He was supposed to die! I want him dead! I want to kill him myself!"

"Calm down, will you?" I snap. Shannon is crying.

"You must get him back," Azazel says.

"And how am I to do that?"

"Use that mighty brain of yours!"

I sigh and turn to Shannon. "Why don't you go take a rest, my dear?" I say gently. "Have your cuts tended."

"Yes… yes…" she mumbles as I summon Guardians to take her away.

When she is out of earshot, I turn my gaze to Azazel. "You do have a card to play."

"What card?"

"*Her.*"

His face brightens instantly. "Her. I forgot about her."

"Of course you did. I am here to remind you. He might be willing to give himself up—in exchange for her life."

A slow smile spreads across his bronzed face. "Bring her to me."

Chapter Thirty-Seven
Grace

The lights blare on, startling me awake. Why am I so sleepy all the time? I feel groggy, like my head is full of cotton. Maybe they are putting some kind of drug in my food. If I never see another grilled cheese sandwich in my life, I'd be happy.

"Ralph?"

No answer. Is it morning already? Day and night mean nothing here in this place. Only dark and light. Sometimes the dark seems endless; sometimes, like now, it seems to pass in the blink of an eye.

"Ralph?"

Still no answer. The little window in my door is closed. I frown. That's never happened before. Are they not allowing us to talk anymore? Talking to Ralph is the only thing keeping me sane. Hearing his voice, changed and broken as it is, and reminiscing about the good old days—not that we had many of those, but at least we'd always been together—made me feel as though I were still connected to the world, that the world as I knew it wasn't just a dream. For now, my existence feels more like a dream than a waking reality.

I'm pretty sure the purpose of this imprisonment is to drive me crazy. When the lights come on, I'm bombarded with holos. The white walls of the cell virtually disappear into reel after reel of Grigori propaganda. Black-hooded "Jehovians" with assault weapons attacking innocent people and fire-bombing businesses and government centers while the Peacemakers valiantly battle them in the streets. There are plenty of shots of Jared fighting in the arena, so beautiful and strong, or standing by Zazel before those adoring crowds, a beatific smile on his face. My mother's movie, *Katrina Kross and the Curse of the Jehovians*, plays every day, in between scenes of her appearances at rallies and on talk shows, promoting the GEM. And, of course, they repeatedly show the death of the *Voice* and the rejoicing in the streets as a result.

When the holos end, the dark returns.

Every once in a while, water spigots open in the ceiling, dousing the cell. That's why my mattress is made of rubber. Once I'm thoroughly soaked, high-velocity fans come on to dry everything out. Sometimes a new set of prison garb—a green baggy jumpsuit—is passed through the slot in my cell door. That's where my meals come from too. A voice directs me to send out my dirty dishes and clothes. Sandy hasn't returned in quite a while. I kind of wish she would. She's annoying as heck, but at least it would break up the monotony.

Today, there is no shower. No holo. Instead, there is a click followed by a hissing sound, like the release of air pressure. The door glides open.

I hold my breath. *Jared?*

A Guardian stands in the open doorway. I shrink back on my cot, my heart thudding with fear and disappointment. These guys still give me the creeps. Were they ever human? Are those hoods surgically implanted or do they just grow that way?

The Guardian's form goes in and out of focus. I shake my head to clear my vision. "What's up? Breakfast in bed? How thoughtful."

Another Guardian enters the cell, zip cuffs in his hand. He quickly binds my wrists together and hauls me to my feet. He's so strong, I think he could lift me over his head and toss me like a paper airplane. The cuffs seem pretty unnecessary. He drags me out the door and down the pristine white hallway to the elevator. Is this it? Am I going to my death? Already? My heart races out of control. The guillotine. I'm not ready.

Please Lord, not yet, not yet. Not until I've seen him.

Two giant steel doors slide open, and the Guardians pull me in.

"You don't have to be so rough, you know. I'm not going anywhere. It's not like I've been able to work out my escape plan yet what with all the drugs you keep giving me. What is that, by the way? Xanax? Valium? Or have you goons invented something new?"

They don't answer. They don't look at me. I wonder if they even understand English.

We take a wild ride that makes me want to vomit. I almost wish I could, just to see if I could get a reaction from them.

"You know, you could charge money for this ride. People would pay top dollar. Oh, I forgot. You don't have money anymore. Still, it's better than Disney World. Is there still a Disney World? Or is it called Grigori World now? Just curious."

My head spins even worse by the time we get out. It takes me a minute to understand where we are. Even then, I don't believe it.

A garden.

This must be Azazel's fake Eden. It's so like him, too—overblown, phony, choked with so many flowers and trees it's hard to breathe. The air seems to glow as if brimming with its own light, and the scents of so many flowers compete for supremacy in a kind of floral stew. Then there are the creatures—hybrids out of nightmares. Azazel is desperate to be a true creator, but in the end, he can only imitate. Badly.

Still nauseous from the ride, I stumble along a neatly made path, flanked by the Guardians, to a central area where a vine-draped gazebo stands on a high dais. The first thing I see is a lion with wings. The second thing is Grigori Zazel.

Azazel.

The last time I saw him in person, I stuck a sword in his eye. I think he's still sore about that.

He looks quite different now from the twenty-foot fallen angel I encountered in the Abyss, but he's still huge, with that combination of beauty and horror the Grigori do so well. He's stretched out languidly on a hammock, wearing a thin robe that barely covers his overly muscular body; that's probably how he thinks gods are supposed to dress. Or maybe it's just his bathrobe.

I blink, clearing cobwebs from my brain. Could be just a holo, after all. Why would he want to see me in person? Information? Torture, perhaps? I look around, hoping to see Jared. He isn't there.

Azazel says something to the Guardians. They haul me up the steps to the gazebo.

"Grace Fortune." His voice is soft and reedy, his smile filled with scorn. He swings on the hammock. "Thank you for joining me."

Is he speaking English, or am I just able to understand him? I swallow but say nothing.

"It's been a long time, hasn't it? Since last we met."

When I took out your eye, you mean?

"You thought you had defeated me. You and my son Baldyr. But all that has changed. I am the king of the world. You are a prisoner awaiting execution. And Baldyr is mine now. All mine."

I bite my lower lip. "Liar."

His one sculpted eyebrow lifts in mock surprise. "Do I lie? If he still loved you, wouldn't you see him here, rejoicing to find you alive?"

"Does he even know I'm here?"

"You wanted to see me, Father?"

I whirl at the new voice, deep and flat but oddly familiar.

And he is there. Jared.

I blink, my whole body going cold and hot at the same time, my limbs suddenly like lead weights. He's so… tall. So huge. Like a comic book character come to life in his gladiator armor, his broad chest bronzed and slick with sweat, his long white hair fashioned into dozens of braids. I take him in, unable to breathe for what seems like a full minute.

"Jared?"

He looks at me. No, he looks *through* me, as if I didn't exist. His face is granite, his blue eyes like lasers.

"Jared! It's me! You… remember me, don't you?" My heart hammers.

His gaze shifts to Azazel. "Who is this person?"

"She is the leader of a rebel faction known as the YBR," Azazel says in a slow drawl. "We caught her in New York. She claims she is your wife, so I thought it best for you to meet her and clear things up."

Jared looks from Azazel to me and scoffs. "I've never seen her before."

I gasp in shock. Something is wrong. "Jared, look at me. I'm Grace. Your wife. You remember, don't you? Maybe not the part about the temple because you were kind of dead then, but before, the Mansion! Forlorn! The Hobbit Hole—"

"What are you babbling about?"

His eyes are so empty and cold I feel my blood begin to freeze. This cannot be happening. He has to know me. I realize then that I can't hear his heart. I've always been able to hear his heartbeat when he is near me. Now, there's nothing.

"Jared, look at me. *Look. At. Me.* You know me. We're married. Remember the ceremony in the little chapel in the woods? Please remember!"

His face is like stone. He starts to turn away.

My legs begin to shake. I lunge at him, raising my cuffed hands so I can grab his arm. "Look at me!"

His arm flinches, throwing me off, and suddenly I am falling, slamming into the edge of the gazebo. Pain shoots through my shoulder, and for a moment, I am sure something is broken—besides my heart.

"What are you going to do with her?" asks the stranger in Jared's body.

"She is slated for execution at the Games."

"Good."

Good.

I lay on the floor, unable to rise, gasping for breath.

"Was there something else you wanted of me?" Jared asks, and I hear eagerness in his voice, a desperate desire to please.

"Oh... just to tell you what a wonderful job you did in training today. But please, take it easy on my trainers. You are going through them a little too quickly."

"I will. And thank you. Father." He sounds positively delighted with this praise. He brushes past me to the steps and strides purposefully down the garden path.

I blink, watching his disappearing form, the pain in my shoulder nothing compared to the pain racking my soul.

"It's better if you just face the truth." Zazel's voice floats in the air like motes of dust. "Take it to your grave. I know it hurts. But do not fear. You will not have long to suffer."

"Let me see my mother." I sound so pathetic, grasping at straws.

"Your mother? You have no mother. You have no father. You have no one, Grace Fortune. You *are* no one. You no longer exist. I just thought I would tell you these things so you don't hold out hope. Because even I am not that cruel." He makes a clicking noise, and I feel my arms wrenched by Guardians, uncaring of my pain, as they pick me up and drag me down the garden path to the elevator. I don't even bother trying to walk now. My only wish is that the games were held today—the sooner, the better.

Part Three
Zion

"Nations will fear the name of the Lord
All the kings of the earth will fear your glory
For the Lord builds up Zion
He appears in his glory"
Psalm 102: 15

Chapter Thirty-Eight
Jared

An ancient lyre sculpture marks the entrance to the City of David. Something stirs within me as I stare at this stringed instrument, not so different from my guitar. The lyre was David's way of pushing back the shadows and cleansing his soul. I understand that.

Past the grand stone archways of the entrance lies a multi-leveled courtyard studded with trees and flowers, now mostly dried up and dead. Yet a remnant of their beauty remains, softening the edges of the pale Jerusalem stone.

Ari shows me the way up the steps to the observation deck so we can get an overview—the ruins of David's palace just below us, the Valley of Jehoshaphat, the deserted neighborhoods of Silwan, the Mount of Olives to the east, and the Temple Mount to the north.

"This used to be a parking lot." Ari indicates the archaeological dig where the remnants of ancient walls and columns have been uncovered. Three sets of bleachers stand at the bottom of the ruins, built for tourists to watch light shows projected on the ruins at night. He takes me into the catwalks constructed over the top of the ruins. "No one knew this place existed until about a hundred years ago. But this is the original Jerusalem, the place David conquered and made his home."

Ari shows me the water shaft built by the ancient Canaanites. "David entered Jerusalem this way," he says as we go deeper and deeper until we come to a larger, open space, the Spring Citadel. "He was a brilliant tactician. He knew he couldn't break down the walls of such a massive fortress. So he went under them."

"It's amazing," I say.

"It is. King Hezekiah built a tunnel to divert water from the Spring Citadel to the Pool of Siloam in case of enemy attacks. A monumental achievement for ancient men with nothing but pickaxes."

"This will be a good place to hide if needed," I say thoughtfully.

"Every Israeli house is built with a safe room," Ari says. "This will be ours."

"And the water supply is plentiful."

"Yes, as long as we can keep the pumps running. Which means keeping the generators running. For that, we will need fuel."

"Davidov can help us with that," I say.

We return to the ruins and end up on what was once a palace watchtower. I gaze around, silent and in awe, feeling thousands of years of blood and death and worship—the lives of millions—vibrate within my bones, just on the other side of the Veil. This place, Jerusalem, is where heaven touches earth.

"It was beautiful," Ari says. He's looking up at the Temple Mount. "That temple. Even I was proud of it. A temple to rival Herod and Solomon. Of course, when the Lord returns, he will not need a building, for He will be our temple. What a glorious... dream." He glances at me. "We need to talk about food and supplies, if we are going to stay here."

"The boys and I have been scavenging in the city." Dozens more refugees have come here, including many teenage boys, mostly shepherds and herdsmen who heard about our little settlement. "They are collecting whatever food they can find."

"The Lord provides." Ari chuckles. "We can use the dry tunnels for storage. The only other matter is… what to do about defense."

I think of Michael's words.

"All we need to do," I say slowly, "is… stand."

Ari cocks his head skeptically. "So we do nothing?"

"Standing is not nothing. In fact, it might be the hardest thing of all to do."

"Fine, fine, but might I make a suggestion?"

I chuckle. "Of course."

"We should build a radio station. Up on the observation deck. I know the electronic shops in the city. If there is anything left of them, we might be able to scrounge enough parts to put something together." He pauses, seeing my puzzled expression. "There are others like us all over the world. Standing. Waiting. They must know we are here—and what we have seen. The Golden Gate, the flood in the desert—our people need to know these things. It will give them hope."

I nod slowly. "I suppose so."

"Good. I will get started on that." He smiles, though it quickly fades. "What do you think Zazel will do next?"

This thought has troubled me greatly. "I don't know."

"With Gadreel and his Dragons destroyed, he won't be pleased."

I almost laugh. Almost. "No, he won't."

***

I prowl the decimated streets of Jerusalem with Nasir and some of his friends. We have a list of items Ari needs for the radio shack. I have something else I need to find.

The city is a shambles. All of the religious and sacred sites have been utterly demolished. We stare in shock at the charred wound that was the Church of the Holy Sepulchre. Azazel chose his targets carefully.

Corpses lie in the open, hardly recognizable as human. Scavenger birds feast upon what flesh they can find. We walk as quickly as we can past these sights.

Nasir keeps up a steady stream of conversation, a welcome distraction. He tells me his story: He and his mother are Syrian Christians. They left Syria because they would have been killed for their faith. Israel granted them asylum. Samir, another of the boys I rescued from the temple, ran away with them. He speaks no English, but he nods along with Nasir's story.

"That night of the attack, we went to the church and prayed. For help. But they found us there, those evil people in the robes, and took us to the temple."

"Who were they?" I ask.

"Grigori cults," Nasir replies. "They were all over the MEU, even here in Israel. They worship Grigori Zazel and offer sacrifices, even before the attack."

This information horrifies me. How did I let this go on so long? I have much to atone for.

Amid the rubble, we find some buildings unscathed. A few markets and small shops. We load what provisions we can find into makeshift carts. But I still haven't found what I'm looking for.

"Do you know where there might be a music store?" I ask Nasir. He consults with Samir, who asks the others. After several minutes of conversation, Nasir beams at me. "Follow us."

I follow the boys down several more blocks to Pierre Konig Street, where they stop before a burned out storefront. I should not be surprised that Azazel targeted music stores.

"Not much left here," says Nasir. "What is it you want?"

"A guitar."

We climb through the broken window and search through piles of charred debris, the remains of instruments and shelving. Nasir makes a noise of triumph and pulls something from the wreckage. It's a guitar, slightly singed but mostly intact. Another boy finds a pack of strings.

"Play something," Nasir demands. "See if it works."

I restring and tune the instrument, my fingers shaking slightly. I try a few notes; to my surprise, they ring out easily, unaffected by the damage. I play a few riffs, my fingers moving over the instrument of their own volition. Nasir laughs and starts to clap along. The others join in. They applaud when I finish.

"Very good!" Nasir says. "You will play for us again?"

"Sure. But let's get this stuff back to the compound."

"As you say, Amir!"

I look at him. "Amir?"

"It means... leader."

Leader.

Once back at the compound, I tell the boys to start cleaning out the houses surrounding the ruins. We need to have space for people to live. They are not happy with the assignment.

"We are fighters," Nasir says. "Not cleaners. That is women's work."

"Not today it isn't," I reply.

He huffs, kicking a stone with his toe. "But we will fight, yes?"

I look these scraggly boys up and down. "Do you know anything about fighting?"

Nasir unhooks a long double piece of leather from around his waist and holds it up. I thought it was a belt, but it turns out to be something else.

"A sling?" I say.

"We are all slingers," Nasir says proudly. "Stones fly very fast, hit very hard. Kill a wolf if hit in the head."

A sling. I got hit in the chest with a projectile from a sling once in the arena. It felt like I'd been shot. Had it not been for my armor...

"Then you'd better start collecting stones," I say, "after you're done cleaning."

He grins and says something to the others, who nod happily.

I take the guitar to my attic room in a house near the excavation site, which I have made into my quarters. There's something else I need to do.

I pull out a small mirror and a pair of scissors, two things I had scavenged in the city. I set up the mirror so I can see myself, and begin cutting off my braids.

***

Davidov arrives a few days later with fuel and other supplies for us.

"What have you done to yourself?" he asks, observing my bad barber job.

"I'm trying to look more... normal," I say.

"Congratulations. You look terrible."

He brought with him two soldiers, Lev and Izik. We share a meager supper of boiled lentils and matzo in the tunnel beneath the visitor's center, for privacy. Davidov looks tired but encouraged by the progress they've made so far.

"We have fresh water, though food is a greater difficulty. We have found some in the surrounding towns; Wadi Musa is full of hotels that have food supplies, but who knows how long it will last. Refugees come every day, from all over the Judean hills. They tell us the water in their towns is fouled from the 'meteor attacks.' They say it is as red as blood." He glances at me. "Imagine that."

I smile.

"We have raided all the military outposts we can reach and stockpiled some weapons. Mostly rifles, grenades, small arms. We brought some rifles for you."

I tell him about the slingers. He nods in approval. "A very good weapon. But you must train your people with the rifles as well. That's why Lev and Izik are here."

I glance at the two men, who have not spoken other than a terse greeting when introduced. Lev is the older one, his bearded face creased from age and sun, though his eyes tell me he is not a man to be trifled with. Izik is younger but equally steely-eyed.

"So you are the gladiator," Lev says in heavily accented English. He looks me over and harumphs. "The prime minister says you are not really the Golden Son. It was all a… ruse?"

"Yes," I say.

"So, why should we believe you now when you say you fight for us? Could that not also be a ruse?"

"I suppose it could be," I admit.

"You look like a Grigori," says Izik. "You brought this destruction on our city—"

"He is with us now," says Davidov, a touch of irritation in his tone. "That is what matters."

A moment of awkward silence is broken by Ari, who clears his throat. "Pardon me, Prime Minister... but I have a concern."

Davidov turns to Ari. "What is it?"

"Well, as you know, when Zazel took over the UE, he took control of all the nuclear arsenals in the world. He did this to ensure peace. No nation would be able to use nukes against any other nation. The UE is the world's sole nuclear power." Ari pauses. "Except for Israel."

I glance at Davidov, who shifts in his chair, jaw tightening.

Ari leans over to me and whispers, "Israel's nuclear capability is a long-held open secret." He straightens. "If we take out the control center in New Asgard, we could prevent Zazel from using nuclear weapons against us."

Davidov shakes his head. "You are dreaming. The Dragons have destroyed all of our missile sites. We have no way of firing a long-range, intercontinental nuclear missile at New Asgard."

"What about dropping an EPW?" Ari asks. The two soldiers perk up, interested.

"EPW?" I ask.

"Earth-penetrating weapon," Davidov says. "Bunker buster."

"You still have planes, don't you?" says Ari. "They could not have destroyed all of them. And I know there are secret sites—"

"Zazel's radar would destroy any plane coming into his airspace," I say.

"What about the B-21?" Ari says.

Davidov narrows his gaze on Ari. "How do you know about this?"

The old man shrugs. "I worked at CERN. I...learned things."

Davidov sighs. "It seemed like an extravagant purchase at the time—so long ago now. I actually opposed the idea. I thought we should invest in more defensive technologies, like the Iron Dome. But my predecessor felt otherwise."

"It won't work," I say. "New Asgard has two control centers that I know about. One is underground, and the other is airborne. You'd have to take them both out in a single strike. That would be nearly impossible."

"I agree," says Davidov. "Besides, Zazel seems far more enamored with his Dragon technology. Ultra pulse lasers are his weapon of choice, aren't they?"

"They are," Ari replies, "but ten of them were destroyed here in one night. Zazel knows who did that. Next time, he must come with more than just Dragons. He must come with every weapon at his disposal."

Davidov leans back in his chair and scratches his beard. "Overwhelming force. Total war," he murmurs.

We are interrupted by a shout from a sentry on the watchtower. We rush through the tunnel, up the ladder into the visitor center, and out to the courtyard. A drone circles overhead. A spy drone? Then why is it in plain sight? Lev raises a rifle to shoot it down. I put a hand out to lower his arm.

The drone drops a payload—a small square package. It lands in the courtyard near David's lyre with a dull thud. We brace ourselves for an explosion or some other unpleasant event. Nothing happens. The drone whizzes away.

"Stay where you are," I say and walk over to the package.

"Careful," Davidov says.

As I get closer, I can see what it is—a black cube, but not an I-Cube. It's bigger than normal and protected by a ballistic cage. I pick it up, carry it inside, and set it on the counter. The others gather around to stare at it.

"What is it?" says Ari.

"Could be a hornet," Davidov says. "A drone bomb."

We all step away instinctively.

"What do we do?" Ari asks.

I have no idea.

"We should get rid of it," Davidov says. He goes to pick up the Cube but jumps back as it begins to glow bright blue. Lev and Izik dive for cover, shouting.

"It's a holo," I say. "A... message."

The cube projects a stream of light that instantly widens to fill the space around us.

And there is Grace, standing before me.

Grace.

She's alive. Ari was right. She's alive! My joy is momentary. For then I see who is with her.

Zazel.

I clutch at my chest, feeling my heart constrict.

She's standing before him. Her hands are shackled. She looks haggard, exhausted, but defiant. She is as I remembered her—almost. The red hair, the green eyes. I want to touch her, hold her, even though she is only a projected image.

"Grace Fortune," Zazel says.

I recoil at the way it sounds coming from his mouth. Zazel is lounging in his hammock, his winged lion at his side, a smarmy smile on his face. I grit my teeth.

"What is this?" Davidov asks.

Then suddenly, *I* appear.

I gasp. We all gasp. I stare in horror as this person who looks like me thrusts my wife away so violently she seems to sail through the air before crashing. She doesn't get up. His words are as cruel as his actions. No hologram could have done that. Could it?

The camera homes in on her face. Pain, horror, unbearable suffering. She is broken, body and soul.

Guardians drag her away.

In the aftermath, the camera returns to Zazel, a lazy smile carving his face as he peers at me with his one golden eye.

"Did you enjoy that?" he whispers. "Oh, I hope so. But it doesn't have to be this way, my son. Come home. Come back to me. Claim your bride. I will send you a Dragonfly tomorrow. It will bring you back to me. To her. You can still save her. If you don't, she will die. What is worse, she will die knowing you have utterly deserted her. It will be the last thing she thinks of before her head falls from her neck and rolls on the ground. Maybe even after. They say the brain continues to function for a few minutes after the head is severed. She will continue to think of your betrayal until the bitter end."

The holo ends; the light winks out.

I slowly fold onto a nearby stool, my legs too weak to hold me anymore. Those around me step back as if afraid I might disintegrate before their eyes.

After a long silence, Ari speaks. "It's a lie. It's fake. He's bluffing."

"I don't think so," Davidov says, his voice grave. I look at him, questioning. "Some of the newer refugees have told us that the Grigori captured a rebel leader from the Free States. It could be her."

"But who was that who looked like you? It must be a trick," Ari says, shaking his head.

"She thought it was real," I murmur. The look on Grace's face was like a sword through my heart.

"But why would he do this?" says Davidov. "Why does he want you back so badly?"

"Probably to kill me. But I have to go," I say.

"No, you must not." Ari's voice is iron now. "You cannot give in to this, Jared. Let us assume, just for a moment, that what we just saw is real. Do you really think he will let her go? Let alone allow you to see her? You know he won't. You will both end up dead. Your mission is here now. You can't help her."

"She thinks I am that—horror. I betrayed her once before. If I do it again—" I can't finish.

"You can't stop that," Ari says. "If you go back, you will make all his lies come true. He will kill you both. We need you here. This is where the Lord told you to be, isn't it?"

"I have failed her too often," I murmur.

"She is in God's hands. Let Him deal with this as He will."

I get up and rush out of the center. I scramble up the steps to the watch tower and drop to my knees, my head in my hands, my jumbled thoughts a desperate prayer.

Lord, save her! Please! Let me leave here so I can go to her.

I hear no answer.

***

The next day, the Dragonfly appears.

It circles overhead before settling atop the Temple Mount, its strange, boomerang shape gleaming in the sun. Its presence makes my stomach turn and my heart race; my limbs feel as heavy as wood beams. Ari gathers some people around me to pray. I feel as though I've been pushed off a cliff, yet the prayers carry me, like a parachute, gently to the ground. I soak them in, my eyes remaining on the Dragonfly. My last hope of seeing Grace alive. Every minute, I want to climb the Pilgrim's Road to the Temple Mount and get on that machine to fly back to New Asgard, to my wife, my love, my death. It would be worth it.

I don't do it.

In the cold light of dawn on the third day, the Dragonfly is gone.

Chapter Thirty-Nine
Grace

"Ralph? Ralph? Are you there?"

No answer.

It's the third day in a row he hasn't responded, although "days" are tough to decipher anymore. The last time we spoke, Ralph had sounded so weak I could barely hear him.

I had told him about my encounter with Jared. He cried for me, though I was done crying.

"I had held out hope," he said. "After all we've been through together. He's been tested so often, and he never gave in. Why now?"

I had no answer for him. I have nothing at all. I still dream of him, though the dreams have turned dark and evil— he's holding me, kissing me, and then he starts tearing my flesh apart with his teeth. Jared is dead; I know that now. He died in the *There*. His shell is inhabited by some other entity, some creature from the deep dark. I am dead as well, dead inside. I'm just waiting for the official seal on my death, the execution. I pray it's soon.

The lights blare on. I blink, shielding my eyes until they can adjust. The slot in my door opens, and a tray of food appears. Grilled cheese. And something else: a black cloth. I pick it up, allowing it to unfold. It's a robe with a hood.

Sandy suddenly appears, wearing a long, white gown with pearls around her neck, her hair done up in a formal style. She smiles brightly.

"Good morning, Grace. Today is the day! The highlight of Grigoralia. Your execution! Please put on this robe. You want to be dressed right for the occasion. Also, don't forget to eat your breakfast! It's the most important meal of the day. You have twenty minutes."

At last!

"Where's Ralph?" I ask the avatar.

"Who is Ralph?" Sandy stares right through me.

"The prisoner in the next cell. Where is he?"

"There is no prisoner in the next cell. Is there anything else I can help you with?"

"There was a prison there. What happened to him?"

"There is no prisoner in the next cell. Goodbye."

She vanishes.

He's dead. I know it. Ralph is dead.

I never got to say goodbye.

I mouth a prayer of thanks to God for sparing Ralph this day.

I have a vision of Jared in the stands, watching me as my head is chopped off. Laughing, gloating, even. My worst nightmare. Can this really be happening? Nothing feels real anymore.

I put on the robe. It's too long for me, and the hood covers my head so completely I can't even see. Perhaps that's better. I ignore the grilled cheese.

It's probably drugged, which would make this ordeal easier, perhaps, but I choose to be clearheaded for once.

I wait, searching my memory for the happy times. The AngelSong forms on my lips, filling me with a strange, unexpected peace.

The door glides open; two Peacemakers enter. They bind my wrists and lead me out of the cell, down a long, dark corridor. A giant steel door opens automatically at the end. I squint, the sunlight almost painful, yet I lift my face to get as much of it as I can. It feels like it's been a century since I've felt the warmth of the sun on my skin.

Peacemakers rush about a high-walled courtyard, corralling other prisoners in black robes toward an egg-shaped vehicle with a glass dome. It looks something like a flying saucer from a sci-fi movie. The door slides open, and a ramp extends to the ground. I gasp. It *is* a flying saucer. It doesn't have wheels or wings. I guess it's some sort of hovercraft.

The Peacemakers shove us prisoners toward the ramp. The dome is pretty low, so most of us have to sit or kneel once we're inside. We're packed in like sardines. The prisoner next to me is a young man with jagged scar running diagonally across his face. He looks at me with empty eyes. I look away, notice a girl about my age with red hair. She holds her head high, as if she refuses to be afraid. I wish I could be like her.

The ramp retracts and the door closes. There's a noise like wind rushing through a tunnel, and the hovercraft rises into the air, wobbling slightly. It turns ninety degrees and then moves forward as the gates of the prison courtyard yawn open.

We pass down a few small streets until we come to a wide boulevard packed with people on both sides. We're part of the parade before the official opening of the games. I've seen these parades on the holo many times—the Grigori leaders riding their golden horses nearly as big as elephants with manes like lions and tails like scorpions. The champion of the arena, Jared, would be next, flying in his own personal Dragonfly. Then Shannon and Vale in their Dragonflies, followed by the rulers of the Council of Ten and assorted other dignitaries in fancy hovercrafts.

This time, there is a new addition. Hundreds of half-naked men riding Grigori horses, wearing golden armor molded to their muscular bodies and carrying long, crystal spears. Their white hair is done up in intricate looping braids, studded with metal spikes. They shout something in unison as they thrust their spears into the air, their horses prancing to the beat of their words.

They look a great deal like Jared.

I feel a lump in my throat. These are the new Nephilim.

The Grigori children have come of age.

The cheers for the Grigori kids turns to jeering when we pass by, with spectators throwing rocks and rotten fruit at the glass dome. The rocks bounce off the glass without so much as a crack. It must be very thick.

I pay no attention to the insults of the crowd. I'm beyond caring. The others don't seem to care either—we all stare dully into space, just wanting this to end.

Make me brave, Lord.

The hovercraft wobbles. I tip over, falling against the boy with the scar. Before I can recover, the hovercraft makes a wild left turn, and soon we are all tumbling into each other. Is this normal? Someone's knee jams in my ribs, then an elbow in my skull. I hear screams as we veer into the crowd on the side of the street. I slam against the side of the glass, a dozen people piled up against me. I can hardly breathe.

People on the ground scramble out of the way frantically as we burst through the barricades and careen down a narrow city street, dodging buildings and pedestrians. I hear the whine of Peacemaker drones behind us. Bullets ping off the glass dome.

"Get down!" I cry out with what breath I have.

I dive to the floor, with a bunch of bodies on top of me. Everyone is screaming. I can't scream—my lungs are being crushed.

A strange sort of calm comes over me. If this is how I will die, it's so much better than the guillotine. Whoever made the prisoner transport go loopy, I could kiss him.

Suddenly there is a mammoth crash. A storm of glass shatters around us. I'm buffered from the impact by all the bodies crushing me, though I still can't breathe, can't move.

Pain ratchets through my chest. I close my eyes, letting go of everything, even the need to breathe. This will all be over soon. *Thank you, Jesus.*

Somewhere in the dimness, the load on me lightens. Death, perhaps. I don't need to breathe anymore. Yet my lungs fill anyway, bringing fresh stabs of pain into my chest. When had breathing hurt so much? Stars spangle my vision.

Something grabs me under my arms, and I yelp with my newfound breath, though I still cannot see a thing; my robe is over my head. I feel myself being dragged, the pain so excruciating I can think of nothing else, not even that I might still be alive.

Sound explodes all around me—a cacophony of sirens and whistles and incomprehensible shouts. Life—the world—has come roaring back.

I'm not sure I'm happy about that.

Chapter Forty
Helel

The Peacemaker trembles as he tries to make excuses for the catastrophe.

"Someone took control of the prisoner transport—unprecedented. We are still looking for the culprit."

"You expect me to believe that?" I keep my voice low and level—it sounds more menacing that way. "A rebel slipped past all the Peacemaker patrols and hijacked a moving transport?"

Peacemakers don't often show fear. It is bio-engineered out of them. But even they cannot withstand this kind of pressure. I stare into the Peacemaker's eyes so intently I can almost see his brain begin to melt. But I stay seated behind the massive glass desk in the Glass Office of the tower.

It's well-named—everything is made of glass, including the walls and the floor. There's no other furniture, only columns of glass molded into the grotesque shapes of human suffering, contorted bodies in various stages of demise. Zazel's aesthetic, probably inspired by his time in the Abyss. He must have reveled in the ability to walk freely around this room, gazing disdainfully at the imprisoned humans. An ironic change of circumstance.

"It would not be possible for a rebel to impersonate a Peacemaker," says the man, shaking his head.

"Then one of your own is a traitor?"

"We are investigating—"

"Why didn't the sniper drones hunt them down?"

The captain struggles for words, his mouth working uselessly. Finally, he speaks.

"The drones were thrown off-course by some force... a shield of some sort. We have been trying to find the source of the anomaly. I will do my best to—"

"Never mind." I know the source of the anomaly. "Round up those prisoners, especially that Jehovian girl. They can't have got far. See to it."

"Yes, Lord."

"And I want all drone footage of the incident destroyed. Make sure none of this is leaked to the media or the HoloNet."

"Already done, Lord."

"And send all Peacemakers on duty today to the camps."

The captain hesitates. "My lord?"

"Normally, I would have them executed. But we need workers in the mines. They are dying at a rather alarming rate."

"But the Peacemakers—"

"Are NPs. They should last longer than the regular humans. You will go with them, of course. As punishment for your failure. See to it."

"I am to await orders from the Supreme Lord alone—"

"You can assume that my order comes directly from the Supreme Lord himself. Now get out of my sight."

The captain, trembling now, bows and exits.

"Guardian," I say, "send in Shavane."

A moment later, Shavane, Master of the Games, waltzes in, a tall, skeletal humanoid with a mop of red curly hair wearing a red skin-tight body suit and chunky high heels. It crosses the vast expanse of the Glass Office, swishing its hips, eyeing the writhing columns with appreciation, before coming to stand before me.

"Your... Eminence." Shavane curtsies clumsily, hands clasped together. No one in New Asgard knows quite what to call me. "May I just say that I am as devastated as you are by this unfortunate turn of events..."

I hold up a hand for quiet. "There will be no executions today." Shavane raises a painted eyebrow quizzically. "As a special gift to the people on the occasion of his birthday, Grigori Zazel, Supreme Lord of the United Earth, has declared amnesty for all political prisoners. Their sentences will be commuted to life in the camps. Make that announcement."

"Of course, Your Eminence. What a great god is our Supreme Lord. May he live forever. His compassion! His mercy! How he loves his people—"

"Get out," I say irritably.

Shavane puts a hand over its mouth, its manicured nails nearly three inches long, looking more like claws. Then it spins and sashays out of the room, winking at the Guardian by the door. The Guardian turns to me, awaiting direction.

"Bring the Supreme Lord's consort to me."

The Guardian hesitates only an instant before going out.

Shannon appears wearing a red gown that hugs her curves, her red hair flowing around her face the way that Shavane likes to imitate. She's come straight from the arena, for her face is flushed, and she looks rather annoyed at having been called away from watching her son perform. The Guardian who brought her stands erect near the door.

"Amon, what's happened? I heard there was a problem during the parade."

"Yes, there was. Someone hijacked the prisoner transport and crashed into a building. The prisoners have escaped."

"What? Grace! Is she—?"

"Unaccounted for."

The look of relief on her face tells me all I need to know, though it's gone quickly, replaced by indignation.

"Well, this is outrageous. Who is responsible?"

"Perhaps you should tell me."

She freezes, eyes wide, indignation turning to fear. "How would I know? I only just heard the news—"

"You deny that you conspired with the Jehovians to rescue your daughter, a rebel leader?"

Shannon steps back, aghast at the accusation. "Of course I deny it! Amon, I would never... You know I wouldn't."

"Yet you are not displeased that it happened."

"Well, I admit I did not want to see my daughter executed. But I could never condone such a thing as this. How could you even think I would?" She comes around the desk and kneels beside me, looking pleadingly into my eyes. "I would never betray you or Zazel. Never."

I gaze down at her and see she is telling the truth. At least, she believes it. But truth has never mattered to me.

I turn to the Guardian in the doorway. "Take her to the prison. Keep a guard on her."

Shannon wails in protest. "Amon! Look at me! I am innocent!" She grabs my arm, trying to force me to face her. I refuse. She continues to plead as the Guardian crosses the room in a flash and pulls her to her feet.

"You have betrayed us," I say evenly. "You know what the penalty is for treason?"

"No, please! Amon, I thought you loved me."

I hesitate only briefly. Did I love her? If I did, it was a sign of my own weakness, which I must rectify now. I am without love. I wanted to own her, to rule her. I was so close; she was putty in my hands. Or so I thought. But she betrayed me. For the love of her child. She could not cope with her regret. I remember another man, over two thousand years ago, who felt the same way. He couldn't live with himself. He chose death. Mysteria must do the same.

I return to the arena to see my creation, the new Baldyr, defeat all challengers to thunderous applause. All is well with the world.

Chapter Forty-One
Grace

"Grace?"

I blink, the amorphous blobs of light and dark slowly coming into focus. Big, brown eyes. Bree's eyes.

I'm dreaming. Bree can't really be here, wherever here is. I left her in New York, running for her life. I was arrested and sentenced to death.

The face looming above breaks into a happy smile. "Thank God you're awake."

"Am I?" I try to sit up and gasp. It feels as though sharp knives are embedded in my ribcage.

"Don't try to move," says the voice. "You've got some cracked ribs."

"What? How? What—?" Any more than one word at a time hurts too much.

Bree laughs. "You'll never believe it. You're on the *Lucille*. Speer's yacht."

I take a half breath and hold it. "Speer?"

"I know, right? It's crazy. I'll tell you all about it later. Right now, you just need to lie still. I'll get you something to eat. Anything you're craving?"

"No... grilled cheese..." I close my eyes.

***

I hobble into the living room of the yacht, Bree holding me steady. Breathing is a bit easier, though every step reverberates in my brain like a pinball machine, jarring my senses. Funny I should think of pinball machines. Speer used to keep his collection of them on this yacht. They're gone now. The rest of the room, which is swimming into focus, looks the same as I remembered: a huge, curved, sunken sofa, a teak bar, giant abstract fish paintings on the walls, a panorama of glass reflecting a sparkling sea. The sea—we must be in the middle of the ocean. I still think I'm dreaming.

Then I see Noah.

He looks nearly as bad as me with a swollen eye and cuts and bruises marring his sweet face. He's leaning on a crutch, one foot wrapped in bandages. I go to him and wrap my arms around him gingerly, tears suddenly gushing out of my eyeballs. He feels real.

"I thought I'd never see you again," I say between blubbering sobs.

"Me too."

He helps me to the sofa, which takes an inordinately long time. Every step radiates pain from my chest and out to my fingertips. By the time I actually sit, I can hardly breathe at all. I notice then that I'm wearing clean clothes: black yoga pants and a T-shirt. Someone dressed me.

Noah sits beside me. Bree sits on the opposite sofa next to Ethan, who smiles crookedly when I look at him.

"Hey, Grace," Ethan says, then winces as if speaking causes him pain, too.

"So... this is all real?" I ask when I can speak again. "We're on Speer's yacht? What happened?"

"What do you remember?" Bree asks.

"I remember being in some sort of crazy crash and suffocating under a mountain of bodies. And thinking I was about to die because I couldn't breathe."

Bree and Noah exchange looks. "I'm sorry about that," Noah says. "I had to crash the transport. Otherwise we had no chance of getting away—"

"You did that?" I stare at him. For one brief, golden instant, I had thought that Jared had come to save me. But no. "How did you do that?"

"It's a long story," Bree says.

What she tells me next is like something out of a spy movie. Once she and Ethan met up with Noah and told him what happened to me, Noah refused to leave New York without me.

"He wanted to sneak into someplace with computers and find out where you were being held," she says. "That's when Ethan showed us that he had a Cube."

I glare at Ethan, who shrugs, shamefaced. "I know. I was supposed to destroy it. I... I couldn't—"

"But it's a good thing he didn't," Bree cuts in quickly. "Because that's how we found out that they were taking you to New Asgard to be executed. The Grigori made a big deal about your capture."

"It's also how they found you in the first place," Noah says.

Ethan bows his head. "I'm sorry, Grace. They must have known about our relationship. They were tracking us the whole time. I didn't think—"

I don't reply, too stunned to be angry.

"We didn't know what to do, then Ethan thought of Speer," Bree says hurriedly. "He thought that if we could get to a ship radio, we could put out a call to him. So we snuck down to Liberty Harbor and searched some of the boats docked there. Most of them looked like they hadn't sailed in ages. But Ethan found one with a working radio and started calling the *Lucille*. It was a shot in the dark. A Hail Mary pass. But then... Speer actually answered." Bree grins. "Can you believe it? Turns out he had sailed to Newport for fuel, but they were out, so he just happened to be sailing into Brooklyn when we called."

"That's amazing," I say. "Where is Speer anyway?"

"Oh, he's on the bridge," Bree says, with a furtive glance at Ethan. "Anyway, the boat picked us up at Liberty Harbor, and we sailed for New Asgard. Right under those big Grigori noses."

On the way, they discussed various rescue plans and settled on hijacking the prisoner transport during the Grigoralia parade.

"I dressed as a street sweeper," Noah says. "There are a lot of those because of all the Grigori horses. No one looks at them. They might as well be invisible."

"Clever," I say, truly impressed. "And no one saw you jump into the transport?"

Noah shakes his head. "They were more interested in those... Grigori kids."

Ah yes, the Grigori kids. They would have attracted all the attention.

"He was supposed to drive straight to the marina," Bree says. "But that didn't go so well."

Noah shrugs. "There was no windshield on that thing. Just a tiny screen. I couldn't see where I was going."

"I couldn't tell," I say, stifling a laugh.

"I figured the only option was to crash into a building. Took me a while to find you. Not sure how we made it to the marina without getting shot."

"Some of the other prisoners followed him," Bree says. "They're here too. Seven of them."

Seven. There were about sixteen in the transport with me. What happened to the rest? *God, protect them, wherever they are.*

"Wow," I say. I can't think of anything else to say. Tears fill my eyes. Tears of gratitude. Tears of joy. Tears of sorrow for those who didn't make it.

I tell them about prison, about Sandy and the grilled cheese sandwiches, and about talking to Ralph and how he and Emilia were both gone. Bree starts to cry. Ethan puts his head in his hands.

"Ralph," Bree says, sniffing. "Emilia. I can't believe it."

And then I tell them about my encounter with Azazel and Jared. Bree's grief turns to spitting anger.

"Next time I see him, I'm going to… to… give him a piece of my mind," she blurts.

I almost laugh at the absurdity of that statement.

"Me too," I say. "If I ever get the chance." I wipe my cheeks. "Is it true? About the Rez? Was it destroyed? Have you heard anything from Penny and Mason? Ripley? Anybody?"

Bree and Ethan look at each other. Bree closes her eyes.

"The fires are still burning," Ethan says. "Eight million acres, the whole of the Black Hills."

"We haven't heard from them at all," Noah says quietly. "We've tried calling on Speer's shortwave. No answer."

I feel the blood drain from my face. The faces of the people around me warp and shiver, like reflections in a pool. I grip the leather of the couch I'm sitting on, just to feel something solid.

Why, God, did you allow this? Why didn't you protect them?

Lean not on your own understanding.

I sigh. "So, where are we going now? I need to speak to Darwin."

"He won't see you," Bree says. "None of us have actually seen him since we came onboard. He only talks to us through the intercom. Lucille won't let us on the bridge, which apparently he never leaves. It's been… a little weird."

"Why? What's wrong?"

Bree shrugs. "We don't know. But Lucille says he will take us wherever we want to go." She pauses. "Darwin suggested Bermuda. Apparently, it's his favorite place now. Not much Grigori activity. Lucille still has immunity, and Darwin is offically dead, but the Grigori might still try to come after us if they figure out what we did. We need to stay under the radar—"

"Israel," I say.

Bree blinks.

Ethan sighs. "I told you she'd say that."

***

"Impossible."

Lucille, Speer's girlfriend, is older and thinner than I remember but as stubborn as ever. She folds her arms and glares at me when we ask her about sailing to Israel. "We saved you, Grace. That is enough. We cannot risk a voyage through the Strait, under the noses of Peacemaker patrols, to take you to Israel, where, in case you haven't heard, the entire world is aiming their guns. The answer is no."

"Let me talk to Darwin," I say.

She hesitates. "Impossible."

"I hear you, Grace." The disembodied voice blares from the intercom on the wall. It doesn't sound at all like the Darwin Speer I knew. It's scratchy and off-pitch, but that could be just the effect of the tinny speakers.

"Darwin?" I say into the air. "Listen, you need to take us to Israel. I'm a Singer, and so is Noah. We are going to be needed there. This is it, Darwin. The final battle. I can't be floating around a boat out of harm's way when that happens. You need to take me there."

Long pause. Then there's a click, followed by a whining feedback noise. Finally, Darwin's reply.

"Roger that."

Chapter Forty-Two
Jared

The *pop, pop, pop* of rifle fire echoes off the distant hills as Lev and Izik conduct training exercises with their new recruits. All these teenage boys: Jews, Arab Christians, Armenians, Greeks. They've come from all over the wilderness, some seeking only refuge and water, others wanting to stand and fight. We have nearly a hundred here now.

They practice with rifles, slings, and bows and arrows. Not for the first time, I wonder what good it will do, remembering the fiery horror of the Dragon lasers. But Lev assures me that, if nothing else, we will be able to shoot down spy drones and protect our food stores from thieves.

"There're plenty of those roaming around the city now," he says. "It's like zombie town down there. Caught two of them just last night trying to get into the tunnel. Took care of them. Don't worry."

But I can't help worrying.

"Want to try it?" Lev holds out a rifle to me.

I shake my head.

"I figured. But I got something for you." He produces a short sword with a leather grip and ball-tipped hilt. "I found it in the rubble on our last scavenging mission. It's a replica of King David's sword. I thought you might like it."

I take the sword, smiling. "Thanks."

"Tell me. Did you really kill a Grigori with your bare hands?" Lev's eyes twinkle mischievously.

"I didn't kill him," I say.

"The people saw you fight him."

"I tried to fight him, but it wasn't me that killed him."

Lev shrugs and sighs. "Whatever you say." He glances at the young recruits. "Perhaps you could teach them some sword fighting when you have time?"

I try to imagine these children in hand-to-hand combat against the Grigori offspring. "What for? Swords will be no use against this enemy."

"It's good discipline. It will build their strength. Confidence. Help them to not give in to fear."

I consider this, glancing down at the sword in my hands. "Fine. Get some practice swords, and I'll come back tomorrow."

I go up to the radio shack on the observation deck to check on Ari, who is training two women to operate the equipment. One of them is Nasir's mother. She has barely looked at me since the incident at the temple and usually scurries away whenever I'm near. Now, she is so intent on Ari's instructions she doesn't even acknowledge my presence.

Ari excuses himself, then comes over to me.

"Have you been able to get through yet?" I ask.

He makes a noise of frustration. "Bah. There is a lot of interference today. It is Grigoralia. All our channels are jammed by Zazel's speeches and news of the games."

"The games... are today?" The blood drains from my face, pooling somewhere in the pit of my stomach. The executions. Maybe they've already happened. Maybe Grace is already...

"I'm sorry, Jared," Ari says softly.

I only just found out she was still alive, and now she is going to die for real. I see her in my mind's eye, her accusing gaze on me as she is dragged up the steps of the platform, forced to her knees, her head on the block. Could she see the imposter me sitting in the stands, watching, gloating? Then the blade... I shut my eyes, gasping for breath. I feel a hand on my shoulder—Ari attempting to console me.

"She will be with Yeshua soon," he says. "We should rejoice."

I wish I could. All I feel is shock and shame.

I return to my room in the attic, set down the sword, and pick up the guitar. I strum a few chords, the words of *Amazing Grace* floating in my mind. *Grace... Grace...* I keep playing, knowing it will take everything within me to get through this moment, this day, without breaking into a thousand pieces.

> *Amazing Grace, how sweet the sound*
> *that saved a wretch like me*
> *I once was lost but now am found.*
> *Was blind but now I see.*

I pray that her final thoughts are not of me.

Chapter Forty-Three
Grace

By some miracle, we make it through the Strait of Gibraltar. Either God made us invisible, or Lucille's immunity order has held up. Whatever the reason, we sailed through in the dead of night without a peep.

The yacht, on the other hand, has been a hive of activity. The *Lucille*'s passenger and crew cabins burst at the seams with me, Noah, Bree, Ethan, and seven other former prisoners in residence. Lucille is losing her mind. It sort of does my heart good.

I've met the other prisoners, some of whom are in worse shape than me. The boy with the scarred face actually says hello to me. His name is Luther. He and his brother Gunther were caught while trying to escape from a work camp in Germany. The girl with the red hair is here too, although I haven't spoken to her. I've tried to approach her a few times, but she always turns away.

"Have you talked to that girl from the transport?" I ask Noah one day while we're drying dishes in the kitchen. Neither one of us are well enough for chores, but Lucille still finds things for us to do. "I think she's French."

"Yes. Her name is Rachel. She was caught in Geneva, stealing supplies from a Peacemaker depot."

"Oh, good. I mean, I don't know why, but I get the feeling she doesn't like me."

Noah doesn't say anything. I look at him and know he's hiding something. "What aren't you telling me?"

He sighs. "She says... that she knew Jared."

I nearly drop the glass I'm drying. "What?"

"She lived in a cave with a bunch of others—a Forbidden hideout. In Switzerland. He turned up there—everyone thought he was a Shepherd. He claimed to have lost his memory."

"Oh my..." I'm shaking so badly I have to sit down. "Why didn't you tell me?"

"I'm sorry. I wanted you to forget him."

"Forget him? Noah, he's my husband!"

"He is one of them, now. It's better that you don't think any more about him."

I burst into tears. "How can you say that? How can you..." I can't finish.

"I'm sorry." Noah leaves the galley.

A few minutes later he returns. I look up to see Rachel is with him. Her eyes are very cold and hard. I dry my eyes and sit up straight as Noah directs her to sit at the table. He says something to her in French and she answers.

Noah translates, telling me how Jared, whom she calls Jean-Luc, showed up in the cave and one of the community elders came up with a plan to send him to the Peacemaker training facility in Geneva. He was supposed to infiltrate the Peacemakers and somehow get sent to New Asgard to assassinate Grigori Zazel.

"I knew it wouldn't work," Rachel tells Noah, who translates for me. "I knew he would turn on us. I was arrested right after we dropped him off in Geneva. Miriam—she's the one who found him and spoke up for him—she's dead. They killed her. They sent my friend Micah and me to different camps. Someone at the camp was from the cave— they had arrested everyone there too. Jean-Luc betrayed us all." Her voice breaks, though she fights back tears. She's not one to cry.

My tears have dried up as well. I am completely numb.

"They say you were his wife," Rachel says, speaking English for the first time. I look at her, surprised, then nod. She tilts up her chin. "Don't feel bad. We all fell for him. I did not trust him, but then… I could not resist him either. I am sorry for you." She gets up and leaves the room.

I look at Noah, who sits silent, focused on the table. "You were right," I say, sniffling loudly. "You shouldn't have told me. At least I would have been able to… hope. A little longer."

"Grace…" He comes over to me and takes me in his arms. I sob loudly, big ugly tears, soaking his shirt.

After a long time, I pull away and attempt a smile. My eyes feel puffy—I must look like a creature from the black lagoon.

"We should get back to work," I say, standing up. I wipe my nose on my sleeve.

Noah stands. "Why don't you go lie down, take a rest. I will finish."

"No. Better to keep busy."

"Grace—"

"I'll be fine. Really."

Even though I won't.

***

I can't sleep that night, so I go up on deck. The air is cold, biting my skin, but it feels good after all those weeks in a prison cell.

I try not to think about Jared, focusing instead on the churning water below and the stars above. All the things I thought I would never see again. I'd forgotten what the outside world looked and felt like—the way the stars wink on one by one as the sky darkens to night, the shriek of seabirds diving for food, the sudden silvery flash of a fish breaking the surface to catch an insect. These are truths I can cling to, rely upon, when everything else in my life spins out of control.

Lord, is there any way to reach him? To change him? Or he is gone forever?

My prayers are feeble. Even now, I can't let go.

"Hey, you." Bree is suddenly beside me. She leans on the rail, a blanket wrapped around her shoulders. "Didn't mean to scare you."

"Hey, you," I reply, smiling at her. "What are you doing up? You should be resting. You're running around all day, taking care of us invalids."

"Yeah, well, Ethan was snoring, and I… couldn't sleep for some reason."

I nod, understanding. "How is he? Really? He looks so… unwell."

Bree's lower lip trembles slightly. "He's not great. This whole… adventure… has been stressful. He was against it from the first. He only agreed to leave because I insisted. He would have stayed. Until he was dead."

"That just doesn't sound like the Ethan I knew."

"It's not, believe me. I've watched the change in him through the years. It got to the point where I felt like I didn't know him anymore. He's lost the will to live, I think."

"Oh, Bree… maybe things will turn around now that he's… away from all that."

"Yeah, at least we got out before the GEM program got into full swing. He was all set to get one of those. You know what a geek he is—always salivating over the latest gadget on the market. He thought the GEM was just the coolest idea ever."

"Seriously?"

"Oh yeah, to be able to just walk into a grocery store, take whatever you want, and walk out? Without stopping at the register? He got really mad when self-service registers became a thing in grocery stores." She laughs.

"Speaking of the GEM... do you know what happened to Judy? Wasn't she with you when you first met Noah?"

"Oh, yeah. With the aluminum foil hat? She's gone."

"Where did she go?"

Bree shrugs. "No idea. After the whole incident in New Asgard, she just disappeared."

I straighten, alarmed. "Why didn't anyone stop her? She could go to the authorities—"

"I don't think so. They would have come after us by now, right? Anyway, she claimed they would kill her if they found her. So maybe she escaped."

"She had the GEM," I say. "She couldn't escape that."

"True."

We are silent a moment, gazing at the water.

"What do we do when we get there?" Bree asks. "I mean, how are we going to get to Jerusalem?"

"No idea. We'll cross that bridge when we get to it."

Bree laughs. "You're so different."

"Am I?"

"You're so... calm. Like you're not afraid of anything."

Not true. I'm terrified. "Just better at hiding it maybe," I say.

She pauses, looking down at her hands. "Where did you go, Grace? I still don't get that. I talked to you on the phone, and you said you were coming home… then poof! Gone. Without a trace. Fifteen years. We thought you were dead. I cried for weeks. What happened?"

I tell her how Jared and I ended up in the *There*. The more I talk, the crazier I sound. Her eyes continually widen and then narrow at the end. She shakes her head.

"Fifteen years gone by in the span of a few hours? No wonder you still look so young. And when you came back, Jared wasn't with you?"

"I woke up at CERN, right where I'd left. Noah was with me. He's been with me ever since. I thought Jared was still dead, still in the *There*. But when I saw the video of him fighting in the arena, it didn't seem real. I thought he must be playing some game, that he had a plan. I guess I was wrong."

I tell her about Rachel and the cave. Fresh tears press against my eyes. I close them, turning my face back to the sea.

Bree sighs and puts her blanketed arm around my shoulder. "Wow. That's heavy. I really wanted to believe Jared hadn't changed, too. I wanted to believe a lot of things. That the Grigori were a force for good. That the world would be a more peaceful and happy place." She bends over, both elbows on the rail, and leans her chin in her hands. "I hope you don't hate Ethan for what he did—getting you caught. He just couldn't let go."

I smile. "Yeah, I was mad about that. And yet, if he hadn't done that, I wouldn't have found Ralph again. So maybe… I don't know. God does work in mysterious ways, doesn't He?"

We both laugh. She threads her arm through mine, pressing close to me. "Noah… is nice." Her tone has changed to flirty and silly, the old Bree.

I laugh out loud. "He is."

"He's perfect for you, Grace. Sweet, capable, strong… he'd make a good husband."

"He would."

"He likes you. Maybe even loves you."

"I know. I love him too. He's saved my life more than once."

"But…"

"But… I'm married. To Jared."

"Jared." She makes a noise of disgust. "There is no more Jared. There's only Baldyr now."

"I know."

"I mean, he looked right at you and pushed you away. What more proof do you need that he's completely… gone?"

I shrug.

"And Noah is here."

She's right. There's no point in hoping anymore. I should forget Jared. Forget he ever existed.

Is that what you want me to do, Lord?

I wait to hear the answer.

All I hear is wind and sea.

Chapter Forty-Four
Grace

All of us gather on the deck of the *Lucille* as it docks in the Ashkelon Marina. From a distance, the marina looked clean and beautiful, a collection of tall hotels and a mall complex of white stone set against the bluest sea and sky. But up close, the picture is quite different. The few boats docked are rusted hulks, many listing badly.

The pier looks equally abandoned. Nothing moves but rolling bits of trash, and most of the windows of the buildings are broken or boarded up. A sandy beach, probably a popular tourist destination once, now looks more like a garbage dump.

"Seems deserted," says Ethan.

"The Grigori killed the boating industry," says Lucille, who has joined us on the deck, probably to make sure we all get off her boat. "Like they killed everything else. 'Degrowth,' they called it. It's all about reducing the use of the world's resources in order to make everyone live more meaningful lives or something. Those that manage to survive anyway."

It's the most I've heard her say since I arrived on the yacht two weeks ago.

"I don't see any cars parked anywhere," Bree says. "Looks like we might be walking to Jerusalem. How far is it?"

"Forty miles," says Ethan, coughing slightly.

"Not too bad," I say. A year ago, it would have seemed like a thousand to me.

"Most of these people can't walk that far," says Noah. "Including him." He points to Ethan.

"There's got to be a car or truck somewhere around here," I say. "Or bicycles or *something*."

Noah and Luther tie down the yacht once it's docked. Once the gangway is in place, I turn to Lucille. "Thank you for the clothes and for... everything," I say.

She harrumphs. "It's going to take me a month to clean this boat after you all leave. Well, it's something to do anyway." She looks at me. "Good luck. I hope... your God takes care of you."

"He's your God too, you know," I say. "It's not too late, Lucille."

She folds her arms and looks away. "Get going," she says.

We file off the yacht and walk up the long pier to a large metal gate. Noah and Luther easily push it aside so we can get to the quay. We head toward the double glass doors of the mall entrance when suddenly they burst open, and three people jump out, brandishing rifles. They rush toward us, shouting in Hebrew with their guns pointed at us.

"We're American!" I yell, even though many of us aren't. "English!"

"On the ground!" shouts one attacker in English, presumably the leader. He's wearing a beret and a black army jacket. The other two—a younger man and a woman—also wear army jackets, though the woman wears striped leggings, and the man is wearing shorts.

"Lie down! Hands behind your heads!"

We do as ordered.

"Look, we're on your side," I say, sticking my head up.

Beret Guy points his rifle in my face. "Down!"

I put my head back down, heart thumping. I glance over at Noah, whose eyes tell me, *Do what they say, Grace.*

They swarm over us, patting us down. I can hear Rachel grumbling in French, not the least bit scared.

"You come on a big boat," Beret Guy says, looming over me. "You are UE. Why do you come here?"

"We're not UE," I say, raising my head to address him. "You can talk to the woman who owns the boat, Lucille, she has full immunity—"

I'm interrupted by Leggings shouting in Hebrew. Beret Guy responds. They seem to be trying to decide what to do with us. Finally, Beret Guy speaks.

"Go back to your boat and sail away. You will not stay in Ashkelon."

"We don't want to stay here! We want to go to Jerusalem." I rise to my knees, ignoring the guns pointed at me. "Please, we aren't UE, we're Forbidden. Jehovians! I'm Grace Fortune—you might know me as M."

"M? M is in prison."

"I was rescued! These people here rescued me."

Shorts says something, then Leggings snaps at him and two start to argue. Beret Guys barks at them and they both go quiet. Then he turns back to me.

"You must leave. Back on your boat. Go away from here."

The three of them force us up and start corralling us back toward the gate, ignoring our pleas. Leggings shoots her rifle in the air as an incentive. Bree shrieks.

"What's going on here?"

The voice brings us all to a dead stop. Darwin Speer stands at the gate entrance, hands on hips, legs splayed.

I gape at him, finally understanding why he didn't appear to us in person. He's a foot taller than he was, his once gangly frame now broad and muscular, hunchbacked. His arms are long, ending in hands that look more like claws. Six fingers on each. His nearly bald skull is elongated and sloping, absorbing his once prominent ears. His skin, what's showing, is scaly and greenish with an iridescent sheen. Only his face is unchanged by this transformation, an all-too-human face on the body of a hulking monster.

"What are you doing to my friends?" His voice sounds just like it did on the intercom, raspy and off-key. Beret Guy, despite his apparent shock and awe at the sight of this lizard man standing before him, raises his rifle. Quick as lightning, Speer moves to him, flicks the rifle away, and grabs him by the neck, lifting him into the air. Beret Guy gasps soundlessly, his feet dangling, arms wheeling.

"Put him down!" Leggings shouts in English as she levels her rifle at Speer.

"Jezzie, no!" says Shorts. But she ignores him and shoots—three loud pops. Bree and I both scream and drop to the ground.

"Speer!" I shout.

Blood trickles from Speer's massive chest. But he hasn't moved an inch, still holding Beret Guy by the neck. He looks at Leggings and says calmly, "Put that down."

The woman seems to shake all over. Shorts has already dropped his rifle and thrust his hands in the air. She moves more slowly, setting her rifle down on the ground.

"Step away," says Speer. The two of them obey. Then Speer sets Beret Guy gently on the deck. He scrambles away to join his friends. The three of them huddle together, staring at Speer with mouths agape. Their expressions are much like our own. Who is this creature? *What* is he? His wounds have already stopped bleeding.

"Okay, here's what's going to happen now," Speer says. "You are going to take my friends to Jerusalem. You got vehicles?"

Beret Guy nods mutely.

"Good."

"But... we have no fuel..." Beret Guy's voice is a hoarse whisper.

"Oh, I'll give you the fuel," says Speer. "As long as you promise to take good care of my friends and get them to Jerusalem safely. You got that?"

Beret Guy glances at his comrades, and all three of them nod.

"Good. You three go on board. My associate will get you what you need."

The three move as one, scrambling up the ramp and into the yacht.

I get up and move to Speer. "Thank you," I say, my voice all choked up.

He looks down at me with a sheepish grin. "No problem, Grace." He pauses. "So... what do you think of my new look?"

"It's... well... definitely new."

"Yes, I think it will be all the rage soon, don't you?" He shakes his head. "It started after I came back from... that other place. What I get for trying to become a god, isn't it?"

I don't answer. I throw my arms around him. He stiffens, shocked I would even touch him. When I let go, I see his eyes are wet.

"Better go now," he says. Then he turns to the others. "Boys, get the guns. Wouldn't want to have any accidents now, would we?"

Noah and Luther quickly pick up the rifles. Everyone avoids looking at Speer.

"Go on with you," Speer says to me.

"Darwin, I..."

"Don't worry about me. I'm just... glad I could do something good. Not sure how much longer..." He pauses, unable to continue.

"I'm sorry."

"Yeah, me too. Take care of yourself, Grace."

I watch as he walks away, back to his yacht. My chest feels tight all over again.

Lord, is he beyond saving too? Is there no hope?

I'm not sure I want to know the answer.

***

The Ashkelon Three, as we come to call them, claim to be ex-IDF—deserters. Beret Guy calls himself Captain Kopel—not sure if that's a real name or not. Leggings' name is Jezzie, and the younger guy, scraggly looking with bad teeth, goes by the name Buck. When I tell him that doesn't sound like an Israeli name, he tells me he got it because he loves Buck Rogers.

"Buck Rogers is the best," he says. Jezzie snickers at that.

"Who is Buck Rogers?" I ask.

Buck looks at me like I am an idiot. "You don't know? Buck Rogers is an American pilot who gets into an accident and is in suspended animation for five hundred years. When he wakes up, the world has been taken over by an evil overlord, Killer Kane, so Buck joins the resistance to fight him in the Hidden City."

"Wow, sounds sort of familiar," Bree says.

Once they get the gas cans from Speer, the Three lead us to a parking lot behind a warehouse where two rusty Jeeps sit in the sun. Kopel fills the tanks and we all climb in for the drive to Jerusalem.

It's a rough ride, as Dragon attacks severely damaged the roads. Noah and I ride with Jezzie, who seems to think she's competing for the Winston Cup. Six of us hold onto the roll bars and pray as she careens around obstacles and gigantic craters. I'm practically on top of Noah, one arm around his neck, the other braced against the front seat. Being so close to him awakens feelings I don't want awakened. I'm grateful for the constant jostling and bumping, which keeps me from getting too comfortable.

"How are you doing?" he asks.

"Good, all things considered," I say with a chuckle. "You?"

"Good, all things considered," he echoes. "Quite a… ride."

"Yeah."

We're quiet for a while.

"Grace…"

"Yes?"

"Speer… what happened to him? Was that because of the *There*?"

I sigh. "Speer was the one who first took Jared's blood to create the Cure. He used it on himself. He had a genetic disease—Huntington's—and the treatment cured him. It made him strong and immune to any disease, but it also changed him in other ways, too."

"Like the original Cure," Noah says.

"Right. He had to have constant infusions. So he kidnapped Jared to steal more of his blood, nearly bled him to death."

"He did that? Yet you are now… friends?"

I hadn't thought of Speer as a friend until this moment. I almost laugh. "Crazy, right?"

"Will that happen to the NPs?" Noah asks. "Will they end up… like him?"

"If they live long enough," I say. "But they usually don't. Anyway, the NPs were only a stopgap measure, I think. Until the Grigori's own children, the natural-born Nephilim, could grow up."

"You think the Grigori will use them as weapons?"

"They did it once before, didn't they?"

Noah doesn't answer.

***

It's fully dark when the journey ends abruptly.

"This is as far as I can go," Kopeck says. "You have to walk from here."

"Where are we?" I ask as we spill out of the Jeep and unfold our cramped legs. The road ahead is blocked by piles of abandoned vehicles. There are no lights except a few flickers on a distant ridge.

"Silwan," Kopeck says. "The City of David is up this hill. That is where the survivors are hiding. Awaiting the end of the world." He chuckles derisively.

"The Hidden City," says Buck in awe.

"Go," says Kopeck. "Follow the road. You will find it."

"You aren't coming with us?" I ask.

Kopeck shakes his head. "They are crazy up there. Waiting to die."

"We stay on our own," says Jezzie.

"I want to go!" says Buck.

"You have to show us," I say. "You promised. We've never been here before. Besides, where are you going to go? Back to Ashkelon? What is there for you? You think you will be spared what's coming? You'd be better off taking your chances with these people here."

"Yes, Captain!" says Buck eagerly. "Come on. We should go. Better to be with others. We are soldiers. We could help!"

"We're deserters!" Kopeck says angrily, pushing Buck in the shoulder. "If there's brass here, what do you think they will do to us?"

"I'll speak for you," I say. "I'll tell them you helped us. Besides, at this point, I don't think anyone cares."

"Captain," says Jezzie in a low voice. "Don't."

Kopek hesitates, looking from Buck to Jezzie. Then he sighs and waves a weary hand to us. "We will take you. Only if you give us food."

I nod. "Deal."

"Come on, then."

We follow the Three up the road, picking our way over piles of broken cars and trash, stumbling in the dark. I hold onto Noah's arm for support, thankful he is there, as always. Noah also lends a hand to Ethan, with Bree on his other side. Ethan's breathing is so labored, I'm afraid he won't make it.

We turn off the road and pass the remains of a brick building, some sort of tower, then climb over a low stone wall. A flickering light illuminates a long series of steps into what seems to be a pool of water.

"What is that?" Bree asks, walking toward the water.

"The Pool of Siloam," Kopeck says. "Come, this way..."

"Let's wait a second, catch our breath," Bree says, leading Ethan toward the pool. She sits with him at the edge. "Just a minute."

Kopeck makes a huffy breath. I go to sit beside Bree.

I hear a noise and look out over the water. Something is floating in the shadows... a log? Or is it a person?

"What is that?" I ask.

Kopek comes to the edge of the pool and shines his flashlight at the floating figure. My heart slows. I stare at the figure, so very familiar, etched in my memory. It can't be. And yet... I blink several times, thinking he will disappear. But he doesn't. He's still there.

Oh Lord, let it be so...

I call his name.

Chapter Forty-Five
Jared

I float in the pool, sloughing off the remains of the day. So many problems—toilets backing up, generators breaking down, food dwindling, constant complaints. This is the only chance I get for peace, these late-night swims. The water is cold, but I don't mind.

I try to relax, yet my brain will not stop. When will the next attack come? Will it be Dragons? Soldiers? Nuclear bombs? How can I keep people strong, keep them from running away in fear? We have fourteen slingers and twenty riflemen. Will anything we do have any effect at all?

I think of the Maccabees, and David, in his early days. One stone killed a giant.

Such thoughts keep Grace from my mind, at least. Though she, too, is ever-present, the leaden weight of guilt in the pit of my stomach, the aching loss, the killing grief. She is dead, but what is worse, she died believing I no longer loved her. Can there be anything more monstrous than this?

When I was a child, my father tried to kill me. He knew I was a monster. I would destroy everyone who dared to love me. That was my fate.

Somewhere, dimly, I hear the trundle of feet on the stones. I don't open my eyes. Voices murmur. A light suddenly shines on me.

Someone says my name.

I right myself and gaze up at the group gathered on the steps. All I see are silhouettes.

"Who's there?"

Suddenly, one of them rushes down the steps and splashes into the water. I see an outline, a face, the shock of red hair caught in a beam of a flashlight. I gasp, my breath gone completely, my eyes now my enemy, for they must be telling me lies. This cannot be real. This is the cruelest of dreams.

She throws herself at me, arms locked around my neck, so we topple backward into the water with a great splash. Water plunges up my nose and down my throat. Her legs wrap around me so tight I no longer know where I end and she begins. And that is the way it should always be.

"Jared," she whispers over and over as we gurgle and cough, choking on water. "Jared. I knew it."

Knew what? What did you know? Her mouth covers mine, so I cannot ask.

Chapter Forty-Six
Michael

The Seven gather on the holy mountain. Gabriel addresses us, the Guardian of the Cherubim, the Messenger of Elohim.

"Elohim has brought his children to Zion," he says in a voice clearer and purer than any earthly trumpet call. "The enemy has begun deployment to the Beautiful Land. Our time draws near."

"Finally," growls Uriel, glowing red with fiery exultation.

"Gather your forces," I say. "We have not only the humans and the Grigori to contend with, but their children as well."

"What is it they call themselves? Light Bringers? We will bring them some Light," says Saraqâêl. He is more shadow than Light, for he is the destroyer, the angel of death. He killed the firstborns and struck the Israelite camps with plague until seventy-thousand died.

"They look like children, but they are not," I say. "And they are led by the False Son. The Unholy One has united the princes of Persia, Syria, and Arabia to attack them."

"And we will let it happen?" Raphael's Light is softer, paler than the others. He loves humanity and hates to see them suffer. "We must intervene—"

"We wait for orders," I say.

"We will pray for the Forsaken One and the Singer," Gabriel says. "Pray that they will stand."

"You have such faith in these humans?" Raquel scoffs. His Light is burnished bronze—he craves vengeance. "They have failed us before."

"Remember the golden calf," rumbles Saraqâêl.

How I do remember that dark day.

"Remember the spies," says Remiel, whose golden Light is brighter than any heavenly star. "Their cowardice. Their lack of faith. Do you think this remnant will act any differently? Once the fear touches them, they will break and run, as they always do."

I say nothing for a moment, wondering. Yes, the fear. It is always the fear that makes these humans turn from the only One who can truly save them. Such irony in that.

"Not all failed," I say. "Think of Daniel. Think of Joshua. Both knew fear but stayed strong."

"What about David?" Raquel counters. "The one after His own heart. He was the worst of all."

"They will not fail," I repeat stoically as if I am convincing myself.

Gabriel turns to me. "So, *now* you have faith in these frail humans?" There is subtle humor in his tone.

My Light flares. "I have faith in Elohim, who chose them for this task."

"As you say," Gabriel replies. "Pray for these children, then. Our power depends upon their obedience. Let us begin."

***

Jared paces the catwalks, trying to walk off his worry. Sometimes, he stops to pray—fragmented prayers, as if he doesn't know quite what to pray for. Direction is what he needs. Assurance. I can give him that, at least. I reach out to him and allow my Light to fall upon him like a warm blanket, settling upon his shoulders. He breathes deep, closing his eyes, his head dropping back as if taking it in. A smile traces his face.

Do you not know, Human, that the One who gave you back your wife is capable of so much more? Of everything?

He feels yet unworthy. He carries his shame still. How is it Elohim always chooses humans like these? Broken by failure? Bowed by trouble?

Jared.

I whisper to him. He looks up. He hears.

You are not alone.

That is all he needs to know.

Chapter Forty-Seven
Grace

My first thought when I wake up is always that moment when I saw him floating in the pool, looking like an apparition in the dim moonlight, a ghost about to disappear. And then I said his name, and he came to life, rising from the water—and it was *him*. I forgot everything then and charged down the steps, plunging into the water, tackling him, practically drowning the both of us. Drowning in joy.

My second thought is always: Noah.

And so my joy is edged with guilt. There's a wrongness to my happiness. Unavoidable, I suppose.

It's been two weeks, and we still haven't talked about him. Avoiding the unavoidable. I keep that subject in the dark corner of my consciousness, papering it over with busyness, the new struggles of living in an abandoned city, wondering what we will eat today, what we will wear, how much longer our supplies will last... and when the battle will begin. Things that seem so much more important than him and me and... the other him.

Jared is gone when I awaken. It's still dark outside, judging from the myriad stars outside the window of our tiny loft. This isn't unusual. He's having trouble sleeping. In the old days, when he was still part angel, he rarely slept. Now he's human, but sleep is still elusive. For different reasons.

I get up and press my face to the window. We live in the attic of a small house that sits on the edge of the ruins of the City of David, near the top of the hill. I have to remind myself that I'm really here in Jerusalem. My first glimpses of the city filled me with sadness—so much desolation from the Dragon attacks, so many people dead or fled. Yet still survivors come, most because they are thirsty and there's no more water to be found anywhere else. We give them water and tell them about the Living Water of Jesus. Some seem interested. Others not so much.

"Hey."

I spin around at the sound of his voice. He's standing in the doorway, a flashlight in one hand, a sword in the other. His body curves like an *S* as if struggling to stay upright. Weariness was something I never saw in him before. Now, it's all I see.

"Hey. What's up?"

"Not much." He sets down the flashlight and sword and stretches out on the piles of blankets on the floor that serve as our bed. There's not much else in the room. A couple of crates that hold spare clothes we've scavenged. Trousers and a few sweaters. A couple of boxes of stale matzo, our main source of food. Two jars of water.

This is our first home together, such as it is. Since Jared was released from his curse, we can be together, finally, as husband and wife. No barriers. No fear. I thought this might scare me more than the curse did. Yet even in this forlorn place, with the whole world crashing around us, it's been... heaven.

I snuggle next to him, needing his warmth. While the days have been cool and mostly dry, the nights are freezing.

"What are you thinking about?" I ask.

"Nothing. Everything."

We've spent much of the last two weeks just talking. He told me everything that had happened to him since waking up in that cave. He was horrified to learn that the cave people had been arrested and Miriam killed. He felt responsible for that, even though he never told the Peacemakers about them.

"Maybe they could read my mind—who knows what they can do."

When he told me that Azazel had sent him the holo of my meeting with the fake Baldyr, it was my turn to be horrified.

"All this time," he said, "I thought you were dead, and it was my fault."

"He was real, that much I know," I told him. "Not a hologram. But who was he? How'd they make a clone of you?"

"I've thought a lot about that," he replied. "I think it must have been Vale."

"Vale? That kid? But he didn't look anything like you."

"No, but they could have changed him. Maybe they can do that."

His reunion with Rachel didn't go so well—she still blamed him for what happened to Miriam and the cave dwellers. She calmed down a little after he explained what happened, but she still believes that he did something to give them away. She refused to speak to either of us since.

I told Jared about Ralph and Emilia. He said he had "glimpses" of them, especially of Ralph as a little boy. It frustrated him that he could not remember more. I thought perhaps it was a blessing. To experience the full weight of losing them was probably more than he could bear now. It was hard enough for me, with the sickening pain of not knowing what happened to Penny and Mason and everyone else at the Rez.

All of this on top of this nagging guilt. I need to get it off my chest.

"Jared, we need to talk."

"About Noah."

He says it so quickly I know it's been on his mind as much as mine. He raises his head to look at me, apprehension clouding his blue eyes.

"He... loves you." The words come hard for him. "He brought you back to me. For that, I owe him everything."

I nod, tears springing to my eyes. "That's true. But I've always been honest with him about where he and I stand."

"But not how you feel."

Heat rises into my face. I turn over so he can't see. "My feelings are all mixed up. For the longest time, I thought you were lost to me. And he was... there. So it might take a little time for me to sort all that out."

He lets out a long breath. "Okay."

He's silent after that. I feel the space between us like a great chasm, unbridgeable. And then his warmth returns. His arms close around me, arms that have grown so strong from gladiator training and whatever else they did to him in New Asgard. I let go of the breath I had been holding and melt against him, letting the tears flow unchecked.

"Do you think this is really it?" I ask. "I mean, are we going to die here?"

He whispers into my hair. "Probably."

"But when Jesus returns, we will be alive again?"

"That's the plan."

"Why is that so hard for me to imagine?"

"Maybe because it's never happened before."

I chuckle to myself. "When I was in that prison, I tried to picture what it would be like, that moment right before the end, you know? When I heard the blade come down. I wondered if I'd panic or I'd be calm and like... at peace. Brave. If I'd see Jesus, and he'd take my hand and whisk me off to heaven. Is that what happens? I mean, how many times have we almost died?

And you *did* die. I held your dead body in my arms. Yet… here we are. This should be easy for me to believe. Right?"

"After all we've been through… yes, it should be easy. I wonder why it isn't."

Silence.

"What if we're wrong?" I whisper.

"About what?"

"What's going to happen next. Maybe this isn't what we think it is…"

"Now who's overthinking?"

He turns me over to face him and kisses me, pulling me underneath him. I wrap my arms around him, clinging to him, pressing in tightly so there is no space between us. This is how it will be, in the end. At least we will be together. We will never be separated again.

***

Ari and Bree sit at the large picnic table in the visitor's center courtyard before a big bowl of scrambled eggs.

"Eggs?" I remark in surprise as Jared and I join them.

"Nasir brought me some chickens," Bree announces cheerfully, scooping eggs onto plates for us. "Who knows where he found them. But we've got eggs now. I just added a bunch of spices, whatever I could find, to liven them up." Bree's taken over much of the cooking duties and organized the daily food distribution, something that was sorely needed from the look of things. She also managed to fix Jared's disastrous haircut. She's a wonder.

I take a bite and nearly choke. "How much spice exactly?" I manage to say.

Ari chuckles. "Tastes almost like the shakshuka my mother used to make."

I'm glad there's no shortage of water. I pour a glass and take a big gulp.

"Where's Ethan?" I ask when I can speak again.

"Still in bed." Bree's tone is more subdued now.

"Is there nothing we can do for him?" I ask.

She shrugs. "One of the women here, Rebecca, used to be a nurse. She said it was probably congestive heart failure. She gave him some water pills the boys scavenged from a pharmacy in the city that may help with the fluid buildup, but otherwise…" her voice trails off.

"God will protect him," says Ari, patting her hand.

I'm still amazed that Ari is here at all. It makes me more and more certain that the other Singers from the *There* are still out there. And that we need to find them.

"And news from Josephine? Or the Rez?" I ask Ari.

"Josephine has been talking, a lot," says Ari. "Camp Zero is full to busting, she says. We've heard from other stations as well. But… still nothing from the Rez." He shakes his head. "There might still be survivors there. You never know. You must have hope, Grace."

"Hope." Lev sits down at the far end of the table. Bree serves him a plate of eggs. "We'll be next. You can be certain. Shot down another spy drone yesterday. The enemy knows we're here. They could come at any time. We're sitting frogs."

"Ducks," Bree says.

"We need more weapons," says Lev. "Something more than rifles and slings."

"We have another weapon," I murmur.

Lev looks at me. "What would that be?"

I take a breath, steadying myself for Lev's predictable reaction to what I am about to say.

"Do you know the story of Jehoshaphat?" I ask.

"Of course," says Lev.

"I could use a refresher," says Bree.

"He was the King of Judah, and he was about to be attacked by a whole bunch of nations. A big alliance. Sound familiar? He knew he couldn't handle it. So he prayed. A lot. And God told him through a prophet that he wouldn't have to fight at all, that God would fight the battle for him. So Jehoshaphat sent out his armies with his choir of singers leading the way, singing praises to God. And then all those allied nations started fighting each other and wiped each other out."

"Wow," says Bree. "Did that really happen?"

"Yeah. When the people looked out at the huge army, all they saw were dead bodies."

"Awesome," says Bree.

"So you want us to... sing?" Lev's tone is all mockery.

"Yes," I say. "We sing."

Lev opens his mouth, then shakes his head. "Foolishness," he mutters.

"I know you may not believe me, but music has a certain power in the spirit world. The *right* sort of music. And one Song in particular. It's an AngelSong. Not everyone can sing it, but some of us can. I can. So can Ari."

Lev turns his incredulous stare on Ari, who smiles sheepishly.

"It was as much a surprise to me as it is to you."

"Noah is also one," I say. "A Singer. There are others too. We need to find them. I believe that God might be raising up more Singers. There could be some here right now. If we can get the message out through the radio..."

"Yes, of course," says Ari. "I should have thought of that myself. The Singers! I'm sure that Veer and Zavier and the others are still out there—perhaps they will be listening! Write the message, and we will send it at once. All night long. But we must all pray that there will be no interference on the airwaves."

"I'll set up a prayer chain," says Bree. "We will have people pray around the clock."

"Good, good," says Ari.

"Veer and Zavier?" says Lev, looking at me sideways. "Who are these people?"

"Ari and I know them," I say, wondering how much I should tell him. "Veer is in India, Zavier is in Brazil. And there's Kato and Finn... and Josephine—"

"You do not really believe that singing is going to fight this enemy," Lev says, interrupting me.

"I do." I stare at him levelly. "Do you believe in miracles, Lev?"

He opens his mouth, but nothing comes out.

"You either do or you don't," I say. "If you believe in God, the God of the Bible, then you have to believe that He can do anything. He can do the impossible. Right?"

Ari leans toward Lev. "You know the story of how shouting and trumpets took down the walls of Jericho?" he asks softly.

"It's a story," says Lev.

"It's more than a story, my friend," Ari says. "It's God's truth."

"I saw the stones of the Golden Gate disappear before my eyes," says Jared. "I saw a barren fig tree suddenly overflow with figs."

Lev looks at Jared then down at his plate.

"We will do our part in this," I say. "Leave the rest to Him."

Lev clears his throat. "So, you have some sort of plan to bring all these Singers here?"

"No, I don't think they have to be here physically," I say. "But I think we need to be connected. Like we were before. It was the connection that made all the difference. Right?" I look to Ari, who nods again with a wry glance at Jared.

"So it did," he says.

Jared listens, a puzzled look on his face. He doesn't remember what happened in the *There* because he was technically dead at the time, though I have told him how the Singers broke Samyaza's hold on me, destroyed his temple, and released him from the control of Moloch.

"The power of the Song is magnified by the number of Singers," I say. "Just like prayer. Because it *is* prayer. A special kind."

"What about the rest of us? Can we sing too?" Bree asks.

"Yes, of course. In fact, worship is going to be the main thing we do now. Just like Jehoshaphat." I turn to Jared. "We will need more instruments. A keyboard, drums, maybe even trumpets. We need to form a band."

"Is *Forlorn* back together?" Bree asks giddily.

I laugh. "Maybe."

***

I find Noah at the pool, sitting on a step with his feet in the water, gazing at the surface as if studying his own reflection.

"Missed you at breakfast," I say, plopping beside him on the step. The more I try to act like everything's the same as before, the worse it feels. "We had eggs."

His head pops up, startled. "Hey. Sorry, I ate early. Had things to do."

"What things?"

"Nasir gave me a sling lesson."

"Oh, how did that go?"

"Terrible. I think you have to be born holding a sling to do it right."

"Stick with rifles."

"Yeah."

After an awkward silence, I start again. "Well, we talked at breakfast about using the Singers, getting them together, you know? Like we did in the *There*—"

"Grace."

I pause, looking at him. "What?"

"I'm leaving."

"What?" My heart does a flip-flop. "What do you mean? Where are you going?"

"Petra. Davidov sent a message with the supply truck. The population there is exploding. They need more drivers and foragers. He asked for volunteers."

"And you want to go? Really?"

He sighs. "It's better this way. For both of us."

I shake my head. "You've been at my side every moment since the *There*," I whisper, my voice breaking.

"But now, you're here. With him. You don't need me anymore."

"That's not true." Tears blur my vision. "I still need you."

He looks at me and smiles. "No, you don't." He reaches up to brush a tear off my cheek.

I throw my arms around him, holding him tight as if this alone can keep him with me. Yes, I *do* want them both. Jared and Noah, whom I love in different but equally vital ways. I'm selfish and stupid and hopeless. And I don't even care.

His hands clasp over my wrists. He pushes me away from him and presses my hands together between us, a barrier, a line no longer to be crossed. He smiles into my eyes, his eyes glistening. He doesn't say the words, but I hear them anyway. *I love you.*

"When?" I whisper.

"This afternoon. I'll go with the supply truck."

Today? He's known probably for days, yet he waited until the last minute to tell me this. My sorrow dissolves into anger, which quickly evaporates.

"You can't go," I say urgently. "I need you here. You're a Singer, Noah. I'm gathering the Singers. If you go—"

"They'll need Singers in Petra," he says, interrupting. "Have you thought of that?"

His words stop me cold. What can I say to that? He's right. Of course, he is.

"Then you need to find more Singers there," I say. "Teach them to sing."

"I will. I promise." He drops my hands gently and stands. "Goodbye, Grace." He smiles down at me one more time before turning and walking away.

Part Four
Armageddon

"The nations rage,
The Kingdoms totter
He utters his voice
The earth melts."
Psalm 46: 6

Chapter Forty-Eight
Helel

It's a beautiful morning when Shannon Snow, Freya, once my Mysteria, ascends the stone steps to the guillotine. I invited the public to witness her execution in the marble courtyard before the great tower. A circle of Guardians separates my former lover from the masses, who jeer at her and call her names. How quickly they have turned on her, these once adoring fans. Of course, any show of support for her would certainly be met with immediate reprisal.

A voice from a drone speaker reads the charges. I had to come up with a reason for this execution without divulging the truth, for no one could know that one of our transports was hijacked by a Jehovian. Instead, I charged her with treason for refusing to get the GEM. People all over the world were horrified that the GEM's main advocate would do such a thing. Especially since refusal is now punishable by death.

My ploy turned out to be a stroke of genius. People are falling over themselves to get the GEM tattooed on their foreheads.

The jeers become louder as the charges are read. My human body tingles with anticipation. To see the blade fall, her head roll away from her body, eyes still moving, mouth still twitching... It will be like Anne of Boleyn, yet better, for this queen was my own.

If only she had chosen differently. Even Mysteria could not overcome the human woman's misplaced affection for that child of hers. Those *two* children, I should say. What is it about motherhood that makes women abandon all sense?

At least she had managed to harness the seed of the Beast to produce the true child of darkness—Vale, my own instrument. Yet even she had not the strength to overcome this abomination, motherhood. All the more reason to destroy that treacherous institution once and for all. Soon, there will be no more mothers. Or fathers. Only birthing people. Surrogates. Vessels. Clones. Test tubes.

A Guardian forces the former movie star to her knees and presses her head down to the block. She weeps loudly. The trumpets blow; the electronic drums roll. My pulse quickens.

"Stop!"

The drums go silent. The blade does not fall. The Guardians and the executioner freeze, their gazes lifting to the sky, where Zazel's head hovers, huge and golden as the sun.

"I, Grigori Zazel, Supreme Lord of the United Earth, have decided to commute the sentence of this condemned one from death to life in the camps. I do this because I am all-powerful and all-forgiving. Freya has served me well, and I have not forgotten her service to me. Though her sin was grievous, she shall not die for it this day. The Supreme Lord has spoken."

The crowd is silent, not knowing how to react. Someone shouts Zazel's name, and soon others join in. "Hail Grigori Zazel! Hail Supreme Lord!"

Once again, that ridiculous demon has stolen my triumph.

Shannon cries out in relief as the Guardians remove her from the block and lead her down the steps. She thinks she has been saved. She doesn't realize that life in the camps will be more miserable even than death. She won't survive six months there.

I burn with rage that can barely be contained by the meager body I inhabit.

Something must be done about Grigori Zazel.

***

"Vale."

"That is not my name." He pummels the giant bag, sweat streaming off his muscles, his braids damp and lifeless. How little he looks like Jared Lorn now. The spark of humanity is gone from his eyes; his mouth is creased in a perpetual frown. His rage leaks from him like bodily sweat—a rage without cause, without purpose, with a will of its own.

My rage.

"Baldyr," I say blandly, "Zazel has sent your mother to the camps."

"Should I care?" He continues to punch the bag.

"I think you should. He's been turning on everyone lately. He's become erratic, unpredictable. He demolished a robot for taking too long to bring him a towel. There is no telling what he will do next. Or who he will unleash his fury upon. Paranoia. It is the disease of kings."

Vale pauses in his punching and looks at me. "You think I will be next?"

"Should you displease him the slightest… I fear you will be. He's failing. Surely, you've seen that? He has been too long in the world. The temple thing was a fiasco. And then the escape of the rebels. I spend all my time putting out his fires."

"What would you have me do?" He sounds annoyed but also curious.

"Do what only you can do."

He hesitates, understanding dawning on his face. "The Guardians—"

"I can take care of the Guardians," I say.

"How?"

"Leave that to me."

"And the Grigori?"

I smile. "They will not lift a finger to help him. They care only for their own pleasures."

He resumes his pummeling, slower now, as he considers what I'm saying. "Why don't you do it yourself?"

"My boy, do I look like a warrior? Can I lead armies? That is not my role. But it is yours. I pass this mantle to you. The true Baldyr. God of Love. God of War."

At this, the boy smashes his fist one last time into the bag so hard he knocks it completely off its hook. I flinch as the bag thuds to the floor, then step close to him and put my hands on his shoulders so I can give him an extra dose of my spirit.

"Do it tonight."

***

I watch from the shadows as Vale enters the garden. It's near midnight, yet the garden glows with ethereal light as thousands of floating lanterns bob and weave through the foliage.

Vale carries a spear.

Good choice of weapon, I think—a fitting choice. A sword would be too obvious. Make Zazel suspicious.

The garden is alive with music and writhing bodies, both human and inhuman—the nightly revelry. The Grigori gather to pleasure themselves with their chosen victims. Zazel oversees the festivities, yet he no longer partakes. He's lost interest in that particular form of human depravity. It's become a bore, as have all human indulgences.

Revelers of undetermined gender glom onto Vale as soon as he appears. He shakes them off. He has eyes only for his father, lying in his hammock, the winged lion at his feet. The lion lurches onto its haunches, curious, perhaps, or alarmed. It watches Vale, wings unfurling. The boy is dressed in full battle gear, his gold armor gleaming in the lantern light. How magnificent he looks! My creation.

Vale drops to one knee and lays the spear on the floor before him. The Supreme Lord glances without interest at the boy and the spear and lies back again.

"What are you doing here?" he says. "I did not send for you. Go away."

"Father," Vale says. "I have come to worship you."

"Oh, if you must." Zazel yawns. "Get on with it."

Vale makes a great show of bowing and prostrating himself, speaking the words of worship taught to all those who come before Zazel.

"Holy are you, God of the Earth, of all creation, conqueror of Men and Beast, all praise and honor and glory are yours, Father of Life..."

Suddenly, Vale snatches up the spear and lunges toward Zazel, thrusting it deep into his naked chest. Zazel screams as his body convulses. The Guardians surge up the steps, aiming their spears at Vale—he spins, kicking the spears away and punching each Guardian so hard they tumble off the dais. He moves like water, slipping around them, beneath them, smooth and liquid, evading their spears and sending them reeling.

More Guardians emerge from the shadows. I raise my hand to them. Suddenly, they stagger and fall, dropping their weapons. They claw at their eyes in agony; blood streaks down their faces. The pain I give them is so horrible they gouge their eyes out of their sockets.

The Grigori finally take notice of what is happening, only half-interested. Zazel lurches to his feet and pulls the spear from his chest—blood spurts out in fountains. He screams in rage and lunges for Vale, who grabs the spear out of his hand and plunges it into Zazel's one naked eye. The Supreme Lord falls collapses, writhing in agony.

The lion lets out a deep purr, wings flapping maniacally, though they are useless wings, for show only. He swings his big head toward Vale, roars again, then bows his head low to his new master.

Vale draws himself up and stands tall, perfectly still. He gazes with utter contempt upon the Grigori, who have done nothing to save their Supreme Lord, just as I knew they would.

The Guardians lie about in heaps, bloody holes where their eyes used to be. Vale removes the spear from Zazel's eye and holds it high over his head in triumph. Blood drips onto the dais.

"This is a new day," he declares. "A new era. No more peace. This is war."

The Grigori are silent for a long moment. Then one named Turiel stands up, his mountainous body towering over the others. He thumps his fist on his chest.

"Hail Baldyr," he shouts. "Hail the Supreme Lord. May he live forever!"

One by one, the other Grigori follow suit, declaring Baldyr their new leader.

"Gather your children," Vale says, once they have all declared their allegiance to him. "The Children of the Grigori. The Light Bringers! We must destroy those who still oppose us. And it begins with Israel. If Israel falls, all will fall. Let us ride to Jerusalem!"

Vale marches through the crowd to a hail of cheers.

I glance at Zazel, lying on the floor, bloody holes in his chest and eye. He still breathes, though he seems unable to move.

"Fine boy you have there, Azazel," I say. "How proud you must be."

Chapter Forty-Nine
Grace

Jared and I are writing songs together again. Setting the psalms to music. It gives me so much joy to see a guitar rather than a sword in his hands. This has always been his real weapon, his true gift. He's a kind of modern-day David that way. David's sling and sword killed thousands, but his lyre slayed demons.

We teach the songs to the population of Mount Zion each evening as the sun sets. We sing, we pray, we worship. I play a keyboard the boys found in the city, while Nasir plays a drum he made himself. My heart leaps to see everyone gathered on the bleachers before the ruins, singing together as the sky glows red and gold as if it were on fire. There is something about the light here in Jerusalem that makes me feel very close to heaven.

"I have one more song to teach you," I say one evening after our worship session. "This is a special song. Not everyone here will be able to sing it, but I believe some of you will. If you can hear me, come and join me."

I pause, surveying their expressions. Perplexed, expectant. I clear my throat, close my eyes, and open my mouth to sing the Song that has been in my head for as long as I can remember. My heart beats faster. I have not sung it out loud in so long. And I've never sung it just for its own sake, without needing it as a defense against the darkness. Does it even work that way? There is so little I understand about the Song, yet it is a part of me, like an internal organ. It is not something I command; it commands me.

It bursts from me like a butterfly emerging from a cocoon, unfurling its wings, filling every corner of my being, every empty space. The words are ancient, a language only known to angels, and yet I understand them in a way I have understood little else. It's as if the strains of melody have altered my brain waves, snapping them into a whole new pattern of understanding. Singing this Song, I feel a oneness with my Creator that cannot be explained or even understood. Only experienced.

Gradually, other voices intertwine with mine, each one delicate and singular, weaving around and through my own melody. I open my eyes to see a dozen or more people, some very young, standing before me. They are all singing, different songs, yet in harmony with mine. Ari. Luther. Rebecca. Many more. I'd thought the AngelSong a rare gift, but perhaps, in these last days, it has been poured out on many.

We continue to sing, louder, more confidently, our voices creating a tapestry of sound only we can hear. The air above us seems to warp and waver with the music, as if creating an invisible shield around us. I weep, my heart full to bursting. Yet the expressions of the others remain perplexed, confused.

Lord, I pray silently, *please let them hear it. All of them.*

And then, He does. I see their faces change suddenly, their eyes grow wide and their mouths drop open in astonishment. For one shining moment, the whole world is filled with music, and every ear can hear it. The Song builds, catches fire, explodes into heaven.

Thank you.

For the first time, I have hope. Real hope. I know God has not abandoned us.

***

Bree, Jared, and I remain on the bleachers long after everyone else has gone to bed. I don't want this night to end. Bree is so thrilled by what she heard, she can't stop talking about it.

"I was surprised at how many girls were Singers," Bree says. "I mean, didn't you say that all the Singers in the *There* were boys?"

"Yeah," I say. "Except for me and Josephine, but we were there by accident. We hadn't been kidnapped. I thought Samyaza had done something with the female Singers. Like he wanted to do with me."

Bree's eyes grow wide. "What did he do?"

I pause, wondering how to speak this part out loud. "He said something—about his first human wife. She was a Singer, and she had red hair. He implied she was my ancestor."

"Your ancestor was married to a Watcher?" Bree's voice squeaks.

I nod. "She gave him a bunch of children. Nephilim. But she escaped from him, somehow."

"Oh, wow—what happened to her?"

"I think she ended up marrying Japheth—one of Noah's sons."

"She was on the ark?" Bree gasps.

"That must be how the line of Singers was able to continue after the Flood. But Samyaza thought all the Singers would be male because the Watchers only sire male offspring."

"So, he wanted to get rid of all the Singers?"

"Right."

"Whew!" Bree chuckles. "But he knew you were a Singer, didn't he?"

I think about this. "He thought I was *her*. His wife. Like she had come back to him after thousands of years."

"Creepy," Bree says. "Almost as creepy as your brother turning into Jared. So *he* is the real Antichrist?"

Silence. We all look at Jared. His eyes grow glassy.

"He was... a good kid," he says softly. "He gave me a guitar. We played music together, even though it was illegal in the tower. He was the only one I could talk to there. If only I could..." He doesn't finish.

"If he is the Antichrist, then there's nothing you could do," I say.

No one speaks for a while. Then Bree gets up, clapping her hands.

"Well, I don't know about you, but I'm starving," she says. We fasted all day in preparation for the worship service. "Matzo, anyone?"

Chapter Fifty
Jared

My eyes snap open, sweat pouring over my brow. I look over at Grace, sleeping peacefully. She's even smiling in her sleep. The music. It was beautiful.

It was harder for me, thinking about Vale. My brother, my friend. What has Azazel done to him? Once again, I feel responsible. If it hadn't been for me...

There's no use in trying to sleep now. I get up quietly pull on a jacket.

"What's the matter?" Grace rouses drowsily.

"Nothing. Go back to sleep. I'll be back in a minute."

I pick up my sword and stick it in my belt. Lev wants me to carry a rifle, but I don't like the feel of a gun in my hands. I grab a flashlight and make my way out of the house. I walk through the ruins to the catwalks. It's an hour before dawn. The sky is dark gray. A light shines from the radio shack at the top of the observation deck.

Kopek and Jezzie sit at a cafe table in the visitor's center, playing cards by the sickly yellow light of a propane lamp. They jump to attention when they see me. I haven't quite figured them out. Two of the Ashkelon Three, as Grace calls them. They clearly are not interested in our mission, yet they have stayed and even volunteered to help with security. They were not at the worship service, nor do they attend any of Ari's Bible studies. I suspect they are simply freeloaders, here for the food and shelter and promise of safety, but not interested in following God.

"Everything all right?" I ask.

Kopek glances at me. "Fine." He looks away quickly, avoiding my eyes.

"We did the rounds," Jezzie says somewhat defensively. She looks me up and down and smirks.

Izik comes out of the shadows, a rifle slung over his shoulder. He yawns. "Something wrong?"

"No," I say. "Couldn't sleep. Thought I'd take a walk."

"Bad place for a walk at night," Izik says. "Lots of holes to fall into."

"Who's working the radio?"

"Buck, I think."

I smile. Buck is different from these two. "I'll go up and check on him, see how things are going."

"Just be careful." Izik sounds irritated. "Want me to come?"

"No, I'll be fine." I go up the stone steps to the observation deck where the radio shack sits, built of spare wood from surrounding buildings. A tall dipole antenna and heavy wires run from the shack to the electrical room just below the deck. A pale light glows from the single window.

I open the door to see Buck hunched over an array of instruments with his headphones on, listening intently. A small oil lamp is the only light in the room. He sees me and jumps up, startled, shoving the headphones off his ears.

"Golden Son," he says with a crooked smile. He always calls me that.

"Jared," I say, correcting him for the hundredth time. "Everything okay here?"

"Yes. All good. There was a message. From someone in India. Would you like it?"

"Yes."

Buck hands me a piece of paper. It's difficult to make out his scrawl.

We hear and are grateful for the Song! We sing—

"That's all?" I ask.

"That's all I could make out," says Buck. "The signal dropped."

"Well, thank you." I push the note into my pocket. "You don't mind being alone up here?"

"No, no. It's quiet. Peaceful." He smirks a little. "Though my friends don't like it."

"Why not?"

Buck shrugs. "They want to leave. They think the people here are weird."

"And you don't?"

He shrugs again and chuckles. "I like to listen to Ari. He talks about how the prophecies of the Bible are coming true. It's... interesting. But I think this place is like the Hidden City. From Buck Rogers. The last refuge of freedom. Do you know Buck Rogers?"

"I've heard of it."

"You are like him, I think."

I stare at him. "Me?"

"Because Buck Rogers had to stop Killer Kane from destroying the whole world."

"And did he succeed?"

Buck lets out a huffy breath like he can't believe I wouldn't know this already. "Of course! What do you think?"

I laugh a little. "I'm glad to hear that. Well, I'll let you get back to work. Good night, Buck."

"Good night Gol… Jared." He grins and waves.

I leave the shack feeling a little better and head down the steps. People like Buck remind me how simple our mission is here. Suddenly, I'm not so worried. I yawn, thinking I might be able to get some sleep after all—

A tremendous blast explodes my ears and knocks me off my feet. I feel my body flying, landing hard on the stone steps, my back burning hot. I can't think, can't hear, can hardly breathe, the world so full of noise and light it seems to block out all sensation. Finally, I turn over and open my eyes. Flames turn the night sky to day.

The shack…

Footsteps from below. Izik's voice. "What happened?"

"Buck!" I rasp, struggling to my feet. I reel, off-balance, ears ringing. Smoke fills my lungs and I choke and cough, eyes watering. "A bomb… Buckets! Water! Wake everyone!"

Izik runs away barking orders. More voices join his, all muffled, far away. I pull myself upright. I rip off my jacket, which is on fire. I pull the sword from my belt and stumble up the steps back toward the observation deck.

Buck.

The shack is an inferno. I feel a movement behind me and spin to see a dark figure looming over me, a blade flashing in the firelight. I dodge the knife and thrust my sword, feel it sink into flesh. My attacker's head is thrown back, his face illuminated briefly before he slips from my blade and falls to the ground.

Another man leaps from the shadows, this one with a curved sword. He swings at me—I block his strike with my sword and kick him in the stomach.

He grunts and doubles over. I push him down to the ground, pressing press my knee into his chest, and wrench the knife from his grip.

"Who are you?" I say as he struggles to free himself. He answers with a growl and a spit.

"Buck!" Kopek and Jezzie rush up the steps, take in the scene, the fire, me with my prisoner. Jezzie turns around and runs away. Kopek just stares. Izik appears with a bucket of water and shoves it into Kopek's chest.

"Help us!" he orders and goes back for more water.

Lev appears at the top of the stairs and aims his rifle at my prisoner, who suddenly stops struggling.

"What happened?" Lev asks.

"A bomb." I pull the prisoner to his feet and shove him toward Lev. "Take him to the citadel. Keep a guard on him. We need to put out this fire."

Lev marches the prisoner away. More people come up the stairs, carrying buckets. Kopek is still standing still, holding his bucket. I take it from him and throw it on the fire. Then I hand it back to him.

"Go get more water," I say, screaming in his ear. "Now!"

He blinks and moves, heading for the stairs.

"Jared!" Grace comes up the stairs and rushes to me, a blanket over her shoulders. "Thank God. I thought you... You're bleeding! Oh my—what—how did this happen?"

Another explosion shakes the stones of the complex. Grace yelps. I grab her before she falls. I look around to see the electrical building in flames.

Our generators.

The lights in the compound go out.

The only light we have now comes from the burning shack.

***

The prisoner squirms against his bindings, his eyes all black fire in the light of my propane lantern. I tell Lev to remove his gag. As soon as he can, he spits again. That seems to be his favorite form of expression.

"Do you speak English?" I ask.

He replies with a slew of Arabic.

Lev punches him in the stomach. "Speak English. I know you can," he says levelly.

The captive thrusts out his chin. "I say nothing to you."

"What is your name?" I ask.

No answer.

"Who sent you?"

He doesn't reply. His upper lip twitches, and he averts his gaze.

"What's the matter?" I ask.

"You look like… him," he says.

"Who?"

"The… Destroyer."

I sigh. "I *was* him. Before I realized what the Supreme Lord—your Madhi— really is. A liar. A demon."

His eyes snap to meet mine. "*You* are the liar. You are an impostor. Madhi has given his armies to the Golden Son. He leads us. He will defeat you. He will destroy Israel forever. So say the prophecies."

"Our prophecies say something different," I say. "Did Grigori Zazel send you to attack us?"

His expression becomes cagey. He looks away. "We do all for the Madhi. For his justice. You are spreading lies." He smiles haughtily. "I will be greatly rewarded. As will my brother, who died by your hand."

"So, your Madhi knows of your actions?"

"Madhi is all-seeing, all-knowing."

I turn to Lev. "Keep guards on him day and night. But not Kopek or Jezzie." I look at the prisoner. "We will talk more later."

"More will come!" the attacker shouts as I walk away. "You cannot stop us! You think you are safe here? You think your God will protect you? Did he protect you this night? You are doomed here! You cannot stand against the great Madhi! You will die!"

I can still hear him, even after I've entered the tunnel and returned to the visitor's center. I hear him all night long.

***

The rain comes. At first, it is welcome. The rain finally douses the fire, which has raged through the night. In the smoldering aftermath, we learn that the radios, the generators, the pump station, and several houses have been destroyed. Four people besides Buck are dead, one of them a teenage boy.

I gather Buck's body from the ruins, though it is hardly recognizable as something human. We bury him and the others, including the other bomber, near the Royal Quarter in the pouring rain. Ari says a few words and recites Psalm 23. Grace and Bree sing a hymn.

I can't sing. Exhaustion has taken over every fiber in my body. I'm still not quite used to this part of being human. Of feeling weighed down by sleeplessness and grief.

Kopek and Jezzie do not attend the ceremony.

Everyone disperses to find shelter once the funeral is over. Grace tugs on my arm, takes me back to our attic room, and silently cleans the soot and bits of shrapnel from my face. We huddle under several blankets for warmth. The light is fading. The night will be cold.

"Why?" she says finally, in the darkness. "Why did God allow this?"

I feel her tremble and know she is crying, though I can't hear it. My ears are still ringing. I want to tell her that everything will be all right. That God is still in control.

I remember something.

I search my pockets and find the piece of paper still shoved in there. I pull it out, smooth it as best I can, and give it to Grace.

"Buck gave me this just before he… Anyway, he said it came from India."

She looks at the paper, her brow furrowed slightly. She takes it and reads it.

We hear and are grateful for the Song! We sing—

"Veer." She looks up at me, smiling through her tears.

Chapter Fifty-One
Helel

"Israel has defied us for the last time," Vale declares, seated on the Cobra throne, his now famous spear in hand. They've even given it a name: King Piercer. "They destroyed our Dragons and decimated our temple. The whole world has seen the utter destruction they have wrought upon innocent people who had been celebrating their freedom on the Temple Mount. Israel refuses to bend her knee to the Supreme Lord, the Savior of the World, and for this, she must be wiped from the face of the earth."

Hassan is the first on his feet, applauding wildly. The others follow suit more reluctantly. They were told that the Supreme Lord had appointed his Golden Son to rule in his place, though they have no idea why. Their questions have been met with stony silence.

Vale continues to bellow. "I call upon each one of you to commit all the troops and weapons at your disposal to the one goal of the destruction of Israel."

"Your Eminence," says the Chinasian ruler, Lee, "is such a force really needed? From the images we have seen, there are barely a handful left in

Israel. They have no weapons to speak of. Why bother with troops on the ground? Your Dragons could dispatch them—"

"They may *look* weak," Vale snaps, "but believe me, they are not. They have a weapon far greater than even our entire arsenal of Dragons." He doesn't mention what that weapon is. The union lords gaze at each other in wonder.

"Greater even than your nuclear arsenal?" Lee says skeptically. The others murmur to each other.

Vale slams his spear on the floor—the sound echoes hellishly through the vast room. "I have spoken! Do you dare to question me?" His voice is so loud it makes the sun above him shiver. The lords are suddenly quiet.

Vale rises from his chair, fist in the air. "Let all the world hear this! I want it repeated to the ends of the earth! We are coming for you, Israel! Destruction is now upon you!"

"Death to Israel!" Hassan shouts, fist in the air. Others join in the chant. "Death to Israel! Long live the United Earth!"

I smile in satisfaction. Even the Singer and her husband the Betrayer will not be able to stand against this onslaught. They will crumble, and when they do, even the Eternal One will not save them.

Chapter Fifty-Two
Jared

We gather for the first time since the bombing. The rain has abated to a steady drizzle. I see questions on the faces of the people huddled on the bleachers, a gnawing fear. We had begun to feel safe here. That false sense of security has fled. Lev reported that several have left us to take their chances in the Judean wilderness.

"This has been a hard week," I say to them, struggling for words. I wish Yosef were here, but we haven't been able to contact Petra since the fire. We have a few portable radios with shorter reach, but their batteries won't last long.

Grace has been unnaturally quiet. The loss of the radio station seems to have broken her. Her plan was for all the Singers to be connected. She thought that was essential to our defense. Now that plan seems impossible.

I clear my throat and continue. "We lost friends. Brothers and sisters. We've lost… a great deal. I know you feel as though God has abandoned us. But He hasn't. He never will. I promise you that." Are my promises worth anything anymore? "Our only choice is to stay strong. Stay together. No matter what happens, we have to *stand*." It's the one word that keeps coming back to me.

I wait for a response. A cheer, an amen, even a nod from the crowd. They stare at me blankly. They look so tired, ragged, worn to the bone. They don't believe a word I say.

"They say you captured one of the bombers," someone shouts. "What are you going to do with him?"

Dark murmurs ripple through the crowd. I look to Lev, who rises to speak.

"Yes, we have a man in custody," he says, sounding unusually subdued. "We are interrogating him."

"Kill him!" yells someone. "A life for a life!"

Kopek jumps up, his face red with rage. He points to me. "Kill *him!* He brought this on us. He brought us to this place where we will be killed. All of us!"

Everyone looks at me, suspicion in their eyes. A nest of doubt churns in my stomach. I glance at Grace. Her anger flares in her reddened cheeks, and her fists curl in her lap. I shake my head.

"You can't blame Jared for this," says Ari, rising. "It doesn't matter what he did in the past. He is here now to help us, so we don't fall when the day of evil comes."

"Prophecies!" scoffs Kopek. "So high and mighty, aren't you? Thinking you are fulfilling prophecies. This is nonsense. When the Dragons come, they will burn us to hell and back. That will be the end of this story. Like Masada. You remember Masada? Such heroism. We will stand! In the end, they all died. So will we."

Everyone shouts in response. Many agree with Kopeck. They are frightened, panicked. Up until the bombing, they somehow thought we would be impervious to harm here. We have been spared the plagues that ravaged the rest of the world. But we will not be spared all of them.

I try to get control of the meeting, but no one is listening anymore. People scurry back to their hovels, whispering among themselves. Grace takes my hand and leads me up the steps to the courtyard. We sit at a table in gloomy silence. Ari joins us.

"That went well." Ari chuckles.

"I don't blame them," I say. "We are on borrowed time now. And cut off from everyone."

"We will keep the portables going as long as we can and scrounge around for batteries."

"Hey, guys. We have something to show you." Bree leads Ethan to the table and helps him sit. I stare at Ethan, who looks so pale and shriveled. He rarely gets up from his bed anymore. He smiles at me wanly and stifles a cough.

"What is it?" I ask, fearful of what they have to say. Can things get any worse?

Ethan takes several breaths before he can speak. "I think I can help with the radio thing."

Grace, who had her head on the table, suddenly looks up, interested. "How?"

Ethan takes an object from his pocket and places it on the table. It's an I-Cube.

Grace recoils. "I thought you got rid of that? You know how much trouble it got us into before."

"I took out the battery and disabled the internal chip. But something told me to keep it. That it might be needed." He wipes a bead of sweat from his brow.

"You just couldn't let it go, could you?" Grace snaps.

Ethan puts up a hand to silence her. "Just listen for a second. The Cube connects to the Skylink satellite internet system, which is connected to UECOM in New Asgard. That's the thing with globalization. Everything is centralized—*everything*. All Cube communications have to go through one hub, UECOM, including the internet and the HoloNet."

"We know all that," Grace says. "All the more reason to destroy it."

Ethan runs his tongue over his lips. He speaks haltingly, yet he seems excited at the same time. "I thought so too… except somehow the *Voice* got around the internet censors. It bothered me. How did they do it? They must have been accessing an alternative network with a gateway browser like TOR, which would pass their signal through several relays to keep them anonymous. But it's not foolproof. The UE could still see them entering TOR and shut them down. So they had to have a way of getting past the UE Firewall and entering TOR undetected… a bridge."

"A bridge," I say. "Can *you* do that?"

Ethan nods slowly. "The *Voice* used a sort of disguise—a cloaking signal— it made them look like someone else. I was working on this before I left New York. I had it figured out—but then I had to take out my chip." He holds up his hand to show his scar. "The Cube is activated by the chip. I didn't know how to get it working without that."

Grace frowns. "So you can't use it, after all?"

"Well, I may have found… a workaround." He pauses to catch his breath. "The chip works kind of like a remote control, on a radio frequency. So I got Nasir and his friends to get me some parts and I built one."

"A remote control?" Grace says. "Why didn't you tell us about this before?"

"Because I knew you'd freak out and try and stop me," Ethan replies. "But now… it might be our only hope."

"Are you saying you can operate the Cube and get on the internet?" I ask. "Without being detected?"

Ethan nods. "Yeah, I think so. Of course, if they do find me, they will shut down my Cube and that will be that. But if they don't, then we can at least get news of what's going on. What their plans are. And maybe even… post on social media."

Grace sits up straight. "You mean, like a message?"

"Yeah." Ethan gives Grace a lopsided grin. "The battery in this thing is solid state. It could last for weeks if we're careful."

Grace suddenly smiles. She jumps up and throws her arms around Ethan, nearly knocking him off his chair.

"Thank you," she says. "Thank you."

"Get some messages ready to post," Bree says. "We need to tell the world that we're still here."

***

"You're going to want to see this."

Ethan has called us together to report on what he's learned from the Cube. We gather around the table as he operates his remote control. The Cube shoot up a beam of light that expands into a shaky holo of jumbled-up images. Then the images stabilize, and I see… me.

"It's the new Baldyr," Ethan says.

He's standing on a stage lined with Grigori banners and shouting to a large crowd of spectators. I swallow hard, watching him.

"What's he saying?" Grace asks.

Ethan looks to Bree to answer for him. She sighs and rubs his back while answering.

"Just a lot of warmongering," Bree says. "Talks about how we took down his Dragons and are murdering people left and right. And also about the Light Bringers. Some super soldiers, I guess. The deployment has started though. All ten unions. Going to muster at Jericho in days."

"Days," I murmur.

"Jericho?" Grace asks.

"It's how the Israelites first entered the Promised Land," says Ari thoughtfully. "He sees himself as a liberator. A rightful conqueror."

Grace touches my arm, but it seems she wants to steady me more than seek comfort for herself.

"Ten armies," I murmur.

"Light Bringers," Bree says. "What a name."

"They still have a hundred Dragons," says Lev.

"Dragons will be useless in Petra." Ari scratches his beard thoughtfully. "If people stay in their caves."

"They have enough troops for a ground assault," says Lev, leaning back in his chair and folding his arms. "The Siq will not hold them back for long. Or they will use tactical nukes."

A shiver goes through all of us.

"Would they do that?" Bree asks. "Drop nukes on Petra?"

"Why not?" says Lev. "Petra is nothing to them. It is remote, isolated. And what a display for the holos. It will bring all the holdout nations to their knees."

The news is sobering. This is really happening.

"There is something else you need to see," Ethan says in a different voice. He looks at Grace. "This is not easy." He makes some adjustments to the Cube. The holo jumbles then stabilizes. Grace gasps.

A group of prisoners sit in a large pit, pounding piles of rocks with mallets. The camera zooms in on one in particular. A woman wearing a turban, her clothes in rags. Her movements are listless, as if at any moment she will collapse from exhaustion. A few strands of red hair escape from her head covering. She looks up at the camera, her green eyes, once so beautiful and fiery, now vacant. The mallet falls slowly as her gaze returns to the rock at her feet. A voiceover drones in Norwegian.

Grace reaches out a hand to touch her mother's face. Her fingers slide through the image. She draws back, pulling both her hands to her chest.

"What… happened?" she whispers.

"She was going to be executed for refusing the GEM," Ethan says. "But Zazel commuted her sentence to work in the mines."

"Executed for refusing the GEM?" Grace says the words as if they have no meaning.

"Apparently, it is now a death penalty crime," Ethan says.

Grace's lip trembles. She presses her hand to her mouth. "Shannon," she whispers as if the woman in the holo can hear her. "Mom."

"That's enough." Bree presses something on the remote, making the image disappear. Grace continues to stare at the empty air as if she could still see her mother there.

"Those… people," Bree says through gritted teeth, "are worse than evil."

"Excuse me…" Grace jumps up from the table and dashes off. I watch her go.

"I figured she had to know," says Ethan. "I didn't think she'd take it that hard, considering."

"Ethan, you are such an oaf sometimes," says Bree.

"But thank you for all you're doing," I say.

"You're welcome," he says. Then adds, with a sardonic smile that looks somehow familiar: "Blondie." He coughs, the smile gone in an instant. The color drains from his face, and he slumps slightly, clearly exhausted by his presentation. Bree puts a hand on his shoulder.

"We're gonna go rest now," Bree says brightly as she helps Ethan to his feet. They shuffle out.

I go to Grace. She's sitting on a bench in the courtyard amid what was once a little flower garden, clutching her oversized cardigan sweater around herself. I sit beside her. We are silent awhile. Finally, she speaks.

"I don't know why I feel so… sad. She never loved me. I hated her most of the time. She was an awful person."

"But she was your mother."

She sighs. "Yeah. And in the end, I think she was really trying… to make amends." She shakes her head. "I don't believe the GEM thing. She would have done anything for Doyle. I could see it in her eyes. She was like his… slave. I think maybe they used her as a scapegoat for my escape. Ironic, isn't it?" She puts a hand over her mouth to stifle a sob. After a moment, she continues. "My last words to her were so… angry. I blamed her for what happened to me. And it wasn't even her fault."

"She's still alive," I say. "There's still hope."

"How? In that place?"

"God will make a way. Isn't that what He does?"

"Yeah." She leans over, her head on my shoulder. "I feel like every time I get a handle on things, get back on my feet, something knocks me down again. I'm tired, Jared. Tired of fighting. I just don't see the point anymore."

Her words fill me with fear. She's always the one who seems so sure of our mission here. I rely on that. If she is having doubts…

A story comes to mind.

"You remember that story about Moses fighting the Amalekites? All he had to do was hold his arms up, and the Israelites were winning. But as soon as he let his arms drop, they started losing. He was tired too. All day, holding up his arms. He couldn't do it on his own. But other people came along and held up his arms for him. That's why we're here. To hold each other up. All the way to the end."

She sniffs. "I get that. But what if... we're wrong? What if we lose anyway?"

"Do we even know what winning and losing look like anymore? Who are we to judge? Let's not think too far ahead, okay? Let's just deal with one thing at a time. This moment—and how to get to the next one. We can do that, right?"

She looks at me. "This moment."

I nod. "This moment. What do you want to do right now?"

"Eat a bucket full of chicken wings."

I sigh. "What else?"

Chapter Fifty-Three
Michael

The armies gather at Jericho.

I cannot help but think of the first battle I witnessed here, which was not much of a battle at all. Jericho, the walled city of palm trees, a lush oasis in a blistering desert, thought herself impervious to all attackers, and indeed she was, until she met her match in Elohim. I remember how Joshua fell to his knees when I stood before him and gave him his instructions. How he stared at me in wonder, because he could not believe what he was hearing could possibly be right. March around the city for seven days? Blow trumpets? That was no way to win a battle. And yet it was.

Joshua was one of the few who never lost his way.

Will Jared do the same? Will Davidov? Will Grace?

Jericho was never supposed to be rebuilt after its destruction. Yet it was—several times. It is the oldest city in the world and also the lowest, sitting almost a thousand feet below sea level. The perfect earthly location for one such as Helel.

Jericho is not what it once was. A few palm trees have survived, lining streets of rundown stone and stucco buildings, abandoned since the water went bad, cars flipped over and looted for battery parts and copper wire. Trash is everywhere. The city is little more than a garbage dump. Its infamous walls were never rebuilt.

Fifty Leviathans have landed in the desert on the outskirts of the city, pot-bellied planes disgorging supplies, equipment, and hovercraft. Grasshoppers, personnel transports, arrive, carrying hundreds of striking, white-haired soldiers, the children of the Watchers, the Light Bringers. In their gleaming gold armor, with their ice-blue eyes and long white braids, they are the image of their brother Jared Lorn, the former Baldyr.

"Light Bringers," says Remequel, my captain, at my side. His Light is blue as ice, a warrior of the wasteland, yet he can turn to fire in an instant. "They should be called Death Bringers."

The desert fills with soldiers from every corner of the world, housed in tents and Quonset huts that disappear into the horizon. Does Helel really believe he can build an army so big not even Elohim can defeat it?

I suppose he can. Because he knows Elohim does not operate in a vacuum. Elohim has chosen to work through the humans He created. That is our limitation. The bigger and scarier the enemy, the more the humans sitting on Mount Zion will falter. If they fall, all will fall. The diamond and mineral-rich nations of southern Africa, the few pockets of resistance in the Baltics, and the remaining Free States in America. Israel is the symbol of the True God, Elohim, Lord of Lords. Its destruction will vanquish the Forbidden and put a stake through the soul of the rebellion.

"Will they stand?" Remequel knows my thoughts.

"If the Human One can keep them together," I say.

"And what about Davidov? Does he listen?"

I don't answer at once. Davidov has always relied upon his own strength.

"I sent Remiel to him. Remiel knows how to speak to one such as Davidov."

Remequel chuckles. "I may have to go over there and spy out that conversation. I hope Remiel puts on a good show for him."

"Knowing Rem, he will."

***

Raphael travels over the land to a large lake of black sludge in Inner Mongolia, where a woman trudges knee-deep in mud, a sack upon her back amidst hundreds of slave laborers. Her breath is ragged from weeks of inhaling toxic fumes, and her eyes are rheumy from dust and sleeplessness, for she works twenty hours a day. She is skin and bones, this woman who was once a queen.

She pauses, swaying, and collapses slowly into the mud, as if she has decided that this is as far as she will go and no more. Raphael sits beside her. She glances up, marveling at the whiteness, the cleanness of his clothes, so bright she has to squint.

"Hello, Lily."

The woman's eyes open wider. She has not been called that in a very long time.

"My name is Shannon... no... Freya... no..." Her voice is a scrappy whisper. "Mysteria?"

"I do not speak to Mysteria," Raphael says, his tone more commanding now. "I speak to Lily. Lily Sova. Do you remember your real name?"

The woman shakes her head and then slowly nods.

"Your Father is calling you, Lily," Raphael says. "To come to Him. Your true Father. Your Father in heaven, who has always loved you, no matter what you have done. Will you come to Him?"

"My... father?" Lily's eyes open even wider. "My father is dead."

"Let me tell you about your real Father." Then Raphael tells her the whole story of Elohim and His Son, The Risen One, the Savior. How He came to save humans from their sins and how He is coming again, to judge the world and rule forever. "All you need to do to be a part of His kingdom," Raphael says, "is to accept Him as your Lord and Savior and to ask for His forgiveness."

"He will take me out of this place?" Lily asks.

"In time," Raphael says.

Lily shakes her head. "Only Zazel can take me out of this place. Or Amon. Can you talk to them? You seem like a powerful man. You must have connections. Can you tell them to get me out of here? I don't belong here. I didn't do anything wrong. I'm innocent."

"No one is innocent," says Raphael. "But your true Father will save you if you humble yourself and repent."

Lily looks confused. She doesn't understand this kind of talk. "But I *am* innocent! I didn't do anything wrong! I shouldn't be here!"

"Your Father in heaven offers you eternal life if you will turn to Him."

Lily shakes her head. "Please, go to the Supreme Lord, go to Amon Doyle, plead with them for me. You are an important person, I can tell. They will listen to you. Please."

Raphael sighs. He gazes at her tenderly. If he had a human heart, it would be broken.

"I am sorry, Lily."

Lily blinks, looking all around, wondering where the beautiful, important man could have gone so suddenly. She has little time to consider it before an overseer grabs her by the hair and pulls her roughly to her feet.

"Get moving!" he shouts.

Lily trudges on, though she continues to call out to the man in white who spoke to her. "Please! Please! Speak to them! I'm innocent! Help me, please!"

***

Jared stands on the watchtower of David's palace, alone. It's close to midnight. He's praying. Asking for guidance. Again. I remember David himself coming to this tower on the nights he felt most alone, most afraid. I spoke to him on those nights, words of comfort and courage. He carried all of Israel on his back, as Jared does now.

I appear to the human man now in my true form, Michael, the warrior angel, the general of the host armies, protector of Israel. He jumps back, fearful, startled, as he should be. He drops to his knees, shutting his eyes against my brightness.

"Human One."

His eyes open at the sound of my voice. He raises a hand to shield his eyes from my brilliance.

"Michael," he whispers.

I dim my Light, so he can see me more clearly. "They are coming soon," I say.

He nods, slowly, lowering his hand.

"There is something I must tell you now, something that will hurt you, though it is meant to help you."

His head tilts, brow furrows.

"Your son leads this army."

His eyes widen; his mouth drops open. He makes a sound. "Wha—?"

"Vale. The one who has become you. He is your son."

He stares at me. His lower lip trembles. He shakes his head, falling backward on his haunches, a hand reaching to his forehead. "No." He strokes his forehead as if trying to draw out a memory. "No." Less certain now.

"Shannon Snow drugged you and used you in an occult ritual to conceive a child. The Moonchild, also known as Antichrist." I reach out to touch his brow, opening his memory. He gasps, eyes suddenly wide, then keels over as if struck in the heart. He understands now. The Antichrist was born of the Scarlet Woman and the Beast. He was the Beast. Once.

He rocks slowly, holding his stomach, his shoulders trembling.

"He is very strong," I say. "Stronger than you. You cannot overcome him in your own strength. The power of the Adversary is in him. He is fueled by a rage you never had. His heart demands vengeance. Your life. But if you fall, all will fall."

Jared shakes his head, mumbling to himself. "No, it can't be up to me. I can talk to him. Explain what happened. We were friends. Brothers. He'll listen."

"He listens to only one voice now," I say.

"What should I do?" he asks.

"They've taken much from you," I say, softer now, my compassion for him outpacing my reason. "Your blood. Your seed. Your very body. But there is something they cannot take, something that is only yours to give. Your soul. Do not give in, Human One. Do you hear me?"

After a moment, he nods.

"I will tell you something else, Jared." I call him by his name. "When I first became aware of your existence, that day in the school—you remember that day, don't you? I was going to kill you myself. My arm was stayed. I was forbidden. Elohim said no. I asked why. I knew what you were. We all did. I knew what your very existence would mean for the world. Elohim chose to let you live." I pause to let my words seep into his storm-tossed soul. "Perhaps you should consider why."

I soar into the heavens, leaving him alone.

He puts his arms over his head and bends over, groaning, an agonizing sound coming from deep within. His groan is a prayer, the kind of prayer that is too deep for words.

I pray, too, that Elohim will answer.

Chapter Fifty-Four
Jared

Vale. My brother. My friend. The boy who traded his most precious possessions to get me a guitar. Who loved music as much as I did. The boy who looked up at me with starry eyes. The boy who wanted to *be* me.

He is my son.

Shannon… I cannot think of it. This was the one blessing my loss of memory granted me. Forgetting this one fact that now I shall never be able to un-know.

I had thought myself free from the curse over my life. But I was wrong. The curse remains.

I don't know what to do with this knowledge. Tell Grace? It would destroy her, destroy us. Why did Michael tell me this? Why did I even need to know?

So I am prepared, he said.

Elohim chose to let you live.

Why, why, why?

From the moment I learned what I was, I have longed for understanding. Why was I allowed to exist? I had thought in these last months, with all that has happened, I was seeing a glimmer of reason. I had a purpose here. I had a mission. I could undo all the damage my being born had created. But the truth is clear to me now. I have only made things worse.

A song comes to mind. Not one I wrote. An old song, from days gone by.

Let my life be a light shining out through the night
Let my life be a light on a hill.

Where did I hear that song before? I can't remember.

Give me wisdom and power every day, every hour…
Guide my footsteps a-right through the dark, stormy night…
Give me peace, give me joy, give me love…

That bluegrass hymn has become my story now.

Let my life be a fire…

"It's because of you he's dead."

The voice is harsh, angry, female.

Jezzie.

I feel the barrel of a gun pressed to the back of my head. I'm still kneeling, helpless. I have no weapon.

Is this what you meant, Lord?

"You and your Jesus. Your prophecies brought us here. Buck believed in you. Now he's dead."

"I'm sorry," I say, not knowing what else to say. "But I—"

"I don't want to hear your excuses. You and all these other freaks here. You are going to get us all killed."

"Probably," I say.

"But if I kill you, then it will all be over."

"Will it?" I turn around slowly so that the rifle is now pressed to my forehead. Jezzie's eyes shine in the moonlight, so fierce yet so filled with hurt. "In that case, you should pull the trigger."

I stand up slowly. She takes a couple of steps backward and fiddles with the trigger nervously. "You betrayed the Supreme Lord," she says through gritted teeth. "You will betray us too."

"So, you worship the Supreme Lord. Does Kopek know? Did Buck?"

"Kopek doesn't believe in anything," she retorts. "Buck believed in you. Now he's dead. Shows what believing in you gets you."

"I don't want anyone believing in me."

"Ha! That's what they all say. But it's a lie."

"Jezzie—" I take a step toward her.

She backs away. "Stay back! I'm not done talking."

"I'm tired of talking. If you want to shoot me, do it. I'm unarmed. I won't stop you."

I stare into her eyes without blinking, then take another step toward her. Then another. I'm inches away from the barrel of her gun. How much she reminds me of that school assassin Derrick Holder at this moment—the torment behind her eyes, the demons screaming in her ear. I could reach out and grab the weapon from her hands. I don't. For this one instant, I believe that this is the best possible outcome. For everyone. Even for Grace.

She pulls the trigger. Nothing happens. She tries again and again. Frustrated, she turns the weapon to fiddle with the trigger mechanism. After a minute, she throws the rifle on the ground.

"Stupid thing."

I pick up the rifle, cock it, aim it at the sky, pull the trigger. The report makes Jezzie jump a foot backward. She stares at me, eyes pulsing.

"How did—?"

"Nothing wrong with the rifle, Jezzie." I hold it out to her.

Her mouth opens, then closes. She looks from the rifle to me and back to the rifle again. Then she utters a curse and runs away, down the steps toward the visitor's center.

I glance up at the sky. "Thanks."

A brisk wind blows in my face. I smile.

***

Jezzie and Kopek are gone the next morning. No one saw them leave. The news makes me sad and a little shameful. Was there anything I could have said to Jezzie that would have helped? But I didn't even try.

We spend the day hauling up water in buckets from the citadel. Everyone is exhausted. Hungry. We live on lentils and matzo, and our supplies are dwindling fast. No more eggs, the chickens have stopped laying because we can't feed them. The supply truck is long overdue. I can't help but wonder if Davidov's trucks were destroyed by bombers as well.

Late in the evening, Ethan brings us the latest holo from his Cube. The news is not good: the armies are gathering at Jericho, not forty miles away. Grace's nails dig into the flesh of my arm as we watch the holo—the children of the Grigori standing in formation, their golden armor glistening in the sun. So many of them. A thousand, according to the reports Ethan managed to dig up.

But it's the Dragons that are the most frightening—a hundred black machines dotting the desert for miles around like monstrous insects ready to swarm.

"I guess this is it," Grace says, her voice hollow.

"Not quite," Ethan says. "Something else happened that is... well... pretty freaking unbelievable."

He fiddles with the remote. The images changes from the Judean desert to the futuristic spires of New Asgard, the great tower with the garden crown at the top. Dragonflies whir around the tops of buildings. The sky is a perfect dome of blue. And then something strange *does* happen—a small explosion, a puff of smoke at the base of the tower. The tower trembles, its glass walls exploding outward as it begins to topple, almost in slow motion. The entire tower tips over with a tremendous burst of smoke and dust, crushing everything in its wake. The blue sky flickers then disappears, revealing a thick bank of clouds.

"Is that real?" Grace asks when she can speak.

"I think so," says Ethan. "I checked some of the media posts on the internet. The tower collapsed. I doubt the Grigori would fake that."

"Did... God do that?"

"I think it was Davidov." I glance at Ari, who shakes his head and chuckles.

"He did it," Ari says. "He must have found someone to fly that plane."

"He was supposed to target the nuclear control center," I say. "But that isn't in the tower."

"Perhaps he missed. Or changed his mind about the target," says Ari.

"That means Zazel is dead," says Bree, almost gleefully. "He's dead! The war is over, right? I mean, if the Antichrist is dead. It's over!"

I shake my head. "It's not over. Azazel might be dead, but Vale isn't. He's here. Not forty miles away from us."

"So there are two Antichrists?" Bree's nose wrinkles.

"The scripture says the Antichrist has many heads," says Ari. He glances at me with a look that says, *Weren't you one of them?*

"So even if the tower is gone, they might still be able to access the nukes?" Ethan's face falls.

Ari nods. "The prophecy says the world will end in fire."

Fire. Did that mean a nuclear holocaust? Would God let that happen?

"Don't tell anyone about this," I say to Ethan. "It's better if they don't know what's coming. Let's focus on getting our messages out… while we still can."

"How is that going?" Grace asks. "Are the messages being seen?"

"They get taken down pretty quickly," Ethan says. "Which means they are being noticed. I have to create new accounts so I can repost, but so far the Cube hasn't been deactivated. They haven't found me yet."

"You're a genius," Grace says.

"I always told you, didn't I?"

***

I take Ethan's Cube to the spring citadel, where we are holding our friend, the bomber. Lev has told me he refuses to eat and won't talk to anyone except to say the Supreme Lord will destroy us all. He did tell Lev his name: Farouk.

I don't speak to him. I set the Cube before him and operate the remote as Ethan showed me to play the holo showing the collapse of the tower.

Farouk stares at it for a long time. Then he shakes his head. "This is not real."

I shut off the Cube to save the battery. "It came from the UE's own satellite linkup."

"Who did this?"

"We did."

"Ha! That proves the evil of you Jehovians," he sneers.

"Maybe it proves that the Supreme Lord is not who he says he is. That there is still one greater. The God of Israel."

"Anyone can drop a bomb."

"Would the Madhi destroy his own stronghold?"

"Did not your God kill his own son?" Farouk retorts. Yet his voice breaks slightly. The holo has unnerved him.

"Jesus died willingly, for the sins of all mankind. He could have called down legions of angels to free him from the cross, but he didn't. Instead, he died for us. And then he rose from the dead."

Farouk scoffs. "Fairy tales."

"Are you sure of that?" I ask. "You don't have to believe me. But here is a simple truth. You are here now, on this mountain, with us Jehovians. The Supreme Lord is coming to destroy us. If we die, you die."

"I will go to heaven with my ancestors," he replies, jutting his chin.

"How do you know? You committed murder."

"Murder of a Jehovian is not a sin. Madhi teaches that killing one of your kind pays our ransom from hell."

"So if you kill a Jehovian, you will go to heaven? According to Grigori Zazel?"

He nods. "Yes."

I shake my head. "And you think this is... a good thing? To murder your way into heaven?"

He hesitates before nodding.

"I am a murderer too," I say.

He peers back at me, curious.

"I've killed people. Not always intentionally. But there is only One who has the power to forgive me. To clean my slate. To give me a new heart. He gave His life willingly to save mine. He would do the same for you. He will give us eternal life. The Supreme Lord cannot give you that. He is an impostor. And from the looks of this holo, he is most likely dead."

"The Madhi cannot be killed. He is immortal."

"Okay." I stand up. "I just felt I should tell you the truth, so when you stand before the True God, you will have no excuse."

"Why?" he says gruffly. "Why do you tell me these things? I killed your friend. You should have killed me already, for what I did. Why do you try to... convert me?"

"Because," I say, "It is what Jesus commands."

"Oh, yes. Love your enemies. Such *khara*. If you were to love your enemy, then how can he be an enemy anymore?"

I smile. "Exactly."

Chapter Fifty-Five
Grace

I lie in bed, feeling too sick to get up. It's been like this nearly every morning. I can't keep food down, not even the dry matzo. Maybe it's the rain, or the cold, or the despair in my heart. I pull out Veer's message and reread it—it's the only thing that gives me hope. If Veer heard our messages, then maybe the other Singers did too. This is my prayer.

Lord, please, let them hear us. Let them sing.

Last night in Bible study, Ari taught the story of Gideon. God had given him an impossible task—go and fight the Midianites. Gideon was no warrior, and the Midianites were unbeatable. Gideon was filled with doubt, too. So he asked for a sign, not once but twice. God didn't rebuke him for his doubt. God answered his prayer.

Okay, Lord, I'm asking you now. Give me a sign. It doesn't have to be a wet fleece or anything. I don't have any fleece lying around anyway. Just… something.

I wish I could think of something more specific. Turn these ratty blankets into a thick, soft mattress? Fix the generator so we can have heat and light? Or maybe just turn our stale matzo into dry, crusty bread.

I feel stupid for asking. Why do I need a sign anyway? Isn't it enough that I am here with Jared? That I survived nearly being executed? Haven't I seen enough of God's provision? Well, Gideon was visited by an actual angel, and he still had doubts. We humans need a lot of convincing.

I hear the worship service begin on the bleachers outside. I should get up, go down there. I don't feel up to it. Fewer and fewer people are showing up to the services. Everyone stays inside now, fearful of another attack. Jared has had his boys searching all the tunnels and streets of the city for more potential enemies, but so far, they haven't found anyone. Still, no one feels safe.

I hear the lilting music of Jared's guitar. His voice carries above the wind, singing Psalm 139.

> *Where can I go from your Spirit?*
> *Where can I flee from your presence?*
> *If I go up to the heavens, you are there;*
> *if I make my bed in the depths, you are there.*

I get up, ignoring my lurching stomach, throw on two more sweaters and head to the bleachers. I sit and listen, not singing, just allowing Jared's music to enter me, fill in the dark, empty spaces, block out the discouragement, the corrosive doom in my soul. God is with us, even when we don't feel it. That's what the psalm says. For a moment, I believe it. I meet Jared's eyes—he chose this one for me. I close my eyes and sigh.

My peace is interrupted by the rumble of approaching engines, followed by shouts from the sentries at the compound entrance. Jared stops playing. What is this? Has the attack begun? Yet the sky is empty. No drones, no Dragons. No, this sound is more ordinary—trucks.

Jared puts down the guitar and heads up the steps toward the visitor's center. We all follow eagerly, hopeful. Three trucks sit idling on the street, just on the other side of the lyre sculpture. My heart thumps—supply trucks from Petra.

To my surprise, Noah emerges from the first truck as Jared goes to meet him. There's a woman is with him—Rachel. My throat tightens. I wondered where she was—she must have gone to Petra too.

Another man emerges from the passenger side of the truck. He's older, with a scruffy beard and curly black hair, in black militaristic dress.

"Is that Davidov?" I wonder aloud.

"He looks important," Bree says.

Noah, Jared and the older man converse for a few minutes as others emerge from the vehicles, a couple dozen people who gaze at us with intense curiosity. What are they all doing here? Was Petra attacked too? Are they survivors? A thousand questions roll through my brain all at the same time. I catch Rachel's eye, and she actually smiles at me. That's weird. I don't think I've ever seen her smile.

Finally, they all come into the compound—the crowd gathers around them. Jared and the older man walk right up to me.

"This is my wife, Grace." Jared says to the man. "Grace, this is Yosef Davidov."

"Grace, good to meet you, finally. My friend Noah has told me much about you."

I glance at Noah, who offers me a shy smile but says nothing. It's like the first time I saw him in the *There*. He barely spoke then. We're starting all over again.

I force a smile and offer my hand. "Nice to meet you, Prime Minister. Is everything... okay?"

"Call me Yosef," he replies, taking my hand. "That title seems a little... absurd at this point." He looks weary, yet his eyes sparkle and his smile is warm. "We are safe in Petra. We were concerned because we lost contact with you."

"Oh, that's why you came."

"Oh. So that's why you came."

"That is not the only reason." Davidov glances at Noah, who smiles encouragingly. "I… I mean, we… I brought many people with me… we wish to be baptized."

My jaw drops open so far I almost have to grab my chin to push it back up. "Baptized?"

"In the Pool of Siloam, as were the new converts on the Day of Pentecost."

"Wow," says Bree.

"Our time is short, from the look of things," Davidov goes on. "Whether we live or die is not up to us, but to God. However, from what I have seen and heard these past many days, I have come to believe that Yeshua is who He says He is. I—we—wish to be counted among His followers. And then, if it's all right, I'd like to take some of the water back to Petra to baptize those we could not come with us."

"Oh, yes," I say, though the word is a squeak, I'm so choked up. "Yes, that would be wonderful."

We escort Yosef and the others from Petra to the Pool with many of our own people following along. The mood is suddenly brighter, cheerful even, everyone talking and laughing. I feel like a thousand pound weight has been lifted from my shoulders.

"I'll be there in a minute," Jared says to me. "I've got to do something." He takes off before I can ask what he's doing.

When we get to the pool, Ari, clutching a battered Bible, tells the newcomers to get in the water. "And anyone else who would like to be baptized!"

It's still cold and drizzly, yet Davidov is the first in the water. The others follow a little more slowly, some yelping at the temperature. To my surprise, Noah joins them. The rest of us gather on the steps.

Ari opens his Bible and reads. "Peter said to them, 'Repent and be baptized every one of you in the name of Jesus Christ for the forgiveness of your sins, and you will receive the gift of the Holy Spirit. For the promise is for you and for your children and for all who are far off, everyone whom the Lord our God calls to himself.' The Lord has called all of us to himself this day. It is with great joy that I baptize each one of you in the name of the Lord."

Ari asks Davidov if he has repented of his sin and believes that Jesus is his Lord and Savior. Davidov nods and says yes. Ari says a prayer, grasps Davidov's shoulders, and pushes him underwater. He emerges sputtering and shaking his head, but smiling. He raises his arms in the air as everyone applauds.

Ari continues to baptize everyone in the pool to much applause and laughter. Noah and Rachel get baptized, side by side. I see the way Noah looks at her, and my heart does a little twist. I decide I'm happy for them.

I stand up and wade into the pool alongside the others. My teeth chatter and my feet go instantly numb, but I don't care. "Baptize me," I say to Ari.

He gives me a sidelong look. "You have not been baptized?"

"I was as a baby, but I don't remember. Is it okay to do it again?"

"Of course." I shiver in the icy water, my heart hammering, as Ari asks me the same questions before dunking me. When my eyes are cleared of water, I see many more people jumping into the water as well—our own people, including Bree and Nasir and all his friends. Ari baptizes all of them. When the baptisms are done, Ari sings the doxology, and we all join in.

Praise God from whom all blessings flow
Praise Him, all creatures here below
Praise Him, above the heavenly host
Praise Father Son and Holy Ghost

Everyone is hugging and laughing. I wade over to Noah and Rachel. "Hey," I say. "I'm so glad you both are... here." I feel awkward, suddenly.

"We are too," Noah says. He glances at Rachel and smirks.

"I'm really happy for you both." That sounded ridiculous, but Noah smiles, grateful.

"Thank you, Grace."

"Yes," says Rachel. "Thank you." I notice then how pretty she is, the bitterness and anger gone from her eyes. She says: "God is good."

That seems like some kind of miracle.

Suddenly, everyone stops talking. I turn around to see Jared standing on the steps beside a bearded, disheveled man in ragged black clothing. Murmurs pass through the gathering, everyone backing away nervously.

"This is Farouk," Jared says. "He attacked us and killed our friends." Gasps. "He has something to say."

No one speaks, no one moves. I look around at the faces of those in the pool, some stricken with horror, others skeptical, even hostile. The mood has changed instantly from festive to somber.

Farouk looks at Jared, then at us. He straightens and lifts his chin, taking a deep breath. "To you, I am the enemy," he begins, faltering a little in his broken English. "I have hated you—Jew, Christians—all of my life. I was taught to hate. This man," he points to Jared, "told me Yesou says to love your enemies. I thought this… stupid. Weak. Now I see… it is strength." He glances at Jared. "This man could have killed me for what I did. Instead, he showed me… mercy." He hesitates, as if even saying the word 'mercy' is painful. "I did not want mercy. It disturbed me. Why did he do this? Why did he not kill me? I could have died with honor. Then that one," he points to Nasir, "gave me a book in my language. The New Testament. I did not want to read it, but I did. And I… wept. All night long. I wept, because knew I would never be allowed to enter this Yesou's kingdom. But in the night, he came to me. Maybe it was a dream, but it felt very real. I know it was Him. He told me I was welcome. If I would repent of my sin and believe in Him." He pauses, licking his dried lips. "I have done that. I know Yesou has forgiven me. But I ask you, as well, for your forgiveness. And I ask, please, for you to baptize me in His name."

Tears stream down the cheeks of this hardened terrorist. I find myself weeping, too. All the hate I had stored up for this man evaporates in a moment.

Jared guides Farouk into the pool. Ari wades over to him and puts a hand on his shoulder.

"Farouk, you say you want to be baptized in the Holy Spirit. Do you repent of all your sins?"

"I do." Farouk's voice quivers with emotion.

"Do you accept Yeshua, the Christ, as your Lord and Savior?"

"I do."

"Then I baptize you in the name of the Father, Son, and the Holy Spirit."

Ari puts his hand on Farouk's forehead and presses him backward into the water. Once righted again, Farouk sputters a little and looks around with wide eyes, as if the world suddenly looks different to him. He turns to Ari.

"You are a Jew?"

Ari smiles. "We are as one now. There is no distinction between us anymore. For Paul has said, there is neither Jew nor Greek, slave nor free, male or female, for all our one in Christ. I would add to that. There is no longer Jew or Muslim or Arab or any other thing that separates us. We are all one family now, one people, one body in Him who redeems us. So, I welcome you to the kingdom, dear brother."

Ari puts his arms around Farouk and draws him into a hug. Farouk sobs uncontrollably, pounding Ari's back as he returns the embrace. Bree moves toward them and puts her arms around them other. Then Nasir, then Luther, then all the rest. We gather around and form one gigantic group hug.

Thank you, I whisper through tears. *Thank you, thank you.*

This was the sign I needed.

***

Later, drinking hot tea in the visitor's center, wrapped in as many blankets and sweaters as we can find, Davidov tells us that he had a similar experience to Farouk.

"I had been talking to Noah about all that had happened since Jared came to Jerusalem. I had seen things with my own eyes. But still, I was stubborn. I was a Jew. Jews believed certain things. I could not change that. One night, I had a dream. A man in white telling me to come to him. Every night I had this dream. For a week or more. As it turned out, many other people had that same dream of the man in white. They would go to Noah and ask him, who is this man in white? He said it was Yeshua." He chuckles to himself. "It was such a strange thing. How could so many people have the same dream? But I was struggling. I had to know for sure. I decided I should pray to God and ask him what to believe. I had not prayed in many years. I went into a cave, alone, and I prayed well into the night. A man showed up there. I had not seen him before. I never saw him come into the cave—he was just there. He sat beside me and asked me why I refused to believe that Yeshua was Messiah. He asked me why I had such a stubborn heart. He knew things about me he should not know. We talked for a long time. He told me many things. Some things I cannot even remember now. Then suddenly, he went away. I searched the whole camp for him, but I never saw him again."

"An angel," I murmur.

Davidov glances at me. "I take it you have met one as well?"

I smile and nod.

"That is when I decided I needed to be baptized. We brought as many people as would fit in the trucks."

"Wow," I say.

"None too soon," Ari says. "Since the attack on the tower in New Asgard." He pauses.

Davidov looks at him. "So, you know about that? Yes, we did that. It didn't go as planned. We never could find the location of the control center, but hitting the tower seemed more symbolic. It might even have been a better choice. Since the fall of New Asgard, the global markets have collapsed. It's worse than the Great Depression."

"The fall of Babylon," murmurs Ari.

"But the army is still on our doorstep," Jared says somberly.

"True," Davidov replies. "Still, it's hurting them. They are struggling to transport troops and supplies. We have learned that the North and South American Unions have yet to deliver any soldiers at all. And their water supply is critically low."

"That will only push Baldyr to more extreme measures," Jared says.

"Let us not dwell on such things," says Ari. "Let us rejoice in our new brothers and sisters. And give praise to God, for His goodness and mercy." He raises his cup of tea. "Shalom!"

Chapter Fifty-Six
Michael

The armies move over the landscape like floodwater, filling every empty space. They swarm the eastern slope of the Mount of Olives, fill the Hinnom Valley, and line the northern ridges of the Holy City.

It is sunrise in Jerusalem. The sky is streaked with pink and gold and every shade of red. It looks peaceful, beautiful, as it was meant to be. The City of God. And then the Dragons appear, forming a circle in the sky around the decimated Old City, unfurling their long, spindly limbs, aimed at the small gathering on Mount Zion.

Grace Fortune stands on the observation deck, her Singers huddled against the chill of the morning, the chill of what they see coming. An army perched on every ridge. A sky filled with death. Grace's face is calm, serene, almost as if she welcomes this day and what it will bring. It will be a long one. Their voices might give out. They must not grow weary.

The choir on the bleachers sings Psalm 46, a call to arms:

The Lord of Heaven's Armies is here among us;
the God of Israel is our fortress.

Therefore we will not fear though the earth gives way,
though the mountains be moved into the heart of the sea,
though its waters roar and foam,
though the mountains tremble at its swelling.

On mountains all over the world, the Singers join in the Song.

Little Veer and his group perch on the highest hill in Gangkok, India, projecting their voices into heaven. Kato has a band on the mountain called Mafinga in Zambia. Finn built a small settlement on the hills above Lillehammer where his group sings every day, not knowing which day will be the last one. Josephine sings into the radio, transmitting the Song to all who can still hear. Noah gathers his Singers in Petra on top of the Monastery. My forces carry the Song to Jerusalem.

From David's watchtower, Jared's gaze drifts to his wife. Admiration and love well up in his eyes. He fingers the hilt of his sword anxiously. He would rather be holding a guitar.

Lev has positioned his slingers and snipers at the lower end of the City of David, hidden on rooftops and in upper-floor house windows. They peer with anxious expressions at the Light Bringers perched on the Mount of Olives across the valley. A thousand shining warriors, their armor glinting in the rising sun. Dragons hover over their heads, unfurling their deadly limbs, the tips glowing white.

A cry comes from the Mount of Olives, a battle cry, strange and frightening as a thousand Light Bringers shout in unison. The white tips of the Dragon limbs point toward the small band of rebels on Mount Zion.

The Singers raise their voices. The Song makes the air around them warp like summer heat. Our swords burn with Light.

The first pulses of laser energy emerge from the Dragon limbs.

I call my legions to action. We lift our swords, shooting flames across the sky, igniting the air, piercing the Veil. I rise above them and spread Light across the heavens. All shadows are extinguished. Demons squeal in agony. Helel himself cowers in horror at the Light we bring to bear on this fragile earth.

The humans below shield their eyes against the blinding light. They think it is the fire of the Dragons that has come to destroy them.

But it is something else entirely.

Chapter Fifty-Seven
Grace

The Song is all around me, darting and weaving, lifting me so I feel I am floating somewhere above the earth, unable to feel my own body anymore. All I feel is heat and light.

Light.

This must be the end. This must be what it's like to be hit by a pulse laser. Heat, so much heat. I've been cold for so long, the warmth is welcome. Soon, I know, the heat will become unbearable, a burning sensation that will tear through my skin and boil every ounce of water in my body, cooking me from the inside out. I hope it will be quick. I hope I lose consciousness before the pain comes. Pain is something I've never been good at.

I wait. But nothing happens. My skin doesn't bubble up and explode. My brain is not on fire.

Finally, I open my eyes to something... wondrous. Great whorls of undulating light fill the sky—blues and greens and reds and yellows—all the colors of the rainbow locked in some celestial dance. Oohs and aahs replace the Song as everyone looks up into a spectacular, aurora-filled sky.

Are we dead? Is this heaven?

"Ari?" I whisper.

"I'm here."

"What is happening?"

"Could it be…?" He doesn't finish. The small radio in his hand seems to ignite, the spark traveling down the makeshift antenna he'd rigged. He drops the radio, shaking his hands as if he'd been shocked. The radio bursts into flame. We both jump back. Above us, the Dragons move erratically, their black limbs flailing.

"What's happening to them?" I ask breathlessly.

"They seem to have… lost control," Ari stammers.

Sparks burst from the Dragons' tentacles. They tilt and whirl, some spinning in circles, others rocking like ships on a stormy sea. Pulses of light spew from their tips, yet none of them hit us. In fact, they are aimed at each other.

Screams rise from the valley, cries of fear and terror as Dragons burst into flame, exploding like fireworks. Fiery Dragon parts fall onto ridges and valleys where thousands of soldiers stand helpless to elude them. Huge balls of flame ignite the whole earth around us, creating storm clouds of dense smoke. I'm almost grateful for the smoke—it hides the scene of devastation, the horror of human beings crying out as they are burned alive.

"Take cover!" Jared's voice rises from the watchtower. "Grace! Get down from there!"

I can't move. I stare at the scene as if watching a movie. Singers all around me jump up and race for the stairs, covering their ears. I can no longer hear the men's screams—they have been swallowed up by fire and smoke and death.

God, help them.

Perhaps it is too late.

A Dragon crashes much closer to us. I feel the heat and wind of its destruction on my face, searing my eyes shut. Metal shrapnel rains down around me, still on fire. I remember a time I sat too close to fireworks and felt burning ash fall on my arms and legs.

"Grace!" Strong arms surround me, hauling me into the air. Jared. He throws me over his shoulder and races down the steps to the courtyard. The rest of them are huddled there, arms around each other, praying out loud for deliverance.

Yes, Lord, deliver us from evil. Deliver us from destruction. Deliver us through this madness.

A terrible noise rises outside, even louder than the sound of Dragons falling into earth. I've never heard a plane crash, but this sounds to me like a hundred planes crashing at the same time.

"This is it," I whisper into Jared's chest as he sets me on the ground. "I love you, Jared. I love you—"

"I love you too." His voice is a mere thread.

"Do not worry!" Ari shouts to be heard. "We do not die today!"

I turn to him, questioning. "What do you mean? What's happening?"

"What you have witnessed is a sign from God. A celestial EMP." Ari raises his voice to address everyone. "A solar flare. A coronal mass ejection from the sun. The resulting geomagnetic storm has likely knocked out all electronics as well as satellite and internet communications. Baldyr can no longer control the Dragons. That is why they shoot each other." Ari laughs with glee. "Do you not see? God has saved us! Praise Him!"

A hush falls over us. Someone laughs. Someone else shouts, "Hallelujah!"

I look at Jared. "Just like the day you were born," I whisper. "Only bigger this time. Much, *much* bigger."

His blue eyes are so wide with shock I could drown in them.

God had, indeed, saved us.

***

Night falls. The sounds of destruction and death outside have faded. We remain in the courtyard, sheltered from the violence.

I lay curled up in Jared's arms, sometimes dozing, sometimes listening to his heartbeat. Hardly anyone has spoken for hours other than stolen whispers. There is something reverent in this moment, something so awesome no one wants to shatter it with ordinary speech.

We wait for the morning, although the sky is still so bright I'm not sure how we will know it's morning.

Finally, Jared untangles himself from me and gets up.

"I'm going up to see what's happening," he says. "Stay here. Stay calm."

When he leaves me, I feel cold, bereft. I fight the urge to go with him. Bree leaves Ethan, who is curled into a fetal position, and crawls over to me.

"That was terrifying," she says, using her favorite word from our teenage years. Everything back then was terrifying—but this takes the cake.

"But beautiful," I say, looking up at the glorious sky through the courtyard trees. I think of Psalm 19: *The heavens declare the glory of God.*

"What does it mean?" Bree asks.

"It means the Lord has leveled the playing field," Ari says. He's close by, though I had not noticed him. "This would have been a worldwide event. Power grids zapped, and internet and cellular service destroyed. The whole world plunged into darkness. Despite this magnificent light."

"Do you think the army is wiped out too? The soldiers?" Bree asks.

Ari sighs. "Many must have been killed by the falling debris. But not all. However, I suspect they will not be of much use to Baldyr."

"Why?"

"Their biometric tattoos. It connects their brains directly to the grid—that is how they are controlled. They may be out of commission altogether. Incapacitated."

"So God… wiped out the entire army?" Bree says, growing excited. "In like… a minute?"

"Less than that," Ari replies with a low chuckle. "However, they still have the Nephilim. The Light Bringers. They are under the direct control of Baldyr, and I assume they were not given GEMs."

"So they can still attack us," I whisper. "And they will."

Ari nods. "But God has delivered us, this day. He will deliver us again. Either from the fire or… through it."

His words dampen my joy.

Jared returns, looking shell-shocked. We all gather around him.

"I couldn't see much," he says. "So much fire and smoke. But nothing is moving in the valley. No signs of…life."

For a moment, no one says anything. Then Nasir jumps up, his fists in the air. "God beat them! God took down the Dragons!" He breaks into a spontaneous song, a song of praise. Psalm 48.

How great is the Lord, how deserving of praise,
in the city of our God, which sits on his holy mountain!
Mount Zion, the holy mountain, is the city of the great King!

Soon everyone is singing, our horror and fear melting away in a burgeoning sense of relief—God has saved us.

You destroyed them like the mighty ships of Tarshish
The city of the Lord of Heaven's Armies.
It is the city of our God; he will make it safe forever.

I turn to Jared, but he has suddenly disappeared. I search all over until I find him, back in our attic room, the guitar in his hands. He strums without singing, a haunting melody I've never heard before. It sounds like weeping.

I sit beside him. "What's the matter?" I ask. "You should be happy. God gave us victory today."

He stops playing and looks at me. "Vale is still out there. With the Light Bringers."

"So? If God rescued us today, won't he do the same tomorrow?"

"Yes. But I can't help but wonder... how."

He returns to playing.

I listen for a while, trying to understand his fear. I think I understand. Jared's real question is, *Lord, what will this cost me?* It's a question I've asked many times.

I hum along with his song, searching for the words.

The LORD your God is in your midst,
a mighty one who will save;
he will rejoice over you with gladness;
he will quiet you by his love;
he will exult over you with loud singing.

The words of Zechariah spin in my brain, finding a home in Jared's melody. He sings with me, a gentle harmony, an echo of my own voice, and I think for a moment I can hear all the angels of heaven singing too.

Chapter Fifty-Eight
Helel

I admit I did not see this coming: The world plunged into darkness. Our Dragons destroyed. Our soldiers now useless zombies, their brains turned to mush. All our beautiful machines—both human and nonhuman—lie in wrecked heaps, spewing toxins into the air. Dead satellites spin through the upper atmosphere and crash into each other. New Asgard has fallen, the city a hollow shell, the tower destroyed. Gabriel descended with his minions to drag Azazel and the rest of the Grigori back to their prison cells in the Abyss.

Lesser beings would be discouraged. Perhaps even give up. But I am not one of those.

I still have Baldyr and the Light Bringers, each one an army in himself. And I had made sure that our atomics were heavily shielded from any celestial attack. We may have lost the first battle, but we will still win the war. I will achieve my goal: the total annihilation of this world the Almighty had made. He did most of the work for me.

Baldyr, however, has yet to be convinced. He rages in his palatial quarters, built literally overnight, overturning chairs and smashing tables to smithereens.

"How are they doing this?" Baldyr turns on me, his face a prism of fury. "Why did we not know they had this power?"

I raise my hands in surrender. "I did warn you that, however weak they appeared, our enemy is not without… allies."

"Allies? What allies?"

I bristle at the comment. "They call him Elohim, Lord of All. He and I have had a difference of opinion on that front."

Baldyr's mouth drops open. "You speak of the Jehovian god."

I nod, reluctantly.

"You told me he was a fiction!"

"Well, I may have exaggerated. But listen, that is not important. Focus, Baldyr. Our plan has not changed. We expected—opposition. But you still have a clear advantage. The Light Bringers will make quick work of the hold-outs. No fancy tech, just a good, rollicking blood bath. It will be fun." I don't tell him about the ultimate ending I have planned. Better for that to be a surprise.

Baldyr growls in reply, unconvinced. I try a different approach.

"You are the Destroyer. They used to call *him* that, didn't they? But he never was, not really. He was too weak, too soft. Too… *human*. You don't have that problem. *You* are the true Destroyer. That is what you were born to be."

He straightens as I speak, his chin lifting.

"Destroyer," he murmurs.

"Would the Destroyer give up now? You are wounded, yes, but you are not defeated. You have life, and you have the Light Bringers. Moreover, you have me. This is the fight you have been waiting for. You. Against him."

He turns to face me. "Me. Against him."

I go to him and put my hands on his shoulders. "My boy," I say. "You have a new father now. Your real father abandoned you. Your fake father ignored you. I am your *true* father. I created you. I gave you my own spirit. I will never leave you nor forsake you. You will have victory, if you trust in me. Do you trust in me?" I cup the side of his face, as I assume a father would a child. He responds as I hoped; his eyes begin to glow, and his body trembles. He nods.

"Good. Now, my boy, my *Destroyer,* don't you want the chance to face your betrayer and give him what he deserves? In front of all his people?"

He nods again, his eyes shining now with my own dark fire.

I smile. "Then listen carefully. I will tell you what you must do."

Chapter Fifty-Nine
Jared

"Unbelievable."

Lev stands beside me on the watchtower, surveying the carnage. Fires burn along the entire valley while enormous flocks of birds feast upon the dead. It's a gruesome sight. The city continues to smolder; whatever was left of it now utterly leveled by the falling Dragons. Not one stone stands upon another. Jerusalem is gone.

"The Lord surely has a sense of humor, doesn't he?" Lev chuckles to himself. "They have nothing to fight with except swords and spears against our rifles and slings. This is going to be more like the Last Crusade than World War Three."

"The Light Bringers are not ordinary soldiers," I say.

"So you say. But an uphill assault through those fires and all that wreckage—even the Romans would not have attempted something like that."

"Someone's coming!" A sentry from the observation deck shouts. Several snipers on duty train their rifles on a lone figure riding through the fiery valley, the horse leaping easily over mangled Dragons and dead men. A Light Bringer. He carries a white banner on the tip of his crystal spear.

"Hold your fire," I shout.

"What's he want?" Lev growls, reaching for his sidearm.

"To deliver a message," I say. "They can't use their drones anymore."

Resisting the urge to run down to meet him, I wait as the rider makes his way up the slope. He rides fast and easily, without caution, as if he does not care at all about the guns trained upon him, as if they could not hurt him. He might not be wrong about that. His armor appears molded to his body, made of some sort of flexible material revealing every muscle and sinew. His horse is also armored, probably fireproof. His face is hidden within a striking winged helmet like that of a Norse god.

He stops before me, the great horse snorting and stamping. He's so big that Lev takes several steps backward.

"I am Hermod, messenger of Baldyr, Divine Lord of the United Earth," he says, his voice somewhat muffled from the helmet.

"Divine Lord?" I say. A step up from Supreme Lord, I guess.

"The Divine Lord gives you this message. He demands that you, Impostor, False Son, and Betrayer, meet him in a contest of single combat, to the death, at first light tomorrow morning. You may choose one weapon. If you fail to take this challenge, you and your people will die."

I take a breath, though my chest is so tight that no air gets to my lungs. "And if I win, you will retreat?" I ask.

The messenger hesitates. "Correct. But if he wins, the insurrectionists must surrender and submit themselves to Baldyr, Divine Lord of the United Earth. They must take the mark and worship him, or die."

"Where do we meet?" I ask. Lev, behind me, makes a noise of protest. I raise a hand to silence him.

"You will meet the Divine Lord on that mountain at dawn tomorrow." He points to the Mount of Olives.

"Tell him I accept."

Lev gasps. Hermod spins his horse and trots back down the hill. I gulp in a bit of air and let it out slowly, trying to untwist my insides.

"Are you insane?" Lev bursts out. "Why did you do this? Even if you win, they will attack anyway."

"I know it."

"And we will not surrender."

"I know that, too."

"Then why?" He's beyond exasperation.

"I must do what I must do," I say.

Lev makes a noise and stomps away. I can't even imagine what Grace is going to say when she hears this.

***

"Are you insane?" Grace shouts while I sharpen my sword in our attic room. "You can't do this, Jared. Listen to me!"

"I have to," I say stoically for the tenth time. "If there's a chance it will avoid a war—"

"What happened to 'Stand?' Let God do the fighting! He saved us once. He'll do it again!"

"Maybe this *is* His plan," I say.

"Has He told you that?"

I don't reply. I haven't heard from God or Michael on this subject.

"I knew it. This isn't God's plan. This is *your* plan. You couldn't pass up the chance for another heroic fight. Even if you end up dead."

"That's not it," I say. "I have to see him. Face-to-face. He's giving me a chance, don't you see? A chance for... something. Reconciliation. Forgiveness. He called me brother once. I have to believe that the boy I knew is still there, somewhere."

"You are so naïve!" She throws up her hands. "He's a monster, and he hates you. Why can't you just accept that?"

"Did you accept that about me? When you thought I was on their side?"

She pauses, the fury leeching out of her. "No," she whispers. "I believed it. But I never accepted it." She throws herself down on the blankets. "But this is different, Jared. I can't lose you now. I can't—" She stops. I look at her, seeing she is about to say more. She can't... what? But she doesn't finish the sentence. Instead, she rolls over and buries her face in the blankets.

Tell her now.

Is that Michael speaking? God? Or my own divided heart?

Maybe knowing the truth will make this clearer.

I get up, put aside the sword, and sit beside her on the blankets. I take a breath. "Grace."

After a moment, she turns over to look at me. Her eyes are red from crying.

"There's something I need to tell you. About... Vale."

She blinks, saying nothing.

"Vale is my... son."

She sits up suddenly. I study her face, watch her eyes widen to saucers, then flatten, compress, her brow furrowing.

"What are you talking about?"

I tell her. Everything.

She is brave. She doesn't cry. Doesn't scream. She's playing the scenario in her mind, terrible, awful images, the horror moving across her face in waves. Her lower lip trembles slightly. She lets out a breath.

I wait.

"How long have you known this?" Her voice is hollow.

"I might have known before, but I didn't remember it. Michael told me."

"Michael. An angel told you." She closes her eyes. "Why?"

"I think he wanted me to be... prepared."

"So that's what this is about."

"Grace—" I reach out to touch her. She recoils, slides away from me, and heads for the door. She hesitates in the doorway but doesn't look back. I hear her breathe out.

Then she is gone.

I return to my stool, my blade. Pick it up again and set it against the stone.

This is what my life has come to. This blade. Where did everything go so wrong? Was there never any chance for me? For us?

The face of another man comes to mind, a face startlingly like mine. And a name as well. Lester Crow. Memories return in a flood—a man determined to beat me, a man who also became like a brother to me, a man I failed to save in the end.

A sob rises from the depths of my soul, and I throw the sword across the room. It clatters against the wall. A strand of golden sunlight falls upon the metal, reflecting in my eyes, taunting me still.

Grace. Crow. Vale. People I have loved. People I have failed. That slim blade is all I have left.

Chapter Sixty
Michael

I met Helel here once before, at this very place, the Mount of Olives, the night he came in the vessel of Iscariot, the true Betrayer. That was thousands of human years ago, yet it feels like mere moments. My Light had been bound then for a purpose even I did not understand. I remember his delight, his unspeakable joy at his apparent victory. And his boundless fury three days later.

He comes now in the shape of Amon H. Doyle, though his darkness overflows that painted shell, dense and limitless. How beautiful he was once, how glorious in his fullness. How brokenhearted I still am at the memory of the choice he made.

Why does he never learn? I wonder at his hubris. He knows his end. He knows he cannot avoid it. And yet he thinks that by turning even one of Elohim's children away from Him, he can delay the inevitable. Elohim is slow to anger, slow to judge, and desires to wait for all His children to return to Him. But even the Almighty One will not wait forever.

And so Helel has poured his spirit into Vale, now called Baldyr, and directs him to lead the destruction of the world, starting here, with my city, Jerusalem. The Light Bringers gather on the ridge of the Mount of Olives, their giant horses stamping and snorting, their golden armor sparkling in the myriad colors of the auroras overhead. Doyle stays close to Baldyr, whispering in his ear.

Helel comes near to me. I raise a shield of Light to keep him at bay.

"Is your boy coming?"

"He will come," I say.

"You made a mistake in telling him the truth. It will weaken him."

"The truth is never a mistake."

I make a path through the fire for Jared to walk through the valley and up the long hill of sarcophagi, his black trousers and shirt in sharp contrast to the whiteness of the tombs. His eyes are downcast.

He carries no sword.

"This is going to be such a disappointment," Doyle says with mock sadness.

Baldyr growls something, then dismounts and descends the switchback to the lower level as Jared approaches. Even the horses go still, sensing a change in the atmosphere.

I gather my legions, as does Uriel and Raquel who are stationed on Mount Zion. Saraqâêl and Samael take up positions between the two camps. Raphael and Remiel remain with the Remnant at Petra. Gabriel oversees all, having dispatched Azazel and his Grigori to the Deep.

Father and son stare at each other for a long moment.

"Where is your sword?" Baldyr demands.

"I didn't come to fight. I came to talk."

"That was not our deal."

"Vale—"

"My name is *Baldyr*. And what should I call you? *Father?*" He laughs.

"Please, will you listen? I came to ask for your forgiveness. I never wanted to hurt you. I loved you like a brother, and now that I know you are my son, I love you even more—"

"Why should I believe anything you say? You have been lying to me from the moment I met you."

"Yes, I have. About some things. But not about this thing—"

Baldyr's barking laughter cuts Jared off. "You expect me to believe that? When all this time you have been plotting to kill me?"

"Not you," Jared says. "Only... him. You were as much his slave as I was. I wanted you to be free—"

"Do I look like a slave?" He sweeps an arm toward his Light Bringers. "*I* am Champion of the Arena now. I lead an army of supermen. What do you lead? A pathetic band of rebels? You made your choice, *Father*. And you did not choose me. Now, I give you another choice. To save yourself and your loser friends. Your only chance." He turns and shouts for a sword. Doyle grabs one from the nearest Light Bringer and tosses it down. It lands at Jared's feet.

Baldyr speaks in a savage whisper. "Pick. Up. Your. Sword."

Jared shakes his head. "Vale, listen, this is not who you are. You used to love music, remember that? We would sit together and play the guitar... I was teaching you to play. Now... what do you love? Nothing. All you feel is hate. It's eating you alive—"

"Pick it up!"

The Light Bringers begin thumping their spears and chanting Baldyr's name. Jared tries to speak, but his voice is drowned out by the cacophony.

With a loud cry, Baldyr launches himself, sword raised for a strike to Jared's head. He darts out of the way in time. Baldyr picks up the sword from the ground and throws it end over end at Jared, who catches it without thinking, pure muscle memory. Baldyr slashes again—Jared raises the blade to deflect the blow. Over and over Baldyr attacks—Jared defends himself but offers no counterstrike.

"Your boy doesn't want to play?" Helel sneers.

"He will not kill his own son," I reply.

"Ha! That's the problem with your kind. Too many rules."

Helel calls in reinforcements: Dark Ones swarm over Jared, clouding his vision, weighing down his strength. He stumbles, taking a slashing blow to the thigh, then another to the shoulder. Blood seeps from the wounds.

My legions descend to drive the Dark Ones off and crush them into oblivion. Yet more come. An unending number pour out from the shadow of Helel.

Baldyr's attack is relentless, pressing Jared up against the railing. He manages to push Baldyr off and flip backward over the railing, landing on a tomb ten feet below. His ankle twists and he collapses. Baldyr leaps on top of him.

They tumble off the tomb onto the ground. Baldyr is up first, slashing with his sword.

I throw a shield around Jared to protect him—the Dark Ones glom onto my shield and burrow their way through. My warriors struggle to pick them off, yet still more and more Dark Ones come, overwhelming our efforts.

And then, from Zion, comes music. Bree and her choir singing.

The Lord All-Powerful is with us;
the God of Jacob is our defender.
He stops wars everywhere on the earth.
He breaks all bows and spears
and burns up the chariots with fire.

The sound is faint, barely noticeable over the chanting of the Light Bringers and the discordant rant of the Dark Ones. Then Grace and her Singers join in with the AngelSong—it wafts through the valley and swirls around the tombs of the Mount of Olives, filtering into Baldyr's ears. The Song is magnified by the Singers on other mountains all over the world—it breaks through the Veil and enters the atmosphere, igniting every molecule of air. The Light Bringers stop their chanting, covering their ears and shrieking in pain. Dark Ones scurry for cover as my legions rush in to finish them off.

Baldyr pauses in his attack, shaking his head as if struck. He staggers and swings his sword aimlessly. Jared staggers to his feet.

Helel curses and swoops in to block the Song from his ears. Baldyr, released for a moment from the power of the Song, swings his sword, connecting with Jared's right side.

Jared falls to his knees, dropping this weapon. He hunches over, grabbing his side—blood seeps through his fingers.

Baldyr raises his sword for the killing blow.

I hurl my flaming sword at Helel—he screams in agony as the blade splits his essence. He loses his grip on Baldyr, who hesitates, sword in midair. The Song bursts upon him once more—his eyes bulge and his mouth twists in agony.

In that moment of hesitation, Jared moves. With the last of his strength, he lunges at his son and throws his arms around him, using his weight to pin him to the ground.

Baldyr flails against him, hitting him again and again with his sword. More wounds appear on Jared's back, deep cuts soaking his shirt, but Jared does not let go.

I throw a coil of Light around them, fusing them together. Baldyr is stronger than his father, but he is not stronger than me.

Doyle screams to the Light Bringers. "To Zion! Kill them all!"

With a great war cry, the Light Bringers descend from the ridge on their huge horses and swarm down the slope into the valley where Uriel and Raquel stir up the flames ever higher.

The Song wavers—a few of the Singers seeing the coming charge stop singing and run for cover. Grace keeps singing, her arms up high, her gaze focused on something unseen in the swirling sky above. Tears stream down her cheeks. She cannot see what is happening to her husband, but she knows now that his battle must be over.

Jared grabs Baldyr's sword arm with his left hand and squeezes, forcing the sword from his grip. Baldyr frantically grasps his weapon. Helel dives to help him, but I hold him off with my Light, burning ever brighter from the power of the Song.

"How dare you!" Helel rages at me. "He is mine!"

"If you want him, try to take him," I reply.

Helel tries, to no avail. Darkness cannot overcome Light.

The Light Bringers leap into the fires of the valley, burning so bright and hot now that many of the beasts burst into flame. Yet they still come, trailing flame, unmindful of the pain, charging up the slope. When the horses collapse, the Light Bringers continue on foot, running as if nothing could hinder them.

"Fire!" Lev shouts. Shepherd boys standing on rooftops sling their stones at over one hundred miles per hour at the golden warriors. Raquel removes all air resistance and guides the stones to their intended targets. Despite their armor, the Light Bringers fall. Snipers positioned in open windows aim mainly at the surviving horses, forcing more of the enemy to continue on foot. The Song slows their progress, as if they are moving against a hurricane wind.

"We don't have to do this," Jared whispers to his struggling son, nearly spent himself, his blood still flowing from his many wounds. "Let it go, Vale. Let *him* go."

"He loves me..."

"No, he doesn't. He can't love anyone but himself. But I love you. That's why I came. And God loves you. Please, Vale, listen to me..."

A movement from above catches my attention—Doyle raises his arm, something gleaming in his hand.

A gun.

He takes aim at Jared's body and fires. I throw my Light upon the bullet, slowing it, changing its course. At the same time, I release the coils holding Jared and Baldyr together. With a burst of strength, Baldyr throws Jared off him and lunges for his sword just as the bullet slams into his back. He gasps, eyes wide with shock. He is frozen for a long moment, his sword slipping from his fingers. And then, slowly, he falls.

Jared catches him and cradles him in his arms.

Doyle, seeing what his bullet has done, lets out a wail of agony that seems to stop time. All beings, Light and Dark, are frozen by the sound.

The ground rumbles. The covers of the tombs shiver on their mountings. Loose stones tumble downhill. The Mount of Olives booms, the sound like a thousand freight trains colliding. The mountain splits open into a wide crevasse, breaking apart the Hotel of Seven Arches.

Shock waves spread to Mount Zion, tottering the fragile buildings around the City of David. Slingers tumble off roofs. The shooters jump from collapsing buildings and flee. All becomes chaos as the warriors in this battle turn from fighting each other to fighting the trembling earth.

Doyle scrambles down to where Jared and Baldyr lie together, bound by blood.

"Give him to me! I can save him!" Doyle shrieks. He claws at Jared's clothes and hair, attempting to pull him off the boy. Jared holds fast, as do I. He's singing into his son's ear. A song I know too well.

Baldyr's eyes close. His breath is ragged. I touch his head, resting my Light upon him, drawing out the darkness within him. He is willing now—his spirit lifts to meet my Light. The Destroyer, fades. His body shrivels, his white hair darkens.

"No!" Doyle shrieks. Helel, caught on the end of my sword, wails in despair.

Vale's eyes open suddenly. He stares into space, a smile suddenly curving his bloody mouth.

"Father..."

Then, with a shuddering groan, his breath leaves his body one last time. Jared wraps his arms around him, holding him close.

From the heavens come the pure note of a trumpet call, forcing all other sounds to silence.

Chapter Sixty-One
Jared

I hold my son in my arms.

My blood seeps from my body, mixing with his. It's as if we are one person now. He is part of me, more than the brother I thought he was. My son. My *son*.

I hold him close as the ground beneath us lurches and trembles, and the lids of the tombs shiver and pop. A deafening roar seems to emanate from deep inside the earth. I glance up to see—what do I see? The entire mountain breaking, cracking open like an egg.

Something tugs at me, trying to pull me off him, but my own body is too heavy. It refuses to move. I am made of lead, stone. I put my head close to his and listen for breathing. *Vale. Vale. Don't go yet.* I sing to him. A song we once sang together, in the underground. A song he didn't know I wrote, Grace and me.

Dear God, won't you
Take me away to a place
Where the dragons don't watch us
like birds of prey?

What started this? I had been sharpening my own sword, prepared to meet him, prepared to fight, and instead, I prayed. I asked for an answer. It came clearly: *do not fight*. This is madness, I thought. If I lose, everyone will die. *Do you not trust me?* said the voice.

So I went to him with nothing. Prepared to die. Trusting. What has that wrought? Not my death but his. Why does it have to be this way?

"Let me have him!"

A voice assails me, demanding I give him up. Who is that? It doesn't matter. I won't give him up. Not now. Not ever.

I feel his life seeping away. Then I hear a word from his lips.

"Father..."

He is not looking at me. What does he see? Which father does he mean?

"Give him to me! I can save him!" The voice rages in my ear. "He wants me! Give him to me!"

I feel my son let out a rattling breath, his last. I close my eyes to weep.

Something shifts—is it me or the world? The noise of battle and earthquake dissolves into a single sound, the clear note of a trumpet, filling every corner of my being.

Against all possibility, I open my eyes again.

All I see is... light.

Chapter Sixty-Two
Grace

Jared and Vale. Father and son. I spend all night trying to come to terms with that.

My mother—I swallow the bile that rises every time I think of what she did. The nausea will never go away.

I should hate her all over again. What I feel instead is... pity. Maybe that's worse.

I should have stayed with him. Talked it out. Even told him what I really wanted to tell him, but didn't. Perhaps he wouldn't have left. We could have faced this final battle together.

But I walked away. Now, he is alone on that mountain, surrounded by evil.

Lord, protect him and save him.

My prayer feels empty now. A meaningless arrangement of words.

I close my eyes, raise my hands though they feel like dead weight, and open my mouth, praying the Song comes forth. It does, somehow. My body fills with it, driving away the consuming dark. My arms go higher. The others join in, their melodies weaving with me, forming a tapestry of music as ethereal and brilliant as the colors of the sky.

Tears stream down my cheeks. *Jared, I love you. I will see you soon...*

The Song seems to take on shape, dimension, weight. It's louder, brighter, more resonant than ever before—I realize I am hearing it not just near but from afar. Other voices, from mountaintops all over the world. We didn't need the radio to connect us, after all. I open my eyes and look at the sky to see the auroras twisting and turning in rhythm with the Song. I am staggered by this feeling of oneness, the spiritual and physical realities coming together, like a dance.

A great cry comes from the Mount of Olives—the Nephilim pour down the mountain. The Song lodges in my throat. Lev shouts orders to his men.

I squeeze Ari's hand and grab the hand of Rebecca beside me as we watch them come. We join hands to keep each other from running. I hear cries from the bleachers below us. A few people scatter, trying to get to the tunnels. *No!* I want to scream. *No!* But I can't break the Song. *Let them come.* I am ready now, I think. Ready to die. *I will be with you soon, my love.*

The rebels unleash their weapons as the Light Bringers crash through the wall of fire. Stones and bullets fly. Enemy horses collapse. A well of hope opens within me.

We sing.

They are still coming, many on foot, some even on fire. But they come. They've crossed the valley and are headed up the slope.

We sing.

I hear a rumble from somewhere, like distant thunder rolling toward us. The olive trees bordering the garden of Gethsemane shiver as if buffeted by a strong wind. But it's not the wind; it's the earth—the ground is shaking.

The Mount of Olives trembles as if it were made of Jell-O. The lids of the tombs launch in the air. The Light Bringers whirl around in confusion.

With a sound like a volcanic eruption, the Mount of Olives... splits open. Right down the middle, a huge crack opens wide like a gigantic mouth, swallowing everything in its wake. Shockwaves rattle the deck under my feet—buildings on either side of the excavation area tremble and fall like houses of cards. Roofs collapse, and walls cave in. The stones of David's palace rock against each other and tumble down into the excavation pit.

I drop to my knees and scramble away from a huge crack that opens in the deck under me.

"Run!" someone shouts.

Ari and I hold onto each other, still singing. I think we are the only ones. I feel secure, enfolded in the Song, which carries above the rising din. The sky, too, has become dark and stormy. The auroras are gone. Shadows fall deep into the valley, cloaking the once-golden Light Bringers in utter darkness.

Below us, I can hear Bree and a few others still singing:

In just a little while, the wicked will be no more.

Only a little while.

I close my eyes and wait.

And then the awful noises stop, as if someone turned off the volume of the world. I stop singing. Only one sound remains, clear and steady, sustaining the world that hangs in the balance.

A trumpet? Not one trumpet. Many. Thousands. Pure and sweet, a sound so beautiful I suddenly want to weep. It fills the sky, the earth, the depth of my own heart. I open my eyes.

The world is full of light. So bright there are no longer any shadows anywhere. The light seems to be pouring out of the space between the mountain halves. Or is it pouring in? I can't tell. It blasts outward, an explosion of light, a supernova. Could be the nuclear bomb we thought they would drop on us. But there is no accompanying fire, no searing heat, no thunderous boom. Only the music.

I stare into the light, which doesn't burn my eyes as it should. Something emerges from the core, something that fills the space from earth to heaven. A white horse. And on its back, a rider draped in red. I can't see his face for the brightness, as if his face were the source of the light itself. The horse's hooves perch on either side of the widening fissure in the mountain. Stars swirl around the rider, banishing all shadow—no, not stars, angels.

And a long blade of fire seems to come out of the rider's mouth. It reaches all the way to the opposite horizon, sweeping over the land, consuming everything in its path. A great bellow of fear surges from the Light Bringers trapped in the valley below. They try to run, but there is no escape. Not for any of us. I watch it approach in its deadly arc and raise my arms in surrender. I feel it pass over me, through me, like a wind on fire, expecting it to sear my eyes and my flesh. I feel no burn. Then the ground beneath me trembles and gives way, staggering under the weight of that burning fire. I am falling. Alone.

Words come into my heart as I let go of everything.

> *We are afflicted in every way, but not crushed;*
> *perplexed, but not driven to despair;*
> *persecuted, but not forsaken;*
> *struck down, but not destroyed*

Not destroyed. Even now.

I will see you soon, my love.

In a moment.

Chapter Sixty-Three
Michael

The King comes on his mighty stallion, as He promised He would. He raises his sword.

"My life for his," Helel cries as he spreads himself over the two humans still locked together among the tombs. "Let me go and I will give him to you."

"He is not yours to give," says the King.

"But, he called to me..."

"Not to you."

In desperation, Helel cowers before the King, pleading. —*Is not Elohim infinitely merciful? Slow to anger? Full of loving kindness?*

—*Do you consider yourself worthy of mercy? Have you shown mercy to any of my own?*

The King reaches out his hand to strike. Helel screams in agony, his earthly vessel burned to cinders. Samael swoops in to take him to the Deep, where he will remain for a thousand years.

The great flaming sword that once guarded Eden passes over the entire world. And the world is reborn.

The King rides toward the gates of the new city, accompanied by his legions, his robe stained red from the blood of his enemies. The resurrected ones follow, all those who died for Him and in Him. They shout and sing with joy, storming the gates.

Jared remains, barely breathing, his big body curled around that of his dead son. I recall the last time I had to do what I am about to do now. As always, just in time.

I touch Jared's shoulder.

"Rise."

Chapter Sixty-Four
Grace

I open my eyes to a vision of blue. *This is heaven.*

Grass tickles the base of my neck. There's grass in heaven? I just want to lie still, bask in the sweet scent, the warm air, the blue sky. It's almost more than blue, deeper and sharper than any color I have ever seen, as if all the colors in the world, no matter how vibrant, were mere shadows of their true nature.

"Grace."

I turn my head. A face looks down upon me, smiling, serene. I take a breath and hold it, unable to let it go.

"Silas?" I sit up, still staring to be sure this isn't an apparition, a ghost, or some AI-generated mirage. I touch his face. His skin is warm. His long silver hair moves in the soft breeze. "Dad?"

"Hey, Kiddo," he says. "Nice of you to wake up."

"Dad!" I throw my arms around him, laughing like a crazy person.

I feel his arms around me, pulling me tighter. "Grace," he whispers in my ear. "My girl."

Tears spill from my eyes, though I'm still laughing. "What's happened? How are you here? Wait, was it all just a dream? Am I finally awake? Like in the Wizard of Oz?"

"'Fraid not."

I pull away to look at him. He looks so much younger than I remember, and he's completely healthy, with no sign of cancer. His clothes are white, a color he never wore before, unless it was covered with paint stains.

"Wow. I'm just… so, how are you here? Is this heaven?"

He shakes his head. "Not exactly. It's more like a new kind of earth."

"Oh? Oh!"

I look around in wonder. The ruins are gone, the houses, the stones, every building that stood here a moment ago. I see nothing but grass and trees now, huge, spreading olive trees, healthy and thriving.

It's a garden.

"Is this still Jerusalem?"

Silas nods. "This is still Mount Zion. As it was in the beginning."

"So…it happened then. He came? Jesus?"

"The King is here."

We walk together up the hill to where the courtyard of the City of David once stood. Now I can see the Temple Mount. I gasp in surprise. A huge building sits there, a palace that extends from one end to the other, with tall golden spires like something out of a fairy tale.

"He's there?" I ask.

Silas laughs, takes my hand, and leads me through the Dung Gate. The stones of the archway are brilliant white, as if they had been sandblasted. The whole wall looks like it was just built yesterday. Which I guess it was.

The street teems with people, most dressed in white like Silas, hugging and laughing and chatting like it's one gigantic family reunion. Among them are people I recognize—Ari and Nasir and several of the people from our compound, all looking as dumbfounded as me. Ari comes over to greet us, shaking with laughter. He looks younger, and his hair is now jet black.

"Grace, Grace… you are alive! How wonderful. It is all… too wonderful."

"Yes," I say, though I'm finding it hard to speak. "This is my father."

"Your father?" Ari looks Silas over. "You are one of them? The resurrected ones?"

Silas grins. "Looks like."

"So good to meet you!" Ari shakes my father's hand vigorously. "So, so good! Everything is good!" He laughs as if he will never stop.

We proceed into the heart of the city as more friends come up to greet us. I'm struck dumb by the city I see before me—no destruction, no fires, no dead bodies. The street is clean; the buildings are bright and new. The whole city, it seems, has been restored.

"Grace!"

I turn to see Bree launching herself at me, followed by Ethan who is walking straight without a cane. Their clothes are as clean as mine. Bree hugs me then hugs Silas. Even Ethan hugs me, beaming from ear to ear. He's got a full head of hair, and his cheeks are rosy as if he's just run a marathon. He can't get a word in edgewise because Bree is talking a blue streak.

"Can you believe it? Of course, you can… Silas… wow… this is incredible… we need to find Ralph and Emilia! They must be here… have you seen the palace? It's so beautiful! Come on! You have to go!"

"Take it easy," Ethan says, though he's laughing. "We just got here."

"Ethan, you're… better?" I ask.

"Better than I've ever felt," he replies. "I can breathe again. And walk. And run. Even my eye sight is fixed. I don't need contact anymore." His smile reaches all the way to his ears.

My heart suddenly feels as though it will burst out of my chest—my body can no longer hold it.

"Where's Blondie?" Ethan asks, looking around.

A stab of pain cuts through my joy. "I don't know," I say.

"He's got to be here somewhere," Bree says. "I mean, everyone is here! I bet Penny and Mason and Ripley and everyone from the Rez are here too! This is so exciting I can't even stand it!"

"Where do we look?" I ask, almost too dumfounded to think clearly.

"Go to the palace," Silas says. "The martyrs returned with the King and will rule with him now."

I glance up at the astonishing palace. "Do you think Jared is in there? You think he's... one of them?"

"Only one way to find out."

"I can't go in there. I mean, I'm not worthy—"

"Everyone is allowed in. All who seek will find."

I blink at my father in disbelief. "He must be so busy today, his first day here. Maybe we should just look around some more. Jared might be in this crowd somewhere..."

"Let's go." Silas grabs my hand again and drags me to the palace on the hill. It's almost too much to take in, the gleaming buildings on either side of the street, the sidewalks lined with flowering trees, the people rushing around in joyful reunion.

Up close, the palace is as big as a mountain. Wide steps lead up to the portico lined with columns. Many people dressed in white with golden circlets on their heads fill the portico. They are singing.

I pause to listen. I don't know the song, and yet it sounds familiar, like a heartbeat, like the rustling of leaves in the trees—all nature singing in praise.

All glory to God alone
Praise to the One who holds the throne
Name above all Names
King Jesus, King Jesus

We walk slowly up the steps. People in the portico turn to look at me. I feel my face redden, knowing they can probably see everything about me. Every horrible thing I have ever done. And then, among them, I catch sight of a familiar face.

"Ralph!" I shriek and run up the steps to fall into his arms. I feel the vibration of laughter in his chest as he picks me up off the ground in a great, bear hug.

"Ha! My girl! We've been waiting for you!"

"I told you she'd be here, didn't I?" says a chirpy, female voice, and I turn to see Emilia's rosy-cheeked face as she joins in our group hug.

"Oh you guys, I've missed you so much. I can't believe this is all really happening."

Ralph pulls away so he can look at me. "I never got to see you during our jailhouse conversations. But I knew that one day, I would see you again. And it would be… marvelous."

"You got me through those days," I tell him. "God knew I couldn't have made it without you."

"I think you would have. But I am grateful for that little gift from the Lord."

"Oh Ralph, Emilia, have you seen him? Jared? Is he here?"

They look at each other. I can't read their expressions.

"Perhaps you should go ask Him," Emilia says, gently steering me to the doors. "*He* will know the answer."

I hesitate. "Wait. What do I say? Isn't there some sort of, you know, protocol or whatever? How do you address the King of the Universe?"

"I'm sure you'll think of something." Emilia gives me a little shove.

My heart nearly leaps out of my chest as I stumble toward that open door. So many people are going through at the same time—I'll probably be in there all day, waiting. Well, that will give me time to gather my thoughts. Think of something not dumb to say. I join the crowd and walk in.

Suddenly, everyone else is gone. I'm alone in a great palace with columns that seem to reach infinity and a floor made of gold and studded with colorful gemstones. I walk carefully down a long aisle, my footsteps making no noise at all, toward a bright light at the far end.

"How can I help you, child?"

The voice is like music... the most perfect of melodies. I stop walking, transfixed. He's there—he looks astoundingly human and let somehow different, *more* than human. His face is kind, though his eyes burn with a peculiar fire. He smiles at me. I open my mouth to speak—nothing comes out. Instead, I fall to my knees, weeping.

I feel a hand on the top of my head, infinitely gentle.

"What's troubling you, Grace?" He asks.

"I... I lost him." Tears spill down my cheeks, unchecked. I feel a hand on my chin, tilting my head up. I force my eyes open and gaze into His face, so bright and clean, so pure, so radiant, so infinitely gentle. "I'm sorry," I blurt out. Why did I say that? It's like looking at his perfection reminds me of my own failures and flaws, of everything I am not. "Forgive me. Please. Forgive me. I was so awful to him—I left him alone. I should have forgiven him. And my mother, too. My heart was so... hard. Have mercy on me. I'm... I'm sorry."

"Give me your hand," He says.

I open up my hand. He places something in my palm. I look down at it. A perfectly round white stone. My fingers close over it. It seems to have a warmth that spreads up my arm and through my body. Not a raging fire, more like a glowing candle. I burst into tears once more, but not with guilt or shame or sadness. With joy. *This* is joy.

"Thank you," I whisper, clutching the stone to my chest. "Thank you, thank you."

"Now, what is it you ask of me?"

"Oh. I'm looking for... my husband. Do you know him? His name is Jared. He went up to the Mount of Olives. He didn't come back. Is he... here?"

"Turn around."

I do as I'm told. At first, I see nothing, just the whiteness and the endless columns. But then shapes emerge, two figures, one quite tall, the other shorter, slimmer. I blink, unsure of what I am seeing.

"Jared?"

Now I can see him clearly. His blue eyes as clear and bright as a summer sky. Clothes as clean as the day they were made. I want to run to him, throw my arms around him, but I hesitate. There is a boy beside him. Shorter, lanky, with red hair, the same shade as mine. This is not Baldyr. Then I remember him from the holos, standing sullenly beside my mother. *His* mother.

Vale.

They stand before me. Jared's smile is guarded as if he's still not sure about my greeting.

"Grace," he says, "this is my... This is Vale."

For a moment I can't think of anything to say. This is my brother. He's also Jared's son. That's too weird for words.

There is so much I don't understand about this moment. What had happened between them on the Mount of Olives? How had Vale become Baldyr and then turned back into Vale again? But maybe it's not important for me to understand everything right now. Maybe none of that matters, after all.

"Hey, Vale." I put my hand out. He hesitates, then takes it. We start to shake, and then impulsively I pull him into an embrace. "Brother," I whisper.

He pulls away, brow furrowed.

"Long story," I say. I turn to Jared. "Jared. I'm sorry…for what I said. I love you…"

He touches my cheek and smiles. "I love you so much."

"Vale. Come here to me."

The King speaks. We turn to look. Vale starts to move and then collapses to his knees, his face to the floor.

"Lord, forgive me… I am a sinner, a murderer… I've done so much evil…"

The King kneels beside the boy and puts his arms around his shaking shoulders.

"You are forgiven," He says. "Look at me." Vale slowly raises his gaze. "You are here, now, because your earthly father refused to give up on you, even if it meant forfeiting his own life. He did that because it is what I did for you and for all who have ever lived. Your sins are great, but My love is greater."

The King takes Vale's hand, opens it, and places a white stone in his palm. He closes his fingers over it. Vale puts his fist to his chest and mouths the words, "Thank you." The King reaches out to wipe the tears from Vale's eyes. Then he rises and turns to Jared.

"Well done, good and faithful servant." He puts his hand on Jared's shoulder. "You've had a long road, haven't you? Time to rest."

Jared drops to his knees, bowing his head. "Forgive me," he stammers. "I caused so much pain… I brought so much horror to the world…"

"I no longer remember your sins." The Lord takes Jared's hand and places within it a white stone. Jared clutches it to his chest just as Vale did.

"What else do you want to ask me?" The King looks at me now.

He knows what I want.

I swallow hard, afraid to ask the question, afraid of the answer. I tremble as if I am standing before a jury at trial, awaiting a verdict.

"My mother..." I whisper.

The King shakes his head.

I let out a breath I'd been holding for nearly a minute.

"It's my fault," I say. "I should have done something. I should have tried harder. Told her what was going to happen if she... kept going that way. I just thought... we had more time."

"That is what all people think."

"Forgive me," I say. "Please, forgive me for failing her."

"You are forgiven, little one." The stone in my hand warms again, and I feel the crushing weight of guilt suddenly drain out of me like blood, replaced by a new blood, a strange kind of joy, a peace like I have never known. A peace that can't be undone.

I throw my arms around his waist, hugging him tight. "Thank you." I feel his hand on my head, a father's gentle pat of assurance. *It is well with my soul.*

Then suddenly, we are alone, the three of us, in the whirl and mayhem of a city street, surrounded by humanity once more.

I look at Vale who gazes back at me shyly.

"We are going to be... the most awkward family on the face of the earth," I say. He stifles a grin. I pull him and Jared to me in a hug. All this hugging—is this what life is going to be like now? Just a lot of hugging? I think I'm okay with that.

"Grace!"

I whirl around at the sound of that voice—*that* voice. Penny. She barges through a bunch of people and launches herself at me, bowling me over. Mason and Ripley are close behind, along with so many others from the Rez. They all look completely wonderful, with no trace of the deprivation they suffered through the last few years. They are all wearing white and have those gold circlets on their heads. Ripley's beard is neatly trimmed—that's new—this is the first time I've seen him in anything other than a ratty Star Wars T-shirt. We take turns hugging and laughing. I even hug Simon, who for once isn't even sniffling. We are soon joined by Ralph, Emilia, Bree, Ethan, and my father. I introduce everyone to Vale and we do yet another round of hugging.

Suddenly, a light shines out of the palace. We look up to see the sky filled with angels. Angels. Huge and white and terrifyingly beautiful. Thousands upon thousands encircling the palace. A hum reverberates through the sky, a resonant note that soon breaks into many different notes, all in perfect harmony.

A song.

A new song.

I open my mouth to sing. Jared, beside me, joins in. I've never heard this song before, yet it is written on my heart, on all our hearts, a song of angels, a song of wonder and peace and hope and renewal.

Together, we sing.

Epilogue
Jared

We place our three white stones together on a small shelf in our new house. My heart is so full I cannot speak for a long time. Neither can Grace.

I glance at Vale, whose eyes are dry now, his face radiant, filled with light. He meets my gaze and smiles.

"That's a good spot for them," he murmurs.

"Why don't you go check out your room?" I say. "There's something in there for you. A gift."

His eyes brighten. "A guitar?"

I shrug. "Maybe."

He grins and takes off, slipping right through the wall. Grace laughs.

"I'm not sure I'll get used to that."

"We'll have to keep an eye on him, if we can," I say.

"Not only him," she says. "Penny and Mason were jumping through walls just for the fun of it. How are we mere mortals going to have any privacy with these resurrected people all around us?"

"Good question."

Grace laughs again. "There's still so many people I haven't seen yet. Noah, all the people at Petra. Did they survive? Are they coming here?"

"They'll be here," I say. "Ralph used to say that in the new kingdom, everyone will come here, at least for a visit."

"So... you remember that?" She looks at me. "You got your memories back?"

I nod. "All of them."

"All of them?"

"Yeah, but... they don't hurt me anymore. That's a gift."

"Wow." She puts her arm around my waist. "Is this what happily ever after feels like? I used to think about that when I heard a fairy tale, like Cinderella or one of those, and think... what did it mean to live happily ever after? Could this be it?"

"I think so."

"So, I have a question," she says, looking at me more seriously now.

"What?"

"Well, neither one of us actually died before the... end. So that means we're not immortal like the resurrected ones are, right?"

"Right, though we will live very long lives."

"Does that mean we're going to get old?"

I take another, longer, breath. "Yes, I believe so."

Surprisingly, she grins. "Cool. I think I'd like to get old with you."

"Really?"

"Yeah. You know, it's not easy to have a husband that's prettier than you. I think maybe when we do get old, you won't look half as good as me."

I laugh. "I think you're right." I kiss her. We stay that way for a long time.

"Guess what," she says, pulling away suddenly.

"What?"

"I didn't want to tell you. I mean, with everything else going on before. And then later... but... I don't know for sure, mind you... but I think... I think I'm going to have a baby."

She laughs at my expression.

"Are you... serious?"

"Yeah, pretty sure. I mean, all the signs. I had been feeling really nauseous. I thought it was just because of everything going on, and what you told me about Shannon. But then, I thought, maybe it was something else." She takes my hand and presses it to her stomach. "New life. Isn't that something?"

For a long moment, I can't speak, overcome. "New life," I murmur.

Thank you, I whisper to the God of the Universe, who has given me—us—a second chance.

From somewhere I think I hear Michael's sardonic reply.

Don't make me come back there again.

I laugh. Grace looks up at me, questioning. I shake my head. "It's nothing."

"You're happy, though?"

"Yes. I'm happy."

"Good! Well, let's go find more people. Your mom, and your friends from the cave. There's got to be others from your family here, right? And what about the disciples? And Paul? And Joan of Arc? I have questions for her! There're so many on my list—"

"In a minute," I say. I pick her up, hold her in my arms, and kiss her again. She wraps her legs around me, laughing, her fingers in my hair.

Plenty of time, I think, for everything we missed, everyone we love. After all, we have forever.

* * *

Acknowledgements

Whew!

Here we are, at the end. If not the world, at least this series.

First of all, I want to thank you, my readers, for sticking with me through nearly ten long years of spiritual warfare and apocalypse. I'm going to miss you. I'm not sure where the next writing journey will take me, but I hope you will be up for another wild ride.

Thanks to my agent, Julie Gwinn, and my former publisher, Dawn Carrington, for making this series happen in the first place, and for guiding me with patience and expertise. I'm also extremely grateful to Brian Kannard at Ally Press for taking on the monumental task of re-publishing the entire series in record time with astounding skill.

Thanks also to my incredible editors, Kristen Stieffel and Erin Healy, whose expertise and insight took this book, in my opinion, to a new level. Honestly, how does anyone write a book without editors with giant brains? I have no idea.

I also want to thank the members of my writers' group, Damascus Blades, who suffered through a year of submissions and offered invaluable comments: A.K. Preston, L.G. McCary, Katherine Massengill, C.W. Briar, Alicia Peterson, J.F. Rogers, and Tracy Sassaman. May you all be blessed with bestsellers in the near future.

Thanks to Katherine Walton for reading and proofreading, and to fellow writers Jenn Rogers and Susan Miura for offering endorsements. Your contributions are more valuable than gold.

Finally, thank you Jesus, for saving me, for loving me, for forgiving me, for guiding me in the writing of this book. I pray that this series honors You, my audience of One.

The *Forsaken* Playlist

As with all the books of this series, I created a playlist to act as a sort of soundtrack for the novel. You can find it by searching for "The Forever Playlist" on Spotify.

About the Author

Gina Detwiler is the author of the award-winning YA Supernatural series *Forlorn* and is co-author with Priscilla Shirer of the bestselling middle-grade fantasy series, *The Prince Warriors.* Her non-fiction books include *The Ultimate Bible Character Guide* and *The Ultimate Bible Character Devotional.* She's written novels for adults, including *Hammer of God, Avalon,* and *Antillia,* under the name Gina Miani.

She currently lives in Bucks County, Pennsylvania, with her husband, her dog, several imaginary friends, and all of the characters from her books, even the dead ones. She is also the author of three beautiful daughters, for whom she shares credit with her husband, Steve.

Follow Gina on Instagram and Facebook @ginadetwilerauthor and @ginadetwiler on X. Read her blog and find out more about all her books at www.ginadetwiler.com